"WHAT STAKES WOULD YOU LIKE TO PLAY FOR, CAPTAIN KIRKLAND?"

Stephen eyed her with a narrowed glance. "On a previous occasion you mentioned high stakes, my lady."

Patricia raised a brow. "Just how high do you have in mind, Captain? I am sure we are talking about table stakes, are we not?"

Stephen smiled. "I had a different wager in mind, Patricia."

Her eyes locked with his across the table. "And that is?"

"A night together."

She restrained her emotions behind an impassive facade. "An audacious wager! I am not certain I understand it, Captain. Are you proposing I play for the pleasure of your company tonight in my bed, or are you playing for the pleasure of mine?"

Stephen faced her mockery unflinchingly. "If you lose, Patricia, you spend the night with me."

ANA LEIGH

A Kindled Flame

LEISURE BOOKS   NEW YORK CITY

This book is dedicated to my daughters—
Patti and Barb

A LEISURE BOOK®

March 1991

Published by

Dorchester Publishing Co., Inc.
276 Fifth Avenue
New York, NY 10001

A Kindled Flame

KIRKLAND SUCCESSION IN THE COLONIES
CIRCA EIGHTEENTH CENTURY

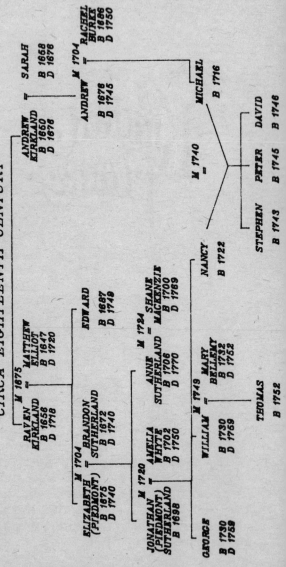

PROLOGUE

Boston
December 16, 1773

It was a dark night, lit only by a thin glow of moonlight that cast mysterious shadows on the many streets and alleys of the town. On the Common, the town crier, a bright woolen muffler wrapped around his neck to ward off the sharp sting of the night, carried a lamp filled with whale oil to light his way as he called out the hour.

Six o'clock.

Despite dreary skies and earlier rain, a crowd had been gathering at Old South Meeting House, their numbers swelling to more than seven thousand people. All through the day, the hall, filled to overflowing, had rung with the inciting speeches of such dedicated revolutionaries as Samuel Adams and John Hancock, despite the attempts by the more moderate Whigs to try to temper the enthusiasm of the crowd with a warning to weigh and consider the ramifications before resorting to actions that would throw the country into the worst struggle it had ever seen.

But words of caution had been in vain and the air was charged with expectation, for most of those assembled knew of the events of the coming evening and were awaiting them eagerly.

A short distance away, in an isolated barn, Stephen Kirkland took a piece of burnt cork and began to smear the sooty residue across the sharp plane of his face. As he worked at the task, his curious glance swept around the barn. The dozen men gathered there, all strangers to him, were engaged in a similar task. Some were using red ocher in a feeble attempt to disguise themselves as Indians, but in its absence, lampblack, burnt cork and even plain soot were serving as a substitute.

A few were dressed in buckskins like himself, but others had simply pulled blankets around their shoulders or garbed themselves in tattered clothing.

"Well, how do I look?" Johathan Kirkland asked beside him.

Stephen grinned, and his teeth slashed a white swath across his blackened face. A dark woolen cap was pulled down to the tip of his cousin's eyebrows, and his customary conservative lawyer's attire had been replaced by a ragged shirt and breeches.

"You look completely out of character," Stephen assured him.

"Good," Jonathan replied. "I have no

wish to be identified. There are many who might recognize me tonight."

"I think the same can be said of many this evening," Stephen cautioned. "You are foolish to join us, Jonathan. Why don't you turn back? You have a great deal to lose if you are apprehended."

"This is my fight too, Stephen. More so than yours. Why would I expect someone else to fight it for me?"

The leader of the small group stepped to the center of the barn and said, "Will all of you come and gather around me?" The ragged band moved to encircle him. "You all know what is expected of you. Remember, no one must call out another's name. Try not even to talk, because voices can be recognized. We have a specific mission. Do not damage or harm anything or anyone. Is that understood?"

The men nodded, their feet shuffling nervously in their eagerness to depart. "Now, good luck to all of you—and down with tyranny!" he cried out fervently.

The impassioned oath was met with supportive shouts.

Stephen Kirkland shook his cousin's hand. "Good luck, Jonathan."

Jonathan Kirkland grinned back at him. "Down with tyranny, Stephen!"

For a moment they lingered with hopeful smiles over their handshake. Then they joined the group of men that had begun to move out of the barn.

The noise began as a faint, indistinguishable shouting, but as it neared Old South, it grew louder until the thousands of people assembled there were able to distinguish the sound as that made by the whooping and howling of wild Indians.

Those milling about outside the meeting house turned expectant eyes on the mob of men hurrying down Milk Street toward the harbor. They numbered over sixty, most of them appearing to be young men. All were dressed in ragged clothing or covered with blankets, their heads hooded or concealed under woolen caps. Most were armed, carrying tomahawks, hatchets, axes, even pistols. The crowd began to follow behind the painted mob as it headed for a designated rendezvous on Fort Hill, where it converged with two other groups dressed in a similar fashion. Their numbers now had increased to more than a hundred men, and they all continued down to the dock. Their destination was the three ships anchored at Griffin's Wharf.

The tide was at its lowest when they arrived, and the three vessels were partially bogged down in muck, lying low in only a few feet of water.

The skeleton crews on board the ships offered no resistance to the mob storming their decks. The men had now quieted, maintaining a prearranged silence, and set about their objective with steadfast determination. The holds of the ships were quickly opened and only the heavy chests containing tea were hoisted to the decks.

The crowd that had followed behind remained on the wharf, watching the operation as silently as the grim men who were perpetrating it. They knew that the eyes of all the colonies were watching to see how the people of Boston handled this latest act of tyranny levied upon them by England's king.

The heavy chests were sheathed in canvas and the men used their hatchets and tomahawks to rip off the heavy binding. The air soon rang with the clamor of hatchets and axes smashing the chests apart after their contents had been dumped into the sea.

In no time at all, huge stacks of tea leaves, as high as the decks themselves, had piled up in the shallow water. Several of the men jumped into the frigid sea and began to toss the tea about as if it were hay, in an attempt to break apart the thick stacks.

The men continued to work silently and efficiently, careful to avoid rendering any damage to any of the vessels.

In their haste, an overloaded hoist

collapsed and one of their number was knocked senseless. A few of his friends carried him off to the wharf, where he soon recovered.

It was hours later before all three of the ships had been emptied and the 340 chests of tea had been completely destroyed. Before leaving, the silent raiders swept and tidied the decks of all debris and released the incarcerated crews.

Once they were on shore, the crisp chill in the air did nothing to cool the spirits of the men as they trudged away. Buoyed by the success of their mission, they no longer attempted to restrain themselves, and the night was rent with the sound of their jubilant laughter and exuberant shouts.

"Lord, Stephen, but I feel like a young man again!" Jonathan Kirkland said as they walked side by side.

Stephen grinned in reply. "I must say, when I came to Boston, I did not expect to attend such an exciting party."

"How long will you be remaining in Boston?" Jonathan asked.

"I will be returning to Virginia in the morning, but I will be back," Stephen said. "I can assure you, Jonathan, Virginia is full of patriots who will not stand idly by and let you people fight this battle alone."

"I hope so, for we have not seen the

end to this night's deed."

As they marched past the residence of Admiral Montague, a British naval officer, he opened his window to call out, "Well, boys, you've had a fine, pleasant evening for your Indian caper, haven't you?"

The men returned his taunt with jeering insults, and the Admiral's window slammed shut again to their defiant shouts of victory. Stephen and Jonathan paused, the frivolity left their faces, and they regarded one another with sobered stares as the Admiral's final words of warning echoed through the night.

"But, you've got to pay the fiddler yet!"

1

The chilling "nor'easter" that had swept across Nova Scotia with devastating ferocity struck Boston that morning, driving the pelting April rain before it.

The creaking buildings that stood in its path appeared to huddle and shiver in the swirling haze that enveloped them. Water ran down the gabled roofs like cascading waterfalls, filling the gutters to overflowing, and ankle-deep puddles quickly formed in the hollows and dips of the cobbled streets. Signs swung hazardously in the force of the gale, and flapping shutters threatened to be wrenched from their tenuous fastenings.

Stephen Kirkland stepped into the protection of a darkened doorway to draw his cloak tighter about him. The raging storm was forgotten when his attention was drawn to three men approaching on the street. Two of them were British soldiers and the wind was whipping at their scarlet coats. Their hands were in a constant battle to keep their tricorns on their heads without letting go of their cumbersome muskets. The wind repeatedly lifted the corners of their hats and threaten to sail them through the air like ascending kites. The third man was obviously their prisoner; his hands were tied behind his back and he was leaning his body into the wind as he struggled to maintain his balance against the fury of the storm.

Stephen Kirkland, grimaced fiercely. Had his friend Jeffrey Cunningham suffered a similar fate? he wondered. His face suddenly broke into an amused grin when several figures broke from a doorway and overpowered the two redcoats, knocking them to the ground. They grabbed the prisoner and sped down the street into an alley. The two soldiers climbed to their feet and were about to pursue the fugitives when one stopped and, with a disgruntled shake of his head at the folly of it, changed his mind. Both men simply picked up their muskets to reluctantly return to their headquarters. As they sloshed, soddened and disgruntled, past Stephen, he could hear them grumbling that they would rather face the wrath of their officer than chase damned Colonial insurgents through alleys in the pouring rain.

Stephen watched the redcoats disappear around a corner before continuing on his way. Within a few moments he reached his destination, a fashionable two-storied house faced with red brick set in Flemish bond.

At his firm rap the door was opened by a tall major domo. A gold ring dangled from his ear. There were very few men that Stephen Kirkland had to look up to, but he felt eclipsed by this powerfully built Moor. Stephen quickly assessed him, as tall men tend to do with one another, and realized that despite the herculean size of the man, there was probably not an excess ounce of fat on him; his body appeared to be solid and muscular.

The Moor nodded politely and stepped aside for Stephen to enter. "Good evening, sir. May I take your hat and cloak?"

Stephen was surprised by the man's speech pattern. It was neither singsong nor nasal, nor did it have the lyrical intonation that was characteristic of the English-speaking natives of India. The Moor's English was rendered in a clear, pleasant timbre with no evidence of an accent.

The man must have sensed Stephen's perplexity, because there was a faint glimmer of amusement in his dark eyes as he assisted Stephen in removing his cloak.

Stephen Kirkland was in for a further surprise when he stepped into the grand ballroom of the house. The large room was opulent in size as well as luxury. A sleekly polished black mahogany bar ran the entire length of one wall. Tasteful pieces of art hung on the walls, and several couches and chairs covered with red and gold velvet were placed around the room. Numerous crystal chandeliers, glowing with candle-light, hung from the ceiling. There were a dozen tables, mainly occupied by British soldiers who had come there to gamble. However, at the moment all eyes were directed to one end of the room where a woman sat on top of a harpsichord, singing in a soft, pleasant voice to the tune played by one of the soldiers.

Stephen reached into his pocket and withdrew a silver case. He took out a cheroot and lit it as he listened to the sound of her husky voice. He found him-self mesmerized by the sight of her. He would not have been able to recall one word of the song she was singing, be-cause his attention was riveted on her face. He drew deeply on the cigar, then exhaled in a silent exclamation of approval, the blue smoke rising in a hazy whirl above his head as he studied her.

There was a patrician delicacy to the woman's face and the way she held her head. The lines of her face and jaw were slender and exquisite, with high cheek-bones, a straight nose, and a slightly rounded chin. A wide, generous mouth was curved into a smile as she sang. She was too far away for him to discern the color of her almond-shaped eyes, but he could see they were tipped with long, dark lashes.

Her hair, a tawny mixture of gold and brown, was pulled back from a high brow and piled high on her head. Two long curls dangled appealingly down a slim neck.

Her dress must have been a Parisian import, because it bore no resemblence to any of the local fashions. The green satin gown clung to a shapely, but not overblown, breast, and the long, lissome line of her legs. A comely ankle encased in black hose peeked out enticingly from the folds of the skirt.

The woman finished her song to a burst of applause, and one of the redcoats stepped forward hurriedly to lift her down. His gallantry was rewarded by a charming smile of gratitude as the activity resumed in the room.

Stephen Kirkland's attention swung from the harpsichord to the woman as she moved across the room, stopping frequently at the tables to speak to the men seated at them. When she disappeared behind a closed door, he quickly crossed to the musical instrument and retrieved an object that she had left lying there.

Patricia Fairchild lifted her skirt and

propped her leg up on the chair to adjust her loose hose. She shook her head in consternation when she realized she was not wearing her garter. *What did I do with it?* she asked herself. She remembered she had been about to slip it on her leg when Charles interrupted her and pulled her into the casino to sing. *Did I carry it into the casino with me? Oh, how could I have been so careless?* she chastised herself. Her head swung around in surprise when the door suddenly opened. A tall stranger stepped into the room and closed the door behind him. The beauty of her face was high-lighted by a deep flush when his glance instantly swung to her shapely leg now exposed to the thigh, and his mouth curled into a suggestive smile.

"Are you looking for this?" Stephen Kirkland asked. A red garter trimmed in black lace dangled from the fingers of his upraised hand. The diamond sewn in the center caught the gleam of the candle-light and sparkled brightly as he slowly swung it back and forth on his fingertips.

Patricia Fairchild lowered her leg and restored her gown to its proper order. She studied the stranger with an interest still shadowed by her initial irritation. The man's arrogance was obvious and the look in his eyes was a familiar one to her.

"So there it is! Just how did you get

my garter?" she asked. There was more exasperation than relief in her tone.

"Not in the way I would have preferred," he said mockingly.

When she reached for it, Stephen flipped it into the palm of his hand in a firm grasp.

Her eyes swung up in surprise. "Really, Mr.—"

"Kirkland. Stephen Kirkland," he said with a charming smile.

Patricia found the stranger one of the most attractive men she had ever seen. He had an exceptionally masculine face—all angles and grooves. A broad forehead and forceful jawline spoke of determination and, probably, stubborness. His nose must have been broken at one time in a fight because the original straight line was interrupted by a small crook at the bridge. She felt, however, that it only added to the complete masculinity of his rugged face.

His most extraordinary feature was the incredible dark color of his sapphire eyes. The small lines that inched from the corners of them, emphasized just then by his roguish smile, attested to the long hours he spent in the outdoors and gave his face an added dimension that was particularly appealing. His face was cleanly shaven except for a dark mustache above a wide mouth with a full, sensual lower lip.

He must have been a guest of the club, and she knew she should be more courteous to him, but her instincts were sending her warning signals to beware of this attraction. She was annoyed with herself for permitting it to surface and she made no attempt to return his smile.

"Well, Mr. Kirkland, in case you failed to notice, this is a private office. You do not have any business following me in here." She knew it sounded outrageously ungracious of her, particularly in view of the fact that he was returning her lost garter. She had no idea why she should be acting this way, but she could feel her irritation with the man continuing to mount.

Patricia took a deep breath to regain her composure. "Thank you, sir, for returning my garter. It was my mother's. It isn't very expensive, but it holds a great deal of sentimental value to me." She mustered a grateful smile despite her resentment toward him and started toward the desk. "Perhaps I can offer you a reward."

"My sentiments exactly," Stephen declared.

Patricia Fairchild was experienced in dealing with over-zealous lechers, so she should have anticipated his next move, yet she was stunned when she was suddenly seized and pulled into the grasp of his arms. Before she could scream, his mouth crushed down on hers. Her struggles to free herself resulted only in his clutching her more tightly against his muscled warmth. She could feel his heated arousal pressing against her, and to Patricia's horror it began to excite her. The compelling persuasion of his mouth forced her lips to part beneath it. She tried to fight him, but the combination of the pressure of his body and lips became overpowering and the sensation that was spiraling out of control from the core of her womanhood became too exquisite to deny.

How long has it been since my passion has been this aroused? she asked herself with startled yearning. *Too long!* she replied in the fleeting seconds of reason. With a shuddering sigh of surrender her head fell back in langour when his mouth released hers and began a tantalizing exploration down the slender column of her neck. His lips returned to hers and his tongue now invaded the honeyed chamber of her mouth in scalding sweeps. She molded herself to him, pressing against the heated swell of him with her own aroused urgency.

Stephen's mouth released hers, and his lips trailed to her ear. "Shall we go upstairs?"

The bawdy allusion managed to penetrate the fog of desire that had held her temporarily in its grip. Patricia's eyes snapped open in shock. She wrenched herself out of his arms and her eyes blazed with indignation as she slashed out and rendered a resounding smack to his cheek. "How dare you!"

Stephen rubbed his smarting cheek and regarded her with amusement. "What a rapacious little tease you are, my dear. I would be impressed with your outraged performance were it not for your ardent response when I kissed you. You're apparently an insatiable little wanton! I would have thought in your line of"— He paused briefly and his voice was edged with mockery, "—ah, business you would be jaded by now, but you are really hungry for it, aren't you, pet?"

His words fueled her mortification, but Patricia forced herself to keep her control. She drew herself up with stately hauteur. "Sir, I did not invite you into this room, but if you do not leave at once I will cry for help, and Salir will come at once."

Stephen Kirkland leaned back on the door and crossed his arms. A brow arched devilishly above his provocative dark eyes. "Salir? Is that the big Moor at the front door?"

Patricia nodded. By this time she had completely regained her composure and her face curved in a smile of satisfaction. "And you know how the Moors treat men who molest their women." She shook her head sympathetically and her eyes shifted suggestively to the bulge in his trousers.

"Are you saying you are Salir's woman?"

Patricia could not understand her reaction to this man. She thought of herself as composed and levelheaded, but, at the moment all she could think about was the satisfaction she would derive from clawing the smirk off his face. Why was this man able to bring out base instincts in her that she was unaware she even possessed?

"I am no man's *woman*, Mr. Kirkland, but Salir has a tendency to be very protective of me."

To her further vexation the lines at the corners of his sapphire eyes deepened as his mouth curved into a roguish grin. "Considering the profession you are in," he said, "it must put quite a strain on his endurance."

Her eyes flashed with indignation at the implication. "And just what profession are you implying I am engaged in, sir?" The air was charged with her anger.

"Why, the oldest and, may I add, the most appreciated profession in the world," he said with a disarming smile.

Patricia's emerald eyes turned to ice. "Are you calling me a prostitute, Mr. Kirkland?"

Stephen raised his hands in mock protest. "Of course not, pet. Courtesan, perhaps, or paramour, or demimondaine. Even, conceivably, concubine. But certainly not prostitute. After that kiss we both know that you derive too much pleasure from it to be doing it solely for the money."

Patricia shook her head in disbelief and regarded him with complete scorn. "You are insufferable, Mr. Kirkland. This is not a whorehouse. Apparently, you have not observed that I am the only woman here. This is a gambling establishment. If you are looking for any other type of diversion, I suggest you take your business down to the dock area."

Her announcement came as a surprise to Stephen, but he concealed it behind a casual smile. He had, however, been so entranced earlier at the sight of her that he had been unaware that she was the only woman in the room.

"And you do not offer any other services?" He shrugged complacently. "As pleasant as it was, I would think you do something besides just sing."

"I run this establishment, Mr. Kirkland," Patricia responded through gritted teeth, "if you are interested in gambling." She appraised him thoughtfully. He obviously was a man of expensive tastes. "Perhaps you would prefer playing in one of the upstairs rooms?"

"With you?" he asked. Once again a brow cocked rakishly, making it evident that he was not referring to a card game.

"I should warn you, the stakes are considerably higher upstairs," she challenged him, deliberately ignoring his innuendo.

Stephen's slow smile said more than any words could convey. "I always play for high stakes, lovely lady, in any game I play."

Without warning he seized her again in his arms and swept her off her feet. He clamped one hand across her mouth before she could utter a sound, and with his other hand laid her on the couch and lifted her skirt. Her eyes widened with shock when he raised her leg and slipped the garter over her foot. Patricia was too stunned to move as he slowly and tantalizingly slid it up her leg to above her knee.

Stephen removed his hand from her mouth and for several seconds their eyes were locked together, her green ones angry and confused; his dark sapphire ones daring and bold. He lowered his head and his mouth covered hers.

The kiss was leisurely and demanding, drawing all the strength from her. Her head felt assaulted by scorching shocks that burned away any thoughts of resisting. Whatever madness their chemistry created, she found herself drowning in her desire for him, swept and tossed helplessly about, clinging for survival to the very person who was creating the danger.

Stephan raised his head, admiring her exquisite face as she slowly opened her eyes. He pulled her to her feet and adjusted her gown and hair. When he was satisfied with the result, he pressed a light kiss to her lips and crossed to the door. He turned with a backward glance, his hand poised on the knob.

"The game's already begun, lovely lady, and we both know what stakes we are playing for."

2

Stephen Kirkland halted outside the door to take some much needed moments to regain his composure. He could not believe how much the woman had affected him. He shook his head in disbelief. He had made a complete fool of himself.

He raised his hands and studied his palms. To his utter astonishment he discovered that not only were his hands shaking, but his palms were sweating. *My God! You're acting like a damned schoolboy*, he told himself in disgust.

For several seconds his gaze swept the room and his mouth curved into a wry grin. "I guess the little temptress is right," he exclaimed, observing the complete absence of any female in the room. Then Stephen suddenly smiled with pleasure at the sight of a tall man with dark hair standing in a doorway on the opposite side of the room. A reunion of sorts was the real purpose of his visit this evening, and he started to cross the floor.

Under other circumstances Stephen

Kirkland would have been aware of the man who had paused at the doorway behind him and who regarded his progress with avid interest. Charles Reardon's eyes gleamed with recognition as he watched Kirkland's tall figure cross the room. He dropped the cigar he was smoking into a brass cuspidor that stood against the wall next to the door and entered the office.

Patricia was sitting slumped in a chair behind her desk when he entered. Her head reared up in indignation. "Doesn't anyone believe in knocking before entering my office?" she spat out. She regretted her outburst the moment she said the words. Her disturbing experience with Stephen Kirkland had left her confused and overwrought. But she should not be venting this frustration on Charles.

Her lovely face flushed with guilt and her eyes deepened with contrition. "I am sorry, Charles. I didn't mean to snap at you."

Charles Reardon smiled down at her with affection. He was a thick-set man in his middle fifties, whose full head of gray hair gave him a distinguished elegance. His clear blue eyes beamed at her from a face that was considered by many to be quite handsome.

Reardon and Patricia's late husband had been business partners until George

Fairchild's death at the hands of an un-
known assailant two years earlier. He
had been stabbed to death and his body
had been found on the wharf, robbed of
even the ring Patricia had slipped on his
finger the day they were wed.

George Fairchild had been forty
years her senior when Patricia and her
father arrived from England. Her father
had become Fairchild's clerk in his
shipping office. When he died, leaving
Patricia orphaned in a strange new
country, Fairchild had taken the
frightened child into his own home.
Patricia had been only twelve years old at
the time. Four years later, at the tender
age of sixteen, she had married the kindly
widower. He had made very few demands
on her physically. Other then an
occasional visit to her bed, he had left her
alone, continuing to treat her more like a
doting father than a passionate husband.

A few years before his death, George
Fairchild had entered into a business
relationship with Charles Reardon that
had resulted in the construction of the
existing gambling establishment.

Patricia had been twenty years old
when her husband was murdered and she
had stepped into the partnership. Now, at
the age of twenty-two, she and Charles
Reardon ran a successful and lucrative
gaming house, despite the Puritan
society that surrounded them. The house

was frequented mainly by English soldiers and the scions of Boston families who were too confident of their social position to worry about being seen in a gambling establishment. However, because of the nature of her profession, Patricia was spurned by polite society, despite her considerable wealth.

"Well, well! What was the notorious Captain Kirkland doing in your office, Patricia?" Reardon asked curiously.

Patricia leaned back in her chair and regarded Reardon with interest. Stephen Kirkland had intrigued her. There was no question about that. She could not deny to herself that the arrogant stranger had stirred some dangerous emotions in her. As a result, she now felt threatened by him, a feeling that no man had ever succeeded in arousing before. She knew she had to get a firmer grip on her emotions before she faced him again. At the moment, because of his daring advances toward her, he had grasped the upper hand, but she was confident that should their paths ever cross again, she would not allow herself to be put into such a vulnerable position.

And I am confident that our paths will cross again, she thought with a resolute sigh, remembering the farewell gleam in his dark eyes.

Charles Reardon's question finally penetrated her thoughts and she realized that he was waiting for her to reply. "*Captain* Kirkland?" she asked, surprised. "Is he in the Army?"

"Heavens no, Angel! The man is a dedicated Whig," Charles replied with a light smile. "He has been an outspoken critic of His Majesty's government for years. He captains his own ship, and ever since the Crown passed the Port Act closing the harbor to all ships except their own, he has been suspected of smuggling supplies into Boston."

"If he is smuggling, why hasn't he been arrested?" Patricia asked skeptically.

Charles raised a hand and shook his finger pointedly at her. "Aha, there's the rub! The Crown has never been able to actually catch him at it." His glance narrowed warily. "What was he doing in here?"

Patricia was not ready to discuss her scene with Stephen Kirkland to anyone. She blushed and lowered her head. "He was just returning something that I had dropped."

Charles Reardon frowned. He could tell that she was lying to him. Obviously, she did not want to talk to him about whatever had transpired between her and Kirkland, but—could it be something that might be used, somehow, to better serve his purpose? He studied her lowered head as she began rifling through the papers on her desk in a fervor of activity. Charles strode to the door and departed the office, his mind beginning to formulate a scheme to turn this moment to his own advantage.

Stephen Kirkland clasped the hand of his cousin, Thomas Sutherland, and the two men grinned broadly at each other. The family resemblance was noticeable as they stood side by side. Stephen Kirkland's maternal grandfather and Thomas Sutherland's paternal grandfather was Jonathan Piedmont Sutherland. Both men could trace their direct lineage to Robert Kirkland, the seventh Laird of Kirkwood.

Their families lived on bordering properties and Thomas Sutherland had grown up with a case of hero-worship for his cousin. His respect had only deepened when he became first mate on Stephen's ship. Now, at 22, the young man was just returning to that post after completing two years of studies at St. Andrew's University in Scotland.

"So, how did you find everything in Scotland?" Stephen asked as the two men moved toward the long mahogany bar that commanded the length of one wall.

Thomas Sutherland grinned, exposing even white teeth that gleamed brightly against the deep tan of his handsome face. His dark sapphire eyes, evidence of his Kirkland bloodline, glowed with warmth. "The clan's intact, Stephen. Ashkirk still stands, as does Blake House."

Their glasses clinked together as the two cousins raised them in the air in a toast. "*Obair Ro Neach Fein*," Thomas declared.

Stephen grinned in response and repeated the phrase, "*Obair Ro Neach Fein*," their clan's Gaelic motto to serve others before themselves. Then, without hesitation, they swallowed the astringent liquid as if it were water.

"Now, tell me what has been happening here since my absence," Thomas Sutherland said in a hushed tone, after their glasses had been refilled and the attendant had moved away from them to serve someone at the far end of the bar.

"You remember Jeffrey Cunningham?" Stephen asked. At Thomas's nod of confirmation, he began to apprise him of his purpose in coming to Boston.

However, before he could finish, his attention was drawn to Patricia Fairchild as she left her office. Stephen's engrossed gaze followed her graceful movement across the room, until she paused at the foot of the wide stairway that led to the next floor.

Patricia could feel the intensity of his deep stare, and she turned to meet the dark sapphire eyes that were affixed to her. Their gazes locked for an infinitesimal moment; yet, in the swift passage of those seconds, a timeless message was conveyed between them. She felt an incendiary flush sweeping her body and turned hastily away to climb the stairs. When she reached her room, she crossed to the canopied bed that was draped and covered in a delicate pattern of green-and-white flowered silk. She lifted her skirt and quickly pulled off her garter, as if it had become a symbol of his hold on her. Her leg still tingled with the exciting sensation of his fingers. Patricia took a deep breath and shook aside the disturbing thoughts. She moved to her dressing table and threw the garter down in disgust, determined not to allow a complete stranger to turn her into a quivering mass of desire, with no will of her own.

Patricia leaned over and peered into the oval mirror that hung above the table, then gave her hair a few perfunctory pats and picked up a small crystal bottle to lightly add a few drops of perfume behind each ear. Satisfied, she left the room again.

Stephen finished briefing his cousin and, after sharing another drink, he accompanied Thomas to the door. The tall Moor assisted the younger man in donning his cloak, and the cousins shook hands before Thomas Sutherland departed.

Stephen nodded briefly to Salir and moved to the stairway. He hesitated momentarily at the foot, trying to decide whether it would be best if he left also. Casting aside the thought, he quickly climbed the steps. The tall Moor remained at the door, his face inscrutable as he watched Stephen's ascent.

At the top, Stephen discovered that the hallway branched into several wings. He selected the one to his right and followed it to a door at the end of the passage.

Stephen opened it slightly and peeked into the room. It was empty and he began to turn away. Suddenly, he could feel the increased beat of his heart as he realized that this was *her* room. It was spacious and furnished elegantly in soft tones of green and white. Unable to control his curiosity about this incredible woman, he stepped into the room, his greedy gaze sweeping it hungrily. His alert senses caught the faint fragrance of her perfume. It seemed to swirl almost teasingly in an intoxicating dance around his head.

He walked transfixed to the white marble fireplace, his eyes riveted on the portrait of Patricia that hung above it. She must have been about twenty when it was painted, he thought as he studied it intently.

A glimmer of a smile, so faint as to be barely perceptible, seemed to carry from her eyes and touch the corners of her mouth. The artist had captured the exquisite line of her jaw and her flawless coloring. Even the highlights of the tawny mixture of her hair had been strikingly reproduced on the canvas.

Stephen expelled his breath slowly. *The artist was in love with her when he painted it*, he realized.

Feeling like Peeping Tom, he forced himself to turn away from the picture. He knew he had no right to invade the intimacy of her bedchamber, but the inexplicable compulsion that had urged him to mount the stairs now led him to an armoire, beautifully faced with carved panels, standing against a wall. Stephen opened the doors and studied the interior. His fingers ruffled through pieces of wispy undergarments folded in neat piles. He picked up a delicate nightgown of black chiffon. For a few seconds he visualized the provocative sight of its transparent filminess clinging to her lissome curves. With a smothered groan he buried his face against the gossamer sheerness, inhaling the intoxicating scent of her lingering perfume.

Stephen folded the garment and returned it to its proper place. He crossed to the dressing table, running his fingers in a tactile exploration across the smooth surface. He removed the top from a crystal perfume bottle and drew a deep breath of its contents. Like a small child, uncertain of which kind to reach for when confronted with the sight of several kinds of confections, his fingers touched discarded pins, a container of face powder, a comb, and a small music box. He picked up a gilded ivory brush; A long strand of blonde hair was snagged between its bristles. Stephen slowly pulled the single hair through the stiff bristles that held the golden silkiness in its grasp. When he succeeded in releasing it, he curled it around his finger and brought the silken strand to his lips.

His hooded eyes widened in recognition at the sight of the discarded garter. He grinned and picked it up. For several seconds he fondled it. Suddenly he spun around and, with a forceful stride, crossed to the bed and turned down the silk cover. Stephen carefully laid the garter in the center of the pillow and restored the spread to its original order. Then, grinning broadly, he left the room.

The clatter of chips and clink of coins led him to an open door at the end of another hallway. Patricia Fairchild was watching Charles Reardon dealing cards to three men who were seated around the table. She looked up in anticipation when Stephen's tall frame filled the doorway. An inviting smile traveled the lush curve of her tempting mouth and settled in the depths of her emerald eyes.

"Do come in, Captain Kirkland. Have you come to play or merely to observe?" A delicate brow arched meaningfully. "Tonight, we are playing for table stakes only."

Stephen did not fail to grasp the unspoken challenge. His blue gaze deepened in amusement. "I think, lovely lady, that I will just observe and wait until you decide to make the stakes more inviting."

3

The following morning dawned as gray and dismal as the previous day. The rain had ceased for the moment, but the dark clouds hovering overhead threatened to split open at any moment and drench the city with another torrential downpour. The weather outside wasn't any more gloomy than Patricia's mood, as she sat at the table with her chin propped up on her fist. She toyed with a piece of flatware, idly tracing a pattern on the tablecloth with the pewter spoon she was holding. The same thoughts swirled through her head over and over again, and Stephen Kirkland was the center of the turbulence.

It was him! It had to have been him! What was he doing in my room?

Finally, in disgust, she tossed the spoon aside and got to her feet. She picked up the cup that had been sitting on the table, and the aromantic fragrance of chocolate sweetened the room as she poured herself another cup of the flavored brew from a pot that sat warming on the hearth. Patricia walked to the window and gazed out with an abstract stare, taking cautious sips from the steaming Wedgwood mug she was holding.

Would he dare to enter my room un-invited? she asked herself for the hundreth time since discovering the garter on her pillow. Her lovely face softened into a grimace of anger. *Of course it was him. Who else would leave such a blatant calling card! Damn the man's audacity!*

She swung around angrily, and the skirt of the green brocade robe she was wearing swirled around her ankles in turmoil to match her own.

"You look as threatening as those clouds overhead," Charles Reardon declared. He had arrived seconds earlier and was standing in the doorway studying the disgruntled frown on her face.

"Oh, good morning, Charles. It looks like we are going to get some more rain," Patricia responded absently and returned to her seat at the table.

"I didn't realize the thought of more rain could be that disturbing to you," Charles said with a grin. "You look as if you are at war with the world, Angel."

"Do I really look that bad?" Patricia asked with a sheepish smile.

Charles Reardon knew he had to

cajole her out of her mood before he would be able to approach her with his plan. He had not failed to observe the way Stephen Kirkland had looked at her the previous night. There was no question in his mind that the man was attracted to Patricia. Now, if she would only keep an open mind, he was certain that he could manipulate that attraction to his purpose. He knew that he could trust Patricia; her integrity was exemplary. Kirkland was smitten with Patricia. All it would take was to dangle the bait in front of him.

Charles sat down at the table opposite Patricia and eyed her cautiously. She still seemed preoccupied, and it was obvious he had already lost her attention.

"While I was dealing last night, I noticed that Captain Kirkland could not keep his eyes off you."

The mention of Stephen Kirkland's name was enough to immediately catch her attention. Patricia's eyes widened in surprise, but she tried to ignore the rapid increase of her heartbeat.

"No doubt he was checking to see if I was passing signals to you," she said caustically. "The man is insufferable." She did not tell Charles how aware she had been of those penetrating eyes on her last night and the unspoken message in their depths whenever their looks had clashed.

"Do you find him that disagreeable?" Charles asked with a worried frown. "I was hoping you would find him as attractive as he, apparently, finds you."

Patricia's eyes narrowed. "What difference can it possibly make to you, Charles, whether or not I find Captain Kirkland attractive?"

"I was intending to ask a big favor of you, Angel," Charles said.

"I am afraid to ask what it is," Patricia replied. "Obviously, whatever you want involves that odious sea captain."

Charles confirmed her worst fears with a nod of his head. "I am certain he is ready to return to Virginia."

"Well, good riddance!" she exclaimed. "Is that the headquarters for his covert activities?"

"Yes, he lives near Williamsburg on the James River."

"Charles, how do you know so much about this man's activities? You haven't been near Virginia in the time that I have known you."

Patricia eyed him with mounting apprehension. She could sense the tension that was holding Charles in its grip, but she could not imagine why her partner would be the least bit interested in the actions of Stephen Kirkland.

His eyes were filled with anxiety as he faced her. "I lived in Virginia before I came to Boston. The Kirklands are a wealthy and influential family there. Captain Kirkland's reputation is well known. I am surprised you have not heard of him before. He has become a folk hero to the citizens of Boston since he began running supplies past the British navy."

"Well, what do you want from him, Charles?" Patricia asked, still perplexed. "Is there something you want smuggled into Boston?"

"Just the opposite. I don't want something smuggled in—I want it smuggled out."

There was no doubt now in Charles's mind that he held Patricia's total attention. Complete astonishment was written across her face. Her brows arched inquisitively above emerald eyes that now gleamed with curiosity. "What in the world do you want smuggled out of Boston?"

Charles reached across the table and grasped her hands. He looked about cautiously and lowered his voice to barely a whisper. "I mentioned to you earlier than I once lived in Virginia. Well, my brother and his family remained there when I left. Last night I received word that my brother William has been accused of a crime he did not commit. He has been imprisoned and is scheduled to be hanged in less than a week."

Patricia's eyes widened with shock and then compassion at the misery of Charles's eyes. She squeezed his hands in sympathy.

"Surely there is something you can do, Charles, to prevent it?"

"A mutual friend has arranged for my brother's escape, but a great deal of money is required to bribe the gaoler. The only way I can get that money there in time is to send it on Kirkland's ship. I have it on good authority that he will be sailing on the morning tide."

Patricia relaxed and smiled in relief. "Is that what you want of me? Are you in need of money, Charles? Of course, I will give you whatever amount you require."

Charles Reardon shook his head. "It's not the money. I have the necessary amount. The problem is Captain Kirkland."

"Oh, Charles, I cannot believe that rogue would hesitate to take you to Virginia if the offer is tempting enough."

"Stephen Kirkland will not take me. You see, it was his father, Michael Kirkland, who brought the false charges against my brother. The family is bitter and deceitful. Obviously, they are disguising their own guilt at the cost of my brother's innocence. I am certain Kirkland would attempt to thwart the plan if he discovered my intentions. That is where you come in."

"In what way?" Patricia asked warily.

"If *you* ask the Captain to take you to Virginia, I am certain he would not refuse you. He is smitten with you, Angel. You need not tell him your true purpose in going. He will probably do anything you ask of him," Charles said.

Patricia drew back in dismay. The thought of asking that arrogant rake for a favor was completely repugnant to her. Charles Reardon saw the look on her face and guessed what was passing through her mind. He clutched her hands in a crushing grasp.

"I wouldn't ask this of you, Angel, if it wasn't a matter of life or death," he pleaded. "William is the only relative I have left, and you are the only one I can trust to carry such a large sum of money. I would do it myself if I only could," he continued passionately.

Patricia forced a quivering smile to her lips. "What makes you think Captain Kirkland will even return tonight?"

Charles Reardon heaved a sigh of relief. He could tell from the question that she had already capitulated.

"I am certain he will not stay away on his final night in Boston," he said confidently. He neglected to tell her that he had already dangled the bait in front of Kirkland by assuring him that she was hoping for a private game with him that evening.

Later, as she went through the evening's ritual of preparing herself to bathe, Patricia's thoughts strayed toward what the evening might bring.

Stephen Kirkland was a power to be reckoned with. Was she defying the gods even to encourage him?

As she pinned up her hair her eyes stared bemusedly into the mirror, blinded to the loveliness reflected there. There was no sense in trying to deceive herself. She was attracted to him. Her quick willingness to succumb to his seduction in her office was evidence of his power over her. Every instinct she possessed warned her not to even see him again. He was the very pitfall she had made a point of avoiding since George had died—a good-looking and charming roue who saw her as an easy conquest.

But somehow she knew that this time it was different. *Dare she let herself get involved with Stephen Kirkland?* Being with him had made her aware of what it was like to be a woman—an electrifying charge between the sexes that transforms man to male, woman to female; the heady feeling of power a woman feels knowing she is beautiful because a man's eyes are telling her so; but most important, knowing she is wanted by the message his male body transmits.

She had never thought of herself in those terms before and Patricia found herself frightened by the pleasure she derived from thinking about it. George Fairchild had never succeeded in arousing her in all the years she had known him. Stephen Kirkland had succeeded in just a few minutes.

She forced the memory of him out of her mind and stepped into the tub. The warmth of the water curled around her like a protective mantle and she could felt the tension ease from her body. Patricia yawned and stretched, tawny and golden like a long, lean jungle cat. She almost purred with contentment.

Unfortunately, that feeling was short-lived. By the time she finished soaping herself, the mellow mood was replaced by a vision of the natural grace in his long panther stride. *That walk is not deceiving*, she admitted grudgingly to herself. *He is all sinew and might—a latent intensity just waiting to spring.*

Her hands curled around the sponge she was holding as she recalled the feel of that lean flat stomach at her fingertips, the strength in the thighs that had pressed against her. Patricia's eyes closed in pleasure at the memory of the power in the arms that had held her.

Suddenly her eyes flew open. "What

are you doing to yourself!" she said aloud. "He's arrogant! He's smug! He's lecherous!" She slapped the sponge into her bath water to accentuate her point. "He is a deadly and predacious force!"

Patricia shot out of the tub and toweled herself angrily. She strode naked to the armoire and began to pull undergarments out of a drawer and fling them haphazardly on the bed.

"But what more can I expect from a man who is a damned, sneaky pirate to boot!" she ranted, as she rifled hurriedly through her dresses, selecting a black gown of silk and a pair of shoes.

Returning to the bed Patricia pulled on the undergarments and hose that were lying there. She slipped into her shoes and crossed to her dressing table.

Her tirade continued as she applied a light touch of rouge to her cheeks and darkening to her lashes, until she finally funneled her remaining anger into a vigorous brushing of her hair.

Now calm and composed, and somewhat embarrassed by her irrational behavior, she was about to slip on her dress, but pulled back aghast at the sight of her image in the full-length mirror that was hanging on the wall. Her mouth gaped in astonishment at the hodgepodge of color confronting her. A green chemise! A yellow petticoat! Red shoes!

"Damn you, Stephen Kirkland!"

She shook her head helplessly. *I don't think I can go through with this, Charles. How can I possibly be civil to that man!*

Patricia pulled off the offending garments. Completely disgusted with herself, she returned to her armoire and found matching black undergarments, then removed the red shoes and replaced them with a black pair with jeweled buckles. In a short time she completed her dressing to her satisfaction.

Then she slumped down on the edge of the bed, the picture of complete dejection.

4

Stephen Kirkland approached the stately mansion that stood at the top of Boston's Beacon Hill. The white-columned house, built by David and Anne Kirkland, had seen some minor changes since its erection in 1651. During the reign of Queen Anne a brick facade had been added to the front. Later, a great-grandchild had added a wing and replaced some peeling wallpaper; but other than a fresh coat of paint whenever necessary, the house maintained the original elegance bestowed upon it by Anne Kirkland.

After David and Anne Kirkland abandoned it, the house had stood empty until their son Simon had returned to America in 1685 with his Viennese bride. She had died the following year while giving birth to their only child, a son Peter.

Upon the death of David Kirkland in 1690, Simon had forsaken the house and returned with his son to Scotland, to claim his titles and the ancestral estate of Blake House.

From that time the house had been inhabited only occasionally, until Peter Kirkland's youngest son Jonathan arrived in 1750.

Stephen Kirkland had been to the home of Jonathan Kirkland on numerous occasions, whenever his covert activities had brought him to Boston. Last night he had agreed to join Thomas Sutherland at the house for dinner.

He raised the heavy brass door knocker and rapped several times. The door was opened promptly by a six-year-old boy. The stern frown of concentration on the lad's face attested to the seriousness the youth placed on the task that had been allocated to him. The look was a far cry from his usually bright and inquisitive expression.

Behind him, the mellow chimes of a stately clock, in delicately carved walnut cabinetry, pealed a gracious welcome as it tolled the hour.

"Good afternoon, sir," the lad said solemnly.

Stephen drew back in surprise at the formal greeting. His dark eyes danced with amusement. "Well, good afternoon, Jamie. I must say I am not used to such formality from you," he said affectionately.

"You wanna know something, Stephen?" Jamie Kirkland asked, with the charm of childish innocence.

Stephen hunkered down, shifting his weight to the balls of his feet, so he could meet the lad at eye level. "What is it?" he asked, noticing a familiar glint of devilry in the lad's eye.

"Father and Mummie are furious with me," the lad confided. "Father swatted my bottom and told me I can't ride my pony for two weeks as punishment."

Stephen tried to contain his grin. His brows knitted together as he regarded the child with a stern frown. "You must have really done it this time, Jamie!"

"I didn't do anything 'cept dump the honey jar on Barbara," he declared piously. "And how come he swatted my bottom and then tells me I can't ride my pony? That's two punishments, not one," he reasoned with the logic of a six-year-old.

"Now, Jamie, I am certain your father would not punish you so severely for accidentally knocking over the honey jar onto your sister," Stephen said with a dubious frown.

Jamie Kirkland's eyes were as wide as saucers. "I never said it was an accident, Stephen. I dumped it over her head."

"Her head!" This was more than he thought the little scamp capable of. "Whatever possessed you to do that?"

The youthful face screwed up in disgust. "You know how uppity she is. Always bragging about how much smarter she is than me, and how I got no manners! Well, she was sitting at the table telling me I was clumsy, just 'cause I knocked over my glass of milk, so I picked up the honey jar and poured it over her head." A low roll of pure satanic laughter rumbled from his throat. "You should have seen her! She was all sticky and gooey 'cause the honey was running down her face. Then a big horse fly got stuck to it, and she began crying and screaming at the top of her voice." The lad was convulsed with laughter recalling the scene.

Stephen shook his head in disbelief. Although he did not agree with Jamie's appraisal of his sister, he could not contain a grin at the sight and sound of the child's infectious laughter.

"Mummie had to cut off her hair and wash it 'bout five times before she got all the honey out of it." A deep dimple came into play in one cheek. " 'Course I didn't 'spect them to have to cut off her hair, or I wouldn't have done it."

Stephen straightened up and grinned down at the lad. "Where is your sister now, Jamie?"

"Oh, she's up in her room crying. Says she'll never be able to face her friends again. I heard her tell Mummie that she wants to go to Virginia with you until her hair's growed back."

Stephen glanced toward the top of the stairway. He was fond of the seventeen-year-old girl and hated the thought of the mental anguish she was suffering. "I think I will go up and speak to her for a few moments. Will you tell your parents I will join them shortly, Jamie?"

Jamie Kirkland nodded amicably and scampered off.

Stephen mounted the stairs two at a time and paused outside one of the rooms that lined the hallway. He tapped lightly on the oak door.

"Who is it?" an anguished voice cried out.

"Barbara, it's Stephen. May I come in?"

"Oh, Stephen!" the voice wailed pathetically.

He heard the key turn in the lock and the door opened a few inches. Barbara Kirkland's tear-streaked face peered through the crack. Her round brown eyes were puffy and red from crying.

"Are you alone?" she asked, sobbing.

At Stephen's affirmative nod she opened the door just wide enough for him to slip through, then locked it hastily behind him. A white towel covered her head, and a few dark brown ringlets had slipped from beneath it and lay on her forehead in curls.

She rushed into his arms and buried her head against his chest. Stephen's arms closed around her consolingly and he let her spend her tears. When her sobs ceased, he pressed a light kiss to her forehead and placed a firm finger under her chin, forcing her troubled eyes to meet his sympathetic gaze.

"Now tell me all about it, honey," he said tenderly.

Barbara Kirkland's face screwed up in distress. "Oh, no! How can you make fun of me!" she wailed pitifully.

Stephen suppressed his grin. "I wasn't making fun of you, honey."

"There you go again. I never want to hear that word mentioned again!"

"Now, hon—sweetheart," he said, catching himself in time before uttering the objectionable word, "it can't be as bad as all that."

"Oh, Stephen, look at what that despicable little toad has done to me now! I've borne the burden of his putting snakes in my bed and frogs in my bath water, but what am I going to do this time? I look horrible," she cried. "Robert Tysdale will laugh at me if he sees me like this—although I doubt that he will because I never expect to let him see me again!"

"And just who is this Robert Tysdale?" Stephen asked tolerantly. He did not recall hearing the name before, but he was certain it was just another name in the steady stream of beaux who came to court the adorable girl.

"He's the man I'm in love with," she said. "But when he sees me without any hair, he is going to laugh at me."

Stephen immediately conjured up the image of some pubescent youth covered with pimples. He took Barbara's hand and drew her over to a full-length mirror that was standing in the corner and turned her shoulders to face it.

Barbara's hands instinctly went to her head to halt the movement when Stephen began to remove the towel. At the look of reassurance in his eyes she lowered her hands and he pulled the towel off her head.

The dark brown hair that had once hung to the middle of her back in heavy, lustrous curls was now clipped short and lay in soft waves on her head. It gave her a winsome part-woman, part-gamin appearance.

She was small and slender in stature with a delicately shaped chin and a slightly upturned nose. Round brown eyes were set wide apart in her appealing face, made more so now by the tumbled mass of curls that covered her head and hugged her flushed cheeks.

Stephen stood behind her with his hands on her shoulders. "No *man* would ever laugh at that face, little one. It's beautiful," he said gently. He smiled, a look of genuine love carrying to the deep blue of his eyes.

Barbara Kirkland held a special spot in his heart because she bore an astonishing resemblance to his dead sister; Stephen Kirkland had appeared to Barbara like the older brother she had always yearned for. As a result, these two people had gravitated toward each other from the moment they met the previous year.

Barbara turned in his arms and smiled up at him through her tears. "Will you take me to Virginia with you, Stephen? I want to get away. I can't face any of my friends. I look more like a boy than a girl."

"You are being foolish and emotional, child. Your hair will soon grow back," Stephen consoled her.

"Please, Stephen," she pleaded. "I have never been to Virginia. I have never met any of my relatives who live there. It will be a good experience for me. I will return to Boston when my hair has grown back."

Stephen was helpless to resist the entreating look in her eyes. "I will discuss it with your parents," he relented grudgingly.

The relieved smile that suddenly broke the saddened face spread rapidly to the round brown eyes. She raised herself on the tips of her toes and flung her arms around his neck.

"Oh, thank you, Stephen. I love you. I love you," she repeated excitedly, bestowing kisses on his cheek.

Stephen laughed and removed her arms from around his neck. He set her apart from himself and regarded her with a serious frown. "I am not making any promises. I said I would ask your parents. But only if you join us for dinner. There will be another guest tonight."

"A guest!" Barbara moaned and retrieved the towel that had fallen to the floor. "I can't let anyone see me like this." She quickly replaced the towel around her head.

"He is a very distant cousin, Thomas Sutherland. He has just returned from Scotland."

Her face constricted. "Well, I don't want him to see me like this."

"Honey, if you return with me to Virginia he is going to be on the ship. He's my first mate. Besides, his family lives right next door to mine. He will undoubtedly have occasion to see you quite often."

"Oh, what' the use!" she wailed despondently. "I can't bear this!"

Suddenly Barbara's eyes lit up with inspiration. "I know what I can do. I will become a nun! I will cloister myself in a convent."

Stephen threw back his head and roared with laughter. "You wouldn't last a week, you little minx. Now rinse your face and I will take you down to dinner, or our bargain's off."

Barbara's shoulders slumped in dejection at the sight of her image in the mirror. She turned back to Stephen.

"You go ahead. I promise you I will come down," she said sadly.

Stephen bent over and placed a light kiss on her cheek. "Trust me, little one. You are still as beautiful as ever."

By the time Barbara entered the drawing room, Jamie Kirkland had produced a model of a sailing ship and Stephen was teaching him the proper name of each sail, Jonathan Kirkland and Thomas Sutherland were discussing the political picture in Scotland over their third glass of Madeira, and Joanna Kirkland, the mistress of the house, was stealing nervous glances toward the clock as she fretted over the overdone roast beef she would have to serve for dinner.

Barbara's hair was concealed beneath the folds of a starched white linen scarf. Faint traces of puffiness still lingered in the corners of her eyes, but on the whole, she looked quite fetching.

To Barbara's annoyance, every time she glanced up during the meal, she discovered the intense blue-eyed stare of Thomas Sutherland on her. She knew she looked ugly, but did the man have to be so insensitive to her plight? Finally, she was no longer able to control her annoyance with him.

"I find your fascination with my hair to be quite annoying, Mister Sutherland," she blurted out angrily.

Joanna Kirkland's face was the picture of shock. Jonathan Kirkland regarded her with a look of parental censure.

"Young lady, need I remind you this gentleman is our guest? Your remark was rude and I expect you to apologize immediately."

"That is unfair, Father. Why should I apologize to him when I have had to bear his ridiculing stare throughout the whole meal. I knew it was a mistake ever to come down for dinner!"

She jumped to her feet and started to race from the room. Joanna Kirkland rose to follow her daughter in the hope of easing her distress.

"One moment, young lady," Jonathan Kirkland's voice boomed out in an obdurate command that caused Barbara to freeze in her tracks. "And you, madam, will please remain seated," he added with a glance in his wife's direction.

His glare returned to his daughter who was standing in the doorway with a bowed head. "Now, young lady, you have not asked to be nor have you been excused, from this table. You also have not issued an apology to our guest for your discourteous remark to him."

He threw his napkin down on the table in frustration. "God's truth, I have just about had enough of this household being disrupted by the juvenile actions of you and your brother! When your childish behavior begins to be reflected in the manner with which you treat our guests, I will not abet or tolerate it."

Jamie Kirkland watched, fascinated, during his father's tirade. Stephen Kirkland sat with downcast eyes, sympathizing with the girl, but knowing he could not interfere. It was Thomas Sutherland whose suffering appeared to be greater even than Barbara's. His face wore a look of complete chagrin.

"Really, sir, it is all my fault. Mistress Barbara is not to blame. I *was* staring, sir," he apologized, in an attempt to placate his host before more sanctions were placed on the undeserving girl.

"That still does not excuse my

daughter's bad manners, sir," Jonathan Kirkland declared.

Barbara returned to her seat and raised her head. There were tears glistening on the tips of her thick lashes and her chin quivered with emotion, but her voice was steady as she addressed them. "I apologize, Mr. Sutherland, for my rudeness. I am not feeling well, Father. May I be excused?"

Jonathan Kirkland nodded his consent.

Thomas Sutherland immediately jumped to his feet and assisted Barbara with her chair. He drew back in surprise at the blazing scorn in the brown eyes when their glances locked.

There was an uncomfortable silence in the room after her departure until Jamie Kirkland, with an intrinsic sense of self-preservation, wisely asked to be excused before the wrath of his father again fell on his slim shoulders. He knew he was still in troubled waters where his father was concerned.

The three men rose to their feet when Joanna Kirkland decided to follow suit. After her departure they moved to the library where Jonathan poured them each a brandy, and he and Stephen lit cheroots.

However, Thomas Sutherland could no longer constrain his thoughts. "I do insist upon apologizing, sir, for I did stare at your daughter during the meal." His glance swung to Stephen. "I couldn't get over how much Mistress Barbara resembles Beth. Aren't you aware of it, Stephen?"

Stephen smiled and nodded. "I noticed it the first time I ever saw her." He turned to Jonathan Kirkland to explain. "Beth was my younger sister. She was just Barbara's age when she died. She was lost at sea while journeying to Scotland with my parents four years ago."

"That still doesn't excuse Barbara's rudeness," her father said, unrelenting.

"I think you're being too hard on the girl, Jonathan," Stephen said. "She has been devastated by having to have her hair clipped. She was just reacting to that emotional upheaval."

Stephen tossed the cigar he was smoking into the fire. "Perhaps this is the appropriate time to plead her cause. Barbara would like to join me when I return to Virginia, Jonathan. I know my parents would be overjoyed to have her. It would be like having Beth back again."

Jonathan Kirkland shook his head in doubt. "I don't know, Stephen. Despite my chastisement, I love the child dearly. Her mother and I would miss the lass."

"Jonathan, right now she is heartbroken and ashamed about her appearance. Allow her this time to heal her wounds, not to mention meeting some of her relatives. As distant as we may be," he added.

Jonathan Kirkland's face reflected the inner struggle he was waging. "What if your ship comes under attack?"

"Why would the British attack a ship bound for Virginia? Our ports are all open. The Crown's quarrel is with the people of Boston. How can they find anything illegal in transporting a relative?" he added with a wicked grin.

"Well, let me talk to her mother on the matter," Jonathan said hesitantly. "When do you intend to sail?"

"I was planning to leave on tomorrow morning's tide."

"Are you certain you know what you are doing, Stephen?" Thomas asked with a rueful grin after Jonathan Kirkland had left the room to seek his wife. "I sympathize with the girl's misfortune, but you must admit she is something of a termagant!"

"It will do her good to get away from Boston for a while," Stephen declared.

The two men were still laughing over their shared joke when Jonathan returned with his arm around his wife's shoulders. Joanna Kirkland had been heartbroken at the thought of losing Barbara for a few months, but agreed that it would do the girl good to get away for a while.

A short conference followed and it was decided that early the following morning Thomas Sutherland would take Barbara to the cove where the ship was anchored.

5

By the time Stephen Kirkland arrived at the club, the rain that had finally begun to fall in the early evening had been reduced to an annoying drizzle.

Salir nodded a silent greeting and assisted Stephen off with his cloak. He shook out the dampness and tiny beads of water fell from the cloak in a sparkling spray and glistened like diamonds on the highly polished floor.

Heightened with expectation at the thought of seeing her again, Stephen hurried to the entrance of the main room. *Good Lord! I don't even know her name. I have never wanted a woman so badly in my life and I don't even know her name!* he thought in astonishment.

Stephen paused at the doorway and his buoyed spirits sank as rapidly as if engulfed by a wall of sea water. She had just finished her song; *Damn, I wanted to hear her.* Disgusted with himself, he cursed his late arrival.

His eyes devoured the slim figure across the room. He had hoped that, somehow, his memory of her had been fallacious and he had allowed his previous night's passion to blind him to the reality of the "next morning"—like a drunken sailor awakening in the clear light of dawn to the garish sight of the blowsy whore in his bed.

But this was not to be. She was as beautiful as he remembered and he felt a stab of pain in his loins.

Patricia Fairchild's heartbeat quickened when she caught a fleeting glimpse of Stephen Kirkland the instant before she was encircled by a ring of admiring males. Her glance returned to the doorway as soon as the group around her had thinned, but there was no longer any sign of his tall figure.

She felt her spirits droop when she found him gone. As much as she hated to admit it to herself, the sight of the man excited her, for reasons she still was not ready to acknowledge to herself, or to anyone for that matter. This was a dangerous game they were playing with each other and she feared she would be the one to suffer from it. If only she could avoid him! But she knew that was an impossibility if she were going to honor her promise to Charles.

What if he had already left? If necessary, she would seek him out. Her heart began a rapid flutter at the thought of it. Should one just approach him out-right and ask the favor?

Nay, that folly would immediately put me at the disadvantage. I will have to continue to play out the game. But to my end, Stephen Kirkland, not yours, she vowed.

Patricia drew back in surprise when she stepped into the foyer and discovered that the very specter that haunted her imagination was engaged in conversation with Charles Reardon. At the sight of her, Charles put a comradely hand on Stephen's shoulder and, with a friendly wave, motioned for her to come in.

Patricia felt like a sacrificial lamb, but she forced a smile to her face and joined them.

Charles slipped an arm around her waist and pulled her to his side. "Patricia, love, Captain Kirkland informs me that you two have not been properly introduced. You must permit me to do the honors. Captain Kirkland, my business associate, Madam Fairchild."

For a second Stephen's dark gaze swung to Charles' arm looped familiarly around Patricia's waist. The compelling blue eyes were inscrutable when they met hers. If the news that she was a married woman came as a surprise to him, he concealed it beautifully behind a mask of courtliness.

Stephen bowed slightly and his dark

head dipped as he brought her out-stretched hand to his lips in a light kiss.

"My pleasure, Madam Fairchild."

At the sight of several British officers departing, Charles excused himself to say good-bye to them. Now they were alone. The dark brows arched over the sapphire eyes and the sensuous mouth curved slightly. "*Madam* Fairchild? Your husband must have the trust of a saint, Madam, to tolerate your absence."

"Do call me Patricia, Captain Kirkland. Everyone else does," she replied. "My husband is dead. He was brutally murdered two years ago."

Patricia immediately chastised herself for being a fool. Perhaps the man was governed by a code of ethics and married women were taboo to him. Why hadn't she allowed him to keep that impression? Subconsciously, did she want him to know the truth?

Patricia was unaware of the disturbed frown on his face as she caught her lower lip between her teeth.

Stephen saw her troubled look. "I am sorry, Patricia, if our conversation forced the unpleasant memory of your husband's death to the front of your mind."

She eyed him warily. "Thank you for your concern, Captain, but I fear my unpleasant memories of you are more fresh and repugnant in my mind. I was reminded of your boorish conduct in my office last night." She would be damned before she would let him know how distressed she was over his bold move in her boudoir.

"Madam, my apologies, but you must take some of the blame."

Patricia's eyes flashed in anger like green jewels. "I, sir?"

The handsome face slashed into an appealingly crooked grin. "You're too damned beautiful, Patricia. I was powerless to resist you."

"Resist me, Captain? That would imply that I intentionally provoked you into following me into my office." She blushed faintly, recalling the events that followed. "Nor did I invite your unchivalrous advances."

He shrugged his wide shoulders. "I won't apologize, Patricia. My only regret is that we didn't finish what we began."

"We?" she mocked. Patricia shook her head derisively, but could not contain a nervous laugh. "I swear, Captain Kirkland, your flagrant misuse of pronouns is amazing!"

Before more could be said between them, Charles returned to her side and again slipped his arm around her waist. "Has Captain Kirkland told you he is most anxious to play tonight?"

Patricia's eyes sparkled with amusement. "The Captain has made that point quite clear, Charles."

"I hope you will forgive me, but I promised Captain Kirkland you would deal tonight's game." There was a culpable smile on Charles's face.

"You what?" she asked, astounded.

"I was certain you would not object. You know you are a much more accomplished player than I."

Her hostile glance swung to Stephen Kirkland and was met by an amused smirk. She knew he was deliberately trying to goad her, but she would never give him the satisfaction of seeing her angered.

Patricia took a deep breath and met his distracting grin with a serene smile. "I am sure that would be a pleasant diversion, if the Captain has no objection to playing with a woman."

Stephen's face broke with an irresistible grin. "We are talking about a card game, are we not?"

Damn the devastating rogue! she thought with grudging admiration. "Why, what else, Captain?" She knew she was flirting outrageously with him.

She could feel the tension ease out of Charles. "Then let the games begin," Charles decreed like an annointed Caesar. He took her arm and directed her to the stairway.

Patricia climbed the steps slowly.

She could feel Stephen Kirkland's eyes boring into her back as he followed behind. She felt like a Christian about to be fed to a hungry lion. Patricia glanced back at him and met the diverting gleam in his dark eyes. *No, that gleam is more wolfish than leonine!*

To her further consternation she could see that Charles was oblivious to the byplay. He was practically purring with satisfaction, just short of rubbing his hands together with pleasure. *He looks like a greedy miser who has accidentally stumbled on a hidden cache of gold*, she thought resentfully.

Patricia shook aside her waspish thoughts. She realized she was permitting her agitation at seeing Stephen Kirkland again to be channeled into resentment toward Charles. After all, she had willingly agreed to help him. The poor man was desperate. He was only trying to save his brother's life. Whatever happened to the meaning of human compassion? Besides, she was allowing herself to become overwrought. Where was her self-confidence? She surely was capable of beating that arrogant clod in a card game any night of the week.

Her face wore a loving smile as she slipped her arm around Charles's waist. He glanced down at her and gratefully pressed a light kiss to her cheek. It was a tender moment between them and it did not go unheeded by Stephen Kirkland, following closely behind them.

Stephen picked up the deck of playing cards and began to examine them carefully when he was seated at the table. Patricia's eyes glinted in amusement.

"You have my assurance, Captain Kirkland, that the cards are not marked."

"I am only checking to make certain they carry the Crown's stamp," he said mockingly. "I can see they are imported. I would hate to think that the outcome of our game would be declared void by law because of a legality."

"You may be certain, Captain Kirkland, that the import tax has been paid on the cards we are using." Her lovely face curved into a genuine smile of amusement. "I wasn't aware that you were that conscientious. Your activities would certainly indicate your aversion to paying the Crown's taxes."

Stephen's eyes widened in surprise. "You do me an injustice, Madam Fairchild. I have no aversion to paying taxes—only to paying unjust taxes."

"And I imagine you consider any taxes levied by the Crown to be unjust," she rebutted.

Stephen chuckled warmly. "I'm a Virginian, madam. We Virginians have had our own legislature since 1619. The House of Burgesses was the first self-governing legislature in the Colonies." He cocked a rakish brow. "That is the government I recognize as my own. I willingly pay any tax it levies on me."

"Your talk has a ring of treason to it, Captain." Charles Reardon said cautiously. *Damn! All these accursed Colonials wanted to do was argue the worth of the King!* But he was in need of this man's services, and this was not the time to argue politics with him.

"Treason? To whom, Mister Reardon? My loyalty to Virginia is unquestionable. It would appear that it is you people in Boston who suffer from mixed loyalties."

Charles laughed nervously and threw a pleading look in the direction of Patricia, who sat quietly listening to the discussion. Stephen Kirkland was no fool, she thought reflectively. Charles was foolish in believing he could be easily duped into taking her to Virginia with him. He was wary and not about to risk his freedom simply to try to win her favor.

She began to shuffle the cards. "Are you joining the games, Charles?"

"I think not," Charles replied, relieved that the subject had been changed.

Patricia turned to Stephen with a temperate smile. "And what stakes would you like to play for, Captain

Kirkland?"

Stephen eyed her with a narrowed glance. "On a previous occasion you mentioned high stakes, my lady."

Patricia raised a dubious brow. "Just how high do you have in mind, Captain? I am sure we are talking about table stakes, are we not?" She glanced up at Charles with a mocking smile. "We certainly are not interested in your wagering the deed to the old homestead in Virginia."

"Oh, I am certain that won't be necessary, Patricia." Stephen's dark eyes gleamed tauntingly. "You see, I don't expect to lose. I am much more interested in hearing what you are willing to stake in this game."

"Well, I admire your confidence, Captain. Shall we set the limit at 5000 pounds?" she offered boldly.

Stephen smiled. "I had a different wager in mind, Patricia."

Her eyes locked with his across the table. "And that is?"

"A night together."

She restrained her emotions behind an impassive facade. "An audacious wager! I am not certain I understand it, Captain. Are you proposing I play for the pleasure of your company tonight in my bed, or are you playing for the pleasure of mine?"

Stephen faced her mockery unflinchingly. "If you lose, Patricia, you spend the night with me."

"And what if I win, Captain?"

"Name it," he answered succinctly. His dark eyes were inscrutable as he faced her.

"I am in urgent need of a quick passage to Virginia. I understand you have a vessel sailing tomorrow."

"You have been misinformed, my lady. Surely, you are aware that Boston Harbor is closed to all but British ships. It is treasonable to violate that law."

Patricia nodded in concession. "Very well, Captain, perhaps I should rephrase my statement. I want your assistance in procuring a passage for me on any ship that is leaving tomorrow for Virginia."

"I am unfamiliar with the shipping schedules, my lady. I could never presume to guarantee such an arrangement."

"Oh, I think you can, Captain," Patricia said.

Stephen reflected on her words for several seconds. "Do I understand that you are willing to spend the night with me if I win, on the condition that I will guarantee your passage tomorrow on a ship to Virginia, if I lose?"

Patricia threw Charles an anxious look. The moment of truth had finally arrived. Charles Reardon took a handkerchief from his pocket and mopped his sweaty brow. He was too ashamed to meet her eyes. This was a turn he had not anticipated. He had not expected the cad to be so bold as to actually make such an outrageous proposition to her. He turned his back to them and quickly poured himself a glass of whiskey from a nearby sideboard, gulping it down in one nervous swallow.

Patricia remained silent, hoping for a sign from Charles that would release her from her promise to him. When he turned his back, she realized that the hoped-for gesture would not be forth-coming—his back was the telltale evidence that he expected her to go through with the horrifying wager.

Stephen Kirkland was not a fool. He had known all along that Reardon had deliberately lured him into tonight's game. His thoughts went back to the meeting he had attended just an hour earlier on the second floor of a brick tavern on Union Street. Avowed Whigs such as John Hancock, John Adams, James Otis, and Joseph Warren had been present, as well as their acknowledged leader, the master politician, Samuel Adams.

Charles Reardon had long been sus-pected as a British agent, and his obvious interest in the movements of Stephen Kirkland had led the group to encourage Stephen to play along with the Englishman to determine what purpose was behind it.

Stephen had had time to study Samuel Adams, this famed leader of the Sons of Liberty, while he listened to the man's plan. Adams was only fifty-two years old, but Stephen was surprised to see that his hands trembled constantly and his voice quavered with palsy. His intuitive grasp of politics, however, had made him the undisputed leader of this somewhat pretentious band of dignitaries. It was obvious to Stephen that Adams completely dominated and manipulated his fretful younger cohort, John Hancock, who certainly was not an ignorant man. This led Stephen to realize what a tremendous force Samuel Adams would have been to reckon with, if his energies had been directed toward the Crown's cause, rather than the Whigs'.

Now, as Stephen saw Patricia's frantic look shift toward her partner, he realized that she was not acting on her own accord. Whatever she was doing, she was doing for Reardon's sake. This realization came as a blow to his vanity. He had not realized until this moment that Reardon had misled him into believing she was a willing participant in whatever scheme he had in mind. Was she so much in love with Reardon that she would wager her honor for him? If so, she would have to pay the price for that love.

"I warned you previously, Patricia, that I always play for high stakes. I am waiting for your answer, my lady," he demanded coldly.

Patricia hesitated momentarily, then with a resolute sigh pushed the deck of cards to the center of the table.

"Shall we cut for the deal, Captain?"

She did not raise her head at the sound of the door closing behind him as Charles Reardon fled from the room.

6

From its inception, the game's outcome seemed a foregone conclusion. It was as if Lady Luck were firmly ensconced on the side of Stephen Kirkland. Patricia waged a gallant battle, but was completely demolished by Stephen's exceptional run of good luck, which, in a two-handed card game, made the upshot inevitable.

Patricia could feel the loose rein she had held on her self-control slipping away with every turn of the card. While Stephen, on the other hand, sat back calmly in his seat, inflicting each painful jab with the confident premeditation of a matador inciting a bull with wounding pricks before rendering the fatal thrust.

After the final losing turn of the card, Patricia closed her eyes and leaned her head against her crooked arm. Her body felt numb, and her mind wrestled with a grim reality—it was time to pay off the wager. *How can I possibly go through with this outlandish bet?* she asked herself. *What can I offer to make him amenable to changing the wager?*

Stephen sat quietly, watching the torment she was suffering. "Perhaps we should have tried chess?" Strangely enough, he had not meant it as a taunt, for he was absorbed in studying the perfect line of her delicate profile. *Lord, but she's beautiful,* he thought admiringly. *If only everything could be different between us!*

She opened her eyes and met the passionate gleam that had begun to deepen in the dark sapphire eyes. "Captain, I am not going to beg."

"Please don't, Patricia. We made a wager, which I would have honored had I lost."

"Perhaps there is something of value that I could offer you?"

"I might have guessed you would renege on the terms." There was no anger or emotion in his voice.

Patricia raised her head and faced him. A glint of resentment sparkled in her green eyes. "I am not reneging, Captain, but surely you must realize how painful this is for me." Her chin quivered with the intensity of her emotion. "I am not a whore, Captain Kirkland."

"You became one, madam, the moment you put your body on the betting block."

She blushed at his candor and felt

her hopes crumbling. "Then you are not enough of a gentleman to release me from the wager?" she asked hopelessly.

"I am afraid not, Patricia. I always pay off my bets, and I expect others to pay theirs in return." He pushed back his chair to get to his feet. The screeching sound of it, as it scraped across the wooden floor, raised the hair on her arms.

"The night isn't getting any younger, my lady," Stephen said gently. He walked around the table and assisted her with her chair. Patricia raised a trembling hand and placed it in the outstretched one waiting to help her to her feet.

His hand closed warmly around her trembling, frigid fingers. "Your hand is cold, Patricia," he said with concern. Stephen reached for her other hand and clasped them both between the warmth of his own as he hugged them to his chest.

Patricia's legs were trembling as much as her hands and she felt more weakened by his nearness. As if in a stupor, she felt him drawing her unresistingly out of the room and down the hallway to her chamber door.

The lamp burning on the bedstand cast a warm golden glow over the chamber, giving it a snug and secure atmosphere. Patricia found this to be a bizarre contradiction to her plight as she helplessly surveyed the room, only to return to the tall figure standing before her.

Stephen reached for her slowly and drew her into his arms. She remained mesmerized as he lowered his head to hers with a leisured deliberation.

The contact of his mouth was blistering. The apathy that had encompassed her mind and body was reduced to ashes and her torpid senses were shocked into awareness.

With awareness came resistance.

Patricia's instinct for survival was greater than her responsibility to that preposterous wager, and she began to struggle to break the kiss.

Stephen raised his head. "What is this, Patricia? Resistance?" he asked with a tinge of scorn. His expression was wary as he assessed her reaction. He did not release his hold on her and she met his bemused stare with glaring defiance.

"Captain Kirkland, let's be realistic about this. The whole wager was insane, and you know it!"

"I know nothing of the kind," he disclaimed, exasperation evident in his tone. He released her so suddenly she almost lost her balance. "The *reality* is that you wagered yourself in the hope of procuring a passage to Virginia. Is it your intention to now weasel out of that agreement?"

If there was any of her previous

torpor still lingering, it was completely dissipated by his words. Patricia was now painfully aware of the ominous position in which she had placed herself and it was time to come to terms with it. Her eyes flashed angrily, mirroring this awareness.

"Very well, Captain Kirkland. A bet is a bet. If you insist upon going through with this, let's get it over with as quickly as possible."

In her anger she began to release the buttons on her gown, her previous trepidation now replaced by indignation.

Stephen crossed his arms and watched her. "Your indignation is amusing, my lady. However, it is also unprofessional. You made a wager which you obviously did not have any intention of honoring."

"I didn't think I would lose," she retaliated honestly. Her gown dropped to the floor and she kicked it aside angrily. "But I honor any bet I make." Her shift quickly received the same impious treatment as her gown, and she now stood before him in a lacy corset, her long legs encased in black hose.

His eyes swept her body in a slow, scorching perusal. She felt the warmth from the flush that began to engulf her at the sight of the naked passion that deepened his eyes. His smoldering gaze stopped at the sight of the red and black garter gleaming above a shapely knee of her right leg.

A pair of strong arms enfolded her and pulled her against the muscular length of him. Slowly a warm hand slid up her slim neck, forcing up her chin. Helpless, she watched his lips descend and her eyes closed in a languorous gesture of surrender.

Her senses were alerted now to everything about him; the musky male scent of him was provocative, the hard feel of his body, stimulating. Now, the female in her had become attuned to his overpowering masculinity as she stood in the confining intimacy of his arms. The insistent pressure of his lips forced her to part her own and accept his probing tongue; her mind began spinning with pleasant sensations. In seconds a mounting anticipation of the pleasure to follow replaced her previous resistance.

When his hand began to randomly sweep the curve of her spine, she felt a responsive trembling to the igniting touch. Stephen Kirkland was the only man who could elicit this heady response from her, and with a throaty groan, she surrendered to the provocative promise of it.

Lord, I'm depraved! she found herself thinking, but she molded herself tighter to him; the need to bring this moment to its fulfillment was greater than any previous reservations. The wager was forgotten, along with any resentment or indignation she had harbored.

His name was a sensuous sigh on her lips when, once again, his mouth closed over hers. Her arms slid around his neck when he lifted her up and carried her to the bed. She could feel the power in the arms holding her and her hands slipped down to his shoulders, her fingertips tingling at the feel of the corded strength concealed beneath the fabric of the coat that was tailored so expertly to his wide shoulders.

Stephen lowered her gently to the bed, their mouths still clinging together. When he finally released her and stepped away, she lay back, reveling in the exquisite shocks that were spiraling through her. She had never been so aware of her own sensuality until this man, and now every nerve within her was responding to his electrifying male essence.

"So it's really this important to you to get to Virginia?" he said scornfully.

Her lids fluttered open in surprise and, at the sight of the contempt in his eyes, all her soaring anticipation instantly plummeted in an anticlimactic descent.

Patricia sat up, stunned. Stephen shook his head sadly. "Believe it or not, madam, I had really hoped you wouldn't go through with this."

He clutched her shoulders in an angry grasp and pulled her to her knees as he jerked her against the hard wall of his chest. His mouth ground down on hers in a cruel and punishing kiss. She struggled to free herself from under the painful offense of it.

Stephen raised his head and shoved her away. She fell back on the bed in a despondent heap and lay there, drowning in a sea of mortification. She felt as base and contemptible as he thought her to be.

"Our sleeping together is inevitable, Patricia Fairchild. We both know that. But I'll rot in Hell before I give you the satisfaction of thinking that a God-damned bet was the reason that you climbed in bed with me. No," he snarled, "you're going to have to admit the real reason, if not to me, at least to yourself!"

In a daze she felt him yank the garter off her leg. "I'll just keep this for future reference."

Stephen strode angrily to the door. "Get yourself dressed. I'll be waiting downstairs. We'll leave immediately."

Patricia was uncertain whether she understood his curt commands. She was barely able to force the words out of her throat. "You mean you are still willing to take me to Virginia?"

His mouth curled into a derisive sneer. "That's right, Madam Fairchild.

All you really had to do is ask me properly."

For several moments she sat there in a stunned stupor, the silence broken only by the sound of the door slamming behind him when he left the room.

7

Charles Reardon glanced uneasily at Patricia as she descended the stairway. He had been pacing the floor, waiting for her arrival. The house was empty of everyone except Salir, who was waiting patiently at his usual post at the doorway, and Stephen Kirkland, who was leaning against the far wall smoking a cheroot. Neither man had spoken to the other since Stephen had come downstairs.

Despite the nonchalance Stephen was displaying, he had been studying Charles Reardon with a great deal of interest. He was uncertain how much of a hold Reardon had on Patricia Fairchild, but he was convinced that whatever urgent business was taking her to Virginia was somehow directly related to this man.

Charles met Patricia at the foot of the stairway with a relieved smile. "Thank God you won. I can't tell you how bad I felt when you were forced into that wager," he said apologetically.

She shrugged off the arm he had swung around her shoulders. "I lost the wager, Charles," she said unemotionally.

Reardon drew back in surprise. "I don't understand. Then why are you leaving—?"

"It's all very simple, Charles. I lost the wager but Captain Kirkland has agreed to take me with him just the same." She felt a painful knot in her chest at the sudden smile of relief on his face. *My God, he really doesn't care about my welfare at all!* she realized.

Charles drew her aside where they were concealed from the watchful eye of Stephen Kirkland. He pulled a thick packet out of his coat, took the reticule that was dangling from her arm, and shoved the packet inside it. Drawing it firmly closed, he returned the purse to her.

"When you get to Williamsburg, go to the King's Inn and ask for a man by the name of Emil Thackery," he whispered conspiratorially. "Tell him I sent you and give him this packet."

"What if he's not there?" she asked, distressed. "Where else can I find him?"

"He'll be there, Patricia," Reardon said impatiently.

He smiled sheepishly at the disturbed look in her eyes and his own swung around the room in a covert glance. "I'm sorry, Angel. I didn't mean to upset you," he whispered apologetically. "It's just that a great deal is resting on your delivering this packet."

"If that is the case, Charles, why don't you tell me where else I can locate this Emil Thackery?"

"Just leave your name at the Inn and he will find you," Reardon assured her.

"How can he possibly find me, Charles? He doesn't even know who I am," she protested.

"He's been here before, Angel. He knows what you look like. He'll find you," Charles assured her.

At the sight of Salir assisting Stephen Kirkland with his cloak, Charles put a hand on her back and directed her to the door. He leaned down and placed a kiss on her cheek.

"Have a pleasant journey, Angel."

"This isn't a holiday, Charles," she reminded him sharply.

Only Salir was aware that Stephen Kirkland had suddenly spun around and was staring at her with a completely stunned look, his normally tanned face white with shock. *Angel.* How many times had he heard that name on Jeffrey Cunningham's lips?

Salir took the brown cape she was carrying and placed it over her shoulders. "Are you troubled, Missy?" he asked with concern. He had been observing the unusual actions of the three people and it was obvious to him that something was amiss that was affecting his beloved mistress. "Can I be of service to you?"

Patricia smiled gratefully up at him. "I'm fine, Salir. I will be going to Virginia for a short stay."

The Moor's wide face grimaced in surprise and he eyed Stephen with suspicion. "Shall I accompany you, Missy?"

She put a reassuring hand on his arm. "That won't be necessary, Salir."

"We must hurry, my lady," Stephen said curtly, moving to her side and putting the hood of her cape up protectively over her head. Her glance widened in surprise at his sharp tone, and she responded with a quick nod.

Salir opened the door for them and Stephen took her arm as they stepped out into the rainy night. A carriage was waiting; he assisted her into it, then climbed in and sat down opposite her.

Patricia turned back for a final frightened look at the club. Salir was still standing in the open doorway with a reflective frown on his face. There was no sign of Charles Reardon.

Stephen did not make any attempt to speak to her as they rode through the night, which was perfectly fine with Patricia. Under the circumstances, she would have found it very difficult to carry on any sort of trivial conversation with him and she certainly would not have considered a more personal one.

The heavy rain made it impossible to see anything—not that Patricia noticed. Her mind was trying to muddle through the confusing events of the night. Whenever she threw a surreptitious glance in the direction of Stephen Kirkland, she found him deep in thought.

At one time the thought crossed her mind that he had lost all sense of time and direction, but she shrugged it aside with indifference. What did it really matter? At the moment she was at his bidding.

The rocking sway of the carriage and the steady patter of rain on the roof lulled her into a state of drowsiness, and soon her eyes closed. Patricia was unaware when Stephen shifted to her seat and rested her bobbing head on his lap. She curled up contentedly, deep in slumber.

Stephen stared down at her sleeping profile, his eyes clouded with torment. He didn't want to believe the full implication of his suspicions. His fingers reached out and gently traced the delicate outline of her cheek as she slept. His own face was marred by a grim frown when he finally leaned his head back against the seat and closed his eyes.

The far horizon gleamed with a faint

glimmer of red and gold as the first rays of dawn began to streak the sky. Stephen shook Patricia and she awoke instantly. She sat up quickly, embarrassed to have found herself sleeping with her head in his lap.

He stepped out of the carriage and she saw him join a small group of people standing a short distance away, awaiting his arrival. Patricia had no idea where they were, but she guessed it must be a secret cove that Stephen used for his privateering. She could see a ship bobbing on the water in a snug harbor just a short distance away. Everyone's attention was on the longboat that was approaching the shore. She stepped out of the carriage and stretched her aching limbs. The rain had stopped and the air felt fresh and revitalizing. She remained at the carriage until Stephen separated himself and returned to her side.

"We'd best hurry, my lady."

Without any further word, he led her to the boat that had beached on the shore. The others were already seated and Stephen lifted her in his arms and waded into the water. He swung her onto one of the seats next to a young girl, then pulled himself up into the boat. A quick nod to the boatswain and the six crewmen began to row back to the ship.

Patricia looked around her curiously. The young girl beside her had a brightly colored scarf wrapped around her head and tied at the nape of her neck. She looked as crestfallen as Patricia did, and the two women smiled fleetingly at each other before the girl returned to gazing out to sea.

Stephen Kirkland was talking in muted tones to the man beside him. Patricia instantly recognized him as the same man whom she had seen with Stephen several nights before at the casino. They were clearly discussing her, as both of the men's attention was directed toward her. She began to feel like a specimen in a bottle as they continued to study and discuss her, so she pulled her cape tighter and turned away.

In a short time the bow of the boat bumped against the side of the anchored vessel. One of the crew grabbed the rope ladder that was dangling from the rail of the boat and held it taut while the women boarded. The young girl, who had wisely dressed in a pair of boy's trousers, quickly scampered up the shaky contrivance, but Patricia, encumbered by her long gown and cape, climbed it more cautiously. Several times she lost her toehold and her foot slipped through the woven rope, but Stephen Kirkland was always there with a steadying hand to assist her.

Within a few minutes she found herself in the confines of a small cabin. Two of the crew gave her friendly nods as they carried in a trunk. When they departed, she peeked into it and discerned that it belonged to the young girl, who had disappeared somewhere with Stephen as soon as they came aboard. It wasn't until that moment that Patricia realized, much to her consternation, that she had neglected to bring along any change of garments for herself.

She removed her cape, but just as she was hanging it on one of the wooden pegs on the wall, the ship gave a sudden lurch and began to move. Patricia clutched at a nearby chair and held on tenaciously, in order to keep from being thrown across the cabin.

When she was confident she could maintain her balance, she released her hold on the back of the chair and hurried to the porthole. By standing on the tips of her toes, she was able to peer out. This was not her first sea voyage, and under any other circumstances, she would be looking forward to it. She had always found a peace and tranquility at sea that could never be attained on shore. The ocean stretched to the far horizon, where a rising sun was sending golden streaks shimmering across the surface of an aquamarine sea.

She turned away from the breathtaking spectacle of it when the door opened and the young girl entered. Patricia gave her a warm smile of welcome. She could not see any purpose in taking out her displeasure with Stephen Kirkland on everyone else around her. "I'm Patricia Fairchild. It appears we're traveling companions."

Barbara Kirkland returned her smile and eyed her curiously. She did not understand what this woman was doing on Stephen's ship. Stephen's explanation that he was taking her to Virginia had been too casual to satisfy her curiosity. Barbara's brown eyes widened with renewed interest. Could she be Stephen's mistress?

"How do you do," Barbara replied politely. "I'm Barbara Kirkland."

The announcement brought a similar gleam of curiosity in Patricia Fairchild's eyes and she studied the girl with a new regard. *She looks too old to be Stephen's daughter. Of course, he could have married young. Maybe she's his sister! Of course, that must be it!* she told herself with a nod of assurance. "Are you Captain Kirkland's sister?"

Barbara shook her head. "No, we're very distant cousins." Too late, she remembered that Stephen had cautioned her not to discuss her relationship with anyone outside the family.

"Well, shall we decide who gets the top bunk and who gets the lower one?"

Patricia suggested, in an effort to ease the tension.

"It really doesn't matter to me. You can have whichever you prefer," Barbara said graciously. Her eyes danced with excitement. "Isn't this all exciting! This is my first voyage and I love it!"

Patricia remembered the excitement of her own first voyage, when she had come to the Colonies with her father. She could not help but get caught up in the girl's enthusiasm and responded with a gay laugh.

"It looks like a beautiful day for sailing. You shouldn't waste it down here in the cabin."

"You're right!" Barbara said. "Let's go up on deck."

The smile disappeared from Patricia's face, replaced by a closed look. There was no way she would go on deck and risk encountering Stephen Kirkland. She was certain he would be up there bellowing commands from the top of his voice. "On second thought, I think I will just remain in the cabin for a little while," she said.

Barbara took the time to study Patricia carefully while the woman tidied herself at the mirror.

Barbara Kirkland tended toward impetuosity, which often led her into mishaps. She also was notorious for jumping to conclusions. Her first impression of Patricia Fairchild had been favorable. She liked her instantly and found her to be the most beautiful woman she had ever seen. Her instincts, however, had also told her, just by the way Patricia had spoken Stephen's name, that her relationship with him was not a casual one.

"Have you known Stephen a long time?" she asked.

Patricia turned her head and threw Barbara a skeptical smile over her shoulder. "Too long, as far as I am concerned," she responded grimly.

The statement was like tossing a ball to a frolicking puppy. It was snatched in the air before it could even hit the ground!

"Oh, I knew it!" Barbara gushed. "You and Stephen are lovers and you've had a spat!" She hopped up on the upper bunk, crossed her legs and tucked them under her. Then she propped up her two arms and leaned her chin on them; her pert face was radiant with expectation. "Oh, this is glorious! You must tell me all about it!"

Normally, Patricia would have been offended by such audaciousness, but Barbara's spontaneity was too infectious and Patricia's mouth curved into a wry grin.

"Does brashness run in your family, Mistress Kirkland?" The humor in her eyes tempered the harshness of the question.

Barbara remained unruffled, although she did frown reflectively as she pondered the accusation. "Well, my mother says that a true Kirkland is born with three B's—*black* hair, *blue* eyes, and *brash* manners." She giggled delightfully. "And Father says that what I lack with the first two, I more than make up in the third."

Patricia laughed responsively. "I think your father's right."

"Does this mean you're not going to tell me about your spat with Stephen?" Barbara asked, completely crestfallen.

"Sorry to disappoint you, my dear, but I haven't anything to tell," Patricia responded lightly.

Barbara shifted to allow her legs to dangle over the edge of the bunk. "Well, I'm sure you'll tell me later, but I have to say that you're wrong about Stephen. He's quite wonderful."

Patricia shook her head in disbelief. *You poor, naive, misguided, trusting little ninny,* she thought affectionately. *What a waste of loyalty on someone so undeserving!*

"Now, if you had been referring to Thomas Sutherland, I would have to agree with you. The man is a complete dolt!" Barbara continued with an emphatic shake of her head. "But that isn't true of Stephen." She jumped down from the bunk as if to emphasize the point.

"And just who is Thomas Sutherland?" Patricia asked amused.

"He was the man in the longboat, who was talking to Stephen this morning."

"Oh, you mean that good-looking, dark-haired one," Patricia said slyly. Her eyes were warm with amusement.

"Oh, I really hadn't noticed. Do you think he's good-looking?" Barbara asked with an indifferent shrug of her shoulders.

"I certainly do," Patricia replied. She was really enjoying the conversation. It had been a long time since she had had the pleasure of a girl-to-girl talk. Reflecting upon it, she realized how much of her life had been spent surrounded completely by men. This captivating gamin was a welcome change.

Her eyes suddenly sobered. For a few moments she had even been able mentally to put aside the circumstance that had brought her to this moment. She had been swept up in the girl's innocence. Her face heightened with color as she remembered what she had been prepared to do to gain passage on the ship. How could she ever justify such actions in the eyes of this girl? *Youthful innocence,* she thought sadly. *When did mine disappear?*

Lost in thought, she crossed her arms over her chest in an unconsciously protective gesture and sank down into a chair. *Enjoy it, Barbara Kirkland. Enjoy every moment of it while you can.*

Barbara saw the sudden shift in Patricia's mood and sensed her sadness. Her young heart reached out to Patricia, and she realized how childish she must have sounded to her.

"I think I will go up on deck. Are you sure you wouldn't like to join me, Patricia?" she asked kindly.

Patricia shook aside her grim thoughts with a gentle smile. "Not this time, dear."

Barbara paused at the door and threw a glance over her shoulder. She smiled shyly. "I don't know what trouble lies between Stephen and you, Patricia, but I truly hope that it is not serious enough to prevent us from becoming friends."

The warmth of Patricia's smile carried to the depths of her eyes. "I hope so too, Barbara."

8

After Barbara's departure, Patricia lay
down on the bunk and, despite her
mental turmoil, fell into a deep sleep. She
was awakened hours later by a rapping
at the door. She sat up, disoriented, and
the circumstances of the previous
evening came flooding back to her.

Whoever was at the door was apparently not be thwarted, because the
hammering became more insistent.
Finally she opened the door.

A young boy, no more than eleven or
twelve years of age, stood there holding a
tray of food. The lad had a pleasant face
with a generous smattering of freckles.
He was wearing a sleeveless waistcoat
and breeches made of gray homespun. A
white shirt with full sleeves covered his
slender chest. Despite his slimness, the
legs, covered with a pair of coarse white
hose, were muscular and well-formed.

The lad smiled broadly at the sight of
her. Patricia suspected it was more relief
than greeting. "I'm Daniel, ma'am. I've

brought you a tray. The Cap'n asks if you're ailing, since you didn't attend the midday meal. He says to tell you if you're sick, you have his condolences, but if you're not, I'm to remind you that this is not a Grand Tour. Them's his words, not mine, ma'am," he added apologetically. The boy had already stepped into the cabin and had put the tray down on the table in the corner.

Either she had become impervious to Stephen's nastiness or she was suffering from an advanced stage of hunger, because Patricia ignored the affront. "Tell Captain Kirkland that I am fine, Daniel, and thank you for your service."

The lad backed to the door and doffed his tricorn, exposing bright red hair combed back neatly and tied at his neck with a black ribbon. "Will you be in need of anything else, ma'am?"

"Not at this time, Daniel," Patricia said with a grateful smile. "Thank you."

She sat down and quickly poured herself a cup of tea. The trencher held a generous portion of what appeared to be a stew. She sampled it gingerly and discovered it was quite tasty, so she relaxed and buttered a biscuit and consumed the savory dish.

Patricia was just enjoying her second cup of tea when Barbara Kirkland burst into the room with the galvanic effect of a whirlwind. Her face was aglow with animation.

"This is positively the most exciting experience I have ever had!" she exclaimed as she plopped down in a chair opposite Patricia. "I can't believe that I have lived in Boston my whole life and have never once sailed on a ship before." She clutched Patricia's hand in her enthusiasm. "Oh, Patricia, you must come topside and see how beautiful the ocean looks."

"Wait a moment," Patricia cautioned with an indulgent laugh. She struggled to return the cup she was holding to the table without spilling its contents. "Topside?" she asked with a dubious brow. "For someone who has never been to sea, you seem to have grasped the terminology well enough."

"Oh, Tom has been explaining it all to me." She jumped to her feet again, too excited to sit still. "The front of the ship is called the bow and the back is the stern." Barbara raised her arm in the air. "The left hand is the port side and the right hand is starboard side," she declared, gesturing appropriately. She then turned to Patricia, seeking her commendation for her feat.

"I am impressed," Patricia laughed. "I have never been able to keep that straight in my head. But what happens if you're facing the opposite direction?"

"Don't you dare try to confuse me," Barbara warned with a merry twinkle in her eye. "I've just gotten all of this straight. Do you know that they keep water in a part of the hold? They call it ballad or ballast, or something like that. That's how they keep the food and the drinking water cool. They float it in barrels on top of that water. Isn't that amazing?"

"Well, I think the real purpose of the ballast is to keep the ship stabalized, honey," Patricia said with a tolerant smile.

"Well, next I'm going to learn the sails. I don't know if I'll ever be able to learn them all. The foresail! The topsail! The mainsail! The mizzen! The spanker! They're endless! How do sailors ever remember all of them?" She threw her hands up into the air in a hopeless gesture. "But Tom says if I don't learn them by the time we reach Virginia, he will take me sailing again."

"Tom? Is that Tom, 'the Dolt'?" Patricia teased. Her eyes were alight with amusement.

Barbara's brow puckered into an adorable frown and two dimples suddenly bore a groove into each of her cheeks. "Well, maybe I was wrong about him. He is quite good looking, especially when he laughs. And he smells divine!"

Patricia had just raised the cup of tea

to her mouth. "He what?" she choked, trying to swallow the liquid.

"He smells divine," Barbara repeated, unabashed. "Robert Tysdale always smelled like—well, like a bar of camphor soap. Whereas Tom has a kind of musky, masculine scent—like Stephen's." She turned her round brown eyes to Patricia. "Do you know what I mean?"

"Seductive," Patricia volunteered.

"Exactly," Barbara lamented.

The two women shook their heads sadly in mutual accord.

Patricia had lost all sense of time. She knew it was very late. She had not ventured out of the cabin the entire day and, as a result, she had dozed on and off all day, so that now any possibility of sleeping evaded her. Barbara was asleep in the upper bunk. She had collapsed gratefully into the bed after her first exhausting day at sea.

Patricia paced the floor restlessly. The air in the cabin was oppressive and seemed to hang like suffocating, transparent gauze around her head. The prospect of fresh air was too tempting to resist, so she left the cabin and climbed the companionway to the deck.

It was a beautiful night. Patricia strolled along the deck admiring the bright stars overhead and breathing the fresh smell of the sea. The ship was exceptionally tidy. There did not appear to be a barrel or length of rope that was not put in its proper spot. She made a point of staying away from the quarterdeck, where she was certain Stephen Kirkland's cabin would be found.

Therefore, she was unprepared for the deep voice that challenged her unexpectedly. "Well, well, the elusive Madam Fairchild. May I assume you spent your day checking the hold of my ship for contraband?"

Patricia spun around in chagrin as Stephen Kirkland stepped out of the shadows.

"You may assume whatever you please, Captain Kirkland, since supposition is apparently your forte." Her blazing retort was as fiery as his had been icy. "But I am not the least interested in what you are carrying in the hold of this ship. I suggest you have this discussion with Barbara, as she is fascinated with everything about it." She walked away but he followed.

"And just what does bring you out on the deck at this time of night, madam?"

Patricia replied with feigned artlessness. "Why, the need for fresh air, Captain. What else? Is there something overly suspicious about that, too?"

"At this late hour it is unusual, to say the least."

"Then I am truly intrigued to hear what you suspect has brought me out. I actually think you believe that I am spying on you!" The remark was laced with astonishment.

"That is for you to say, madam."

"I have already said what I have to say, Captain, so I believe this conversation has ended." She turned away from him like a queen dismissing her audience and leaned over the railing of the ship to peer down into the murky darkness below.

However, Stephen Kirkland did not take to the role of court lackey, and a muscle began to twitch in his cheek as he fought to contain his anger. "Madam, I must insist on an answer." This time the request was made authoritatively.

Patricia spun back to face him. "Captain Kirkland, I think it is time I make myself clear."

"Ah, at last. The long-denied confession," he said with an unamused, mocking smile.

Patricia's green eyes were blazing with anger. "Frankly, sir, I am getting sick and tired of your storming around me like some tyrant. Believe me, Captain, I am not intimidated. Nor, may I add, do I feel I hold myself accountable to a damned swaggering pirate!"

"Privateer!" he corrected her, annoyed.

"Pirate!"

"Privateer!"

Their heads were face to face, mere inches separating them. Their eyes were locked together in combat, her chin thrust up in defiance, his head lowered in fury.

Stephen clenched his fists to keep from grabbing her and shaking her until her teeth rattled—or better yet, to seal that vituperative mouth with his own and channel the force of her passion into a heated exchange that would ignite their bodies into flames.

In total frustration, and to keep from touching her, he turned and began to stride away.

However, Patricia's control had snapped. He had forced this confrontation and, as far as she was concerned, the last word had still not been said on the matter. She followed and angrily grabbed his arm, spinning him around.

"I will tell you this for the last time, Captain Kirkland. I am not, and never have been, a British spy. That suspicion is ludicrous." She stood glaring up at him, still grasping his arm in anger. Her chest was heaving from the exertion of her tirade and her emerald eyes were blazing their ridicule.

She suddenly became physically aware of the fact that he was there before her. She was near him—touching him! By the shocked look on his face it was obvious that this realization was as startling to him as it was to her. As if magnetized, they suddenly found themselves cleaving to each other, a desperate urgency in the embrace.

Patricia allowed herself the comfort of remaining in his arms, feeling the lean strength absorbing all her pent-up emotion. When his lips closed over hers, all their hungering desire exploded in a fiery demand. Her arms encircled his neck and now they both trembled, locked in each other's arms. Her senses were reeling with her need for him, and he was staggering under the urgency of his masculine lust for her.

Stephen was frowning when they finally pulled apart, still unable to rid himself of the suspicion he harbored. "Damn it, Tory, I didn't want this to happen."

All Patricia wanted was for him to kiss her again. She knew the danger of the game they were playing, but she did not want to hear his angry censure. She still was unsure of what she wanted to hear him say, but she knew it was not more accusations and condemnations.

She stepped out of his arms and turned her head away from him. "It was very foolish of me to come out here tonight."

His fingers forced her head around to meet his stare. She became aware of the deep anxiety in his eyes. "It would appear that we are at an impasse, Tory. As two rational, level-headed adults, we should be able to work out this situation to our mutual satisfaction." There was a tender huskiness in his voice that tugged at her heartstrings.

Her eyes glowed with amusement and, for the first time since they met, Patricia's smile was sincere when she looked up at him. "Stephen, if we were rational level-headed adults, we would not be in this situation."

Stephen saw the irony of his words and the disturbed frown on his face was replaced by a grin. "Then let me rephrase my statement, Tory. Somehow, despite my blustering, I feel there are worse things that could happen to me than having an emerald-eyed, tawny-haired woman, whom I find very desirable, as a passenger on my ship. I am certain I am intelligent enough to be able to handle it. What about you?"

His smile was boyish and appealing and she was helpless to resist it. "I guess I'm just too independent. I'm not used to taking orders from anyone, Captain."

"Then I must try to remember not to bare my fangs for the remainder of this journey. Do we call a truce, Patricia?"

For a few seconds before replying, she stared into the dark eyes that were studying her so intently. Finally capitulating, she reached out her hand to seal the bargain.

"A truce it will be. Shall we shake on it?"

At the sight of her outstretched hand his brow quirked with amusement. "Surely you jest, Tory. There is just one way to seal this bargain."

She stepped back to meet his eyes; his look was laden with desire. He drew her slowly into his arms and lowered his head to hers, claiming her mouth with leisured sensuality. The kiss was long and lingering—and exquisitely gentle.

When they parted, their eyes met in a message that was clear to both of them; this desire for each other was growing with a ferocity that neither of them would be able to resist for long. Causes be damned!

"Goodnight, Tory."

The words were wrenched painfully from his throat; then he turned and walked away.

9

Having made a temporary truce with Stephen, no matter how tenuous it might be, Patricia was now free to enjoy the remainder of the trip. She saw very little of Barbara Kirkland, who seemed to spend every wakeful hour with Thomas Sutherland. Once Patricia saw Barbara actually scaling one of the masts until Stephen Kirkland bellowed at the top of his voice for her to come down.

There was no question that the girl had found a new love, but, whether it was the sea or Thomas Sutherland, was still unclear to Patricia.

She was standing on deck pondering the question as she watched Barbara and Tom at the helm on the quarterdeck. Barbara was guiding the large wheel of the ship as she stood within the circle of Tom's arms. A sudden gust of wind caught the mainsail and the ship lurched to port. Barbara looked up and laughed in delight as they both grasped the wheel to steady the ship on course. She twisted her head to laugh up at him with eyes glowing with laughter, and his own deep blue eyes were smiling down into her up-turned face.

"I think they're in love," Stephen said unexpectedly at her side. She had not been aware of his approach.

"I think you are right, Captain. They make a beautiful couple, don't they?" Patricia agreed, with a wistful smile. "He seems like a very fine young man." She threw Stephen a jaundiced glance. "He doesn't suffer from your bad manners."

Stephen chuckled warmly and drew back his head as if to dodge the sting of her gibe. "I thought we had declared a truce, Tory?"

Patricia laughed up at him. "You're right. I apologize, Captain Kirkland."

"If you have a similar desire to pilot the ship, I will be more than happy to instruct you." For a few breathless seconds their eyes locked in a warm gaze. Each of them visualized themselves changing places with the young couple at the helm.

The tinkle of Barbara's laughter floated on the air like the cheery lilt of a sleighbell, encroaching upon their temporary illusion. Why was it that they could never carry on even an ordinary conversation without an underlying physical awareness of each other?

"Thank you, Captain, but I prefer to leave such tasks in the hands of those who are capable of doing them." She nodded amiably and strolled away.

Stephen remained at the deck. The expression in his dark eyes was obscured beneath a hooded stare as he watched the graceful sway of her hips disappear into the companionway.

Patricia awoke the following morning and, to her surprise, discovered *The Liberty* had slipped into the harbor sometime during the night and was now berthed as snugly as a newborn baby in swaddling clothes. She woke Barbara and the two women dressed quickly in preparation to disembark.

"The first thing I am going to do when I get to Williamsburg is buy myself some new clothes," Patricia announced, as she donned again the brown worsted gown she had put on so hastily the night she left Boston.

"You know you are more than welcome to wear anything of mine that fits you," Barbara said.

"I have already borrowed a pair of your hose, which I will return as soon as I purchase another."

"Will you be coming to Ravenwood with us?" Barbara asked her. There was a hopeful gleam in her eyes.

Patricia shook her head. "No, I have some business to transact in Williamsburg. Then I will attempt to find passage back to Boston as quickly as possible."

The news came as a complete shock to Barbara. She dropped the garment she was packing and spun around in surprise. "You mean I won't be seeing you again?" Her eyes brimmed with tears and she put her arms around Patricia and hugged her tightly. "We have just become friends, Patricia. I didn't expect us to have to part."

Patricia was feeling the same remorse at the thought of parting. "It will just be for a short time, honey. I am sure you will be coming back to Boston soon. After all, that is where your home is."

Barbara looked stricken. "I am in love with Tom Sutherland, Patricia. I don't ever want to leave him."

"But what about your parents, Bab? Don't you plan on ever returning to them?"

"I am hoping Tom will ask me to marry him. When he does, they can come here for the wedding. We certainly cannot plan on getting married in Boston with the situation there the way it is right now."

Patricia took her hand and pulled her to a seat at the table. She sat down opposite her. "My dear, aren't you rushing your plans quite a bit?" she cautioned. "Has Tom even hinted of marriage as yet?"

"Well, he said he might consider marrying me whenever 'I take the damned kerchief off my head.' Those are his words, not mine," she added with a giggle.

"I know it is really none of my business, but didn't you tell me you just met Tom a short time ago? Are you certain you know what you are doing?" Patricia asked with a worried frown. She was afraid her new-found friend was acting too impetuously.

Barbara saw the doubt on her face. "Oh, I know I have been acting like a child and you probably think I really don't know what I am doing. But I'm not a child, Patricia. I am a woman, the same as you," she said earnestly. "I am seventeen years old. I've been of marriageable age for over a year. Why, many of my friends have children already."

She halted to observe Patricia's reaction to her words. Her round brown eyes sobered. "Back home I always had many beaux because it is natural for a girl to have romantic fantasies. But no matter what the fantasy, I could never see myself married to any of them. It was all just a game I was playing, and I suppose, therefore, I acted like a child."

Patricia sat silently, watching the shifting expressions on Barbara's lovely, gamin-like face. "I don't want it to be just a game where Tom is concerned. It's not a game to me anymore, Patricia. I love him and I want to marry him. I pray that he doesn't look upon me as just a child."

Patricia smiled in understanding and patted her hand. "Oh, I've seen the way that young man looks at you. He definitely doesn't think of you in those terms. But what worries me, Bab, is that perhaps you are being swept away by his glamour. He is rugged and handsome. He lives a very exciting existence. Perhaps that is why he appeals to you."

"Patricia, Tom and I have spent long hours in conversation. I have discovered a great deal about him. He has a very serious side to his nature and intends to give up the sea very soon to become a lawyer. In fact, the only reason he sails is because of Stephen. He would never ship out under any other captain. Tom said that as soon as the trouble with England is settled, he is going to read law."

She stopped at the pained expression on Patricia's face. "He and I know what we want, Patricia, and are willing to admit it. Why don't you and Stephen do the same?" Her eyes softened. "Why do you challenge my love for Tom when it is you and Stephen who are really acting like children? Why can't you two be honest with each other for a change?" Her face was wreathed in fear that she had been too candid with Patricia.

"Honey, don't expect anything ever to come of the relationship between Stephen Kirkland and me. We are very attracted to each other, but the mulehead is convinced that I am a spy. There is nothing that I can say or do to convince him to the contrary. That is why I am going to conduct my business as quickly as possible and get back to Boston where I belong."

"You mean you are running away!" Barbara stated with a mischievous gleam in her brown eyes. "If Tom asks me to marry him immediately, will you remain in Virginia to witness the ceremony?"

"If that handsome rogue proposes marriage, nothing could drive me away—not even Stephen Kirkland," Patricia said, giving Barbara a reassuring hug as they got to their feet.

Arm in arm, the two women hurried out of the cabin.

Stephen Kirkland was reading a letter when they reached the deck. He tucked it into a pocket of his waistcoat at the sight of them.

"Why didn't you wake me sooner?" Barbara posed the question that was foremost in her mind the minute she saw him. "I feel as if I have slept away half the day." She flashed a special smile of greeting in the direction of Thomas Sutherland, who was standing next to Stephen.

"Stephen, Patricia has told me she will not be coming to Ravenwood with us. Can you convince her to change her mind?"

Stephen doffed the cocked hat he was wearing and bowed slightly from the waist. "It would be our pleasure to have you as our guest, Madam Fairchild." There was a glint of devilry in his eyes that belied the courtliness of the invitation.

"That is very kind of you, Captain Kirkland, but I have already explained to your cousin that I have urgent business to attend to in Williamsburg. Then I will be doing some shopping and I hope to return to Boston shortly."

The line of Stephen's jaw sharpened as he was reminded of her purpose in being there. The warmth instantly left his eyes, to be replaced by an angry frown.

"Then please allow me to get you a carriage, Madam."

She nodded gratefully. "I would appreciate that, Captain." They had both retreated behind grim masks.

"Well, I must insist that we accompany you to an inn to be certain you are properly ensconced," Barbara declared.

"That is really not necessary, Barbara. I can take care of myself. I have been doing so for a number of years," she added firmly.

"I am certain you can, Madam, but Barbara has reminded me of my manners. We are in Virginia now and down here we conduct ourselves with a particular code of chivalry," Stephen asserted. "We would be remiss in our responsibilities if we abandoned a lady to her own auspices."

"Very well, if you insist," Patricia relented. *Damn!* she cursed silently. She didn't know how to avoid allowing them to accompany her. It had been her intention to contact Emil Thackery upon her arrival. Now it appeared she would have to allow this whole entourage to accompany her to an inn before even attempting to find him.

"And I will go shopping with you," Barbara said. "I find that I, too, am in need of some additional clothing."

"How could you possibly be?" Tom teased. "You have me convinced you never wear anything except boy's breeches and that red kerchief on your head."

"Well, that certainly tells me that I have a greater reason to visit the shops," she responded. "Can we remain in Williamsburg this afternoon?" she asked Stephen.

This scheme fit perfectly with his own, and he smiled in relief. "Why don't we allow Madam Fairchild to conduct her business and then we will return to

the inn. Does that meet with your satisfaction, Madam?"

Patricia thought it was an excellent
idea. She would like to take more time to
bid Barbara a proper farewell. She was
certain that all she would need would be
the balance of the morning to locate
Thackery.

She nodded her approval. "I would
like that very much, Captain Kirkland."

Within minutes Patricia found herself being assisted into a carriage by
Stephen Kirkland. Barbara joined her,
followed by Tom Sutherland. They sat
down side by side on the seat opposite
her and immediately joined hands.
Stephen had no choice but to seat himself
next to Patricia.

The length of his right side was
pressed against her on the narrow seat,
emanating a warmth that soon was
blazing through her as if his body were
the nucleus of a fire.

The carriage stopped at a three-
storied white building with a red roof.
Barbara and Thomas remained in the
carriage while Stephen escorted her into
the building to the registration desk.

The hostler seemed well acquainted
with Stephen and he sent several
meaningful glances in Patricia's
direction while Stephen registered for
her. *He thinks I'm Stephen's whore*, she

thought in disgust, as she met the man's lascivious smirk. *It doesn't come as a surprise. I am sure I am not the first woman he has brought here.*

"I expect Madam Fairchild to be given your finest consideration," Stephen ordered. "You are to put any of your facilities at her immediate disposal, or you will have to answer to me for your negligence."

"Yes, sir," the hostler assured him. "We will do our best to see that any of Madam Fairchild's desires are satisfied." He handed her a key. "I hope you enjoy your stay with us, Madam."

He then picked up a tiny silver bell and shook it. A young black boy immediately appeared from the kitchen. "Joshua, assist Madam Fairchild with her baggage."

"That will not be necessary. I have no baggage," Patricia replied.

The clerk's brow arched and his mouth curved unpleasantly. "I understand."

Patricia could not help but blush under his pointed stare and the implication of his words.

"And just what do you understand, Johnson?" Stephen snapped angrily, unaware that he had raised his voice. "I suggest you apologize to Madam Fairchild immediately."

Patricia wanted to sink through the floor in embarrassment. Several people seated at nearby tables were beginning to regard them with curiosity.

"Oh, let it be, Stephen!" she said hastily. Mortified, she turned and began to mount the stairway as rapidly as possible, just to get away from him and the whole humiliating scene.

Her hand was trembling as she unlocked the room. She sank down on the side of the bed for several minutes to try to compose herself. Finally, she got to her feet and crossed to the window. She drew aside the curtains and was in time to see the carriage pulling away. With a sigh of relief she picked up the key and hurried from the room.

10

Patricia stopped at the desk and Johnson eyed her with hostile reserve. He had not as yet composed himself from his recent confrontation with Stephen Kirkland. Now here was his woman back, probably prepared to add more fuel to the fire.

"Is the King's Inn within walking distance?" Patricia asked him.

"Hardly, madam," he replied, looking disdainfully down his nose at her. "It is near the wharf."

"Then will you please summon me a carriage," she said politely.

"Surely, madam, it is not your intention to go there!" he responded, shocked.

"As a matter of fact, it is."

"Unescorted?"

Patricia found the man's condescention very irritating, but she tried to remain gracious. "I am certain I can take care of myself."

"I am certain you can, madam," he added insolently. His former suspicions of her were confirmed. No lady of quality would ever consider entering such an unsavory establishment. Why, everyone knew the place was frequented by nothing but cut-throats and thieves—and harlots, he thought with a pointed glance in her direction. "Very well, madam, as you wish."

He rang the bell and once again the young boy appeared. In a matter of minutes a carriage containing Patricia was rumbling down the cobblestoned street.

Stephen Kirkland stepped out onto the street from the shadows of an alley. He had been within hearing distance and heard her tell the driver her destination. His jaw set grimly, he mounted his horse and followed her.

Unlike the innkeeper, the driver of the carriage recognized quality when he saw it. "Are you certain you want to go in here, ma'am?" he asked worriedly, as he assisted her out of the carriage in front of a disreputable-looking building on the waterfront. "It's an unfit place for such a fine lady as yourself, ma'am."

"I have urgent business within," Patricia replied with a grateful smile. "I would greatly appreciate your waiting for me."

"Oh, I'll surely do that, ma'am," he said, doffing his hat with a friendly nod. "Would you like me to accompany you?"

"That is kind of you, sir, but my business is brief. I should be finished soon."

Her heart was hammering in her chest as she approached the entrance. Two sailors, who had over-imbibed, came staggering out of the door. A waft of the foul air accompanied them and her nostrils were immediately assailed by the pungent odor of stale smoke and ale.

Patricia stepped cautiously into the tavern. The place stank! The stale air was strongly laced with the smell of unwashed bodies. She brought her handkerchief to her mouth to avoid gagging. Clouds of smoke hung in the air like gray clouds, and tiny motes of dust could be seen swirling around in the air like snowflakes in the filtered light.

She looked neither to her right nor to her left, but walked directly to the bar. She could feel a multitude of eyes following her.

A grizzled bartender, dressed in a shirt stained with food and perspiration, which had not seen soap and water in days, if not weeks, was mopping the top of the bar with a soiled rag. A black patch covered his right eye, but his left one was riveted on her with curiosity. She certainly was not the type of female he was used to seeing come through the door. She was the kind of woman who spelled trouble as far as he was concerned. Most likely she was some woman looking for her husband, who was probably upstairs with Belle. Why didn't she stay home where she belonged, he thought disgruntled, and let a man do what he has to do?

"Wha' be yer business 'ere, lady?" he inquired suspiciously in a guttural voice.

Patricia lowered the handkerchief she held clutched to her mouth. "I am looking for Emil Thackery. I was told I might find him here."

To her consternation she was standing too near to him and was forced to cover her mouth and nose again when he raised his arm and pointed to a table in the far corner. With mild relief she turned away.

The man seated at the table studied her approach with restless black eyes. She paused before him, but he remained slouched in his chair.

"Mr. Thackery?"

"Yea," he muttered through thick lips set in a swarthy face.

"Are you Mr. Emil Thackery?"

"I already told you as much," he snarled. The black eyes flashed in anger under a scowling brow.

"Do you have something with which to identify yourself?" she probed cautiously, hesitating to turn over Charles' packet to him without some proof of his identification.

"What for, lady? I know who I am," he snorted.

The remark brought a raft of laughter from those within earshot, all of whom were watching and listening intently to their conversation.

Patricia wanted a private moment alone with this totally disgusting person, but she knew it would be impossible in this odious place.

"Perhaps we could step outside and I can discuss my business with you."

"Lady, you can state your business here as well as outside," he objected.

"I prefer some privacy, Mr. Thackery. Does the name Charles Reardon mean anything to you?" Patricia had a moment of satisfaction when she saw an acknowledging gleam in his eyes. She had reached the limit of tolerance with this horrendous place and spun on her heel and strode to the door.

Emil Thackery got to his feet, quaffed the few remaining drops of ale in his tankard, and followed her out.

Once outside Patricia leaned against the building and took several deep breaths of fresh air. She felt as if she had just been released from prison.

Thackery stepped beside her and clutched her arm, forcing her into the alley. The coachman saw the move and was about to step down to come to her aid but Patricia waved him away.

"All right, lady. You be Madam Fairchild, ain't you?" he said with a grudging smile. "I recognize you now in the bright light."

Patricia certainly did not recognize him. She could not believe she would have forgotten this unsavory character if she had ever seen him before.

"You say you came here on business for Charles Reardon?" His restless black eyes had taken on a feral gleam.

With a resigned sigh, Patricia released the drawstrings on her reticule and drew out the packet Charles had given her. She quickly handed it to him.

"I am sure you understand what Mr. Reardon expects of you," she said coldly.

"I'm sure I do, lady." The thick lips curled into a gloating smile that revealed yellow, tobacco-stained teeth.

She wondered how Charles could ever trust this man. What would keep him from just taking the money and disappearing with it? What recourse would Charles have then? It was proof of Charles's desperation that he had to depend on such a revolting rogue.

"Then I will bid you good-day, sir," she said. She felt relieved that the whole covert affair was over. A heavy weight had been lifted from her shoulders.

Patricia returned to the street and the driver hopped down to assist her into the carriage. Had she looked back, she would had seen a figure on horseback watching the whole exchange with interest.

Stephen Kirkland frowned grimly and his warm sapphire eyes hardened to blue ice. He dismounted and quickly followed Emil Thackery, who was scurrying down the alley.

Stephen Kirkland was not with Barbara and Thomas when they appeared at Patricia's door a few hours later. Tom took them to a couturier, and after introducing them and promising to return in two hours, he immediately disappeared.

A green-and-fawn walking dress had caught Patricia's eyes the moment she stepped into the salon. She examined it with interest. The tightly fitted jacket of moss-green velvet had long sleeves and a peplum that flared out over a fawn-colored full skirt. A velvet flounce, the color of the jacket, was joined to the bottom of the skirt with a narrow band of ruffled ecru lace. There was a ruffle of the same lace at each wrist of the jacket.

Monsieur Galbraith, the couturier, was a small man with a pencil-thin mustache and a pair of dark, flitting eyes that never seemed to rest on anything or anyone, but darted from side to side in his head as rapidly as his hands moved through the air. He flittered around them, pointing out the fine quality of the lace on the jacket and the extraordinary workmanship on the corded frogs that closed it.

When Patricia nodded her acceptance, he clapped his hands and two seamstresses appeared from the back room. Patricia was hustled off to a tiny fitting room, where she was assailed from head to toe by a methodical army of tape measures.

At the same time, in the salon, Monsieur Galbraith addressed his attention to Barbara.

"Now, *Mademoiselle,*" he said sternly, "I am certain I am abreast of the latest fashions and I know of no such style as that which you are wearing. The kerchief on your head offends my sensitivity."

Barbara reached up and planted her hands firmly on each side of her head, as if she expected the Frenchman to snatch the scarf off her head.

"I have a serious problem which I am trying to . . ." She faltered, groping with the proper way to explain to this stranger the embarrassing episode of the honey pot.

Galbraith raised a finger in understanding. "Disguise," he offered with a conspiratorial wink.

Monsieur Galbraith frequently had to suffer the vanity of his female clientele. It was often the problem of a too-large waist or too-small breasts. This was an unusual situation for him and he doubted this girl had cause to hide anything.

Barbara acknowledged his remark with a slight blush. "I know it's very vain of me, but I would like to keep my head concealed until my hair grows a bit longer."

"I quite understand, *Mademoiselle*. He shook his head sorrowfully, visualizing this adorable little gamin ravished with the fever that probably caused the loss of her hair. "Your recovery has been remarkable, Mademoiselle Kirkland. You look quite enchanting. I think I have the very thing you are seeking."

"Recovery? Recovery from what?" Barbara asked, perplexed. She had no idea what he was talking about. But the Frenchman had already scurried across the room and produced a small hooded cape.

The garment was a brown taffeta capuchin with a deep rose satin lining. It was cowl-shaped and the skirt of it flowed to shoulder length.

Barbara removed the red scarf from her head. Her eyes shifted self-consciously in his direction. "My hair is so unstylish," she apologized.

Monsieur Galbraith's expressive face remained impassive as he watched her put the brown hood on her head. He did not understand why this captivating beauty tried to disguise herself under the cumbersome and uncomely scarf. With such round brown eyes, he felt there was no need to attempt to conceal even the minutest part of her face. *She is enchanting! What a youthful glow*, he thought with admiration. The pure glory of it could never be diminished because of the length of her hair.

Women! he thought with a sad sigh. *When will they learn that there is no relationship beween beauty and the fickle dictates of fashion. Fashion? What is fashion?* he thought with unsuspected disdain for a man in his profession.

"Mademoiselle Kirkland," he said kindly, "I have recently returned from France, where the women are hideous with their fashionable high hairdos." He threw up a hand in digust. "*Mon Dieu!* Their heads are larger than their bodies!"

Barbara could not contain a giggle at the sight of his eyes rolling in revulsion. "You are very kind, Monsieur Galbraith."

"You must excuse me, *Mademoiselle*," he said when a seamstress came to the door and called for his attention.

The velvet jacket needed a few nips at the waist, and Monsieur Galbraith assured Patricia it would be accomplished while she continued to browse through the salon. She was so relieved at the thought of a change of clothing that she willingly agreed to it. Quick hands helped her to redress and she joined Barbara in the salon.

Patricia's breath caught in her throat at the sight of a bolt of ivory-colored satin. "This is exquisite, Monsieur Galbraith," she exclaimed. She picked up a corner of the material and began to examine the intricate stitchery. The smooth, glossy fabric was embroidered with pale pink, white and green flowers.

The Frenchman's eyes flitted heavenward and he raised his hands in prayerful praise. "*Oui, Madame.* Exquisite! It has just arrived from the Orient. Is it not superb workmanship?"

"I would love to have a dress made of it. I only wish I had the time."

Galbraith frowned with concentration and his eyes seemed to spin in their sockets as he calculated feverishly. "Two days, Madame. I can have you a gown in two days."

Patricia sighed forlornly and let the fabric slip from her fingers. "I am afraid I must leave Williamsburg and return to Boston."

The Frenchman's eyes twinkled like

candles and he almost choked in his haste to get the words out of his mouth. "There is no scheduled ship departing for Boston for seven days. I can have you a complete wardrobe in that time."

"Seven days!" Patricia exclaimed. "Are you certain, Monsieur Galbraith?"

"Indeed, Madame. There are only English ships that sail from here to Boston, and the next one is not scheduled to arrive for five days. It will then depart in another two following. This I know, Madame Fairchild, because I have a shipment of plumes arriving." His small mouth had curved into a satisfied smile.

"That's wonderful news!" Barbara exclaimed. Her lovely face was vibrant with joy. "This means you will have to extend your visit here."

Patricia slipped her lower lip between her lips as she reflected on her plight. She had never been to Virginia before and this would be a good opportunity to explore it. *Actually, why not?* she asked herself objectively. *I haven't been away from the casino since George died and I need a holiday from Boston.*

"Well, Monsieur Galbraith, if I must remain here another week, I certainly will need some more gowns, as well as some undergarments and accessories."

The Frenchman rubbed his hands

together in pleasure. He looked like a cat eyeing a bowl of cream. "My staff and I are at your disposal, Madame. I also have additional seamstresses available for such emergencies." He took her arm and began to lead her to the backroom. "Come, I have some flowered silk that I am certain you will appreciate."

Within a short time Patricia had picked out fabrics for several more gowns, and some batiste and silk chiffon for chemises and petticoats.

She accepted Monsieur Galbraith's suggestion for a narrow pannier to give the ivory gown a needed fullness, but insisted on a quilted silk petticoat for the other garments.

By the time Patricia finished chosing some plumes for hats and some jet and ribbons for shoes, the seamstress had finished the alterations on the jacket.

Patricia's final purchase was a large beaver hat. The fashionable chapeau, trimmed with brown satin ribbon, was cocked toward the front and turned up in back. It sported a colorful green-and-rust plume.

Monsieur Galbraith clapped his hands exuberantly and his roving eyes flashed with respect. "Ah, Madame, your taste is faultless," he said reverently. "It is the very touch you need for the walking gown you have chosen."

Barbara had not been idle while Patricia had been occupied. Several bolts of material had caught her fancy and she selected some suitable pattern boards to make them into gowns.

"I don't know when I have felt so good!" Patricia exclaimed to her. "This has really been a treat."

"You spent a duke's ransom, Patricia. It's a good thing you are not married, or your husband would be furious," Barbara laughed.

"My late husband left me very well provided," Patricia declared. "I must say, other than the casino, which has proven to be a very lucrative investment, I have not had much occasion to spend money, except on clothing." Her green eyes flashed merrily. "And I don't know when I have ever bought so much at one time. I feel as if I have done something wicked."

Monsieur Galbraith rushed over to Barbara with a troubled frown. "*Mon Dieu, Mademoiselle Kirkland*! We do not have your measurements!" He grabbed Barbara and hurried her into the fitting room, then returned to Patricia. "I think it would be wise if we checked your measurements, Madame. Due to the limited time we have available, neither of us can afford to make a mistake. It would be too costly for both of us."

Patricia found herself stripped of her gown and once again, the seamstresses reappeared with their tape measures in hand to reaffirm her waist, bust, and arm measurements, as well as her height, the width of her shoulders and the size of her foot.

11

The first thing Patricia did after leaving Thomas and Barbara was to order a hot bath. After pinning her hair on the top of her head, she luxuriated in its warmth, contented and relaxed. The whole disgusting situation was behind her now and she could just enjoy herself and get on with her life.

What about my life? she reflected as she idly sponged herself. *Should I be thinking of marriage again? I'm only twenty-two years old. Surely, I do not want to spend my life alone! What of children?*

She realized she had not had much opportunity to be around little children. Her whole life up until now had been men—men with their smoking cigars and their glasses of brandy, men with their talk of war or their invitations to share their beds. She leaned her head on the rim of the tub and wondered what it would be like to cook a meal each night for her husband, to tuck her children into bed each night with a goodnight kiss. Her lovely face clouded with wistful yearning. *What would it feel like to be invited into the proper drawing rooms of these Virginia mansions? How would it feel to have the respectability of being a married woman in the community, rather than the reputation for "marrying an old man for his money" or being "the harlot who runs a gambling house?"*

Funny, she thought with a derisive smile, *I have never before regretted the way I lived. Why am I doing it now?*

Patricia shook her head. *You're deceiving yourself. You have allowed a brief friendship with a woman who is socially acceptable to delude you into believing you would be welcomed into the same drawing rooms. That is laughable! These people down here would accept you no more willingly than those bigots in Boston did. Stephen Kirkland. The hostler. Those men have no problem recognizing you for what you are. Why dwell on it any longer?*

Patricia climbed out of the tub and, after towelling herself, wrapped herself in one of the mammoth white linen towels.

The snug bathing alcove, containing a wooden tub, commode and mirror, was sequestered from the sleeping chamber by a pair of heavy muslin curtains strung on a rod.

She drew them aside and then froze,

the air escaping from her with a startled gasp. A tall figure stood leaning against the opposite wall.

"Stephen." Somehow his name seemed to catch in her throat and came out as a breathless sigh. Strangely enough, she was not offended by his being there. This unexpected sight of him filled her with a sweeping warmth.

For what seemed endless moments, the two stood staring at each other. She drank in the long muscular frame, her eyes swinging back to the sculptured line of his tanned face. It seemed that every time she saw him, he was more handsome. Her gaze lingered hungrily on the sensuous lips before swinging to his incredibly blue eyes.

Stephen's eyes seemed to devour her. She felt naked as his hungry perusal seem to strip away the towel that inadequately shrouded her from his scorching inspection. Finding her breath, she finally broke the silence between them.

"What are you doing here, Stephen? How did you get in here?"

Why was it that everything she said sounded like breathless stammering in her ears?

Wordlessly, Stephen held up a key in response to her question.

"I don't understand." Patricia's eyes clearly reflected her bewilderment as she stared at the key that dangled from a ring held loosely between his fingers.

"This is *my* room. I keep it available for whenever I am in Williamsburg on business."

Was it her imagination, or was there an apologetic tone in his declaration? For a few seconds her head whirled in confusion, before everything fell sickeningly into place.

Stunned, Patricia walked to the armoire as the realization hit her. "And it has come time to settle our unfinished business."

In a daze she slowly removed the pins from her hair. She had hoped to put the memory of that nefarious bet behind her, but it was just another delusion. The depth of her bitterness forced her eyelids closed, and she fought to restrain her tears.

Stephen was behind her instantly, and his arms enfolded her, pulling her back against his length. Patricia stiffened in his embrace, fighting her desire to relax against that familiar warmth and lose herself in the excitement of those arms.

His breath was warm and tantalizing against her ear. "I stayed away as long as I could stand it, Tory." There was no disguising the raw passion in the sensitive apology.

Helpless to ignore it, Patricia turned

in his arms and raised imploring eyes to him.

"Must it be this way, Stephen?"

A smothered moan was the only answer before his lips plummeted down to close over hers. Even if she had wanted to resist the kiss, she would have been powerless to do so, for Stephen's lips were exacting a response from hers.

She was aware of wanting this moment as much as he wanted it. For the past week she had existed in a mindless void, but now his touch and lips were reviving her, making her feel agonizingly alive again, as every nerve end throbbed with a mounting need for this man who was holding her.

Patricia's arms slid around his neck as Stephen's hands pressed her closer. Breathless, she was forced to pull away and she buried her head against the solid wall of his chest. His lips were at her ear, then trailed to the hollow of her throat. His hands explored the nape of her neck, before cupping each cheek to tilt her head up to meet his tender gaze.

"I tried, Tory. I really tried," he rasped hoarsely. Patricia felt incincerated by the heated intensity of his look.

His words reminded her of the reality of their relationship. "I don't want you like this, Stephen. Why must you cheapen anything we could share, by forcing it this way?" A tear began to trickle down her cheek.

She watched his face run a gamut of emotions as it changed from wretched bewilderment to incredulous skepticism, before finally darkening with scorn.

"The bet! My God, are you talking about that damned bet?"

His hands slid to her shoulders in a forceful grip. Patricia cringed under the crushing pressure. "Forget that damned bet. I have!" His eyes flashed angrily in disbelief. "Do you actually believe that is why I am here?"

Patricia wrenched away and turned her back to him, unable to face the fury in his eyes. "I want you, Stephen. I want you as much as you want me, but there are problems between us that must be resolved before I can ever willingly give myself to you."

"I told you I'm canceling the bet, Tory," he said irritably.

Patricia spun around angrily. Her hair tumbled to her shoulders, and her eyes seethed with emerald fire.

"You really are incredible, Stephen Kirkland. You must believe that you are the only one with pride. Well, I have my pride, too." A slim finger poked at his chest, angrily beating out each word. "I will rot in Hell before I climb into bed with a suspicious, paranoid pirate who thinks my only purpose in sleeping with him is to ferret out military secrets!"

"Privateer," he retorted through clenched teeth.

"Pirate."

"PRI—VA—TEER!" he roared.

Patricia put her hands on her hips and lifted her head defiantly. "That which we call a wolf in sheep's clothing, by any other name would smell just as foul!"

For several seconds he stood speechless while she waited for his retort. She could tell by the furious expression in his eyes that he was struggling with the urge to either strangle her or smack her in the middle of her defiant face. But she knew deep within her that as much as he wanted to, Stephen was too much of a gentlemen to impart any bodily harm to her.

He walked to the door and when he turned back, his face bore a calm and serene expression. It was hard to believe that just seconds before it had been etched in fury.

"Please pack at once. You will be leaving here."

"Oh, don't worry, Captain Kirkland. I do not intend to remain one moment longer in any quarters that belong to you."

"You do not understand, Patricia. I am taking you to Ravenwood with me."

The announcement left her at a

temporary loss for words. She could only gape at him in astonishment. She began to stammer, unable to disguise her pleasure. "But that is your parents'— Why would you take me? Why would you want me to. . . . ?" She faltered helplessly, then cleared her throat and took a deep breath. "Ravenwood? Isn't that your parent's home?"

Stephen saw her confusion and his dark eyes gleamed with devilry.

"And do put on something more conservative, Patricia. You would make a greater impression on my family if you were wearing a little more than a towel."

12

Barbara jumped to her feet when Stephen swung Patricia on the deck of the sloop and rushed over to throw her arms around her.

Stephen stepped lithely on board behind her, and at his nod, Thomas Sutherland struck the sail. The small ship began to glide smoothly into the channel of the James River as the swirling water surged at the sides of the vessel.

Thick forests lined the water's edge. Occasionally a pier broke the wooded shore and a stately manor could be seen through the thick foliage.

Tom and a black man named Abraham busied themselves with the sail, while Stephen steered the ship through the rapidly flowing river.

Patricia and Barbara sat talking quietly. Barbara was ecstatic that Stephen had included Patricia on the trip to Ravenwood. It convinced her that Stephen was truly in love with Patricia or he would never have considered taking her home with him.

After about an hour on the river, Abraham produced a large straw hamper and they dined on pieces of cold roasted chicken, hard-boiled eggs, and a tasty corn relish. Thick slices of a moist gingerbread cake were also wrapped in bright red-and-white checkered napkins. There were even a bottle of wine and a container of cold milk.

As they passed many of the docks and boats that lined the route, people would wave and shout a "Welcome home" to Stephen and Tom when they recognized them. Barbara and Patricia both noticed that there seemed to be a considerably more enthusiasm among the young females than from the males.

Finally, after several hours on the river, Stephen steered the vessel to a long wharf and Tom dropped the anchor. Abraham quickly jumped out and tied the ship to a piling.

The ladies peered through the massive oaks and dogwoods and glimpsed a huge two-storied red brick house in the distance. Several people had started down the worn path leading to the pier. At the sight of one of the men, Tom Sutherland's eyes sparkled with excitement.

"Grandfather!" he called out and

began to wave frantically. He swung Barbara off the ship, then ran up the path toward an old man who was approaching. A negro man was walking cautiously beside him.

Tom hugged the old man and smiled down into the wrinkled face of his grandfather, Jonathan Piedmont Sutherland. Now in his late seventies, the old man's blue eyes still twinkled with boyish warmth; his once-red hair had turned to white, but he still walked straight and unbowed with a spring to his step.

"So, you're home, Tom," Jonathan said. The simple sentence conveyed the deep emotion he felt.

"I said I would always come back to you, Grandfather," Tom replied, smiling tenderly at the man.

"Let me look at you, Son," Jonathan said.

Tom stepped back and the old man's eyes scrutinized the tall, younger man. "You've filled in some, and you're a man now," he said, his eyes beaming with pride. What was left unsaid was the strong resemblance Tom bore to his father, William, Jonathan's son, who had been dead for fifteen years.

Jonathan Sutherland's eyes shifted to the dock. "Do I see that rogue Stephen?" he asked with a warm chuckle.

"Yes, Grandfather. We came home together."

"Has he got himself a wife yet?" he asked with the privileged irascibility of the old.

Thomas threw back his head with laughter. "Not yet, sir, but I think he is working on it. Wait right here, Grandfather, I have someone I would like you to meet."

He hurried down to the dock where Barbara had just met Stephen's parents, Michael and Nancy Kirkland. He shook his uncle's hand, embraced his aunt and bestowed a quick kiss on her cheek, then grabbed Barbara's hand and pulled her up the path to where the old man was standing.

"Grandfather, this is Barbara Kirkland. She is a distant relative from Boston."

Barbara dipped in a curtsey. "It's a pleasure to meet you, sir." Her brown eyes were round and warm and two dimples danced across her cheeks as she smiled a greeting. A few brown curls were peeking out of her forehead from under the brim of the brown taffeta capuchin. The rose-colored lining enhanced the lovely glow of her face and she made a stunning picture to the eyes of the old man.

"Are you going to marry this girl, Thomas?"

"I am considering it, sir—when she decides to grow up," Thomas affirmed.

"It appears to me she's done enough growing. The trouble with you and that rapscallion Stephen is that you spend so much time gallavanting around the world, you're never around when these young buds start to blossom. Marry her, Thomas, while she's still able to give you some sons. Our house has been empty for too long."

Barbara's face turned a shade deeper than the lining of her hood. At the sight of her Tom began to chuckle with amusement. "Well, Mistress Kirkland, I think you have finally met someone who is more brash than you are," he taunted.

Barbara was too spirited to suffer a loss of words for any length of time. She recovered as soon as her blush faded.

"Well, Grandfather Sutherland, I am not certain I am ready to marry your grandson. I think I have a few years remaining in me before I am put out to pasture." Her eyes glowed with affection for the old man.

"If that darn-fool boy don't speak out for you, I'll claim you myself," he chortled. "After all, I am the reigning patriarch of the clan. I do have certain privileges."

"Well, if that's the case, you old rascal, I must protect my own interests," Tom interjected. He turned to Barbara and doffed his hat with a sweeping bow. "Mistress Kirkland, will you do me the honor of becoming my wife before my lecherous old grandfather spirits you away?"

Barbara's dimples tucked bewitchingly into her cheeks as she tapped a finger on her chin and regarded the two men. "I am afraid I have to think about this, Mister Sutherland. It isn't every day in the week that a young girl gets two such appealing proposals of marriage." She slipped her arm through Jonathan Sutherland's. "I think we might have to talk about this, Grandfather." She threw Tom a sassy smile over her shoulder as, arm and arm, she and Jonathan Sutherland began walking up the path to the house.

For a few seconds Thomas Sutherland stood watching them, shaking his head in amusement before he followed behind.

Patricia stood aside self-consciously as Stephen greeted his parents.

Nancy Kirkland was radiant with happiness over the safe return of her son. Patricia marveled at her beauty. In her early fifties, Nancy was still an elegantly attractive woman with a slim figure, blue eyes, and stunning gray hair.

Patricia paid equal attention to Stephen's father, Michael. Charles

Reardon had indicated that this was the man responsible for his brother's dilemma. Charles had painted the man as a conniving schemer, but she could not see anything in the way he greeted his son to substantiate such an accusation.

Michael Kirkland, although not as tall as his son, still stood over six feet and was a handsome and well-built man. It was apparent he did not suffer from indolence. Despite his distinguished bearing, there was a down-to-earth friendliness about him that was not only on the surface. She sensed it in the manner in which he greeted her when Stephen introduced them.

The color of his eyes was as deep as Stephen's, and when he smiled she could see a strong resemblance in their mouths.

Nancy Kirkland's welcome was just as sincere, although Patricia sensed a more curious and perhaps speculative assessment from her. However, she seemed genuinely pleased that Stephen had brought Patricia with him.

"Are you certain I won't be an imposition?" Patricia apologized. "I feel so awkward about your having no advance warning that I was coming." She darted a glare in Stephen's direction, but he shrugged it off.

"I gather Peter and David are not home," Stephen said.

Nancy Kirkland shook her head sadly. "It's ridiculous! I haven't seen either of your brothers in two years. Peter is in New Orleans and David is as far west as he can go, in California." She shook her head again. "I just don't understand it. Are their lives so miserable here at home that all my sons had to stray to all these strange places?"

"Now, now, Nancy," Michael Kirkland cautioned. "Before you know it, you are going to be in tears." He bent down and kissed her cheek. "You just raised three sons who have no desire to become planters."

"Well, when I look at our friends, surrounded by their children and grandchildren, what do I have in comparison? A few letters tied with a ribbon in a steel box! It's a small comfort."

She turned to Patricia with an apologetic smile. "I am sorry to bore you with this family prattle."

"I sympathize with you perfectly, Mrs. Kirkland, and I admire your fortitude. I am not certain I could bear having my sons in distant places."

Nancy patted her hand. "Thank you, Patricia. You don't mind if I call you Patricia, do you?"

"Oh, please do, Mrs. Kirkland," Patricia assured her.

"I can't tell you what a comfort it is to have a woman with whom I can air this grievance. Do you know what it is like to be completely surrounded by men? Men don't seem to recognize it. They consider these exploits to be noble and courageous." Her lovely face screwed up in a disgusted grimace.

Patricia wanted to tell her she understood it perfectly, because, she too, had lived in a womanless world.

"Now, Nancy, all we have ever said is that it's perfectly natural for a man to want to find out what is on the other side of the mountain," Michael Kirkland said indulgently.

"Come, Patricia," he said, putting his arm around her shoulder. "Or she'll keep you down here at this dock bemoaning her lot all through the night. Stephen, you escort your mother back to the house while I take care of this lovely young woman you have brought home with you."

Charmers! Patricia groaned to herself. *All these Kirkland men are incredible charmers! They must be a menace to the entire female population of Virginia!*

"Your home is beautiful, Mr. Kirkland," Patricia exclaimed as they approached the huge structure.

"Thank you, it was built by my grandfather, Matthew Elliott, near the end of the last century."

The big, two-storied brick building had gabled windows and a wing on each side of the house. As they came nearer Patricia could see several of the many outbuildings that surrounded it.

The stables, spinning house and grist mill were easily identifiable, but she had no idea what the other buildings contained.

The houses were surrounded by a multitude of massive oaks, box cedars, pines, huge elms, and dogwoods. Patricia was so used to cobblestone streets and blocks of shops that she thrilled to the splendor and dignity of the structure. What a totally different way of life!

The interior of the house was as gracious as its exterior. Patricia was dazzled at the sight of a Waterford chandelier hanging in the central hall. A myriad of colors danced on the opposite wall as the setting sun reflected off the crystal teardrops that hung from the chandelier.

The huge rooms, with twelve-foot ceilings, were furnished in elegant splendor. Panels of hand-carved mahogany reached from floor to ceiling, and the wooden floors had been polished until they shone. Patricia had heard stories about the opulent luxury in these Virginian mansions and this house gave credence to such rumors.

Patricia felt like an interloper the moment she stepped through the massive double oak doors.

13

When they sat down to dine later that evening, Grandfather Sutherland insisted on sitting between Patricia and Barbara.

As they waited to be served, Patricia's eyes swept the room with interest. The dining room was as elegant as the rest of the house. They were seated at a long mahogany table; a huge pewter chandelier hung above it, and a mammoth rug that Stephen had brought from Persia covered most of the polished wooden floor.

The walls of the room were papered in Wedgwood blue and lined with shelves holding pewterware and attractive pieces of Wedgwood china. The workmanship of the finely-crafted pieces was superb. Pewter tankards and chalices were interspersed on the shelves with the warm richness of Wedgwood bowls and cups. Large pewter trenchers and plates stood on end lining the walls and delicate pewter spoons hung across the front of the shelves.

A servant carried in a tray holding two roasted ducks that had been simmered in a savory bourbon sauce and then coated with an orange glaze. They were perched on a nest of wild rice; thick slices of oranges dusted with brown sugar and sauted in butter garnished the platter.

Jonathan Sutherland carried on an outrageous conversation with the two women during the whole meal to the complete chagrin of his daughter, Nancy Kirkland. She was relieved when the ladies could excuse themselves from the table and leave the men to their cigars and glasses of brandy.

Once alone in the comfortable drawing room, she had a chance to observe the two women who were her guests.

Barbara Kirkland was an unexpected delight sent to her from heaven. The strong resemblance between the vivacious girl and her dead daughter Beth was unbelievable. It was as if Beth had returned home. The fact that her nephew Tom was so openly smitten with the girl was an added assurance that she would have the company of the elfin-faced sprite in the years ahead.

Her gaze lingered longer on Patricia Fairchild with a motherly curiosity. She found her to be an exquisitely beautiful woman. There did not seem to be a flaw in her lovely face. However, there was no doubt that the woman was uncomfortable in her presence. Nancy did not know what she had done to cause this uneasiness.

Stephen had not told her a word about her. She was the first woman he had ever brought home with him. Was it possible her errant son had finally fallen in love? Glory be! she thought reverently.

Several of the daughters of local families had chased Stephen outrageously for years, but none had ever seemed to hold his interest for any length of time. As much as he tried to disguise it, it was obvious to her that Stephen could not keep his eyes off this woman. Yet Nancy sensed, with a mother's intuition, that a serious problem existed between the two.

She handed Patricia a cup of tea and, as the young woman reached for it, their gazes met. Nancy Kirkland smiled graciously and Patricia returned a nervous smile. *Why is she so uncomfortable?* Nancy wondered.

Patricia sipped her tea, waiting for the questions she was certain would follow. She had not failed to observe Mrs. Kirkland's interest. Patricia knew that in a matter of moments Stephen's mother would get to the inevitable questions and then the masquerade would be over, and there would be the usual look of scorn and disapproval. *Damn Stephen. Why couldn't he have at least made it easier by telling his mother the whole truth about me?* she thought resentfully.

"Have you lived in Boston your whole life, Patricia?" Nancy Kirkland inquired.

"Only the last twelve years. My mother died when I was ten years old, and that is when my father and I came to America."

"What a coincidence!" Nancy exclaimed. "My mother died when I was ten, too. Do go on, Patricia," Nancy added.

"My father died when I was twelve. I married George Fairchild when I was sixteen years old."

Nancy Kirkland's eyes widened in surprise. "I didn't realize you were married, my dear."

"I am a widow, Mrs. Kirkland. My husband died two years ago."

"Oh you poor dear. It always is so tragic when death strikes down the young."

Patricia put down her cup to brace herself for what was to follow her announcement. "Death is a tragedy anytime it strikes, Mrs. Kirkland. My husband was sixty years old when he died. He married me when he was fifty-six." Patricia's eyes remained downcast. She didn't want to see the shock and condemnation in the woman's eyes.

Nancy put down her own teacup. Her stricken glance swung to Barbara, who had remained silent, in sympathy for her friend.

Nancy moved over and put a comforting arm around Patricia's shoulder. "You've had to bear a great deal of grief, for one so young. I am so sorry, my dear," she said kindly.

Patricia looked up in surprise. There was no censure, no sign of disapproval. There was only sympathy in the woman's eyes.

"You don't understand, Mrs. Kirkland. Mine was not a love match, it was a marriage of convenience. I was all alone and George Fairchild was like a father to me. He wanted to take care of me."

"Nonsense!" Nancy Kirkland declared. "It's obvious to me you loved him very much, and he certainly loved you, or he would not have been concerned about your welfare. The desire to protect someone you love is one of the greatest evidences of love there is. Aren't you confusing love with passion, my dear?"

"I never did, Mrs. Kirkland, but others certainly did. You see, my husband was a very wealthy man. Therefore everyone considered it a very sordid relationship. They assumed I married George just for his money."

Nancy studied her with kindly regard. "Do you believe you did, Patricia?"

"Of course not," Patricia disclaimed. "George Fairchild was the kindest and most gentle man I have ever known. I loved him very much."

"How did he die, Patricia?" Nancy asked gently.

"He was robbed and brutally murdered one night on the waterfront."

Nancy shook her head sadly and clasped Patricia's hand in the warmth of her own. "How tragic! There is so much grief in people's lives."

"Tell me," she asked on a lighter note, "how you met Stephen. Was it through Barbara and her family?"

Patricia knew that up to this moment Nancy Kirkland had been incredibly tolerant and understanding about her past, but now there would be no way this gracious lady would be able to accept her profession.

"I operate a casino, Mrs. Kirkland. I own it jointly with my husband's previous business associate."

This announcement was as much of a surprise to Barbara as it was to Nancy Kirkland. Both of the women's eyes widened with shock.

"Do you mean a *gambling* casino?" Nancy asked.

"I can't believe it!" Barbara exclaimed. "Patricia, why didn't you tell me this before? How absolutely exciting!"

Patricia was grateful for Barbara's continued support, but she was conscious of Mrs. Kirkland's silence. She raised her head defiantly. "Yes, it's a gambling casino. That is where I met Stephen. But you don't have to worry about your son, Mrs. Kirkland. I have no designs on him."

Nancy Kirkland's blue eyes flared. "I beg your pardon, Patricia, but it's a privilege of motherhood to worry about a son or daughter, no matter how old they may be. So I will be the judge of whether or not I worry about Stephen. And I can tell you honestly, I *will* worry about him. But not for the reason you would like to believe.

"I don't worry whether he's eating properly, or if he's clothed warmly in a rainstorm. I hope I raised him well enough for him to make those kinds of judgments for himself.

"And I can tell you that I definitely do not worry whether or not the woman he loves is good enough for him, because he is the only one who can make that determination. When he does, if *he* thinks she's worthy of his love, that will be all that will be necessary as far as his father and I are concerned.

"But I will tell you what I do worry about. I worry every time his boat disappears around the bend of the river whether or not it will be the last time we will ever see each other. That is my worry about Stephen." Her eyes were glistening with tears.

"If you expect me to pass some kind of judgment on you, I am afraid I am going to disappoint you, Patricia. I have been surrounded by the love of my family my whole lifetime. I have had them to lean upon and support me during my moments of grief. Do you think I would censure a woman who has had to bear life's misfortunes alone? God forgive me if I even try!" Nancy declared vehemently.

"I am sorry if my attitude has offended you, Mrs. Kirkland. It is just that in Boston I learned to expect censure and I guess I anticipated the same here," Patricia said contritely.

Nancy Kirkland gave her an affecionate squeeze and rose to her feet. "You're in Virginia now, honey. You've come to the right place to start enjoying your life before any more of it passes by."

"I'm only here for a week, Mrs. Kirkland," Patricia said, laughing lightly. "I don't think we can accomplish miracles in such a short time."

"Well, we're going to try—beginning tomorrow. The church guild is holding a tea tomorrow afternoon. It's going to be a pleasure to introduce you ladies. My goodness!" she said with a gay toss of her gray head, "the appearance of you two lovely ladies is surely going to set a lot of worried tongues wagging!"

When they left the drawing room the men had just finished their cigars and Jonathan Sutherland, over Nancy's protests to remain the night, insisted upon returning to his own home and bed. Tom and Barbara agreed to escort him and the three disappeared in a carriage.

Patricia willingly accepted Stephen's offer for an evening stroll. The moonlight cast a bright gleam of light on the fragrant garden. The aroma of lavender, columbine, yellow jasmine, and the roses Nancy Kirkland's loved best, hung pleasantly on the air.

Patricia and Stephen meandered silently along a path of neatly trimmed hedges, both deep in thought.

Patricia's thoughts were still on her conversation with Nancy Kirkland. Were all the people in Virginia this liberal-minded, or was it just this wild Kirkland clan? And why was Stephen so different from the rest of his family? They all believed in 'live and let live'—all, that is, except Stephen!

"Your grandfather is an enjoyable old man," she said warmly.

"I hope he doesn't take you in with all his bawdy suggestions. He's a big fake. He hasn't even glanced at a woman since my grandmother died over forty years ago."

"He certainly didn't fool me, and I am certain he didn't fool Barbara either," she laughed. "It's strange, though, that he never remarried. He must have been widowed very young."

"There is a saying in our clan that there can only be one love in the life of a Kirkland male. It seems to have proven true through the years," Stephen said solemnly.

They halted at a small spinning house, and Stephen showed her the looms and spools of flax before they moved on to the a grist mill, a dovecote, a cooling house, the barn, and, finally, the stables. Patricia found it all fascinating. It was like a little community within itself, she thought as they paused at the stall of one of the sleek horses.

"Do you ride, Tory?" Stephen asked.

"Yes. I always made it a practice to take a ride each morning in Boston. I love it," she responded with eyes aglow.

"This is Vulcan. How are you doing, old boy?" He began patting the neck of the powerful black stallion. The horse tossed his head in response to the attention. "I think riding is the thing I miss the most when I'm at sea."

Patricia chuckled lightly. "That would never have been my guess."

"Is that right, Madam Fairchild!" He propped an arm up on the wall on each side of her head, pinning her back against the stable door. "And just what would have been your guess?" he challenged. His head lowered dangerously, nearly to hers.

"A woman, of course, Captain."

"We do touch port periodically," he said huskily.

Her eyes were locked with his. "I said a *woman*, Captain, not women." In a mere flicker the sexual tension that lay between them had sprung into awareness. "I mean a particular woman."

"Don't you know that the only woman in a sailor's life is his ship?" he taunted. His head dipped lower and his lips brushed her ear. "She's a very possessive mistress."

"Then we must not do anything to incite her wrath," she chided him and, ducking under his arms, she stepped away.

Stephen followed dociley behind her with an ambiguous smile as they returned to the house.

14

Tom and Barbara entered the library of his home after turning Grandfather Sutherland over to one of the servants. The house was soon quiet after his grandfather and the servants retired for the night. A low fire glowed in the fireplace and Tom lit a lamp that stood on the desk. "Just make yourself comfortable, Bab. I promised Stephen I would check some figures in the ledger. It shouldn't take me too long."

Barbara began to wander aimlessly around the room as he rifled through several ledgers that were lying on the desk. She pulled a book of poetry from one of the shelves and sat down in an upholstered chair in front of the fireplace. She attempted to read, but her eyes constantly strayed to the broad back of Thomas Sutherland, as he worked over the books.

There was an exciting intimacy about the interior of the room and Thomas's masculinity seemed more overpowering to her as she studied him beneath half-closed lids.

The dim light cast him in abstract shadows and Barbara stared in fascination. He leaned across the desk and pulled a heavy book off a shelf. His lithe movement was like that of a leopard, whose effortless grace of motion hinted at the contained strength that could be unleashed in a flickering of an eye.

Thomas suddenly turned his head toward her. "You look as if you are going to fall asleep," he said with a devastating grin.

"No, I'm not sleepy," she denied quickly. "I have been studying you."

"I know," he answered softly, "I can feel your eyes on me."

She blushed slightly, embarrassed by the knowledge that she was so transparent to him. "Does it make you nervous?"

Tom rose from his chair and walked over to stand above her. "Yes, it makes me nervous, but not for the reason you may think. It excites me, Bab. It drives me crazy when you do it." He took the book from her hands and put it aside.

Barbara's heart began thumping against the wall of her chest as he reached down and took her hand, pulling her to her feet. He sat down in the chair she had just vacated and pulled her down onto his lap. The heat from his thighs scorched her as he began to examine each of her fingers intently. This new and unexpected intimacy with him was disturbing and she tried to still her trembling, but it was an impossible task.

"May I ask what is so fascinating about my fingertips?" she asked nervously. Just his touch was causing a heady reaction in her.

"I intend to get to know every inch of you," Thomas said softly. "I am beginning with your fingertips, since they are the only things accessible right now."

Barbara could not contain her immediate blush at the suggestiveness of the remark. Thomas saw her discomfort and his face softened with a slight grin.

His mouth was a throaty whisper at her ear, and an erotic shiver swept through her as she felt the stimulating warmth of his breath against her skin. "Have you ever been kissed, Bab?"

"Yes," she replied hesitantly.

"Did you like it?" His mouth slid down the slender column of her neck.

"Not always," she answered truthfully.

"Then you are aware that you are about to be kissed again." He chuckled lightly, the warm timbre of it as a provocative to her as his touch.

He pulled her across his lap, his

mouth firm and exciting as he kissed her. It was a kiss far different from any she had ever known. She felt secure and contended as she lay in his arms, yet every nerve in her body was responding to him. Her look worshipped him as she gazed up; his hand tenderly caressed her face before he slowly pushed the scarf off her head.

She remained still, studying every nuance of his expression, looking for a sign of disappointment in his eyes. All she saw was adoration gleaming in their depths.

"Do you mind that my hair is clipped? That it's so unstylish?"

He shook his head. "Of course not."

"I want to be so beautiful for you, Tom. I want everything to be very special." Now that their hour had begun, there was no question in either of their minds as to its final outcome.

"You are beautiful to me, sweetheart," he said tenderly, tossing the flattened mass of dark curls with the palm of his hand. He smiled down into her worried eyes. "I love the way you look, Bab." He picked up a stray curl and played with its silkiness. "I love every one of these little curls on your head." He pressed it to his lips and kissed it.

"I should let you up because I know I am not going to be able to keep my hands off you tonight. You would be wise to get the hell out of here right now and get back to Ravenwood," he warned in a husky whisper.

Barbara had no intention of leaving. She had been waiting for this moment between them and was not going to attempt to pretend maidenly modesty. She was in love with Thomas Sutherland, in love with all the intensity her young heart was capable of and she wanted him with an equal passion. She no longer felt young and awkward. Tom had made her aware of her own womanhood. She was no longer the foolish girl who had left Boston. In his arms she was the woman she was destined to become.

And she knew for that reason, she was ready for this moment, that this moment was far and beyond any other consideration. No matter what lay in the future, there never would, and never could, be a more *right* moment between them. Her woman's intuition told her as much, and she recognized it for its absolute rightness.

Barbara smiled secretively. "I don't want to leave," she half-whispered, unaware the words had even slipped through her lips. There was a mysterious and diverting smile on her face, as mysterious and alluring as an ancient sphinx.

At the sight of it, Tom whispered

huskily, "I fear that I am the one who is at your mercy, my lady."

The sight of his tender smile caused her to reach up and stroke his cheek, as if to capture his smile in the palm of her hand. For a breathless moment their gazes were locked together. Her fingers wove through his dark hair, forcing his head down to hers. This time the kiss was deeper, she the agressor.

Thomas forced himself to pull his mouth away from hers, but continued to stare down at her. His breathing had become labored. His eyes had deepened, mirroring the battle he was waging with himself. "Are you certain you know what you are doing, Bab?" he whispered hoarsely.

"Tom."

His name on her lips was like an urgent plea for him to continue. His finger slowly traced the delicate outline of her mouth. His lips parted in a breathless offering, as though his fingertips were transmitting a sensation from her lips to his own.

She stopped the motion with a shuddering breath, grabbing his hand away from her mouth. "That's driving me crazy, Tom. I don't understand everything I'm feeling at this moment, but I hope you are seducing me because I—"

She never got any farther because

his lips closed off her words. He covered her mouth and face with light kisses. She closed her eyes, and as she lay back in his arms, she could feel the flutter of her heart each time his lips pressed a kiss on her eyes, the pulse of her temple, the hollow of her throat—or took a lazy slide to toy with her ear. Always they returned to reclaim her lips again and again. The fluttering in her chest became a wild throbbing when his tongue began to trace the outline of her lips.

Their kisses deepened, his tongue exploring and probing, seeking and finding hers as they began to lose themselves in the fervor of their escalating passion.

His hand was warm, arousing, as it released the buttons of her bodice and slid beneath her chemise. She moaned aloud when he began to fondle a quivering breast. Its fullness filled his hand and the feel of its hardened crest was not satisfying enough. In his urgency, he pushed the bodice off her shoulders.

Thomas' head dipped and his mouth, warm and moist, closed around each peak, as he concentrated on first one, then the other. Barbara was trembling and arched achingly against the pressure of his mouth in response to the arousing titilation. When his tongue joined the play and began curling and tracing lazy patterns around them, her body began to writhe with erotic sensation.

She lost her hold on reality and surrendered to the feeling consuming her. He lifted her in his arms and lay her on the rug in front of the fireplace. His eyes worshipped her as he slipped the gown down the length of her, then removed her petticoat and stays.

Barbara watched shamelessly as Tom divested himself of his clothing. Her wide round eyes were slumberous with the weight of passion. She lay silent, trusting but flushed with the expectation of what was to follow.

His body appeared awesome to her, the muscular litheness of a man who was no stranger to hard toil. The curled hair on his chest pressed against her now, creating a new and excruciating ecstasy against her naked breasts.

She burst into flame and had no idea when or how he removed her remaining clothing. Her ears were deafened to her own pleas when his hand began to explore her intimately. Mindless, her head became a whirling mass of flashing, indistinguishable colors that seemed to blot out everything except the sensation mounting within her.

How could anything building toward such a dangerous eruption fill her with such exquisite, unrestrained rapture? In the throes of passion, she unknowingly squirmed and writhed beneath the long muscular length of him.

Her uninhibited response presented an obstacle to him, because her spontaneous sobs, roaming hands and searching lips were raising him to the same incredible heights in which she was swirling about helplessly.

A shudder swept through her as he pressed the throbbing evidence of his passion between her thighs and began to probe the thin layer of resistance. She gasped with the shock of pain when he forced his entry, but his lips immediately swooped down to cover hers before she could cry out. The rhythm of his thrusts began to increase and his tongue combined with them until she found herself soaring to incredible heights of ecstasy that she was certain would be impossible to attain ever again.

Her body exploded in a glorious release as he discharged the heated moisture of his love into her, as if to blend with the life-sustaining blood of her body.

They remained entwined for a long time afterward. Their breathing steadied and they were able to speak of what their bodies had so eloquently expressed only moments before, two lovers now speaking words of love that their breathlessness had prevented them from uttering during their lovemaking.

Barbara had no feeling of modesty as Thomas's eyes devoured her nude body. Lying on his side with his head propped in his hand, he could not seem to get enough of the silken feel of her, and his hand continued to fondle her in caressing sweeps.

"I want to marry you, Bab," he said. "Now, as quickly as possible."

"I have my parents to consider, Tom," she replied.

"We will send word to them. You know as well as I it would be too awkward to try to get married in Boston. The situation there is too explosive." He sat up and began to gather her clothing together. "Come on, brown eyes. Let's get dressed. I want us married before *The Liberty* sails again."

He stopped suddenly, as if stunned, and his eyes swung back to her in alarm. "You do want to marry me, don't you, Bab?"

She nodded, a diverting dimple appearing in each cheek, forcing him to lean down and begin kissing each one. She slipped her arms around his neck and sighed deeply.

"Oh, yes indeed, Thomas Sutherland. I do want to marry you."

Once again their lips melded and soon their bodies, too, were fused together in a blissful consumation.

15

At tea the next afternoon Patricia and Barbara sat facing the avid interest and blatant resentment of some of the young maidens in the parish.

It was obvious that several of the ladies had looked forward to the home-coming of Thomas Sutherland and Stephen Kirkland, only to have their expectations dashed by the presence of these two interlopers from Boston.

Patricia was thankful that, although her riding habit was not actually appropriate for the occasion, it was, at least, new. Clothing a woman in a new gown and bonnet was equivalent to arming a warrior with a shield and sword—it fortified her for combat.

Barbara was dressed in a becoming gown of pale yellow taffeta. Its full skirt flowed over a pannier and a ruffled chemise peeked out from a scooped neckline. The sleeves flared at the elbows into lacy ruffles and an elegant apron of white linen covered the front of the gown. Her short hair was concealed beneath a low crowned hat made of white linen with green and yellow crewel embroidery. A lace-edged kerchief was tied around the hat and under her chin in a bow.

Several of the younger girls engaged the newcomers in conversation as they sipped their tea.

"How long will we have the pleasure of your company?" a dark-haired belle with a sugary smile inquired of Barbara.

"I haven't put any limit on my stay," Barbara replied, returning the smile. "It is such a pleasure to get to know all my relatives, as distant as they may be," she added.

"Are y'all related to them too, Miss Patricia?" one of the ladies asked.

Patricia shook her head. "No, I came down here on business and Stephen was considerate enough to invite me to Ravenwood. It is such a beautiful plantation. So different from Boston. Don't you agree, Miss Barbara?" she asked lightly.

"Oh, yes indeed, Miss Patricia, I am not certain I ever want to return to those crowded streets again," Barbara chirped. At the look of disappointment on several of the women's faces, she added, "Tom is insistent I remain." Her brown eyes rolled suggestively. "And I am sure some of you know how persuasive he can be."

"Have y'all known Stephen very long?" the woman pursued. It was clear that she had more than just a casual interest in Stephen Kirkland.

"Not at all. I met him for the first time just a few days before we sailed," Patricia replied.

"My goodness! And he asked y'all to Ravenwood! Ah do declare, that is quite astonishin' for Stephen!"

A young woman with golden hair hanging almost to her waist and a cleavage that was awesome to behold, eyed Barbara curiously. "I notice, Miss Barbara, y'all appear to be wearin' your hair unusually short?"

"Do you think so, dear?" Barbara asked with a forced smile. "It's the latest style in Boston. Long hair is considered to be extremely unfashionable."

The young girl curved a brow in disdain. "Well, Boston women have never been famous for their style," she simpered. She grasped some strands of her hair that were dangling over the huge mounds of her breasts. "Why, ah would feel positively naked without my hair! Ah have often said, ah would surrender my virtue before ah'd give up my long hair." Her long lashes fluttered above the fan she brought to her mouth with a nervous giggle.

Barbara's face was wreathed in a friendly smile. "I certainly admire your determination, if not your discrimination, Miss Mary Sue." She turned to

Patricia. "I wonder how many times she has already tested that theory?" she whispered sotto voce to Patricia behind her own fan.

"Will y'all be joinin' us tomorrow at the bazaar? We're engagin' in a fudge makin' auction for charity. All the proceeds go to support the orphange. It's a very worthy cause."

"Well, I really have no idea what Aunt Nancy has planned for us," Barbara said.

"Of course, we understand. If y'all have never made fudge before, it can be very difficult," one of the young ladies piped in. "Tom Sutherland says ah make the best fudge in the entire county. My Daddy says he and my momma named me Divinity because ah'm as sweet as a piece of candy. Would y'all believe anything so silly, Miss Barbara?" Divinity preened.

Patricia was admiring how well Barbara was restraining herself during the whole conversation. Knowing the younger girl the way she did, she was certain that Barbara must have been biting her tongue.

"Well, I don't think it's silly, Miss Divinity, because you certainly are," Barbara agreed. "Why I said to Miss Patricia just a short while ago, 'Isn't Miss Divinity the sweetest thing you have ever met?"

Patricia had just taken a sip of her tea when all eyes swung in her direction, apparently waiting to hear what had been her reply. She gulped down the tea and said sweetly, "Yes she did, and I agreed that I don't know when I've met anyone sweeter. Except Miss Barbara herself," Patricia added with an affectionate smile in Barbara's direction.

Divinity Forsythe raised her fan to her mouth with a self-satisfied smile. "Tom Sutherland always bids on my fudge. It was always so embarrasin'! Why, he would bid the most outlandish price to get it! Sometimes as much as fifty pounds!"

Barbara's head bobbed in agreement. "Well, that certainly sounds like Tom, Miss Divinity. Generous to a fault. He believes that no sacrifice is too great as long as it's for charity. As a matter of fact, he did the same thing while he was in Boston—at a charity cotillion. He insisted on bidding an outrageous amount of money just for the privilege of dancing with me." Her brown eyes flashed with a saucy sparkle. "Isn't he the most charitable rogue!"

"Then we can expect y'all be joinin' us tomorrow. It will be great fun, but don't be too surprised if Tom bids on my fudge," Divinity Forsythe declared with a smug simper.

Perhaps Barbara was capable of it,

but Patricia knew she was not going to be able to restrain herself for another moment. "Will you ladies excuse us, please? I feel the need for a breath of fresh air, and I am hoping Miss Barbara will accompany me."

She grabbed Barbara's hand and yanked her out the door. "I don't know about you, Barbara Kirkland, but I have never made fudge in my whole life, so please exclude me from these plans you are making."

"I have never made it, either," Barbara declared with a bland smile.

"Then why in the world did you allow those women to goad you into entering this contest?"

"Because, Miss Patricia, Tom Sutherland has swallowed the last piece of Miss Divinity's fudge he is ever going to eat," she asserted with a positive toss of her head.

"But if you have never made fudge before, how do you expect to be able to do it tomorrow? You'll make a complete fool of yourself."

Barbara Kirkland remained adamant. "I will get the recipe from the Kirklands' cook. I am sure the two of us should have no trouble following it."

Patricia was uncertain she heard her correctly. "Did you say the two of us?" At Barbara's affirmative nod, Patricia threw her hands up in exasperation. "I don't believe you, Barbara. You are absolutely the most audacious person I have ever met. I don't care what *you* do, but I, personally, have no intentions of entering any fudge-making contest! I don't care if Thomas Sutherland grows obese eating Miss Divinity's fudge! That is your problem, not mine."

"But, Patricia, you know I can't do it alone. I need you for moral support."

Patricia was determined not to relent. "And I will give you all the moral support you need—from the sidelines. But there is no way I am going to join you." Barbara just nodded positively, and Patricia knew even as she spoke that tomorrow the two of them would be standing over a stove cooking fudge!

Since the affair was for charity, the following day the whole parish turned out for the occasion. Two dozen brick-enclosed fires had been erected on the lawn of the Exposition Hall. A metal grate was leveled across the top of each one for cooking. An assortment of utensils, such as pots, spoons, trenchers and cups, had been provided at each station.

Under the shade of a mammoth elm there was a table with crocks of butter, syrup, and vanilla, as well as pitchers of milk and water. Huge barrels containing chocolate, sugar, salt, pecans and grated coconut were standing nearby.

Patricia approached their assigned station with all the enthusiasm of a condemned prisoner facing a firing squad. She had never made anything more challenging than a cup of hot chocolate. Now here she was about to make a public spectacle of herself with the whole community looking on. She glanced nervously around and to her dismay, saw Stephen Kirkland and Tom Sutherland lounging indolently against a nearby tree. The lawn was roped off and many of the spectators were sitting on blankets to watch the proceedings. The look of total amusement on Stephen's face was enough to destroy her faltering courage.

Barbara, on the other hand, was like a general surveying the enemy encampment the night before the big battle. Her brown eyes were void of any expression. Whatever she was thinking was concealed behind an enigmatic mask.

She carefully examined the pot and wooden spoons that were the primary utensils needed.

"Yoo hoo, y'all," a voice called out. They swung around to discover Mary Sue Harper and Divinity Forsythe waving to them. "Good luck over there."

Barbara raised a hand and waved back to them, flashing a broad smile as she returned the greeting. "Good luck, Miss Divinity. Good luck, Miss Mary

Sue."

"Good Lord!" Patricia groaned aloud.

Barbara regarded her with a raised brow. "You clearly do not understand, Miss Patricia. I intend to be Tom's wife, so I have to cultivate the friendship—or at least the respect—of these women." Her eyes sparkled with impishness.

"Well, good luck, Miss Barbara, because you'll need even more luck doing that than making this fudge today."

Barbara covertly produced a piece of paper she had tucked in her sleeve, on which she had written Essie's fudge recipe. "Here, read this, but I don't want anyone to see it."

As she was handing it to Patricia, the paper slipped from her fingers and fell on the grill. Both girls watched, horrified, as it flattened itself against the red hot grate. A black smoldering circle appeared in the center, gradually widening until the paper burst into flames.

"Good Lord! What do we do now?" Patricia asked aghast.

"We do not lose heart," Barbara said firmly.

A sudden pistol blast officially announced the beginning of the event. "Oh, yes we do!" Patricia exclaimed.

The crowd cheered and clapped as the ladies rushed to get the ingredients they needed. "I'll get the chocolate and you go and get a half cup of milk," Barbara ordered with a frantic gleam forming in her eyes.

When Patricia hurried back with the milk, Barbara already had the chocolate in a black cast-iron pot setting on the grill. "I couldn't remember whether we're supposed to use two ounces of chocolate or two cups, so I compromised and used one cup," she announced as she poured the milk into the pot and mixed the ingredients together.

"Is this all we need?" Patricia asked dubiously, looking into the pot.

"No, we have to have some syrup, too. Let's keep all the measurements the same, so get a cup of syrup while I get us some salt."

"Well, if you want everything the same, shouldn't I get some more milk? You told me to get only a half cup of milk."

"No. I am certain about that measurement. I remember Essie telling me to use a half cup of milk."

"Well, I think we should match the syrup and milk measurements if we are going to be consistent," Patricia argued.

"Just get the syrup—and hurry!" Barbara declared.

Patricia rushed back to the table to get the syrup and when she returned Barbara was stirring the chocolate mixture. Her pert nose turned up in distaste. "This looks too thick. I think it's burning. Maybe you're right. I think we should put in some more milk."

Patricia shook her head in exasperation and dashed back to the table to get another half cup of milk. "What all do we have in there now?" Patricia asked, as she dumped the extra milk into the mixture.

Barbara passed the stirring spoon to Patricia and began to check off the items on her fingers. "We've used a cup of chocolate, a cup of syrup, a cup of milk and . . . a pinch of salt."

"A pinch of salt?" Patricia asked suspiciously. "Is that how much Essie said to use?"

Barbara's eyes danced mischievously. "No. That's how much my mother says to use. Mother refuses to use more than a pinch of salt in anything she makes."

Patricia frowned and looked back toward the table. "Well, I noticed that some of the other women were taking butter and vanilla. There are also pecans and coconut over there."

"I think the pecans go in when it's through cooking and maybe the coconut is to spread on top," Barbara reasoned. "But Tom doesn't like coconut, so let's forget that. Why don't you go to get a cup of vanilla."

"What about the butter?" Patricia asked.

"Well, bring that too."

"Very well, but I am getting tired of making trips to that table. The next time you can go."

Patricia hurried off while Barbara continued to stir the mixture. She looked over at the next station and noticed they were dropping some of the cooked substance into a cup of water.

"Darn it!" she mumbled, and grabbed a pan and raced across the lawn to get some water.

Patricia returned and added the vanilla and butter and resumed stirring the syrupy mixture. It seemed to be sticking to the bottom of the pot. When Barbara returned with the water she put it down on the top of the hot grill and grabbed a spoon to help stir the fudge.

"What do you need the water for?" Patricia asked.

"I am not quite certain. It's got something to do with testing the mixture to see if it's done. I've been watching the other women and they drop some of the fudge into the water."

"What is supposed to happen?"

"Something about forming a ball."

"Well, shall we try it? This is boiling now. Maybe it's through cooking," Patricia suggested.

They picked up the pan that had been

setting on the grill and dropped some of the syrupy mixture into the warm water. It immediately dissolved into a cloudy liquid.

"Well, obviously it must not be done," Barbara lamented. "We will just have to continue cooking it." She resumed stirring the mixture while Patricia watched anxiously.

"Oh no, it's boiling over," Barbara cried out, as the hot syrup began to roll over the sides of the pot.

Both of the girls grabbed a spoon in each hand and attempted to catch the liquid as it ran down the sides and scoop it back into the pot. They were running in circles around the kettle and grill, scooping up the oozing syrup but it continued to dribble down the pot faster than they could catch it. Some of it was sticking to the grate and the rest was dripping into the fire below.

The odor of burning chocolate and smoke began to permeate the air as the two girls continued with their struggle to retrieve the streaming syrup.

"Get the pot off the fire!" Patricia cried through the smoke that was rising from the grill.

"The handle is too hot to lift," Barbara exclaimed, drawing back with a burned finger.

"Use your skirt then," Patricia shouted, as she continued to scoop up the syrup that was still flowing over.

Barbara finally succeeded in lifting the kettle off the top of the hot grill and she plopped it on the grass, where it continued to gurgle and simmer for several seconds before the mixture finally stopped cascading down the sides of the pot.

They stood with their hands on their hips staring down forlornly at the kettle that began to spit at them with sporadic popping bubbles.

"What do you think we should do now?" Barbara asked with a desolate sigh.

"I think we should get on the next ship bound for Boston," Patricia declared.

Barbara regarded her with a pathetic look and Patricia began to laugh. Barbara soon joined her and within a short time the two girls were hugging each other with tears streaming down their cheeks as they stared at the dismal black pot setting bleakly on the ground.

Finally, wiping away her tears with the skirt of her soiled gown, Barbara picked up the errant pot and returned it to the grill.

The pan of water was now boiling furiously on the grill and they dropped a spoon of the syrupy mixture into it. It dissolved into the water as rapidly as the previous test.

"This just doesn't seem to be getting any harder. Do you think we should add more chocolate?" Barbara questioned. She looked over and saw that many of the other women had begun to beat their fudge mixture. "Why don't we try beating it like those other women are doing? We are surely not getting anywhere with this water test."

"Are you certain the water should be hot? Maybe we would be better off if the water was cold," Patricia suggested.

"Water is water," Barbara shrugged. "What does it matter whether it's hot or cold, unless you're drinking it or taking a bath! I think the problem is that we are not cooking it enough. That is probably why it isn't getting hard. Let's cook it for a few more minutes. After all, who wants to eat raw fudge?"

They both continued to stir the fudge until they were satisfied it had cooked for a reasonable length of time. This time Patricia did the honors of lifting the black kettle off the grill and Barbara took a spoon and began to beat it. When she was too exhausted to continue, she passed the pot to Patricia. The mixture soon became so thick, she could not get the spoon out of it.

"I think we are supposed to spread it on a tray now," Barbara declared.

"Spread it on a tray! I can't even beat it, it's so hard. How are we ever going to spread it?" Patricia expounded.

They began to chip at the brittle substance in the pot. "This is very peculiar looking fudge," Patricia reflected. "I think we must have done something wrong."

"We will never get it onto a platter. Tom and Stephen will just have to eat it from the pot," Barbara panted, as she tried to dig it out. She turned the pot on its side and began to pound on it in the hopes of loosening the mixture.

"Someone give them a hammer," a voice called out sarcastically from among the spectators.

Patricia stole a quick glance in the direction of Tom and Stephen and discovered both men were clutching their sides in convulsive laughter.

A large chunk of the mixture broke off and flew out of the pot. Patricia caught it in her apron before it could hit the ground. The girls succeeded in breaking off several more pieces of the candy by the time the auction began.

Mary Sue Harper's and Divinity Forsythe's neat little boxes of cut squares of fudge were sitting on the table. Barbara put down the box containing the misshapen chunks they were able to salvage from the pot. The rest of the mixture was hard and stuck to the sides and bottom of the kettle.

The two girls stood aside, bedraggled

and exhausted. Their hair was disheveled from the exertion of stirring the fudge and their gowns were spotted and soiled. Barbara was still clutching the heavy cast-iron pot in her hand with the handle of the wooden spoon that was mired in the mixture sticking out of it.

The auction moved swiftly, with the families and beaux bidding for their daughters' and sweethearts' candy. Mary Sue Harper trooped off, with a backward smirk in their direction, on the arm of one of the local bachelors who had bid generously on her box.

"I'll bet he ends up getting a lot more than a piece of fudge," Barbara grumbled to Patricia.

The only boxes that now remained were Patricia's and Barbara's, and the the neat little box complete with a lace doily that belonged to Divinity Forstyhe.

The minister picked up the box containing the effects of the heroic endeavor of the two girls. "Now, what is the bid for this fine offering from our two lovely visitors from Boston?" The announcement produced a series of amused chuckles, jostling elbows and pointing fingers.

Tom Sutherland and Stephen Kirkland were sending the spectators into loud laughter with a histrionic display of reaching into the pockets of their trousers and pooling their combined coins.

Tom raised his hand to make his bid. "We bid two shillings, four pence and two—no, three farthings," he called out, recounting the coins.

The minister brought his hand to his mouth to stifle his laugh. "Now, gentlemen, you must remember this is for a worthy cause."

"Are they required to eat it if they buy it, Parson?" a voice called out from the crowd. It sent another wave of laughter through the spectators.

"I am never going to speak to either of them again," Barbara fumed, as Tom and Stephen joined the laughter.

"I told you this would end disastrously," Patricia mumbled. Barbara was on the verge of tears and Patricia was beginning to feel sorry for the girl. It had meant so much to her.

Apparently Stephen Kirkland also felt there had been enough laughter at the girl's expense. "I bid a thousand pounds," he called out.

The laughter was cut off as if a knife had sliced across it and the hushed spectators began to whisper among themselves. The bid was ten times more than what had ever been offered at these bazaars before.

"I will add two hundred pounds to

it," Tom Sutherland said.

The parson stood with his mouth agape. He drew a handkerchief out of his pocket and mopped his brow, then the inner band of his hat. "That is a very generous offer, gentlemen. The orphans and the church thank you. God bless you, sirs." He raised his voice and called out loudly, "The box of confection from the Boston visitors has been sold for a bid of one thousand and two hundred pounds." His gravel banged down on the table to legitimize the sale.

Barbara forced back the pleased smile that was tugging at the corners of her mouth. "Oh, damn it!" she grumbled.

"What in the world can possibly be wrong now?" Patricia exclaimed.

"The nuts, Miss Patricia! We forget the nuts!" Barbara moaned—and then burst into laughter.

16

The whole household was thrown into a fervor of activity when Nancy Kirkland insisted upon giving a ball at Ravenwood to announce the engagement of Tom and Barbara.

To everyone's surprise, Stephen was initially opposed to the engagement, claiming that Barbara was too young to marry and that her parents hardly knew Tom. Besides, he argued, the Colonies were on the brink of war; there was no time for the frivolity and hubbub of a ball.

Nonetheless, when Nancy complied a list of supplies she wanted from the city Stephen gracefully conceeded defeat and took the sloop to Williamsburg accompanied by Tom, Patricia, and Barbara.

The women were dropped at Monsieur Galbraith's while the men went on to assemble the items on Nancy's list.

As the couturier had promised, their gowns were completed. A few minor alterations were required, and within a few hours, Patricia and Barbara had finished their purchases and were ready when the men returned.

Patricia had changed into an elegant floral silk of rose, green and beige. The bodice was worn over a matching corset and hooked together into a point at the waist. Elbow-length sleeves had a flowing cuff of exquisite lace reaching to each wrist. The full skirt was divided in front and worn over a beige-hooped petticoat. Her hat was a simple band of ruchings in the same fabric, wound around her head with a large rose-colored bow in the back.

After the supplies were stored on the sloop, they all took a carriage to the Raleigh Tavern. The white building with its gabled windows and black shutters was a favorite of Stephen's.

As soon as they sat down, two men approached their table. One was distinguished, handsomely groomed man in his early forties, the other a younger man, tall and thin, dressed quite commonly.

Stephen and Tom got to their feet at the sight of them and shook hands. "Gentlemen, you remember my cousin, Tom Sutherland. He has just returned from Scotland."

"Of course," the distinguished man replied. "How is your grandfather, Tom?"

"He's fine, Mr. Lee. Thank you for asking."

"And I would like you to meet our houseguests from Boston," Stephen said. "Ladies, this is Mr. Richard Henry Lee, one of our distinguished members of the House of Burgesses. Mr. Lee, Madam Fairchild and Mistress Kirkland."

Mr. Lee acknowledged the introduction by bringing Patricia's hand to his lips. He quickly paid the same courtesy to Barbara.

Stephen took the arm of the next man. "And Mr. Patrick Henry, also a member of the Burgesses." Patrick Henry acknowledged the introduction in the same manner as Richard Henry Lee.

"Will you gentlemen join us?" Stephen asked.

"Thank you, Stephen, but we have already eaten. However, I would like to hear what the ladies have to say about the situation in Boston," Richard Henry Lee replied.

"Then at least sit down and have a cup of coffee," Stephen insisted.

The two men quickly pulled up chairs and sat down. As they talked, Patricia studied the more subdued man, Patrick Henry. She noticed not only his plain attire but his back-country accent as contrasted to the smooth speech of Mr. Lee. It was apparent he was not born into the accepted wealth of the other men, yet there was no doubt he was regarded with a great deal of respect among them.

"I must congratulate both of you on being elected as delegates to Philadelphia in September," Stephen said.

"We worked very hard for it, Stephen," Patrick Henry said with a shy smile.

"And now it's a reality. The First Continental Congress!" Richard Henry Lee declared with fervor. "It's long, long past due."

"First Continental Congress?" Barbara asked. "What is that, Mr. Lee?"

"Delegates from the colonies will be assembling in Philadelphia in September. It is the first united assembly we have ever had."

"Mr. Lee and Mr. Henry were instrumental in accomplishing it," Stephen interjected. "Last year, together with Mr. Thomas Jefferson, they organized a Committee of Correspondence. The colonies began to communicate formally with one another on major issues affecting them, in an effort to work out satisfactory solutions."

"You see, ladies, we do not have, and never have had, a need for the British government," Patrick Henry added.

Richard Henry Lee turned his piercing gaze on Patricia. "How tense is the situation in Boston, Madam Fairchild?"

"I am certain you will be well informed of that in September, Mr. Lee,"

Patricia replied. "Much more graphically, and, I am sure, more eloquently then I could ever express it."

"I must admit, I am looking forward to meeting that distinguished patriot, Mr. Samuel Adams," Patrick Henry announced. His sharp features softened with a smile.

"Will any Loyalists be represented at this Congress, Mr. Lee, or just rebels?" Patrick asked.

"Madam Fairchild, many of our own Burgesses are Loyalists. This quarrel with the Crown has earth-shattering complications. It is not an issue easily resolved."

"I am certain of that, sir. I hope only that it can be done without bloodshed."

"You mean without any more bloodshed," Patrick Henry declared. "How can you forget the massacre that occurred in your own city? Or weren't you in Boston in '70? Armed soldiers firing into a crowd of unarmed citizens does not aid the cause of peaceful negotiations!"

"I agree, sir, but I would hope that the tragic event would not cause a nation to take up arms. I prefer to believe and hope that with all your intelligence and wisdom, a more conciliatory solution can be reached."

"Well put, Madam. It appears, Stephen, you have here a politician as diplomatic as Mr. Jefferson and as eloquent as Mr. Henry. We could use her in the Burgesses," Richard Henry Lee replied with a good-natured grin. He rose to his feet. "I am afraid my colleague and I have lingered too long. It has been a pleasure to meet two such lovely flowers from the North."

As soon as the two men departed, Stephen turned glaring eyes to Patricia. "Did you have to attempt to start the Revolution right here?" he snapped.

"I don't know what you're talking about," Patricia said, shocked.

"They are two of Virginia's most distinguished statesmen, and you, madam, were addressing them as if they were rabble!"

Tom Sutherland came to her defense. "I think she was only expressing her opinion, Stephen. I can't believe it isn't shared by most of the women in the country, and I am sure they both have heard the same arguments from their own wives."

"Thank you for your effort, Tom, but I fail to grasp what I said or did that was offensive!" Patricia flared.

"I think we should drop the whole subject," Barbara interjected, with a worried glance in Tom's direction. "I thought we came to Williamsburg to enjoy ourselves."

"You're right, of course," Patricia

agreed, with a scathing glare in Stephen's direction.

Tom and Barbara kept up a light running conversation during the remainder of the meal, but the day had been spoiled between Patricia and Stephen.

Barbara caught sight of a poster advertising a traveling troup of Shakespearean actors. The men finally capitulated to her pleas and took them to a presentation of *Hamlet*. However, Stephen sat stiffly beside Patricia during the whole performance with an exchange of only the most perfunctory conversation.

The sun had long set when they finally climbed back on the deck of the sloop in return to Ravenwood.

17

The mellow strains of a violin danced liltingly above the temperate drone of the voices of the guests as Patricia paused at the bottom of the stairway and looked around her with pleasure.

The huge ballroom of Ravenwood had overflowed, and some of the crowd was standing conversing in small clusters in the hallway.

Patricia felt strange being in a room that was not dominated by the red uniforms of British soldiers. She had been merely tolerated by Boston society while George Fairchild was alive, but from the time of his death Beacon Hill had shunned her completely and she had not attended any gala affairs in years.

The laces, satins and silks of the women's elegant gowns were a sight that her eyes had not feasted upon in years. Even the men were stylishly attired, although only a very few had elected to wear the prescribed white wigs that the formal affair would normally warrant.

The assembled wealth in the room

was evident at a glance. *So this is a sample of a Virginia ball!* she thought, intrigued. There was as much anticipation in the thought as there was curiosity.

In Boston she had often heard of the wealth and luxurious lives of these Virginians. In a country on the brink of a revolution, Virginia appeared oblivious to the dilemma, until Patricia was reminded, usually by Stephen, that many of the strongest champions of that movement were Virginians.

He had always been vocal in reminding her that Virginians might not be suffering the privation that the Port Act had inflicted upon Bostonians, nor did they have to bear the further invasion of their privacy of having to quarter British troops in their city and homes, but many of the previously rich tobacco growers were staggering under the heavy export taxes imposed on their crops, as well as the limitations of being able to ship them only to England.

One look at Stephen Kirkland standing in a far corner with several other men was enough to convince Patricia of that verity. The ring of men closely grouped around him was engrossed in deep conversation. From the frowns on their faces, they could have been in attendance at a crucial session of Virginia's Burgesses, rather than at a sumptuous ball in an opulent mansion.

As Patricia passed them, she did not fail to catch the eye of Stephen Kirkland. His pensive, brooding gaze followed her progress across the hall.

She looked exquisitely beautiful wearing a gown of ivory satin intricately embroidered with pale pink, white and green flowers. The bodice was plain with just a low rounded neckline, and the sleeves were shirred to above the elbows and dropped in ruffles deeper in back than on top, so that they hung down beautifully on her slim arms. The skirt, worn over a matching petticoat, was drawn up and draped over her hips into small panniers. A row of lace on her chemise formed a lacy ruffle around the neckline.

She had brushed her hair until it shone like burnished gold. It curled on top with soft curls hanging on her forehead. The rest of her hair was swept into a thick long curl that hung down behind her ear. Patricia had tucked a tiny spray of white forget-me-nots in her hair at the side of her forehead.

She paused at the entrance of the ballroom. A musical ensemble consisting of a French horn, violin, guitar and harpsichord, was providing the accompainment for the dancers, who were engaged in a minuet.

The first person who caught her attention was Thomas Sutherland, who was dancing with Barbara. He was wearing kilts. She was surprised to see that Michael Kirkland was dressed in the same manner. Her eyes swept the room to discover that several other men were dressed in the same fashion.

Barbara looked breathtaking in a gown of deep rose velvet with a sweeping skirt worn over small hoops. The deep color converted her youthful beauty to a radiance as she smiled up at her fiance while they danced.

Patricia had swept Barbara's hair to the top of her head in a mass of soft curls and attached a woven band of pearls and rose ribbon across the top. She concealed the pins under a flattened bow on the back of her head with the ends of several long streamers trailing down. Now, as they danced, the ribbons bobbed fetchingly on her shoulders.

Patricia was claimed immediately by a handsome young gentleman and drawn into the reel. After several rounds she was so breathless she had to stop. She sat down next to Nancy Kirkland while her partner was gracious enough to get her a cup of lemon punch.

"Are you having a good time, my dear?" Nancy asked with a happy smile. She looked stunning in a pale blue satin gown with a dark blue plume in her lovely gray hair.

"I can't remember ever having such a

grand time," Patricia enthused. "I must admit my feet are beginning to ache." She stretched out her ivory pumps. "I've never danced so much in my life."

"Where is that son of mine?" Nancy complained. "I haven't seen him on the dance floor all evening."

Patricia did not want to admit that she, too, had been watching all evening for Stephen's appearance in the ballroom. Apparently, he was too engrossed in conversation to break away. *Or perhaps he's engrossed elsewhere with one of these Southern belles,* she thought wretchedly. He had been avoiding her ever since their return from Williamsburg.

Her partner returned with a cup of punch, and after thanking him for the courtesy, she declined his offer for another dance.

Nancy Kirkland was soon whisked off by her husband for a dance and Patricia was sitting back relaxing, just enjoying watching the people dancing a reel, when suddenly Stephen was standing before her. She was surprised to see him wearing kilts in his clan's tartan.

"May I have this dance, Madam Fairchild?" he asked with a courtly bow.

Patricia could not help but admire how dashing he looked. He was wearing a short black jacket with a white ruffled shirt. A kilt of red and black Kirkland tartan hung to below his knees and his plaid was draped across his shoulder. Woven plaid knee hose encased his long muscular legs and he was hatless, his dark hair tied in a queue at his neck.

Whatever the man wore always seemed to fit him handsomely, and he always seemed comfortable and at ease. Now, standing before her in his Highland kilts, he looked devastingly handsome and her heart began a familiar rapid flutter at the sight of him.

Stephen's hand was warm and firm when it closed around her own as he led her to the line of dancers. When the dance ended, she found herself partnered with Michael Kirkland, then Tom Sutherland. She nodded gratefully when Tom suggested a cup of punch.

They had just reached the table when Barbara snatched her future husband away for another dance.

Patricia casually strolled along the lengthy table that held several varieties of cakes and tarts. She stopped to sample a small slice of a loaf that tasted of orange and nuts, She did not realize she was nearing Stephen until he called her over to where he was standing with two other men. One was tall, with red hair and not much older than Stephen himself; the other was shorter, with gray hair, probably in his late forties.

"Patricia, Mr. Jefferson is interested in meeting you." She blushed as the tall, redheaded man smiled down at her.

"I must confess, Madam Fairchild, I have been openly admiring you. Stephen tells me you are from Boston."

He had a friendly smile and there was something about the man's manner that relaxed her, even knowing that Stephen was looking on. "May I introduce my mentor, George Whyte," Thomas Jefferson said.

"It is a pleasure to meet you, Madam Fairchild," George Whyte said politely. "Will you excuse me, though? I see Patrick over there and I must speak to him. Come with me, Stephen, as this concerns you also."

"Would you like to dance, Madam Fairchild?" Jefferson asked politely when the other two men hurried off.

"Actually, I would prefer a breath of fresh air," she admitted. "Would you mind terribly?"

"Not at all. I think I would welcome it myself," Jefferson said, taking her arm and leading her through a veranda door.

"I must confess, Mr. Jefferson, your name came up recently in a conversation and you are not what I expected. I understand you were instrumental in creating several important documents, so I anticipated meeting a much older man."

"I, too, have a confession to make,

Madam Fairchild. Your name was mentioned also in a recent conversation and you are everything I expected. Richard said you were a beautiful and intelligent woman."

"Richard? Are you referring to Mr. Lee, sir?"

Jefferson nodded. "He and Patrick Henry were quite taken with you."

She smiled nervously. "I was afraid I might have offended them. In fact, Stephen accused me of as much."

Jefferson chuckled warmly. "Stephen is convinced you are a Tory. Are you a Tory, Madam Fairchild?"

"Please call me Patricia," she replied. "Madam Fairchild sounds so pretentious, even for Virginia."

"Now, Patricia, are you implying that we Virginians are pompous?" he admonished her with a warm chuckle.

"Not at all, Mr. Jefferson. I just meant that everything here seems very grandiose, compared to Boston. Have you lived in Virginia all your life, sir?"

"Well, if I am to call you Patricia, I must insist you call me Tom." He blushed slightly. Patricia could see that basically the man was very shy. She sensed a personal modesty about him that was a freshing change from Stephen's arrogant attitude. "As to your question, Patricia, I was born and raised in Virginia. Stephen Kirkland and I grew up together and attended the same schools, until he elected to go to sea, and I opted to study law under Mr. Whyte. We have been close friends our whole lives." He smiled down at her. "But you haven't answered my question, Patricia. Are you a Tory?"

Patricia regarded him with a troubled frown. "I don't know what I am, sir. I haven't made any commitment. As I told Mr. Lee and Mr. Henry, I just hope this can all be resolved without going to war."

Jefferson shook his head sadly. "We all would like that, Patricia, but an individual's liberty is a cherished natural right with which all men are born. He can willingly surrender it, but no king or man has a right to deny him that privilege until he does."

"I am sure you have slaves, Mr. Jefferson. Isn't that a contradiction?"

"Patricia, I consider slavery an abomination. I have tried to emancipate the slaves in Virginia from the time I have been in the House of Burgesses. Mr. Lee has done the same. And when this conflict with the Crown ends, I intend to continue that struggle. Virginia will one day be the home of true democracy. Mark my words, Patricia."

"So many of you appear so young to take on such a committment—such a responsibility," she argued. "I fear many will perish in this struggle."

"I am afraid you are right, madam. But a spirit of resistance is a necessary limb on a tree of liberty. We cannot saw it off or the tree will not bear fruit."

The tall figure of Stephen Kirkland suddenly filled the door. "Here you are, Tom. Your presence is being sought in the library."

Jefferson kissed Patricia's hand. "This has been a pleasure, Madam Fairchild. If you have the opportunity before returning to Boston, please visit us at Monticello. I know Mrs. Jefferson would enjoy meeting you."

"Thank you, Mr. Jefferson. I hope I will have that chance."

Patricia remained silent after Jefferson departed. "He's a very nice man. He seems so young, though, to be carrying the weight of the world on his shoulders."

"Well, madam, did you succeed in seducing him to your cause?" he said sarcastically.

"Oh, Stephen, please don't start. Can't we get through one evening without an argument?" she asked with a weary sigh. She turned away from him and walked to the railing.

Stephen moved to her side. He leaned on the railing and stared out pensively. "He's only thirty-one, the same age as I. I imagine you succeeded in convincing him that King George will slap our hands if we're naughty."

She looked up at him calmly. "I think he knows that without my having to tell him. I don't wish to appear sacrilegious, Stephen, but I never gave too much credence to the story of David and Goliath. I don't think your little sling shot is going to be too effective against the King's heavy boot."

He straightened up in surprise. "Do I detect more concern than censure? Can it be that the lady cares about my welfare?"

"Well, just look at yourself, Stephen. What are you wearing?"

He looked down at himself in bewilderment. "Are you referring to my kilts?"

"Exactly!" she responded with a feisty toss of her head. "How many others are wearing them in there tonight? From the numbers, I thought we had been invaded by a regiment of the King's Highlanders."

"It's just tradition, Tory. We always wear our clan's colors for formal family occasions. Tom and Barbara's engagement warranted it."

"Tradition! That is the exact point I am trying to make. What are you going to do when war does break out and a troop of Highlanders comes marching across your lawn? Tell me about your traditions then. Are you going to shoot them—or join them?"

A muscle began to twitch in his cheek and he gripped her shoulders. "Damn you, Tory. Don't play Devil's advocate with my loyalties! When the time comes I'll handle it! I'm a native-born American. My father was born in America, and his father before him. My Grandfather Kirkland was part Indian. You can't get more native American than that!"

She glared up at him defiantly. "Well, then don't mock my loyalties either, Stephen Kirkland, because I was born in Suffolk, England! When are you dedicated rebels going to realize that it isn't an easy decision for everyone to make!"

His hands slipped from her shoulders and he stood staring down into her eyes. For a brief moment there was a shared compassion in their locked glances, as each commiserated with the other's internal struggle.

"Nevertheless, Tory, we both have made it, haven't we?" he said sadly and turned away, disappearing through the door.

Long after he left she remained standing on the porch. She refused to cry. The situation between them was hopeless, so why didn't she have the strength to walk away from it? All she had to do was leave, and that would end it. Oh, if only she had never come to Ravenwood—to Williamsburg, for that matter!

Patricia turned to return to the dance and then thought the better of it. The last dance had already been played, as far as she was concerned. Instead, she stepped down from the porch and strolled to the garden. She had grown to love that corner of Ravenwood as much as Nancy Kirkland. Somehow, it was easy to forget the turbulence around her while she was sitting in the serenity of the garden.

She seated herself on a bench and once again lost herself in the turmoil of her thoughts. Dark clouds, marking the passing of time, drifted across the face of the moon, but she sat unmindful of them. The strains of the music had long quieted, the guests had departed, and she sat in her despair.

A sudden breeze swept in from the sea and her body trembled with a quick shiver. She stared down in surprise at the goose flesh that had formed on her arms. Patricia rose to her feet to return to the house, aware for the first time of the hush that now lay over Ravenwood.

She drew up sharply at the sight of Stephen Kirkland blocking the narrow path. He was holding an open bottle of brandy. He took a deep draught and emptied it.

"We were out of cognac, so I was reduced to this," he said. He tossed the empty bottle away and moved toward her. She could see he was unsteady on his feet.

"I hope you didn't drink that whole bottle of brandy yourself, Stephen," she cautioned.

"I hope I did, Tory, but I actually can't remember." There was enough of a slur in his speech to indicate that he certainly did not have complete control of his faculties.

Patricia was not in any mood to cope with him while he was inebriated, so she attempted to step around him.

"Don't run away, little rabbit," he teased.

"I am cold, Stephen. I would like to return to the house."

"Ah! I have just what you need." He released the plaid on his shoulder and wrapped it around her like a shawl, holding an end of it in each hand. "Is that better?"

"It's fine, Stephen. Thank you," she said nervously. "May I pass now?"

"Not yet, Tory. Not quite yet." He began to tug on the ends, drawing her slowly into the circle of his arms. His dark eyes gleamed desire.

"No," she pleaded helplessly. "Don't do this, Stephen. Please don't do this." There was desperation in her eyes as he released the ends of the plaid and his arms closed around her.

Stephen's head dipped and his mouth covered hers. She could taste the brandy on his lips. She wanted to resist the persuasive pressure of his mouth, but it was too arousing to ignore. His mouth left hers and began a moist trail down the slim column of her neck.

"Tory, why must you fight me? Do you think I enjoy always having to force your response? We're both playing the same game. Why can't you come to me?"

His dark eyes mirrored his anguish. "Just once, why don't you force a response from me? Just once, let me feel your arms slide around my neck, or taste the honey of that sweet, sweet mouth over mine? Oh, God, Tory! Free me of that fantasy!" he begged in a smothered groan.

Her heart and body cried out to him in response. Her fingers itched to entwine themselves in his dark hair. Her arms ached with her need to wrap around him, and her body trembled with an urgency to press against him.

Her hand was shaking as she raised it to stroke his cheek. It froze in mid-air at the sound of nearby voices, and her eyes widened, startled.

Nancy and Michael Kirkland hurried along the path. Nancy rushed to her, her blue eyes wide with concern. "There you are, Patricia. We have all been so worried about you. There has been no sign of you for hours, and Barbara even checked in your room." She stopped, at the sight of the distress on Patricia's face. "What are you doing out here? Are you all right, dear?"

"She's fine, Mother. She just came out to smell the roses," Stephen said bitterly, and walked away.

18

Patricia tossed restlessly in bed for
what remained of the night. She made
up her mind that she would leave Ravenwood the following day and return to
Williamsburg to await a passage to
Boston.

There was no sign of Stephen at
breakfast. Tom and Barbara were preparing to take a morning ride, so she
decided to withhold her announcement
until they returned. The thought of a
final ride around the beautiful plantation
was appealing to her, so after they departed, she donned her riding habit and
went to the stables.

The groom warned her that the mare
she was riding was more spirited than
any horse she had previously ridden, but
this held no fear for Patricia, because she
had ridden daily in Boston.

The day was a bright and pleasant
one, and as she rode through the beautiful rolling hills, she realized how much
she would miss it all. The whole experience had been a fairy tale to her. If only

Stephen Kirkland could have been the hero of that fable.

Patricia picked a trail to follow that led to the river. She reined up at the sight of Stephen and several members of his crew engaged in a hushed conversation on a small craft bobbing on the river. The meeting broke up and Stephen mounted his horse. To her horror he began to ride straight toward her and, in panic, she pulled her mount into a copse of trees and dismounted.

Just as Stephen was passing, her horse recognized a stable mate and snorted a greeting. Stephen reined his horse and approached the spot where she was concealed.

He dismounted and glared down at her with eyes as cold as marble as he tied his reins to a tree. "What are you doing here, Tory?"

"I was just out for a ride." She didn't understand the reason for this latest hostility. His moods were imcomprehensible to her.

"Alone?" Stephen asked skeptically.

"Yes. Barbara and Tom have gone off. I didn't feel like intruding upon them." His interrogation was becoming insulting. Did he believe she had purposely followed him?

"Was it because you had more important things to do, Tory? Like spying on my activities, for instance?"

There it was again, she thought with a resigned sigh. The same tune he had sung so often before. And, as before, her temper flared in response to it.

"Why do you insist upon calling me Tory? I am not a part of this senseless struggle you are waging with the Crown."

"Oh, spare me the dramatics, Tory. We both know who and what you are." She drew back in surprise at the razor-sharp edge in his voice. There was no longer any attempt at humoring her.

Patricia was dumbfounded. His scathing announcement took her by complete surprise and she challenged it immediately. "Do you honestly believe that I would betray you to the British, Stephen?"

"Why would I doubt it! Didn't you do the same thing to Jeffrey Cunningham?"

"What are you rambling about now? I don't even know a Jeffrey Cunningham. I have no idea what you are talking about."

A telltale muscle in his cheek began to twitch with anger and the fury in his eyes was frightening. Patricia stepped back instinctively in an effort to avoid him, but was too late to evade the hands that reached out and grasped her. His fingers felt like steel talons as they bit into her shoulders and her struggles to free herself only caused them to dig deeper into the tender flesh.

"You really are a cold-hearted bitch, aren't you! At least give the man the dignity of acknowledging that he existed." His sapphire eyes had hardened to icy marbles as he fought to try to control the loose rein he held on his emotions. "He was so in love with you. The last time I saw him before he died all he could rave about was how much he loved you."

Patricia was shaking her head hopelessly. "I swear to you, Stephen. I don't know what you are talking about. I have never known anyone named Jeffrey Cunningham." Her eyes were pleading for him to believe her.

Her denial only seemed to incite more of his wrath. He began to shake her and her hat and pins flew in all directions and hair tumbled to her shoulders in dishevelment. "Well, let me refresh your memory, *Angel*. Jeff was my age. He had dark hair, brown eyes. He wore a perpetual grin on his face."

The fury in his voice was rising with each word, until he was practically shouting. "He went to Boston and fell in love with a tawny-haired woman with emerald eyes who was called Angel. A month after he met her, his body was found floating in the bay."

He shoved her away and the tree

behind her prevented her from falling to the ground. Patricia stood there, her eyes were wide with fright, uncertain whether or not he had lost complete control of himself. Would he strike her in his rage? Her alarm was mirrored on her face, but in his fury he misread it and took it for frightened guilt.

"I can see that it's all coming back to you now, *Angel*!" he said bitterly. "When I went to Boston and began to investigate his death I was told the British thought he was an American agent. They claim, though, that his death was an accident. That he apparently slipped and hit his head on a piling, fell into the ocean and drowned. What do you think, *Angel*? The Sons of Liberty suspect he was betrayed by the woman he loved and was murdered. To this day, no one has seen or heard from this mystery woman."

Somehow she was able to find her voice and force a question through her lips. "What does all of this have to do with me?"

"I didn't even think to link his death to you until I heard Charles Reardon call you Angel—and then all the pieces fell into place."

The fury in his eyes were rekindled. "Well, you were wrong, *Angel*. Jeff Cunningham was no American spy. He was harmless. He was an idealistic dreamer who loved poetry. He wouldn't have hurt a fly, so you wouldn't have had to kill him." There was as much pain now in his eyes as there was anger. "He was a good friend. We grew up together. He was a lovable, damned fool, who fell in love with a scheming Tory bitch!"

The unjust implication of it was more than she could bear. The fright that had held her immobilized was swept away by a wave of righteous indignation. How dare he! How dare he accuse her and find her guilty before even confronting her with his suspicions!

"That is sheer stupidity," Patricia blazed. "Do you actually believe that I am the only woman that some man in love would call 'Angel'?" She threw her hands up in the air in total frustration. "My God, Stephen, you really are grasping at straws in your effort to convince yourself that I am an English spy."

"I don't think I'm too far out of line," he snarled with a merciless stare. "Jeff said the woman he fell in love with had tawny-colored hair and emerald eyes. That description rather fits someone we both know and love," he taunted mockingly.

She wanted to cringe under the contempt in his voice but was determined not to waver. "And, of course, I am the only woman who happens to have green eyes and blonde hair," she retorted with renewed fury. It was becoming obvious to her that it was useless to try to defend herself. His mind was sealed against anything she had to say in her own defense.

"You happen to be a green-eyed, blonde-haired woman named Angel," he sneered. "Who, I might add, just happens to be a Tory. Couple that with the fact that you live in Boston, which, coincidentally, is the same city where the woman lived who betrayed Jeff."

Patricia refused to cower under his glare and met his scorn unwaveringly. Her own defiant glare returned his contempt. He couldn't help but admire the courage she demonstrated as she faced him. She was trembling—not with fright, but with the pent-up fury that was raging unchecked through her body.

"Well, you're wrong on several points, Captain Kirkland. My name is Patricia. Charles Reardon is the only man I have ever known who calls me Angel. And I am not a Tory. I have not permitted myself to sympathize with either side in this issue. I have too many friends on both sides of that quarrel. I have always hoped the differences would be resolved before they broke into open warfare.

"But if the American cause is going to be waged by blind, pig-headed fools like you, than I think, when the time comes, my choice will be an easy one."

She was unaware of what a physical impact she was making on him. Her face was radiant with color, beautiful to him beyond description. The exquisite line of her jaw was thrust forward in defiance; her green eyes, ablaze with passion, were like gleaming emeralds.

The tawny glory of her hair flowed to her shoulders in wild disarray. She was a tigress, sleek and golden; cornered, but spitting and snarling her defiance, determined to go down fighting.

"You claim to be fighting for justice, yet you don't hesitate to condemn me, unjustly, on inconclusive evidence. Where is the justice in that?"

If she believed her words would somehow help her cause, her hopes were soon crushed.

"Even if I allowed myself to believe that Jeff was not murdered," he said, "that his death was an accident—there was nothing inconclusive about seeing you in Williamsburg with Emil Thackery. That wasn't conjecture, Tory, I saw you with my own eyes."

Her eyes widened in confusion. "What has Emil Thackery to do with this matter?" The unrelenting way he stood there in silent contempt told her more than any words could possibly do. "Are you implying that he is working for the British?"

Her question produced a scornful smirk. "Oh, you didn't know!"

Patricia was beginning to stagger under the weight of confusion. How many more accusations would he throw at her? "I thought Emil Thackery was a gaoler whom Charles was bribing to release his brother from prison. The packet I brought him contained the money that Charles was giving him to do so."

"It also contained the name of a very prominent Frenchman traveling incognito, who was due to arrive in Williamsburg the following day to meet with some of the organizers of our resistance. I know, because I read it! It would have made the American cause very shaky in the French Court if he had met with a fatal accident while in Virginia under our protection. When I arrived, I received a letter warning me of the plot."

"Are you saying Emil Thackery is an assassin for the Crown?" she asked shocked.

Stephen's laugh was laced with contempt. "Oh, Reardon is too clever to directly link an assassination to the Crown. If it could be proven, it could lead to serious ramifications with France. Emil Thackery has no loyalties. He is a mercenary who will do anything for a price. He would slit his own mother's throat for a pound. Fortunately, I saw to it myself that he met with an unforeseen accident before he could do any further damage.''

Patricia was beginning to believe that the whole conversation was part of a bizarre nightmare. Everything he said sounded outlandish.

''Are you saying you had him murdered?''

''No, Madam Fairchild, our cause does not sanction murder. Poor Mr. Thackery overimbibed and landed on a vessel bound for the South Seas. It was an English ship, so he should feel right at home! In a few years, if he behaves himself, he should end up in England.''

Patricia could only shake her head in denial. ''I can't believe one word of what you are telling me.''

''I seem to have the same problem where you're concerned,'' he responded in a voice tempered with quiet emphasis.

Once again indignation ran rampantly through her. Each accusation sounded more ludicrous than the previous one. ''You expect me to believe that Charles Reardon would deliberately use me in a foul scheme to have a man murdered!''

''Oh, you're good, lady, you're really good! No wonder the British use you as a spy! That wide-eyed innocence would convince anyone. But you're wasting your time. Let's not play any more games, Tory." There was a finality to his words that was as cold and grim as the smile on his face.

She was sapped of any will to continue the argument. It was a useless battle and she was merely wasting her breath. "Then there is no way I can convince you of my innocence. Despite everything I say, you are still that certain of my guilt." She closed her eyes in a futile gesture of defeat.

Stephen's voice softened and her head swung up in surprise at the sound of it. "I wish I could say it doesn't matter, Tory. That I could put my feelings for you ahead of my duty. But I can't. There is too much at stake. Too many people who have put their trust and faith in me. They could be harmed if I trusted you and was wrong. I can't gamble with their lives."

He turned away, unable to watch the shifting emotions on her face. Patricia fought to maintain her control, driven by an intense need to convince him of one thing. She looked at the unrelenting back before her and closed the gap between them. Timidly, she raised a trembling hand and placed it on his arm.

"Stephen, if you can't believe anything else I say, I beg you to believe me when I tell you I never knew your friend. I didn't have anything to do with his death. I can't believe Charles did either. He was never in the casino. I know the name of every regular patron, and Jeffrey Cunningham was never one of them."

She could feel the tautness that was holding him in check through the fabric of his shirt. The corded muscles were rigid with tension. "You are not going to betray your cause, nor the people who have put their trust in you, by believing what I am saying. Accept the reality that your friend's death was an accident and not foul play. Sympathize for the woman, Angel, who probably loved him as much as he loved her. Is your loss any greater than hers? You are so enmeshed in politics and intrigue that you suspect treachery where it does not exist."

Stephen turned and gazed down at her. His face was drawn with strain. "I would like to believe you are right just for Jeff's sake alone, but I am afraid I'm just too old to change my beliefs."

Patricia felt overwhelmed with frustration. "You mean you will not accept anything I've said?" He turned away from her without a reply.

She had to get away. She couldn't bear this war between them another second. It was a hopeless situation— his mind was closed to her.

"Then you're a fool, Stephen Kirkland. A damned pigheaded fool!"

Tears were streaming down her face as she ran to her horse. Without conscious regard, she prodded the horse and it leaped into a gallop. Within seconds she was racing across the green meadow toward the white fence that separated the two pastures.

At another prod the mare leaped the fence with the grace and sleekness of a gazelle. Patricia sat the saddle like a champion, her tears of anger blocking out awareness of anything. The mare raced several more yards before Stephen's powerful black stallion thundered up beside her. He leaned over and grabbed the reins of the horse, pulling it to such an abrupt halt that Patricia was almost unseated.

She could not help but flinch under the antagonism of his stormy glare. Even on horseback, she felt dwarfed and intimidated by his size as much as by his overt hostility. There was no attempt at tact in his blazing demand.

"What in hell are you trying to do?"

The surliness of the question was all that was needed to restore her faltering courage. Defiance gleamed in her eyes as they locked coldly with his.

"Damn it, Tory. Are you trying to break your fool neck?"

Unabashed, Patricia raised her chin,

refusing to cower under his wrath. "I am as capable of handling a horse as you are of steering a ship, Captain!"

"Get the hell off that horse," he ordered in a brittle command.

Patricia wanted to scream out her protest. Her hand curled into a tight fist around the quirt she was holding. She fought to repulse the need to strike out with it at the arrogant, self-assured mouth that was issuing these obdurate commands.

"Like hell, I will!" she replied mutinously.

"Are you getting off that horse, or do I have to pull you off?" His eyes blazed a potent warning. "I should caution you, Tory, I have no intentions of being gentle. That's a thoroughbred jumper you are on. It's got more spirit than you, so I don't advise your putting it to any more tests. I will ask you just one more time. Are you getting off that horse, or do I pull you off?" A nerve began to twitch nervously in his cheek as he fought to control his rage.

Stephen's mood was black and dangerous. She recognized the short rein he held on his control. There certainly was no question that it was useless to expect to sway him from his intent. In complete frustration, she slid off the horse.

Patricia strode away angrily and

plopped down on the ground at the foot of a large oak tree. Her hand still clutched the quirt in a tenacious grip and she repeatedly swatted the ground with it as she vented her frustration. Each beat of her heart hammered a thudding blow as intense as those she was venting with the quirt, and the thumping in her chest was deafening in her ears.

She watched sullenly as Stephen gathered the reins of the horses and tied them to a shrub. He sat down beside her.

Patricia took a deep breath, preparing herself for his tirade. It did not come. He did not make any attempt at conversation. He just sat beside her silently, staring morosely at the ground.

She studied him openly. Despite her anger she saw how haggard and tired the tanned face appeared. She had never seen him in such a state of exhaustion and was startled by it. She was even more perplexed that it should bother her.

"I'm sorry, Tory."

Lost in the confusion of her thoughts, she was unaware that Stephen had spoken to her.

"If I repeat it, it will sound like a rhyme." Her glance swung up warily at the sound of his warm, husky chuckle.

"I believe you. I guess in my heart I have believed you for a long time, Tory. I just was not willing to admit to myself. I didn't trust my emotions where you are concerned."

She was uncertain she had heard him correctly. Only moments ago he had denied her innocence. "I do know Charles Reardon set you up, though, Tory. He used you."

She refused to accept that and shook her head in denial. "No, I will never believe that about Charles. It's all just a misunderstanding. Charles would never do this to me. I am certain there is a logical explanation."

"Is he your lover?" he asked softly.

"No, nothing like that. He's just a very dear friend whom I have always trusted."

"How can you still have faith in a bastard who was willing to allow you to peddle your body to serve his purposes?" he lashed out.

She buried her head in her hands in despair. That was the one conclusive evidence against Charles. Stephen's tone gentled at the sight of her misery. "I hope for your sake, Tory, that he does have that explanation you believe exists."

She could sense that he was sincere, that he felt the heartache she was suffering, this enigmatic man whose moods were as shifting as the tides he rode! She raised her head and turned to him.

The sight of him caused the breath to catch in her throat. He was lounging lazily on the ground beside her. Thick spiky lashes seemed to hang suspended above his cheeks as he studied her with a hooded stare.

They regarded each other with a penetrating look and she felt a searing fire surge through her. She wondered if she would ever be able to look at him without being conscious of how much she wanted him physically? Whatever the reason for this macabre fascination, it always managed to blot out her anger and reservations.

She turned away from him, afraid he would read her thoughts. Could he sense this about her? Was it possible he knew that she wanted him to make love to her? Maybe that was why he was willing to play this teasing game with her.

"You take pleasure in humiliating me, don't you, Stephen?" There was no anger, no accusation. She said it simply as a matter of fact.

"No, Tory, you are wrong. I have no desire to humiliate you." There was a gentleness in his tone. All his anger had dissolved, all the suspicions he had harbored about her loyalties, all the indescribable fear he had felt for her safety when he saw her leap that fence. There was only the nearness of her now, and his aching love for her.

"From the first moment we met you have played a cat-and-mouse game with me. Why, Stephen? Why do you do it?"

His dark eyes were brimming with the love he could not voice. "Did you give me any other option, Tory? Did I dare lower my guard with you? I believed you were a British spy."

Tell him, she told herself. *Tell him how you feel about him. Get it out in the open once and for all or it will haunt you to death.* She opened her mouth to speak, but her pride kept her from saying the words that would reveal to him the depth of her love.

Every nerve in her body was attuned to the male essence of him now. The tenderness in his eyes was more of a devastating assault on her than his lips and hands could ever be, and her body began trembling with a passion that was spiraling out of control.

Stephen sat up slowly, his stare fixed on the sensual invitation in her eyes. He slowly leaned toward her, closing the gap that separated them, and his head lowered. Her lips parted to accept the tender and warm mouth that closed over her own.

Every nerve end, every cell in her body ignited in spontaneous combustion. All the pent-up desire she had repressed since their first kiss finally erupted, and her last vestige of resistance was incinerated by the intensity of the heat in their mutual passion.

His lips mercifully left hers, only to blaze a scorching path to the hollow of her throat. His hands had joined the ravishing of her senses; one trailed down to cup the round mound of her breast, while the other played havoc with the tingling nerves of her spine as it repeatedly swept her back, pressing her tighter against his own heated body.

A rapturous moan escaped her as his mouth began a moist trail down the column of her neck. Stephen's hand felt like a flame through the fabric of her gown.

"Stephen." She lay back, his name a sensuous purr on her lips. Her arms slid around his neck, pulling him down with her. Now in an even greater bombardment of her already devastated senses, his weight was on her, the warmth of his long hard body pressing her soft curves into the ground.

He raised his head and stared down at her, his long spiky lashes hooding his passion-filled eyes. At the sight of the tremulous smile on her lovely face, the corners of his dark eyes crinkled with the warmth of his own smile, and he reached up to cup her face with his hand.

Their mouths opened to one another and his tongue electrified her with fiery probes. His hand slid down to her bodice and began to release its buttons.

Suddenly he lifted his head, alerted by the sound of approaching horses. "Damn!" he cursed softly and sat up, easing his weight off her.

Patricia became aware of what had distracted him when two horsemen came galloping across the field. She sat up as frustrated as he, and began to adjust the top of her gown.

Tom Sutherland and Barbara Kirkland reined their horses before them.

"Are you all right, Patricia?" Barbara asked worriedly, as Tom swung her to the ground.

Her face was heightened in color from the ride. She looked radiantly lovely in a long-sleeved taffeta dress of rust and white stripes. A white kerchief of embroidered chiffon covered her head like the hood of a cloak.

"Yes, I'm fine now, Bab. I just rode too vigorously and was resting from the strain of it," Patricia said, trying to conceal her embarrassment.

"You do look quite flushed. I think you should continue to rest," Barbara insisted, her round eyes filled with concern.

Stephen realized how close the moment had come to a possible commitment he was not prepared to make. He rose to his feet and strode to his horse, hopping into the saddle with a lithe movement.

"Will you see the ladies back to the house, Tom?" he said and, not waiting for an answer, rode off without a backward glance.

Patricia sat forlornly, watching the tall figure disappear.

"Patricia, are you certain you are all right?" Barbara asked, troubled. She cast an anxious glance at Tom.

"I am fine, Barbara. Truly, I am," Patricia said quietly, unaware of the woeful picture she made.

He had confused her now more than ever.

19

With an unconscious gesture, Patricia pushed back the strands of tawny hair that had fallen across her face. Her emerald eyes swung to the dark-haired pixie curled up in the center of her bed. Barbara did not have her head concealed and her hair was a mass of wavy curls.

"I don't know when I have had such a wonderful time."

The puckish grin that split the appealing countenance of Barbara Kirkland spread to the depths of her brown eyes. "I have, too. I hate to see it end."

She uncurled herself from the comfort of the bed and walked over to Patricia. Barbara's arms encircled her waist and hugged her affecionately. Her brown eyes shimmered with unshed tears. "I am going to miss you, Patricia. You are the best friend I have ever had."

Patricia's own eyes misted as she returned the younger girl's embrace. It was true that the two women had become very close in the short time they had known each other.

"If for nothing else, honey, I guess I should be grateful to Stephen for our meeting," Patricia said.

Her heart lurched painfully at the thought of the man she tried continually to erase from her mind, but somehow never could: Stephen Kirkland with the engaging grin that always crept to the corners of his eyes, changing his sculptured, chiseled face to winning boyishness; Stephen Kirkland, teasing and lighthearted one moment, hateful and accusing the next; Stephen Kirkland, whose evocative touch and passionate kisses aroused feelings within her which frightened as much as they excited her. *Damn him! I think I hate him!* she swore to herself.

Barbara's voice snapped her out of her stabbing reflections. "You will let me visit you when I return to Boston?"

Patricia smiled fondly at the concern blurring the usually vivacious face. "Of course, honey." She hugged Barbara again impulsively and then turned back to her packing. "But aren't you as convinced as your muleheaded cousin that I'm a harlot, Bab?"

Barbara could not disguise a troubled frown. "You know better than that, Patricia."

Patricia could see that Barbara wanted to pursue the subject, but was torn between mixed loyalties. One was to

Patricia and their friendship, and the other was to Stephen, the man whom she loved like a brother.

"I really don't see why you have to leave at this time," Barbara said petulantly, returning to the bed.

"I have taken enough advantage of the Kirklands' generous hospitality. Furthermore, I think I am ruining Stephen's visit with his family. It really is best for me to leave at this time so he can relax and enjoy it."

Barbara looked up thoughtfully. "But you wouldn't have to go. Stephen is gone. He's sailing tonight." She grimaced in self-disgust. "Oh, I wasn't supposed to say anything. Tom told me that in the strictest confidence."

Her candidness brought an indulgent smile to Patricia's face. "I'll forget you even said it." *So he left without even saying good-bye,* she thought with disappointment.

Across the room a bizarre plan began to formulate in Barbara's mind. "Why don't we go with him?"

"What?" Patricia asked with a disbelieving backward glance over her shoulder.

Barbara sat up. Her mind was spinning as rapidly as a top. "Why don't we go with him? Tom told me they are sailing to Jamaica to get some cargo. I have never been to such an exciting place before."

Patricia knew she had to nip this plan in the bud before the girl could give it any further thought. "That is ridiculous, Barbara. I am not certain whether or not Stephen Kirkland can even stand the sight of me. He would never tolerate my being on board his ship. Besides, I'm sure it is not a pleasure trip. He will obviously be on some more of his nefarious privateering and certainly will not want us to be on board. It could prove to be dangerous."

Barbara jumped to her feet and began to pace the floor, deep in concentration. "Nonsense! What's dangerous about a trip to Jamaica? We can easily get to the dock and sneak onto the ship before they even board." She stopped and swung around excitedly. "They will be at sea before they even discover us." She smiled with smug delight. "Stephen can't very well set us adrift in the middle of the ocean."

"Ha!" Patricia said sarcastically. "Perhaps not you, but I am sure he wouldn't hesitate doing it to me."

"Oh please, Patricia! This may be the only opportunity I will ever have to see Jamaica," Barbara pleaded, with an appealing sparkle in her dark eyes.

Patricia put her hands on her hips and regarded the girl with a reproachful frown. "Just what am I missing here? I can't follow your reasoning. What makes you think you have the opportunity now? Why, Stephen would be furious."

"Oh, I know he would. But he'd get over it. He's got a great sense of humor whether you believe so or not," Barbara protested. "Please, Patricia, I don't dare try it without you."

"You're talking like a ninny, Bab. You don't dare try it with me, either. It's too preposterous." She shook her head and returned to her packing.

That is the last thing I can do, she thought. *Bab has no idea how explosive the situation is between Stephen and me.* She cast a surreptitious glance in the direction of the bed. Barbara looked the picture of misery. She was sitting on the edge of the bed with her arms propped up on her knees and her chin resting in her hands.

The sight of it was enough to work on Patricia's conscience. *I could go*, she thought. *It does sound exciting.* Furthermore, it would be a good way of showing Stephen Kirkland that he didn't intimidate her. *Why not do it? What have you got to lose?* She caught her lower lip between her teeth in a wicked smile. *It is really going to annoy Stephen. He may even think I came along to spy on his activities. And if he makes a big issue of it, I can always pay him for our passage.*

"How can we get on the ship without

anyone seeing us?"

It took several seconds for Patricia's words to penetrate the gray wall of Barbara's thoughts. When they finally pierced her gloom she bolted to her feet. Her face was the picture of incredulous delight.

"You really mean it!" she squealed. She grabbed Patricia in a forceful hug. "Oh, I love you. It's going to be so much fun."

Patricia tried to keep a disapproving frown on her face. "Actually, I am too old to encourage this impetuous streak in you, but it does sound exciting. Now, how do we go about it?"

"The first thing we have to do is get hold of Daniel. I'll send him a message." She sped out of the room like a whirlwind.

Once alone, Patricia's face sobered. Was she making a mistake? Of course she was, she reasoned. There was no question about it. She was on a collision course with Stephen Kirkland. Why didn't she have enough sense to turn around before it was too late?

Patricia sat down in the chair and reached for the lap desk. She began to pen a letter to the Kirklands, thanking them for their hospitality and assuring them, despite Stephen's accusations, that she would never intentionally do anything to harm them or any other member of their family. She had just finished the letter and set the desk aside when Barbara rushed back into the room.

"I have sent a letter with Abraham to Daniel. I told him to come back here so I can talk to him."

"What makes you so certain he will comply with your request?"

"Request? I am not requesting him. I am ordering him. One day I caught the little demon smoking in the storage hold. He knows if I tell on him Stephen will probably replace him. He has a strict rule that no one is allowed to smoke there because they carry gun powder sometimes."

"Well, then, you should have told Stephen, Barbara. After all, that is dangerous. He could blow up the ship and everyone on it."

"Do you think I'm a snitch?" Barbara asked with affront. "Oh, I gave him a proper tongue lashing, all right. One of my father's finest! He would have been proud of me! I am sure the little hellion won't try it again," she said with a confident toss of her head. "I am going to rest now. I am sure we will be up quite late, so I suggest you do the same." She disappeared through the door as quickly as she had entered.

A few hours later she was back. "I can see them coming! Let's go to meet them." And before Patricia could utter a word, the younger girl had grabbed her hand and was pulling her toward the door.

Once outside the house, she released Patricia's hand and raced ahead of her. Daniel had just climbed out of the boat when Barbara reached the pier.

"I hope this is important," the young cabin boy complained.

"You bet it is," she replied enthusiastically. Patricia arrived in time to hear her announce, "Madam Fairchild and I have decided to take passage on *The Liberty.*"

"Well, who cares? Do I look like the Captain? Just what has that got to do with me?" he grumbled.

Barbara threw Patricia a conspiratorial look. "Well, you see, Daniel, we do not want Captain Kirkland to know about it until we're far enough at sea, so he can't put us off the ship."

The young lad had been standing in a hunched-up slouch. At her words his head shot up in astonishment. "You mean you want to stow away!"

Barbara's head bobbed in agreement and two dimples came into play. "Exactly, Daniel, and you're the very lad who will help us to do it!"

"You're daft, lady! Why the Cap'n would tan my hide. I ain't gonna do it."

Barbara drew herself up primly. "Daniel, if you remember, there is a small matter of my discovering your smoking in the hold. I would hate to call it to my cousin's attention because I am certain he would do a great deal more than just spank you."

Daniel's heart took an instant dive to the toes of his boots. The look on his face was heartbreaking to see, and Patricia was beginning to feel guilty about her part in the scheme. Her resolve crumbled when Daniel's frantic gaze swung to her.

"Are you a part of this, ma'am? You know the Cap'n won't stand for anyone's stowing on board his ship, especially you ladies. He'll not take to it kindly."

"Perhaps we should reconsider, Bab. There are endless complications that we haven't really considered."

Daniel's face broke into a smile of relief.

"Patricia, you promised!" Barbara pleaded. "It probably will be the last opportunity I'll have. You know as well as I that soon we will be at war with England, and then it will be impossible." She looked so utterly forlorn that both Patricia and Daniel were unable to resist.

The young lad shook his head in a helpless gesture. "All right, meet me at midnight. *The Liberty* is docked at Pier 4. I'll sneak you on board, but you both gotta swear you won't tell the captain who helped you." They nodded in agreement. "You best dress differently, too.

The sight of two ladies in fancy gowns is sure to attract attention."

Barbara's eyes were wide with joy as she grabbed Daniel and kissed his cheek exuberantly. She drew back in surprise with a worried frown. "Daniel, why are you so hot?" She put her hand on his brow. "Why, you're burning up! You must have a fever."

"I've been feeling poorly all day," he said. "Sure didn't feel much like coming way out here, and now that I heard the reason for it, I'm sorry I did."

Barbara put an arm around his shoulders. "Well, you just go right back and rest. We'll see you tonight."

They watched Daniel climb forlornly into the vessel. He looked pathetic sitting all hunched up on the seat as Abraham struck the sail on the tiny sloop. When it disappeared around the bend of the river, Barbara turned back to her with a smile of satisfaction.

"Now, the next thing we have to do is get us some boys' clothing."

"Barbara, I do not intend to dress myself as a boy. I think that is carrying deception too far. I have my dignity to consider."

Barbara slipped her arm through Patricia's and they walked back to the house. "You're right. We'll just have to pick the right moment to get onto that ship!"

Patricia turned to her with a dubious frown. "I can't believe I ever let you talk me into this insane scheme," she lamented. "I am a mature woman. A widow! I operate a successful gaming house. I am five years your senior, and despite all that, in the last few hours I have been talked into stowing away on the ship of probably my worst enemy and into being a party to coercing a young, and I should add feverish, lad into betraying his captain. The Lord only knows what you next have in mind!"

Barbara laughed and slipped her arm around Patricia's waist.

"Your problem, Patricia Fairchild, is that you missed all of this kind of fun while you were growing up. You take life too seriously."

A very feminine brow arched skeptically. "Are those words of wisdom really coming from the mouth of the woman who runs around with a scarf wrapped about her head because she had her hair clipped too short?" Patricia scoffed good-naturedly.

Barbara grimaced reflectively, her dimples biting into her cheeks. "I have to admit I acted very immaturely. I can understand why everyone treated me like a child. I am never going to wear that hideous red bandana again."

"Then I would guess it's worth the trip," Patricia teased.

Barbara gave Patricia an affectionate squeeze, followed by a delightful
chuckle. "We'd better hurry or we'll miss
the boat."

20

"If'n Mistah Stephen finds out 'bout what ah did, he's gawna whup me good," Abraham complained as they neared the wharf.

Barbara screwed up her pert little nose in denial. "That is pure nonsense, Abraham. You know as well as I that the Kirklands do not whip their slaves. Thomas has told me that they have supported Mr. Jefferson's and Mr. Whyte's attempts to emancipate all the slaves in Virginia. They have voted for Mr. Jefferson's amendment every time he has brought it up in the House of Burgesses."

"Well, eben if he don't whup me, he's sure to boot me of'n da plantation. Where wills ah go den? The old massah has looked afta me my 'hol life."

"Abraham, do you really believe the Kirklands would make you leave Ravenwood?" Barbara asked exasperated. "Don't worry. Madam Fairchild has left a note explaining everything to the Kirklands. They certainly are not going to hold you responsible for our actions."

The girls stepped onto the wharf. Abraham handed Patricia the two satchels they had packed containing their clothing.

"Ya ladies take care, does yer hear me now?" he called out in a warning. "Jus' ain't fittin' fer two fine white ladies ta be here on dis wharf all alone."

"We're getting on board the ship. See, there she is over there," Barbara said confidently, pointing toward the hull of *The Liberty* docked nearby. "Now you'd better leave, Abraham, and thank you for all your help."

Patricia felt the flutter of butterfly wings in her stomach as she watched the boat slide away and disappear into the darkness.

"I don't think we should stay out here on this pier. Someone might come by and see us," Barbara whispered.

"Why are you whispering? There's no one around," Patricia asked. She looked about her uneasily at the deserted wharf.

"Well, let's get nearer the ship. Daniel's probably looking for us," Barbara said softly.

The two women approached the ship cautiously. There did not appear to be any activity on board. They slumped down next to some crates remaining to be loaded.

"Where do you suppose Daniel is?" Barbara asked, after a prolonged lapse of time. "It must be almost half-past the hour."

"Well, why are we waiting for him?" Patricia asked. "We can easily get on board. I have been watching the guard. He is down at the other end of the ship now."

"Do you think we should try?" Barbara asked doubtfully. "We have come this far. I surely would hate to get caught now."

"Well, if we don't get onto that ship soon, the deck is going to be crawling with crew members. It must be getting close to the time of sailing."

"All right, but try not to make a sound," Barbara cautioned.

"Why don't we just walk right up the gangplank as if we were expected," Patricia suggested. "It's too dark to distinguish anyone. Come on, if we are going, let's make our move now."

"I really don't think we should hold hands," Patricia said, breaking the firm grasp Barbara held on her hand. "I think it might not look too proper to the guard."

Barbara started to giggle. "Don't make me start laughing, Patricia." Her body began shaking as she forced back her laughter. Patricia couldn't keep from joining her. She tried to clamp a hand across Barbara's mouth when the laughter erupted from the girl's throat just as they stepped on deck.

"Halt. Who goes there?" the guard challenged and began to move toward them.

"Oh, no!" Patricia moaned. "What will we do now?"

"It's me, Daniel," Barbara called out deeply, in an imitation of the cabin boy's voice. "I am just assisting the ladies with their luggage. Cap'n wants them settled below before we shove off."

The sailor peered at them through the dim light. "Where are you, Daniel? I can't see you." The sudden approach of a carriage caused him to shift his attention to the wharf. "Well, you'd better get them below right away because here comes the Captain now."

"Thanks, mate," Barbara called out. They moved off, as the sailor moved to the rail.

"Where shall we go?" Patricia whispered.

"Well, let's get into Tom's cabin for now. He will be busy on deck until after they cast off," Barbara suggested.

"I would think we would be safer in the hold."

Barbara shook her head. "I don't want to go down there. How about one of the longboats? We could hide in one of them."

At the sound of approaching footsteps Patricia grabbed Barbara's hand. "I think we'd better get out of here."

In desperation they ducked into the cabin of Tom Sutherland. It was pitch dark in the small room and the girls crouched down in a corner. They were convinced their scheme was thwarted when the door was flung open and the lantern hanging in the passageway cast a swath of light across the floor. Thomas Sutherland crossed to the bunk and tossed down his seabag. To their relief he instantly departed, closing the door behind him and once again casting the cabin into darkness.

"We did it!" Barbara exclaimed victoriously. "Oh, Patricia, we did it!"

"We haven't sailed yet," Patricia cautioned.

"Yes, but I just know it's going to work," Barbara enthused.

In a short time the girls' eyes had adjusted to the darkened room. From the sound of the activity above them, it was obvious that the ship was preparing to set sail. Soon they heard the sound of the heavy anchor chain being raised. Both of the girls had dropped into slumber by the time the mainsail caught the wind and the vessel drifted on the tide out to sea.

Patricia's long lashes fluttered in long sweeps against her cheeks, until she finally forced her eyes open. They focused on two black boots looming before her. She followed a course up the boots that were encasing muscular calves and reached black trousers snugly sheathing strong thighs. With foreboding she swung up her gaze to meet a pair of sapphire eyes that had turned black with rage.

Patricia sat up and looked around her in surprise. In an instant the memory of the night's events returned. Barbara was still asleep beside her on the cabin floor, but enough daylight was streaming in through the porthole to give the cabin a dull grayish haze. She could see Thomas Sutherland standing close by with a bemused look on his face. Whatever thoughts were going through his head were concealed behind a mask of bewilderment.

This, however, was not the case with Stephen Kirkland. The air in the cabin was charged with the energy of his fury. Any previous anger she had witnessed in him seemed diminished by the fury which now held him in sway. He reached down a hand and yanked her to her knees. She shrank back instinctively, certain that were she a man he would not hesitate to strike her.

"What the hell are you doing on my ship, madam?" he demanded. She felt impaled as the scorn in his dark eyes pierced her like two lances of blue marble. Patricia tried to force out some words in her defense, but was choked as they constricted in her throat. She could only remain speechless in the face of his enraged passion.

Barbara stirred beside her and sat up rubbing her eyes. At the sight of the scene being enacted before her, she reached out instinctively and put a restraining hand on Stephen's arm. He shrugged it aside, but released the painful grasp he held on Patricia.

"Stephen, you must not blame her, it—"

Before Barbara could utter another word, he turned the full fury of his anger on her. "You stay out of this, Barbara! I will deal with you later. I don't doubt this is your hairbrained scheme, but Madam Fairchild should have had the sense to thwart it immediately. I did give her credit for more intelligence."

Barbara was visibly shaken by this side of her adored hero that she had never before witnessed, or even suspected existed. She was stunned by it all, and like a drowning man, in fleeting seconds she was made aware of what her impetuosity had brought on poor Patricia. The injustice of it gave her an added courage.

"You don't understand, Stephen, it—"

His narrowed glance returned to her. "Shut up, Barbara. Get her out of here, Tom," he snarled.

Tom Sutherland crossed the room. He hesitated at Stephen's side, uncertain whether he should leave Patricia alone with Stephen. Was his anger out of control? Would he attempt to do bodily harm to the woman? His instincts about his captain convinced him otherwise and he reached out a hand to assist Barbara to her feet.

"Come on, Bab," he said gently. The urgency in his eyes pleaded with her not to resist. He was certain it would only incense Stephen more.

Barbara sensed his compassion and accepted his hand. She paused at the doorway for a final backward glance. "No matter what you think, Stephen, this was all my idea. Patricia is not to blame. I will never forgive you if you harm her."

When the door closed behind them, Stephen walked to the porthole and stood staring out of the small embrasure with his hands folded behind his back. His right foot tapped a slow, steady beat on the wooden floor.

Patricia rose to her feet. She attempted to arrange her disheveled clothing. She was feeling completely ridiculous. It had been insanity to go along with the whole preposterous scheme. Why had she elected to ignore her common sense?

As she stood studying the unrelenting pair of broad shoulders, she realized her real motive for being there. She was in love with Stephen Kirkland. She had been unprepared to face never seeing him again and had jumped at any excuse to be with him, no matter how insane it might appear to her now. The hopelessness of it all only added to her vulnerability and made his scorn more unbearable.

She closed her eyes, gripped by an uncontrollable shudder, when he turned back to her with a scathing accusation.

"Is there no limit to your irrational behavior, madam?"

"I don't know what you mean, Stephen. I admit this was a very foolish move on my part."

"Foolish indeed, madam. Foolish and ill-advised," he thundered. "I am aware you and I have been playing a dangerous game, but I naively believed that you would keep it between us. You know, as well as I, that we are going into dangerous waters, waters swarming with hostile vessels. It is no place for women. We could easily be attacked by cutthroats, as well as by English warships. This foolhardy act has endangered the safety of my ship and crew, and I must cry nay. Nay, madam! No more! This time you have gone too far!

"I hold you personally responsible, Patricia. You could have prevented this, or at least informed me, so I could have taken the proper measures. You have seriously abused the friendship of an innocent girl to serve your own selfish purposes."

Patricia had known the futility of trying to defend her actions to him and had prepared herself to suffer his accusations and suspicions once again. But the one thing she had not expected to hear was his attack upon her friendship with Barbara. These latest allegations were too much for her to suffer in silence.

"I am tired of hearing these same repetitive accusations from you, Captain Kirkland," she flared angrily. "But now you have added another one that I will not abide. I love Barbara and I cherish my friendship with her. Don't try to malign that relationship with your warped suspicions."

Stephen's mouth curled with scorn.

"Oh, spare me, madam, for I am certain my accusations cannot be any more tiresome to listen to than the refrain of that damn litany of innocence you constantly chant."

He walked to the door. "For the duration of this voyage, you and Barbara are confined to this cabin. When we reach Jamaica, I will attempt to secure you passage on a ship to Virginia or Boston.

"Unfortunately, because of the limited quarters, I cannot prevent you from associating with my cousin. I must warn you, however, that if you again attempt to corrupt her I shall confine you in the brig. I do not tolerate my authority challenged or my ship endangered.

"You are forbidden to address one word to any member of my crew, or to step one foot on my deck at any time during this passage.

"Fresh water and your meals will be brought to you and Barbara by Mr. Sutherland.

"There is a chamber pot beneath the commode to service your personal needs, and a porthole to dispose of it."

He smiled grimly. "Have I made myself perfectly clear, Madam Fairchild?"

"I think you have, Captain," she replied with a defiant thrust of her head.

He brought his hand up in a quick, mocking salute. "Then do have a pleasant voyage, madam."

He stepped out and closed the door. Patricia slumped down on the bunk, her body shaking with pent-up emotion. *You're certainly right, Barbara. He really has a great sense of humor!*

Her spine prickled at the sound of the scrape of the key turning in the lock.

21

Barbara and Patricia's foolhardy act had more far-reaching effects on others than anticipated. It was difficult for Thomas Sutherland to ignore Stephen's treatment of the woman he loved. At the end of two days, he was no longer able to restrain his objection and decided to approach Stephen on the matter.

That evening, after finishing his watch, he rapped lightly on the door of Stephen's cabin.

"Who is it?" Stephen called out.

"It's the Mate, Captain," Tom replied respectfully. No matter how close his relationship was with Stephen on shore, he never allowed the friendship to affect the discipline and authority that was necessary on board a ship.

"Come in Tom," Stephen replied.

Tom entered the cabin and stood waiting stiffly while Stephen pondered a map stretched out on the desk in front of him. "Trouble?" he asked succinctly, still preoccupied with the chart.

"No trouble, sir. There is a personal

matter that I would like to discuss with you."

Tom was uncertain the captain had heard him, because Stephen did not acknowledge the remark. His attention remained focused intently on the map. But finally, after a lengthy silence, Stephen spun around in his chair.

"I wondered how long it would be before I heard from you," he said brusquely as he faced his young first mate with a stern frown.

"Captain, I know the ladies were wrong in stowing on board, but you are treating them like common criminals."

"Tom, their actions have jeopardized the safety of every man on this ship," Stephen replied. "The Caribbean has become a nest for every scoundrel and cut-throat afloat. If their presence on board *The Liberty* is discovered, we could be in for a lot of trouble. You know as well as I that we wouldn't dare engage a ship in combat for fear the ladies would be harmed."

"Sir, that cabin of theirs is hotter than Hades. The farther south we go, the hotter it becomes. There's no breeze coming through that porthole at all." Tom's face was etched with concern. "Can't you at least let them out briefly at night for some fresh air?"

Stephen's face was set in a grim line

as he pondered Tom's request. "Very well, Mr. Sutherland, a complete stroll of the main deck each night after sundown, but keep them off the quarterdeck."

Tom broke into a broad grin. "Thank you, Captain." He started to leave and then turned back. "You know, sir, it wasn't Patricia's doing. Bab was the instigator of the whole thing."

Stephen looked up at him, his dark eyes still cold. "They both stowed away on this ship, Mr. Sutherland. Therefore, they are equally to blame. Madam Fairchild is aware of Barbara's impetuosity. She should have made a greater effort to temper it."

"Bab's a Kirkland, Stephen," Tom said, for the first time lowering the formal guard between himself and his captain. "It's pretty hard to steer Kirklands up a different channel once they've set their course."

Stephen Kirkland leaned back and looked up at him. A slight smile tugged at the corners of his mouth. "That has a ring of mutiny to it, Mr. Sutherland."

"Not at all, sir." Tom grinned broadly and grabbed the handle of the door. "A complete stroll of the main deck after sundown, and keep the ladies off the quarterdeck. Aye, aye, sir."

Stephen could no longer contain his grin as the young man disappeared hastily through the door.

Tom took the companionway steps two at a time in his haste to reach the girls' cabin. He rapped lightly on the door.

"It's Tom. May I come in?"

"Yes. Thank God!" Patricia cried out.

The smile on his face disappeared instantly at the urgency in her voice. He quickly turned the key in the lock and swung open the door. Patricia was on her feet waiting for him. Her lovely face was stamped with anxiety.

"There's something wrong with Barbara, Tom. she's burning up with fever and her face is red and blotchy."

He rushed to the bunk where Barbara was lying and bent over the sleeping form. Patricia had placed a damp cloth on her forehead. Tom lifted it off and put his hand on Barbara's brow.

"My God! She's on fire!" His eyes shifted worriedly to Patricia. "How long has she been like this?"

"It hit her shortly after her evening meal," Patricia replied. She dabbed the cloth into a basin of water and wrung it out. Tom placed it on Barbara's forehead. "Before that she complained that she ached all over, and she was even more irritable than our confinement had made her anyway."

The young girl opened her swollen eyelids and, at the sight of Tom, managed a weak smile. "I feel miserable, Tom."

"You don't look too well, either, sweetheart," he said tenderly. "Do you hurt anywhere, honey?" he asked anxiously.

"No. Not any more. I'm just thirsty, Tom. Will you get me a glass of water?" she murmured weakly. Her eyes closed as she began to drift off to sleep.

Tom jumped to his feet. "I'll be right back. I'm going to get Stephen."

Within minutes Tom returned, accompanied by Stephen Kirkland. Stephen bent over the bunk and studied Barbara's sleeping face.

"I was afraid of this," he said grimly. He turned to Patricia with a hooded look. "I want you to examine her closely, without clothes."

At Barbara's startled glance, Stephen continued. "Tom and I will step outside while you do so."

As soon as they were gone Patricia raised Barbara's nightgown and drew back in surpise. The young woman's body was covered with the same red blotches that had come up on her face. She covered her hastily and called the men back into the cabin.

"There are parts of her body covered with a reddish rash," she announced.

Stephen nodded, as though he had anticipated what she would say. He released the sleeves of Barbara's gown and slid them up her arms. There were several more of the small spots dotting the arms.

"What is it, Stephen? What's wrong with her?" Patricia asked.

Stephen raised his hand and met the frantic look in her eyes. "Measles. She has a case of measles," he said, trying not to smile.

"Measles!" Patricia exclaimed.

"Measles!" Tom echoed.

"Measles!" a voice rasped weakly from the bunk.

Barbara had awakened in time to hear Stephen's announcement. "Oh, no! Measles is a child's disease," she moaned.

Stephen tried to keep a straight face. He knew she felt miserable enough, and he did not want to add to the poor girl's humiliation. "I received a note from Daniel's parents just before we sailed. He is suffering with the same malady. That is why he missed this voyage."

"Daniel! You mean that obnoxious little demon did this to me? Oh, what a blight little boys are on society!" Barbara wailed.

Tom walked over to her with a relieved smile. "Thank God it's only measles, Bab. I was afraid it was something far more serious."

"It can still be that," Stephen cautioned. "It's quite dangerous to an adult male. Daniel was contagious, so it means he has probably exposed the crew to it. We will have to find out which of the men have never had measles. I remember you had them, Tom, when you were younger. I know I did, too. What about you, Tory?"

Patricia nodded. "Yes, I remember I had measles when I was six or seven years old."

"Then that leaves the rest of the crew to be concerned about. We'll find out in the morning where we stand. In the meantime, I suggest we all get some rest. For now, just keep putting cold compresses on Bab's forehead, and keep the porthole open, until the fever breaks."

Patricia nodded in understanding, and Stephen stepped out of the cabin. Tom lingered for one remaining look at Bab, then he followed Stephen out. Patricia's eyes swung to the door and she was surprised to find Stephen's gaze resting on her. Their eyes locked briefly before he closed the door behind him.

She listened for the sound of the key in the lock, but this time there was only the echo of their retreating footsteps.

* * *

The next day two of the men came down with the infectious disease. Stephen called the entire crew on deck and discovered that over a third of his crew were certain they had never had the disease. This presented a serious consideration for which he was not prepared. When journeying into the islands of the Caribbean, a ship's captain needed every able-bodied man he could muster.

By the following day, three more of the men were flat on their backs with the raging fever, and as Stephen had indicated, an adult male became much more seriusly ill than a child. Besides their high fevers, many of the men suffered with dry hacking coughs. Stephen decided to isolate the cases in the hope of avoiding further complications.

Because of the number of crew members down with the disease, he could not spare any healthy man to care for them. He was forced to press Patricia into nursing duties.

She searched among the ship's limited supply of medicines and found some James's Powders and some ground calamina, both of which she mixed with water and gave to the men, the first internally and the second to soothe their itching skin. But she spent most of her time trying to keep the men as comfortable as possible. Whenever she had a free moment from tending to the more seriously ill, she boiled hot water and scrubbed down their quarters to keep the smell and uncomfortable closeness at a minimum.

Her hands became raw from constantly wringing out cold compresses, scrubbing the bunks, washing the bedding and clothing of the sick men, and applying her diminishing supply of lotion.

She also could not neglect her duties to Barbara, although the young girl's fever peaked early and it became just a matter of letting the rash run its course. Barbara's youth was an advantage that the older seamen lacked, and her major discomfort was simply the itch which resulted from the rash.

At the end of five days Patricia was moving in a trance. She had barely had any sleep, but for the first time since the outbreak of the disease there were no new cases, that morning so it appeared the worst was over.

The discomfort of most of the infected sailors had been reduced to the irritation of the rash, with the exception of one seaman. For the last three days he had lain unconscious. The high fever he was suffering would not break. Patricia had constantly kept cool compresses on him, but with no success. He would toss fitfully in his delerium and she was forced to have Tom tie him to a bunk. This made it extremely difficult for her whenever she had to tend to his personal hygiene.

As she watched the poor soul thrashing about with fever, she was reminded of how lightly they had initially taken Barbara's illness. After all, measles was just a common childhood disease! Now it was easy to see the reason for Stephen's concern and how swiftly an epidemic could strike a ship, rendering the crew useless. She said a prayer of thanks when the raging fever finally broke and, mercifully, the sailor regained consciousness.

The following morning Stephen anchored *The Liberty* in a quiet cove in one of the Bahamian islands to take on fresh water and fruit. The illness had caused an excessive usage of fresh water and their supply was running dangerously low.

In gratitude for her services, Stephen suggested that Patricia accompany them to shore where she could take a refreshing swim. She needed no further persuasion and was seated with soap and towel when they lowered the longboat.

After a cautionary warning for Patricia not to stray away from the small pool he located for bathing, Stephen and the men departed to fill the water casks and gather some melons and papayas.

Patricia immediately stripped to her chemise and inched into the beckoning water. She thought she had never felt anything as wonderful as the refreshing waters of the inland pool. She cleansed her body and shampooed her hair, then refreshed and clean, she sat down under a palm tree and began to brush out her hair.

In the distance she could hear the men shouting back and forth to one another, and occasionally a bird squawked its objection to this invasion of its sanctuary.

The exhausting rigors of the previous days finally caught up with her. Patricia's eyes drooped and the brush dropped out of her hand. In seconds she was fast asleep.

Sometime later, as she drifted in the hazy torper of sleep, she became vaguely aware of a pair of strong arms lifting her up.

"Stephen," she murmured with a contented sigh and settled her head snugly against a firm chest.

From a distance came the faint sound of creaking oars, and she felt the gentle rocking of the boat as it bobbed on the water; but her eyes remained closed and she burrowed deeper against the firm wall.

"Stephen," she murmured again. "I'm so sleepy."

The arms holding her seemed to tighten more protectively around her. "Then sleep, love," a voice whispered tenderly in her ear and she felt warm lips press a light kiss to her forehead.

Patricia smiled and surrendered to deep slumber.

22

When Patricia awoke the following morning she was convinced it had all been a dream. Yet, it all still seemed real to her; she couldn't have dreamed the trip to the island.

Her troubled frown swung constantly to the mirror as she freshened herself, as though the image could reveal some telltale evidence. She realized she had been walking around in a daze for several days, but surely she could not have conjured up the whole thing in her mind.

Patricia raised a hand to her head to see if she were feverish. Was it possible she was suffering some reoccurance of the disease?

I need a cup of tea, she thought rationally. *A cup of tea will clear my head.*

"Good morning," Barbara chirped from her bunk.

Patricia turned to her with a smile. Barbara looked as if her face were covered with a mass of rose-colored freckles. "How are you feeling today?"

The young girl grinned. "I am feeling fine. I'll just be glad when I get over these measles. I'm getting really bored lying in this bunk." She picked up a copy of *Poor Richard's Almanac* that Stephen had given her to read. "Stephen said I should read this in the hope that I gain some common sense from it."

Patricia eyed her with curiosity. "Barbara, I . . . I don't remember coming to bed last night. Do you have any idea what time it was?"

"Oh, I would guess it was about two o'clock," Barbara replied, not raising her eyes from the book.

"Two o'clock in the morning!" Patricia exclaimed. "No wonder I don't remember! I was probably walking in my sleep by that time."

Barbara looked up amused. "I didn't say it was two o'clock in the morning. It was two o'clock in the afternoon," she corrected. "And you definitely weren't walking in your sleep. Stephen carried you in and put you in bed. I don't think you moved a muscle the entire night."

Patricia blushed with pleasure. She hadn't dreamed it. It was Stephen's arms that had held her and it was his lips that had kissed her!

Patricia had good cause to believe she still might have dreamed it all when she next saw Stephen. His face was cast in the same stony mold she had grown to expect from the time she came on board. His manner was curt and businesslike.

"Tom told me you were kind enough to lift your ban on our isolation. Thank you, Captain, and I assure you we will not disturb you or your crew."

"Under the circumstances it would have been extremely ungrateful of me to do otherwise," Stephen snapped. It was obvious to her how difficult it was for him to admit he was wrong.

However, she was not about to allow him to think that she believed he was doing it out of gratitude.

"But I understood, Captain, that you granted us the permission before the outbreak of the measles." She tried not to look too smug.

Stephen looked as if he wanted to throttle her and silently cursed Tom for betraying him. "Well, perhaps I over-reacted at the time. But I haven't changed my belief that it was a foolhardy act for you and Barbara to stow away on this ship," he growled.

"That is the only subject about which you and I are in complete accord, Captain Kirkland." Patricia spun on her heel and walked away.

That evening Patricia and Tom leisurely strolled the deck. The fact that there was no sign of Stephen Kirkland enabled Patricia to relax and enjoy the fresh air.

She did not make any attempt to leave the cabin during the day. When Tom came to visit Barbara in the evening, Patricia would leave to take her stroll, thus giving the young sweethearts some privacy.

It was such an occasion that found her walking the deck alone. She drew a deep, exhilarating breath. The ship was gliding smoothly across the calm water under a full press of canvas. The towering masts rose majestically against a dark sky, dotted with the florescent glow of hundreds of stars, and the lofty masts creaked and swayed as the breeze bellied their surging sails.

Patricia drew back in alarm at the sudden appearance of Stephen Kirkland. "Captain Kirkland! You have a disarming habit of unexpectedly jumping out at me from the dark shadows of this ship," she laughed nervously.

"That would be impossible, madam, if you were not *on* my ship," he offered. She could sense immediately that his manner was relaxed and casual. For a moment, at least, he was no longer the stern and unrelenting sea captain. The man was an enigma!

A strong breeze caught the long silken strands of her hair and she looked up laughing as she brushed them off her face. "And inasmuch as I am on your ship without an invitation, it makes me entirely to blame. Am I right, Captain?''

He grinned charmingly and took her arm. ''My grandfather, Andrew Kirkland, was part-Scot and part-Indian. He was a remarkable man who, despite a successful political career, never lost touch with his Indian roots. When I was a young boy, Grandfather would take me hunting with him and teach me many of the beliefs and habits of his Indian heritage. They were great times. Unforgettable times,'' Stephen said with a pensive smile.

Patricia listened with rapt attention, fascinated by the changing emotions on his expressive face.

''One day,'' Stephen continued, ''Grandfather and I were on our way home. He had shot a duck and we were going to roast it for dinner. Grandfather pointed to a solitary eagle gliding freely in the sky. 'Stephen,' he said to me, 'do you see that eagle? He has wings to soar, so he builds his nest high and remote, away from the reach of man. On the other hand,' Grandfather said, 'consider this duck. He too, has wings to fly. But he seeks his nest on the ground, easily accessible to man.'

''I looked up at him and I said, 'What are you trying to say, Grandfather?' And Grandfather Kirkland flashed his incredible smile and said, 'Well, if you notice, son, there are a damned sight more roasted ducks around than there are roasted eagles!' "

Their walk had brought them to the top of the companionway and Patricia paused, her eyes sparkling with amusement. "I think I get the analogy, Captain. But you are wrong if you think for one moment that I am going to end up trussed and stuffed on the center of your platter. No matter where I decide to nest!" she added.

"We'll see about that, Tory," he chuckled warmly, his dark eyes dancing with mischief.

"Good night, Captain," she said with a saucy nod of her head.

He dipped his head politely. "Madam Fairchild."

Stephen's grin broadened and his dark gaze followed her as she descended the stairway.

Three days later Stephen was busy writing in the ship's log when there was a light tap on the door. At his permission to enter, the door opened and Barbara and Tom stepped into the cabin.

Barbara's rash had disappeared, but her face was flushed with excitement. Stephen grinned at the sight of her.

"You look as if you have suffered a relapse, Barbara."

"It's nothing. I'm just excited," she assured him. "Tom and I have a favor to ask of you."

"I seem to be plagued with requests

for favors," he replied sternly. "Well, what is it?"

"Let me handle this, Bab," Tom said and stepped forward. "I request permission to get married, sir."

Stephen leaned back in his chair. "As opposed as I am to the idea, I believe that issue was settled already in Virginia. You certainly don't need my permission."

Tom's eyes shifted nervously to Barbara's and she gave him an encouraging nod to continue.

"Well, we do, sir—if we want you to marry us now."

"Marry you?" he roared as he shot up in his chair.

Barbara was no longer able to maintain her silence. "Please, Stephen. Tom and I want to marry right away. This voyage would be a wonderful honeymoon for us. We will probably never have a better chance to be together." Her brown eyes were round and wide as she pleaded for his understanding.

"Certainly not!" Stephen declared, jumping to his feet. "There is no way I would consider it! You two are trying to rush into something that requires a great deal of reflection."

"I think we know what we're doing," Tom replied, annoyed. "Bab and I love each other and it seems ridiculous to waste this time that we could be sharing together."

"Tom, you know as well as I that the country's about to erupt into a war. A war that you will have to fight! What if you are seriously wounded, or even killed? Do you want to leave Barbara alone? A widow? What if she has a child?"

Barbara stepped forward, her eyes blazing angrily. "If you understood anything about real love, Stephen Kirkland, you would know that if something happens to Tom I would want to have his child. That is part of what loving someone is all about!"

"I don't expect anything to happen to me, Stephen," Tom interjected. "But let me remind you that I grew up without a mother or father, but I was never without someone who loved me.

"Oh, I know a war is pending, Stephen, and I know I will have to fight in it, but I refuse to allow the prospect of it to keep me from living my life while I wait for it to break out. My God! I could be an old man by that time!" Tom's face was etched with earnestness.

"Is that your problem, Stephen?" Barbara lashed out. "Are you afraid to commit yourself to a woman because of the pending war? Are you so obsessed with it that you are denying yourself a chance for personal happiness? If that's true, Stephen, then you have already become the first casualty of the war."

Stephen stared at her in astonishment. It was as if Barbara had reached down into his soul and tapped the very nerve of his insecurity. It was hard to believe that this young woman who was facing him with such insight was the same person he once thought of as an impetuous child. Was it just a few short weeks ago?

Stephen glanced at Tom and in an instant the young man's life flashed before him as if he were drowning. He had not been aware of when Tom had slipped into manhood. When had it happened?

And who was he? What right had he to deny them their recognition? They were two adults who had charted the course of their lives and were not afraid to make the journey.

"I would be very proud to marry you," he said humbly.

Barbara rushed into his arms and kissed his cheek. "Oh, thank you, Stephen. I love you, you know. Nothing will ever change that."

He winked at Tom who was grinning broadly, over her head. "And just to show you what a nice person I really am, I relieve you of all your duties and you two can have my cabin until we reach Jamaica."

"That is generous of you, Captain, inasmuch as we are due to reach Jamaica tomorrow," Tom replied.

Stephen shrugged innocently. "You can't deny it's still a generous offer."

"Which we will accept," Barbara piped in. Her eyes were sparkling with happiness. "I am leaving now to put on a proper gown for my wedding. Don't either of you go away," she warned.

Patricia threw up her hands in frustration. "How can you do this? I can't find one decent thing for you to wear to a wedding. Where are we going to get flowers in the middle of an ocean?"

"I don't know about flowers, but this yellow gown is a perfect wedding dress." Barbara held up a pale yellow floral silk dress with a corset of the same material showing in the front. Its elbow-length sleeves each had a pleated cuff. A white chemise ruffled above the corset and the full skirt was divided in front and worn over a white petticoat.

Patricia helped her to put on the gown and then took a white silk chiffon kerchief and draped it over Barbara's head and shoulders. She stepped back to admire the result with tears glistening in her eyes. Barbara looked beautiful. Her warm brown eyes glowed in the radiance of a pixie face that was softly framed by the sheer scarf. Deep mahogany curls lay on her forehead.

Patricia donned a plain dusty-rose

silk gown with a round neck and shirred sleeves. A pink chemise filled in the neckline. She brushed her hair and pinned it off her face with two pearl combs.

Stephen held the wedding ceremony on deck so that the crew could witness it. Tom looked handsome in a brown coat and breeches with a gold waistcoat and white hose. His hair was combed neatly into a queue and he wore a black tricorn.

Stephen was wearing his naval dress uniform, which was more ostentatious than his usual working attire. His dark blue coat was cuffed, but collarless, and a white ruffled shirt was concealed behind a red waistcoat that buttoned down the front and was edged with gold braid. He wore black buckled shoes and his long muscular legs were sheathed in white hose. Like Thomas, his hair had been neatly tied in a queue at his neck and he was wearing a black tricorn edged with gold braid.

The crew of *The Liberty* let out a roar of approval when Tom kissed his bride after Stephen announced the couple man and wife.

Before he abandoned his cabin to the newlyweds, Stephen insisted that the bridal party join him for a wedding drink. He poured each of the ladies a glass of Madiera and he and Tom each had a glass of cognac. He raised his glass in a toast of happiness to the young couple.

"God, I hate cognac," Tom complained after the toast. "The least you could have done, Stephen, inasmuch as it was my wedding toast, is offer me a decent drink."

"You will have to develop a taste for cognac, Tom, if you are going to occupy my quarters," Stephen said good-naturedly. "You know that is the only thing I stock." Tom's distaste for Stephen's favorite drink had set off a running battle between the cousins from the time Tom had been old enough to sample his first spirits.

Patricia saw no excuse for lingering in the cabin and excused herself. Barbara and Tom decided to return to the deck to give Stephen the opportunity to change back into the comfort of just a shirt and breeches.

The quiet of the afternoon was shattered by the sound of a scrape of a fiddle and the plunking rhythm of a guitar, which were quickly joined by the twang of a jew's harp.

Barbara was snatched out of Tom's arms by one of the crew into the fast steps of a jig. Patricia was pulled on deck and drawn into the dance. Several casks of ale were broken open for the occasion as the wedding celebration got under way.

Stephen leaned against the rail,

smiling, as he watched Patricia struggling with the quick steps of the dance. She had never had any occasion to learn the brisk jig, but soon her feet and arms were swinging as lively as her partner's, and her face glowed with animation while one member of the crew after another claimed her for a dance. Barbara was kept just as busy, and the bridegroom got very little opportunity to dance with his bride as the celebration got livelier after each draught was consumed.

The ship was under half-sail as the celebration continued into the evening. Patricia was completely exhausted, but she couldn't remember when she had known such fun.

Stephen had claimed her several times for a partner. Now, as he twirled her lightly, his hands spanned her waist, and swung her into the air as if she were a feather. With a laughing shriek her arms encircled his neck and he spun her around. She laughed with delight into his upturned face, her own face glowing with animation.

The music ended abruptly, and Stephen slowly slid her along his long torso until her feet touched the planks of the deck. The movements sent shock waves of physical awareness along her body. The laughter left Patricia's face and changed to desire as they looked into each other's eyes. His message was blatant.

In an instant she was pulled out of his arms by another partner and whisked away.

The newlyweds disappeared and most of the crew had passed out from too much ale. The three musicians began to play more softly; the three instruments mellowed into the traditional music of their homelands. Soon it grew haunting —nameless tunes with no words, no printed notes, just familiar country melodies that had been played and passed on until they became unforgettable.

Stephen had taken the helm and was alone on the quarterdeck. He held the huge wheel and a tankard of ale in his hands at the same time. Occasionally he would take a sip from the tankard. Patricia could not help being drawn to the solitary figure standing at the wheel. She drifted over to him.

The ship was riding gently on the water. Stephen had not raised any more sail, so they were not moving more than two knots an hour. A soft breeze kissed the sail, and the water and starry sky blended into a velvet blackness.

"I feel as if I could drift forever," Patricia said softly. "The sea is beautiful at night."

"Would you like to take the helm?" Stephen asked.

Her heart leaped with excitement. "I would love to. I have wondered what it felt like to steer a ship."

Stephen stepped back and she grasped the heavy wooden wheel. "How do you know which direction to travel?" she asked. "Everything looks the same."

He stepped forward and she found herself in the circle of his arms. He pointed to a bright star up above. "Just keep your eye on that star overhead." His warm breath ruffled the hair on her neck. He brought the tankard to his mouth but remained with his arms around her.

"Would you like a drink?" he asked.

She nodded, hoping he would release her. His nearness was too disturbing. To her consternation he raised the tankard to her lips and she took a few sips of the bitter ale.

Her nose turned up in distaste. "It's horrible. And it's warm!"

"Well, at least it's wet," he chuckled. He continued to sip from the tankard. "I would offer you a glass of Madiera, but unfortunately, my cabin is occupied at the moment."

"That's right, you're without a bunk. Where are you sleeping tonight?" She was beginning to find it impossible to concentrate on the star up in the sky.

His brow raised to a rakish angle. "I don't suppose that is an invitation. Logically, I would sleep in the Mate's cabin."

"The Mate's cabin is already occupied, Captain. I suggest you find where the Mate has been sleeping previously," she announced lightly.

He moved closer and she could feel the heat of his warm thighs through the layers of her gown. Or at least she thought she could feel them, she thought with a nervous gulp.

"Would you embarrass me in front of my whole crew, Tory? They all know I am mad about you." he asked charmingly at her ear.

She deliberately avoided looking up into his roguish eyes. She dared not or she would be lost. "Mad *at* me would be more realistic, Captain."

When Stephen Kirkland attempted to be charming, he was absolutely devastating and she found herself weakening under the potency of that charm.

She slipped out from beneath his arms to make a hasty exit. "I think it is far past my bedtime. Goodnight, Captain." But the temptation was too strong to resist and she glanced up to him once more. His dark hair was rumpled as he looked down at her, flashing his incredible smile.

"Is that your final answer?"

"Final and absolute, Captain," she said with a feigned sternness.

"Nothing is absolute, Tory," he cautioned wickedly · as she strode hurriedly away.

23

The whole crew's spirits seemed to swell with anticipation as *The Liberty* neared the steaming port of Kingston.

Stephen stood on the quarterdeck peering through his telescope at the three ships anchored in the harbor.

"Damn the luck!" he cursed aloud.

Thomas Sutherland, standing beside him, glanced up anxiously. "What is it, Captain?"

"The *Serpentine* is in port. I was hoping that scurvey bastard, Laurette, would be elsewhere. The *China Lady* is there, too. Which means we could have our hands full with Billy Wong." He swung the glass in the direction of the third ship. "There is also another ship, but she's not flying any colors. I can't see her markings either."

"Is she armed?" Tom inquired.

"From the way she's setting in the water, she appears to be weighed down with some armament, or she has a full store in the hold. Swing *The Liberty* starboard, Mr. Sutherland. Let's get a better look at her."

As the ship tacked about, Stephen trained the telescope on the bow. "She's *The Betsy* out of London," he reported to Tom. "She looks to be armed."

He handed the glass to Tom, who peered through it. "Do you think she's a merchant ship? Maybe she's a convoy ship, or even a warship."

"She's too light," Stephen said. "How long do you make her?"

"Looks to me like she's about a hundred feet. I make out six cannon on her port side. If there's the same on her starboard, that's only twelve guns. Looks like two guns at her bow and the same at her stern."

"Apparently, she's just what she seems to be," Stephen said thoughtfully. "She's carrying that armament for her own protection, and not anyone else's."

Tom returned the telescope to Stephen. "I don't like it. *The Betsy*. Have you ever heard of her before?"

Stephen shook his head. "Well, we're here now, so we'll have to take our chances."

"What about the ladies, Captain?"

"I think they should remain on board until we get the lay of the land. We still have to determine why that other ship put in here," Stephen advised.

"Bab's not going to like this delay. I promised to take her up into the hills for our honeymoon."

"I thought you would. And it's just as well. With Laurette and Billy Wong in port, the streets of Kingston will not be the safest place for a white woman."

"After just getting over the measles, Bab's got cabin fever. She can't wait to get ashore."

"Another day won't make that much difference. You want her to be safe, don't you?" Stephen said worriedly. "You know as well as I that Laurette and Billy Wong are both white slavers. They would kill to get their hands on Barbara and Tory."

"You don't have to convince me, Captain," Tom replied with a rueful grin. "Convince Barbara, will you?"

"She's your wife, Mr. Sutherland."

Stephen raised the glass for another look at the ship. "Drop anchor and secure the ship, Mr. Sutherland."

"Aye, sir," Tom replied and turned away and immediately began to issue orders to the crew.

Barbara Sutherland took the news that she and Patricia had to remain on board calmly. Too calmly, Tom thought with a worried frown. It wasn't like Barbara to accept such a disappointment so graciously, especially considering how she had looked forward to going ashore.

The longboat had no more than departed, when Barbara disappeared, too. Patricia attributed her disappearance to the initial disappointment, so she did not make an effort to find her. She felt it would be better to let her adjust to the disappointment.

She put aside the book she was reading when Barbara entered the cabin a short while later and dumped an assortment of men's clothing on the floor. Patricia took one glance at the pile and guessed Barbara's intent. She shook her head and picked up her book.

"No, Bab. Stephen ordered us to remain on the ship. I am not going to disobey him."

"Oh, he's just being overly cautious," Barbara protested.

"He's doing it for our own good, Bab. He says there are two pirate ships in port. I respect his judgment."

Barbara shook her head in exasperation. "I don't expect to go ashore dressed as a woman! We can put on these men's clothes and no one will know the difference."

"I want no part of it, Barbara, and that is my final word," Patricia declared emphatically.

The announcement was met by a deep sigh and a momentary silence. "This is the only adventure I will probably ever have in my lifetime. I am not going to let the opportunity pass me by. I'm going, even if you don't, Patricia." Barbara began to remove her gown.

"What difference will one more day make?" Patricia argued, trying to dissuade her, although she could see by the determination on the girl's face that it was useless.

"If I know Stephen Kirkland, he will load up this ship and sail out of here as quickly as he can, then I will never get to see the island. That's what one day's difference will make," Barbara said decisively. "I have discovered that Stephen is a very stubborn man!"

"Well, it obviously is a family trait!" Patricia remarked, when Barbara began to pull on a pair of men's breeches.

She knew she couldn't let Barbara go ashore alone. If nothing else, there was safety in numbers! Perhaps if she went along she would be able to find Stephen before any problem arose.

A short while later Patricia surveyed her image in the glass doors of Tom's bookcase. "I can't understand how I ever let you talk me into this insane scheme," she lamented. She was wearing a pair of boy's breeches that fell to just below her knees, tied at the waist with a piece of rope. Heavy woven knee-high hose covered her long slim legs. A loose shirt was tucked into the waist of the breeches. Were it not for her hair, from a distance she could easily have passed as a tall, slim young man, until one peered into her face and saw a jaw too delicate and slim to be a man's, and lips too curved and provocative to be masculine.

Barbara Sutherland was dressed in a similar fashion. Being several inches shorter than Patricia, with the added advantage of clipped hair, she made a very convincing young lad.

"What do you suggest we do about my hair? Patricia asked amused. "I certainly am not cutting it off just to go along with this hair-brained scheme of yours." Her eyes sparked with amusement. "No pun intended, of course."

"I found each of us a stocking cap in Stephen's footlocker. They will do just fine as soon as I get your hair pinned up."

Patricia could not believe Barbara's audacity. "You mean you even went into Stephen's footlocker? Not only are you disobeying his specific orders, but you have the nerve to enter his cabin and steal from his footlocker to do it! He is going to throttle you."

"More than likely, and I will deserve it," Barbara said objectively. She tucked a pouch of money into her pocket; her brown eyes brightened with mischief and she flashed a dimpled smile as she grabbed Patricia's arm. "Jamaica, here we come!"

The remaining boat was tied to the ship, bobbing on the water. It was a simple matter for the two women to climb down the rope ladder that was dangling from the railing. Barbara untied the rope and put the end of an oar against the hull of the ship. She gave it a firm shove and they glided out onto the water.

Patricia could only sit, shaking her head. She was still unable to believe that she was again a part of Bab's madcap schemes!

After a short trip to the dock, exhausted but exhilarated, they climbed out and tied the boat to a piling. Barbara squeezed Patricia's arm in excitement. "Isn't this thrilling!"

The two women looked about them with interest. The city seemed to hang on the edge of a jungle. Lofty mountains covered with a green leafy carpet rose in the distance.

The largest of the British West Indies, Jamaica was a tropical paradise abounding in streams and rivers of fish. The native population had been practically exterminated under the cruelty of the Spaniards, and it had become a popular slave market. But then Cromwell had taken Jamaica in 1655 and the island was ceded to England by the

Treaty of Madrid in 1670. With the typical British enthusiasm for gardens, the English turned the island into a veritable orchard of oranges, limes, lemons, plantains, and pineapples.

The narrow streets of Kingston were bustling with activity. The two women wandered unobtrusively through the throng, gawking at the Jamaicans in their colorful native costumes. Occasionally, they passed a sailor, but it was easy to discern the blue-and-white uniform of an English tar from the shaggy shirt and breeches of a pirate, with his glinting eyes and dangling queue.

Barbara poked Patricia in the ribs and pointed to the approach of two of these menacing characters. Scraggly beards hung from their swarthy faces and red bandanas were tied around their heads. Each wore a single gold hoop dangling from one ear.

"I wonder if they had their hair cut too short, too," Patricia jibed.

"I can see where I really made a mistake wearing that scarf," Barbara chimed. At Patricia's nod of agreement, Barbara's eyes danced merrily. "I should have worn a gold earring with it!"

"You ninny," Patricia laughed and jokingly gave her a light shove.

The movement caught Barbara unexpectedly and she lost her balance, staggering into a man who had been standing in front of an inn. A strain of Oriental blood was evident in the pair of black slanted eyes that glared at her. He was wearing a small gold hat on the top of his head. A long queue tied with a bright red ribbon hung down to the middle of his back.

The long trailing ends of a thin mustache curved around his narrow, thin mouth and hung to the end of his jaw on each side of his face. He was wearing a white satin shirt with billowing sleeves, black breeches and thigh-high black boots. A curved cutlass hung below his hips, dangled from a red satin sash wrapped around his waist.

" 'ere, lad. Watch your step," he grumbled. Despite his appearance, he spoke with an English accent.

"Aye. Sorry, Cap'n," Barbara responded in a deep voice. She returned to Patricia's side and the two women started to move on.

" 'Ey, you two lads. Come back here," the stranger called out.

They looked back in distress. The man was motioning for them to come to his side. "What should we do? Do you think we should make a run for it?" Barbara asked softly.

"Let's see what he wants first," Patricia suggested. Reluctantly, the two women returned to his side.

"I'ave need of two lads such as ye," he

declared in a gravel voice. He pointed to a trunk that was sitting on the ground next to him. "I want you to take this trunk upstairs for me."

"Why should we?" Barbara said belligerently, in her best imitation of Daniel.

" 'Cause Billy Wong says ye should!" The stranger lowered his head and snarled into her face.

Barbara's eyes widened in surprise. She had heard that name before. Stephen had repeated it several times in his warning. "And ye be Cap'n Wong?" she asked.

The pirate's face curled into a deadly smirk. " 'at's right, lad. Ye be a pretty little thing, ain't ye?" He began to eye her suspiciously.

Barbara gulped nervously. "A pleasure to help ya, Cap'n. Come on, Mate," she said to Patricia, "the Cap'n 'ere wants 'r 'elp."

"Take it to the room at the top of the stairs. And mind ye, don't be tippin' it," he warned with a fierce frown.

Patricia threw Barbara a disgusted glance as they each picked up an end of the trunk. "This is a fine mess you've gotten us into," she whispered. They managed to get the heavy trunk through the door and found themselves confronted by a tall flight of steps.

"How are we ever going to carry this

thing up those steps?" Barbara hissed.

"Just lift your end—and don't tip it, Matey," Patricia scolded.

"What's he got in here? Rocks?" Barbara complained.

"Save your breath," Patricia panted. "We're only half-way up!"

They finally succeeded in struggling to the the top and opened the door. Two Oriental girls were sitting on the bed. They looked surprised at the sight of Patricia and Barbara and began to giggle and whisper to each other as the girls dragged the trunk across the floor.

"One more giggle and I'm going to pop them in the face," Barbara grumbled through clenched teeth.

"I can't believe that is what a properly reared young lady from Boston would do," Patricia teased.

"I'm sure not," Barbara agreed. "But you forget, Mate, that this one is a Kirkland, too! Let's get out of here. I saw some stairs at the back of the hall."

"Then we're going to get right back to the ship. Do you understand, Barbara? You are going to listen to me whether you want to or not."

"You're right, Patricia. Let's get out of here," Barbara said contritely. "If we're lucky we can get back before anyone discovers we have gone."

They reached the outside of the building and cautiously made their way to the front. Barbara peered around the side of the building and was relieved to see that there was no sign of the sinister Captain Wong. She nodded an all clear to Patricia and the two girls stepped out on the street.

Suddenly a paw, seemingly as heavy as a bear's, clamped down on each of their shoulders.

"Well, 'ere ye be, Mateys! I was feared ye'd run off fore old Billy Wong could buy ye both a draft o' ale fer yer 'elp."

"That'll not be necessary, Cap'n," Barbara said, with a smile that was weaker than her trembling legs.

"I'll nay take no fer an answer," the pirate replied.

He steered them into a nearby tavern. The place was as dark as an alley at midnight and as sour smelling as a pail of week-old milk sitting in the sun at high noon. Patricia's nose curled up in distaste. It reminded her of the King's Inn in Williamsburg.

The tavern was crowded with other members of Billy Wong's crew. They called out a welcome to him when he entered.

"What do we do now? This place is crawling with his crew. We'll never be able to get away," Barbara complained.

"I think I'm going to gag," Patricia whispered.

"Great idea!" Barbara said with an enthusiastic pat on her back. "We can get out that way."

"I mean I really am going to gag," Patricia reiterated. "Have you ever sampled a glass of ale? It tastes worse than it smells!"

Before they could continue to devise a method of escape, a tall tankard of ale was standing in front of each of them on the bar.

"What do we do now?" Barbara asked aside to Patricia. She could feel the panic mounting within her.

"We drink it! What do you think?" Patricia asked, raising her voice slightly louder than she intended.

Billy Wong peered down at her suspiciously, and with a game smile Patricia raised the tankard in a gesture of gratitude.

"Do you think this glass is dirty?" Barbara whispered. She hesitantly raised the glass to her mouth.

"Well, if it's not, it's probably the only thing in here besides us that isn't!" Patricia replied.

"Come on, lads. Drink up," Billy Wong declared, slapping them on the back.

Barbara took a few sips of the drink. "I can't do this, Patricia," she complained. "I know I will never be able to drink this. It tastes terrible. You're going to have to pretend you're sick."

"I don't have to pretend. I am sick," Patricia replied, after taking a few more sips. "You're the one with the ideas. You better come up with one now."

"Let's just close our eyes and gulp it down," Barbara suggested.

"Yes, why don't you do that," Patricia agreed. "I'll just wach you along with all the others."

Barbara took a deep breath, closed her eyes and began to down the tankard of the dark ale to the hoots and shouts of encouragement from the men around them. She slammed the tankard down on the bar when she was finished.

Billy Wong slapped her on the back. " 'ats a stout lad, if I ever seen one!" he called out approvingly. "Give the lad another draught, Jims."

Barbara turned to Patricia and the two girls faced one another with sick looking smiles on their faces.

"Now?" Barbara asked.

"Now," Patricia agreed.

They both turned and bolted to the door.

They raced back to the wharf and were into their boat without so much as a backward glance. Once safe on *The Liberty*, Barbara suddenly paled and rushed to the rail.

The tankard of ale, the fast run, and the boat ride on an undulating sea had blended together in a recipe too potent for her to swallow.

When Thomas Sutherland returned to *The Liberty* a few hours later, he found his very sick new bride still leaning over the railing.

24

It was midday, the following day when Patricia and Stephen waved goodbye to Tom and Barbara and watched the cart taking them on their honeymoon disappear over the top of the hill.

Stephen had rented her a room in a local inn and Patricia was looking forward to a bath and an evening's rest in a proper bed. She was just anticipating ordering the bath when Stephen tapped at her door with an offer to show her the town.

Patricia hesitated. The previous day's folly was fresh in her mind, but she certainly would be seeing it under different circumstances with Stephen at her side. She nodded eagerly.

The town was still swarming with activity and arrayed in a rainbow of color. Tiny buildings in colorful shades of pink, blue and yellow stood thickly at the foot of the steep hills that surrounded the city.

Patricia was beginning to feel uncomfortable. The air was humid and her clothes were tight and confining. Her eyes enviously followed the freedom of the native women as they moved about in their colorful sarongs and bare feet. They were completely unencumbered by corsets, panniers or long hose.

Stephen bore her yearning glances at them as long as he was able, and then took her hand and led her to one of the grass stalls that lined the streeet. She stared dumbfounded as he searched through several pieces of bright cloth, until he found one that satisfied him. It was green with a brilliant print of white and blue.

"Here. Take off those cumbersome clothes you are wearing and put this on," he ordered abruptly. He shoved the garment into her hands.

"Are you insane? I can't wear that! Why—why, it would be scandalous," she sputtered, shocked.

Stephen raised a skeptical brow. "When in Rome, Tory! It's a matter of survival." He flashed a devilish grin. "Besides, who else is going to know? I won't tell."

"Dare I, Stephen?" she asked. "It would feel so wonderful to get out of all these hot and stuffy clothes. But if anyone would ever find out, it—"

"It would just be another scandalous escapade of the infamous Widow Fairchild," he grinned. His dark eyes softened. "Do you really care what those wagging tongues have to say, Tory?"

That was the needed incentive to convince her. She held up the strip of cloth. "I haven't the vaguest idea how to put this on."

Stephen's eyes danced. "I would be more than happy to assist you."

Patricia could feel a hot blush sweeping through her. At the sight of it, Stephen threw back his head, chuckling warmly. "Oh, Tory, you're such a delightful mixture of sophistication and innocence. I never know which one to expect!"

He turned to the native vendor and exchanged a few words of Spanish. She nodded agreeably, and took Patricia's hand and led her into the small structure behind her booth.

Patricia felt ridiculous as the woman began to strip off the stomacher and gown she was wearing. She was then divested of her petticoat, her shoes, her hose, and finally her chemise. With experienced hands the native woman wrapped the wide strip of green cloth around Patricia to cover her breasts and then form a skirt that fell to the calves of Patricia's long legs. She brought the end up, draped it across one of Patricia's shoulders, and secured it.

It was fortunate that Patricia could not see the end results in a full-length mirror or she would have been as shocked as those wagging tongues in Boston. Her shoulders and arms were completely bare. One side of the sarong was raised enough to show one of her long slim legs, which were now just as bare as her shoulders.

"*Muy guapa!*" the woman exclaimed, stepping back to admire the end results. Before Patricia even realized her intent, the native woman had pulled the pins out of Patricia's hair and it tumbled to her shoulders. She ran a comb through it with a few quick strokes, and the hair was shimmering like a golden wave as it hung down her back.

"No, I cannot," Patricia announced, shaking her head. It was bad enough of her to appear semi-naked in public, but she would not allow her hair to flow freely. The woman helped her to make a long, thick braid down the back of her head.

Patricia stepped out self-consciously. Stephen's back was to her and he was still unaware of her presence.

"*Aqui esta la senora, senor.*"

Stephen swung around and froze at the sight of Patricia. He sucked in a deep breath that seemed to catch in his throat. His eyes slowly swept the graceful length of her. They followed a course from her bare shoulders across the rounded swell of her breasts to where her slim waist flowed into the curve of her hips. The dark gaze continued its smoldering trail down her long legs to the naked ends of her toes. His inspection did not seem to miss one dip or curve of her body.

When it swung back up, his eyes locked with hers. She read the approval and passion that was gleaming in the sapphire depths.

He wanted her! It was raw—unmasked! And that knowledge gave her the self-assurance she needed. Whatever some bigoted dowagers in Boston had to say was of no consequence to her. It didn't even matter how it would be accepted in those more enlightened Virginia drawing rooms. What mattered was this man's approval—and she could read that clearly in those incredible blue eyes that were locked with hers.

Patricia smiled at him. A smile that tempted with all the provocative enticement of an ancient Eve, a smile that beckoned with all the irresistible seduction of a Circe, a smile that enchanted with all the bewitching allure of a woman in love.

"You're beautiful, Tory. More beautiful then I have ever seen you," he said hoarsely, visibly shaken.

And the warmth in his eyes convinced her of the truth in his words.

Stephen had bought her a pair of straw sandals while she was dressing, and he kneeled down and slipped them on her feet. Hand-in-hand, they continued to stroll through the dozens of stalls that lined the streets, with their vivid displays hanging from the thatched roofs and facades.

With typical female curiosity, Patricia stopped to investigate some vials of perfume. Stephen took the bottle from her, and, after a few discerning sniffs, he set it aside.

"You smell much nicer, Tory."

In one of the finer shops Stephen discovered a beautiful pair of combs encrusted with pearls. After some firm bartering, they were tucked into Patricia's hair.

She in turn searched diligently for an appropriate gift for him. She found a tasteful piece of ironwood sculpture for his cabin, as well as a bottle of cognac made by some French monks in a monastery high in the hills.

Patricia found Barbara and Tom a lovely trencher of spun-silver as a wedding gift, and Stephen bought them a woven blanket.

As they wandered the streets, they stopped at the various food vendors to sample their wares. They feasted on a savory mixture of chicken, pineapple and peppers wrapped in plantain leaves. Neither was able to resist the tantalizing aroma of baked bananas sprinkled with cinnamon and sugar, still delectably warm from the oven.

They drank tall glasses of lemonade and ate slices of orange marinated in a concoction of sugar and sherry and served on a banana leaf, laughing like children as the succulent juice ran down their chins.

Finally, unable to take another sip or eat another bite, they returned to the stall to retrieve her clothing, and once again, she donned the formal gown before returning to the inn.

"I *must* check on my cargo," Stephen said reluctantly as they halted at the door to her room. "I will return later and we can dine together."

"That sounds wonderful," she agreed, covering her mouth to stifle a yawn. It had been an exhausting day for her.

"Take a nap while I am gone," he grinned, "But be sure to lock this door," he added as a precaution.

Patricia nodded amicably, already overcome with drowsiness. Stephen kissed her on the forehead and she slipped into the room. He waited to hear the reassuring slide of the bolt before turning away.

Patricia fell on the bed and was asleep before her head hit the pillow.

When she awoke the room was pitch

black. She quickly lit a candle as the bells from a nearby church began to peal out the hour. She was horrified to discover it was nine o'clock. She had been asleep the whole evening. Why hadn't Stephen bothered to wake her?

Patricia quickly donned a peach-colored chintz gown with scalloped lace around the rounded neckline. She brushed out the long plait and pinned her hair on top of her head, adding the pearl combs which Stephen had given her. She hurriedly pulled on white ribbed hose and slipped her feet into peach satin slippers with a row of tiny white satin bows lining each shoe from its top to toe.

Patricia had just finished putting the final touch of rice powder on her nose, which had been slightly burned, when Stephen rapped on the door. She grabbed a white chiffon kerchief and draped it over her head and shoulders as she rushed to the door.

They dined at the inn on an excellent dinner of shrimp cooked in a spicy sauce of onions, peppers, and pimentos, topped off with a tasty almond pudding.

She found it strange for just the two of them to be sitting across a dining table from each other. Stephen was tense throughout the whole meal and several times Patricia looked up to find his brooding eyes on her. It was a drastic change from his mood earlier that day.

Finally, unable to bear the suspense a moment longer, she faced him boldly with a determined calmness. "Is there something you have to say, Stephen?"

He took a sip from the glass in his hand and regarded her coldly. "Tory, this afternoon while I was making my cargo arrangements, I was told that there will be a ship leaving for Virginia very shortly."

He didn't have to say another word. The fantasy had come to an end. He was going to carry through his earlier threat of shipping her back. Why had she deluded herself into believing otherwise?

"I understand." She hoped she sounded as calm as she pretended to be. *My God! what an ironic twist! Any given moment today I would have willingly allowed this man to make love to me. Now, here he is, calmly sitting across a table from me and telling me that he is shipping me home!*

She forced a frozen smile to her face. "You told me when the voyage began that when we reached Jamaica, you would send me back. No one can say you are not a man of your word, Captain."

He slumped back against his chair. "You don't understand, Tory."

She interrupted him before he could continue. "I want to pay you for my passage here. And thank you for a perfectly wonderful trip. It was an experience I am certain I will never forget. I am glad that I permitted Barbara to persuade me to come along."

Her eyes widened with shock when he slammed down the glass he was holding. "Damn it, Tory, will you drop this drawing room repartee and wipe that blasted frozen smile off your face. You know what business I'm in. When I pull out of here, *The Liberty* will be loaded with contraband that I'll be trying to run to Boston. Every damned English ship of the line will be looking for me! It's too risky. I can't take a chance with your life."

Her heart quickened with renewed hope. "I am old enough, Stephen, to be the judge of the risks I will take with my life."

"Perhaps you are, Tory, but I refuse to be the instrument you use to implement that judgment."

He leaned over and picked up her hand. "I didn't want it this way. I had hoped we could have some time together, but I can't pass up this opportunity. There is an English ship in port. I am going to seek out its captain tonight, and if I feel I can trust him, I will arrange passage on *The Betsy* for you and Barbara."

Patricia snatched her hand away from his. "Barbara! She's on her honeymoon. Do you intend to snatch her out of

Tom's arms? Doesn't he have anything to say about it?"

A nerve began to twitch in his cheek. "Tom is a member of my crew. Where *The Liberty* is concerned, he must obey my orders. If he prefers to accompany Barbara and you to Virginia, I certainly will not attempt to stop him. In fact, I think I would feel more comfortable if he did. Nevertheless, I do not intend to subject you and Barbara to any danger."

He got to his feet. The issue was a closed one as far as he was concerned. "I will see you safely to your room and then I will try to locate the captain of *The Betsy*."

Patricia rose to her feet. "That won't be necessary, Captain Kirkland. I can see myself to my room. I've been doing so for years. I certainly don't need your assistance. And please don't let me keep you any longer. Thank you for dinner." She hurried up the stairway.

Stephen watched her, tormented. He knew he had handled the whole situation horribly. Why hadn't he told her he didn't want her in danger because he was in love with her?

Oh, well! Maybe it's better she thinks the worst of me, he thought with a resigned sigh. He shoved away his chair and departed.

Stephen had not been aware of the figure that had remained in the dark shadows of a corner listening to the conversation. The black eyes of Francois Laurette had gleamed with cunning when he watched Patricia flee from the table and his thin mouth had curled with a merciless smile when Stephen did not follow her up the stairway. He saw the opportunity to formulate a plan that had been tickling his mind ever since Billy Wong had told him about his suspicions that *The Liberty* had white women on board. Apparently, Kirkland had tired of the wench—and what a wench! That honey-colored hair and golden skin! What a prize she would bring! He knew of a sultan in Constantinople who would give him a treasure for this confection. Laurette's mouth curled with a sinister leer. Of course, that would be only after he was finished with her himself.

His evil eyes narrowed in thought. He would need a diversion to get her away successfully. It was time to find Billy Wong.

25

Stephen stormed down the street in a black mood. Nothing had gone right between Tory and him from the moment of their first meeting. He should have bedded her a long time ago. At least, then he would be abele to think rationally. She had been a burr in his loins from the moment they met.

He loved her. He knew that. But this was not the time for such a commitment, not with America tottering on the brink of a war. Tom was a fool for marrying Barbara at this time. What if he were killed or came back maimed? He wouldn't do that to Tory. A little hurt now would be better than a lot of hurt later.

Stephen entered the tavern that was the favorite haunt of many of the English merchant seamen. It was owned by Matthew Groggins, a retired sea captain whose leg had been blown off during a skirmish with a Spanish ship near Gilbralter.

The tavern was boisterous with

revelry. Stephen approached Groggins, who was standing behind the counter on one leg. His wooden peg was lying on the top of the bar.

"I'm looking for the captain of *The Betsy*."

Matthew Groggin eyed him curiously. "What for?"

"I would like to approach him with a business proposition," Stephen replied.

Groggins picked up his peg leg and pointed with it toward a table that appeared to be the source of all the noise. Two men were arm-wrestling. One was a huge, hairy bear of a man who appeared to have ponderous strength. The other was just the opposite, small and wiry. A Scottish tam o' shanter sat jauntily on his head over long chestnut hair neatly gathered into a queue.

"He's the one in the tam," Groggins said.

Stephen strolled casually over and joined the men who were shouting and cheering as they watched the event. The outcome was the source of wild wagering. Stephen studied the Scotsman intently. The Captain's dark hazel eyes were fixed in a steady and direct gaze on his opponent's face. Despite the difference in their sizes, there was such an air of confidence about the smaller man that Stephen immediately made his

own wager of five pounds on the outcome.

Within ten minutes the small man
had succeeded in forcing his opponent's
arm to the table and the outcome had
been decided.

The captain slapped his opponent
good-naturedly on the back and yelled for
a round of drinks on him. The men began
to drift away and Stephen took the
opportunity to introduce himself.

"Captain, I understand that you are
the master of *The Betsy*. I am Stephen
Kirkland, captain of *The Liberty*. I
wonder if you could spare me a few
minutes of your time."

"Of course, Captain. Do sit down,"
the young Scot replied in a low, soft
voice. His deportment was polite, but
cautious.

Stephen speculated that the man was
probably twenty-five or twenty-six years
of age, twenty-seven at the most. The
expression on his deeply tanned face was
almost fierce, yet he seemed to contain
that energy under a very calm, almost
urbane, manner.

Stephen saw no reason for mincing
words. "Captain, I understand your ship
will be departing soon for Virginia."

"Your information is accurate,
Captain Kirkland. As a matter of fact, I
will be sailing on the morning tide."

"That soon?" Stephen replied with disappointment. The captain regarded him warily, but waited with polite reserve.

"I have two female passengers in need of passage to Williamsburg. I was hoping you would have room for them on your ship."

"It could be arranged easily. However, Captain, as I stated earlier, this is my last night in port. My ship is ready to sail."

"Unfortunately, one of the women is not in Kingston at this time," Stephen lamented.

"Then I am afraid I cannot be of service, Captain. What of the other passenger?"

"I think it would be advisable to keep the two ladies together. Thank you just the same, Captain."

The Scotsman rose to shake hands and Stephen was surprised to see that the man did not stand more than five inches above five feet. He emanated such an essence of self-contained power that Stephen had expected a colossus to rise from the seat.

"Since I can't be of service to you, at least allow me to offer you a drink, Captain Kirkland."

Within a short time the two men were chatting together like old friends.

"I, too, am a Virginian, you know,"

the Scotsman confessed. "That is, since last year."

"But *The Betsy* is out of London."

The Scotsman nodded. "But England does not hold my loyalties, Captain. When I leave Virginia I intend to go to France. Paris offers a comfort that I am in need of."

"Oh, I understand. Your wife, Captain?" Stephen grinned. It was obvious the man was referring to a woman.

"I am not married, Captain. Actually, it is my intention to take a mistress." His hazel eyes flashed mischieviously. "I am attempting to learn French, and I know of no quicker way to learn the language than taking a French mistress."

Stephen threw back his head with laughter. "A good point, Captain, but speaking from experience I am afraid that some of the terms you will learn might not be appropriate on a quarter-deck."

The vein of conversation reminded Stephen of his constant need for Patricia and he got to his feet to return to the inn. The two men shook hands in farewell.

Stephen's step was light and quick as he hurried back. He would give Patricia the news tonight. That is, if she was still talking to him!

Actually, he found himself relieved to know she would be sailing with him.

Despite his concern for her safety, he did not want to part from her. It was selfish of him, but he was a man in love. *And Lord! How I need that woman!* he thought with a wry grin. Despite all their sparring and spatting, he knew she wanted him, too. It was impossible to ignore it any longer.

Ignore it, hell! he grinned. *Who am I trying to fool? I could no more ignore Tory than I could ignore the need to breathe.*

He took the steps two at a time in his eagerness to reach her. He could feel the blood surging through him, but his rapid heartbeat was due to excitement, not exertion. Tonight he would have Patricia—and the nights to follow. The long wait was finally over.

Stephen tapped on her door. "Tory, will you let me come in? I must talk to you."

When she did not reply he turned the knob and, to his surprise, the door opened. Stephen stepped into the darkened room.

Patricia dabbed at her eyes as she sped up the stairway in her haste to get away from Stephen. It was over. She could not bear another of these scenes with him. She wanted to get away from him, away as fast as a ship could carry her.

Once again she had made a fool of herself over him. Well, this was the last time. Never again would she weaken! Thank God she had never actually surrendered to him, or she would be just another conquest he would kiss goodbye before sailing off.

Well, this was the last encounter she would ever have with Stephen Kirkland! She would return to Boston as quickly as she could get a ship out of Kingston. She didn't need *him* to tell her to go!

She continued to brush aside her tears of anger as she entered her room and flung herself down on her bed. *Hold on, girl, no matter how much it hurts,* she told herself, as she stared up at the canopy above the bed.

She refused to cry. As much as she wanted to, she refused. She had shed her last tear over Stephen Kirkland. She would never allow herself to succumb to his deceitful charms again. If he ever again came to Boston she would not remain in the same room with him. The game between them was over.

She had known from the beginning that it was a dangerous move to get entangled with him—just as she had known from the beginning that when it was over, she would be alone and heartbroken.

Patricia lay mentally reliving every moment between them, suffering the exquisite sensation of every shared kiss, every caress.

Oh, God, Why can't the mind dominate the body? Why can't my mind's command to forget him be stronger than my body's refusal?

If she were to retain her sanity, there had to be a way to purge him from her memory. The long trip home would do that. Without the nearness of him, there would be no temptation. In the past there had always been some temptation to melt her resistance—a faint whiff of his shaving soap in the passageway, the sound of his warm chuckle in the distance, a fleeting glimpse of his broad shoulders on the deck, or just the awareness of his brooding dark eyes shadowing her when their paths crossed.

She would find a way to forget!

Patricia lay fortifying her resolve until, wearily, she forced herself to get to her feet and light a candle. She kicked off her peach sandals and slipped off her hose. Her fingers felt numb as she released the buttons on the peach gown and let it drop to the floor. Clad only in her chemise, she moved to the armoire to get a robe.

Her eyes caught the sight of the knob on the door slowly turning and her glance swung up to the bolt. With the paralyzing effect of escalating fear, she realized she had not slipped the bolt to lock the door. She watched, transfixed, as the door slowly opened.

Patricia opened her mouth to scream but the sound remained frozen in her throat at the sight of the spectre who slipped into the room.

Francois Laurette held a long, wicked-looking knife in his hand, the glint of its jagged edge flashing in the gleam of the candlelight. With a motion as mesmerizing as a coiled snake about to strike, he cautioned her to silence with just a menacing flick of the knife. The finger he brought to his lips to indicate she remain silent was superfluous.

As she faced the intruder, his presence generated such an aura of evil that she began to tremble.

"*Bon soir, madame,*" Laurette said with a leering grin.

He stood a few inches taller than Patricia. A scar ran down the right cheek of his swarthy, pock-marked face to the corner of his mouth, puckering the skin to give it the appearance of a perpetual sneer; the evil that shone in his black eyes gave him a sinister quality.

"What do you want?" Patricia managed to sputter out in her fright.

"If you wish to live, *ma cherie*, I advise you to remain silent." He nodded to a cohort, and Billy Wong stepped into the room.

"Well, lad, ye be looking more

appealin'," Billy Wong said with a lecherous smirk. "Now why didn't ye tell ole Billy you was such a pretty wench?" He stepped forward to reach for her.

Patricia backed away from him. "Don't touch me," she warned, on the brink of hysteria.

"Now, Pet, don't be foolish enough to scream or I will have to slit that lovely throat of yours," Laurette warned. "Tie her up, Billy, and put a muzzle on her," he ordered.

Patricia had regained enough of her composure to attempt to scream, but Billy Wong lunged at her and clamped a hand across her mouth. She began to struggle in his grasp and Laurette came to his assistance. The Frenchman bound her hands together behind her back while Billy Wong grabbed her chiffon scarf and tied a gag around her mouth. He picked her up and, with a wicked laugh, dumped her on the bed. She attempted to roll off, but Wong grabbed her and forced her back.

"Tie her ankles together," Laurette snapped.

"Not till I has me fun, Mate," Billy Wong declared.

"You crazy fool," Laurette snarled. "What if Kirkland comes back? We've got to get her on my ship before he returns."

"Sure, then ye'll take 'er fer yerself,

Mate. I get 'er now, or our deal is off,"
Wong insisted.

"All right, but hurry," Laurette
snarled, irritated. He regretted having to
bring the Chinaman into this scheme, but
he knew he might have need of Wong's
help if Kirkland caught up to him before
he could reach his ship.

Patricia cringed in fright as Wong
climbed on the bed and straddled her.
His eyes were narrowed slits as he released the drawstring on her chemise and
slid his hands to her breasts.

"Ah, nice . . . nice, little Matey. Just
right fer ole Billy's 'ands. Wud they be
tastin' as good as they feel?"

Patricia whimpered beneath him and
tried to heave him off her with her hips.
It only added to his perverted pleasure.
"So, ye wants ole Billy to ride ye, huh
Matey?" he laughed.

"Oh, get on with it and let's get out of
here," Laurette snapped. "You act like
we've got all night."

"Well, hold 'er legs for me," Wong
declared. He climbed off her and
Laurette grabbed her ankles as Wong
began to lower his breeches. He swung
around in surprise at a sudden rap at the
door.

"Tory, will you let me come in? I
must talk to you," Stephen Kirkland's
voice called out from the other side of the
portal.

"*Scare bleu!*" Laurette hissed. "What did I tell you?"

The room was pitched into darkness when Laurette yanked the candle out of its holder and picked up the heavy metal candlestick. He crossed to the door and raised it above his head as the door swang open. Laurette brought the heavy holder down on Stephen's head just as he stepped into the room.

26

"Did ye kill 'im, Mate?" Billy Wong asked.

Laurette bent over Stephen's body and laid his head against his chest. Patricia held her breath, waiting for the reply. Stephen could not be dead. Not Stephen! She would never accept that. Stephen was strength. Stephen was invincible!

"He's still alive," Laurette replied. She smiled through her tears with relief, then her eyes widened with alarm when she saw him draw his knife out of his boot. "I'm going to finish him off and be done with the bastard for the last time."

Laying on the floor, Stephen hovered on a fine line between senselessness and awareness. The voice of Billy Wong penetrated the narrow abyss of his consciousness.

" 'At weren't part of 'r deal, Mate. I wants nothin' ta do with killin' Kirkland. We won't be able to come 'ere again if we do. This 'ere's a English colony and if we kills anyone 'ere, every Union Jack will be after 'r 'ides. 'R deal was the wench. I was tu 'elp ye get 'er on yer ship fer 'alf the price ye gets fer 'er. 'At's the deal, Mate!" There was no longer any pretense of geniality in the tone.

"Well, it's your fault we were even here when Kirkland got back," Laurette challenged.

"I'm gettin' out of 'ere now. I wants no trouble," Billy Wong declared.

"At least you can help me get her to the wharf!" Laurette complained.

"Jus' toss somein' over 'er 'ead tu muzzle 'er. I've already 'elped ye, Mate. Jus' be sure I gets me money when the time comes, or ye'll 'ave more than Kirkland snappin' at yer 'eels," Billy Wong warned before he disappeared through the door.

Patricia said a grateful prayer for the existence of Billy Wong. If nothing else, the scoundrel had prevented Laurette from carrying out his nefarious intention to murder Stephen. But it was still no assurance to her that Stephen would survive. How long would he lie there before someone discovered his body?

Her tormented thoughts were interrupted when Laurette grabbed her ankles and tied them together, using the sash from the window drape. He snatched the case off a pillow and pulled it over her head, then picked her up as if she were a sack of grain and slung her over his shoulder.

Stephen opened his eyes in time to see Laurette vanish through the door. "Tory," he murmured, as he tried to rise to his feet. The effort caused an excruciating pain to shoot to his head, and he fought to keep from sliding back into unconsciousness.

He crawled to the bed and pulled himself up on his knees. His head slumped onto the bed and he rested it there for a few moments, struggling to clear his mind. One driving urgency spun through its muddled denseness—*Tory. Tory needed him!*

Stephen painfully raised his head. The door was standing ajar and a slim shaft of light from the hallway sliced a narrow stream across the darkened floor. He focused groggily on it as if it were a beacon.

He grabbed the firm bedpost and pulled himself to his feet. His vision was still blurred, but he was able to stagger to the door. His mind was too fuzzy to formulate any decisive thought, but something within him was driving him to the waterfront with a burning urgency—*Tory needed him!*

Disoriented, Stephen stumbled down the stairway, losing his balance completely and tumbling down the last four or five steps. He got back on his feet and staggered out into the street. None of the people he passed gave him a second glance; he was just another drunken sailor who had over-imbibed.

The fresh air began to clear the cobwebs from his mind, and with the return of lucidity he began remembering snatches of the conversation between Laurette and Billy Wong.

The wharf! Laurette was taking Tory to the wharf!

Stephen reached the pier in time to see a boat carrying Laurette a short distance away in the water. It was headed for *The Serpentine*.

"Tory!" he cried out in a mournful wail. His hand reached out in supplication, but drew back with only a handful of the murky darkness. He keeled over into unconsciousness.

Patricia was suffering her own nightmare of terror. Her mind was still spinning frantically with the fear that Laurette might have struck Stephen hard enough to kill him. *Dear Lord, please don't let him die*, she prayed. In her anxiety for Stephen, she had shoved the precariousness of her own position to the back of her mind.

When they reached the wharf, Laurette tossed her unceremoniously into the bottom of the boat. "Is all the crew on board?" he snapped with a guttural growl.

"All 'cept Spanish Joe. We can't find him," she heard a crewman respond.

"Then we'll sail without him," Laurette announced. "Let's get going."

Patricia was lying in a puddle of brackish water. The foul-smelling liquid immediately saturated her chemise. The pillowcase over her head added a greater dimension of fright to her situation. Being totally in the dark, unable to see, made her feel more at risk and added to her desperation and hopelessness.

The cry of "Tory!" shattered the stillness of the night. Her heart leaped to her throat at the sound of it. It was Stephen's voice! *Stephen was still alive! Thank God! They had not killed him.* With that knowledge came a purpose for living as well as a renewed hope for her own rescue.

If Stephen were still alive, there was hope for her!

She tried to shake the pillowcase from her head and managed to get it as high as her nose. From her position on her back, she could now peer out from under it enough to discern the legs of three men, obviously the two rowers' and Francois Laurette's.

The boat bumped against the hull of a ship and once again she was slung over one of the men's shoulders as he climbed the rope ladder leading to the deck. Peering out from beneath the pillowcase she could see the inky waters of the sea below. *Stephen, please help me,* she prayed desperately.

"Weigh anchor and hoist all sails," Laurette called out.

"Where do you want the wench, Cap'n?"

"My cabin," Laurette shouted. "And tie her to a chair. I've got no time to worry about her until we clear this harbor."

Patricia could hear the crew scurrying into action as she was toted across the deck like a sack. Her captor entered a cabin and plopped her into a chair without any consideration for her comfort. He lit a candle and released her ankles, then tied each of them to a leg of the chair. After releasing her hands, he jerked them around the back of the chair and tied them together. The pirate departed without ever removing the pillowcase from her head.

Patricia began to inch it off by swinging her head in a sideward motion like a dog shaking off its fur after a bath. She finally succeeded in dislodging it.

The cabin was strewn with heaps of soiled clothing. Apparently, Laurette did not believe in laundering clothes. Maps and charts were scattered about, lying among the dozens of other articles on the floor. For a fleeting second she wondered how the scoundrel was ever able to find anything.

She recoiled in revulsion at the sight of a shrunken human head hanging nearby on the wall, an apparent memento of one of the voyages of *The Serpentine*. She had heard of this barbarous practice, but never really believed that people actually committed such heinous deeds.

Patricia lost her awareness of the passage of time. Every moment seemed to pass like an hour. She felt it had to be nearing sunrise, but she was too frightened to sleep.

Her glance spun to the door and her eyes widened with rekindled fear when Laurette entered the room.

"Well, little pigeon, I see you have shed your plume," he sneered. He strolled over and released the gag from her mouth.

She gratefully gasped a deep breath of the welcoming rush of air. Even the stale odor of the cabin was a relief from the suffocating gag she had endured.

"I am anxious to hear how my little pigeon can coo." He snaked out a finger and traced her cheek. She could not bear the thought of his repulsive touch, and drew back to try to avoid his finger. "No, no, *ma cherie*, that is no way to act. Do I frighten you, little pigeon?"

"You revolt me," she flared. Her eyes

blazed their contempt.

The sneer widened. "I think not, *ma petite*. I see fear in those lovely eyes."

Patricia was determined not to cower. The man revolted her, and she knew he was deliberately playing a cat-and-mouse game with her. She thrust up her head defiantly. "You see revulsion, Captain Laurette. The same revulsion you have seen in the eyes of any woman whom you have touched. Go ahead and rape me, since that is obviously your intent, but you are mistaken if you think I am going to beg or cry."

The Frenchman's eyes narrowed with a satanic gleam. "I think different, little pigeon. I think, when I am through with you, you will be begging and crying, too."

His hand slid down and slowly pulled the menacing knife from his boot. The sight of that frightful weapon sent chills down her spine and she clamped her mouth shut to keep her chin from trembling. Laurette grinned evily and lightly tossed the knife from one hand to the other.

She took a shuddering breath and forced her eyes to meet his diabolical gleam. "You don't scare me with that knife, Captain. I have ears, and I heard you and your slimey companion. You aren't going to kill me because you intend to sell me."

"Most perceptive of you, my pet."
Patricia sat frigid, not daring to blink an
eye, when he took the flat side of the
blade and ran it along her cheek to brush
back the hair. He lifted some of it off her
shoulder with the point of the blade.
"And such a pretty ear, too. So pink and
tiny." He shook his head, clucking sadly.
"One would think that such a pink and
tiny little ear could not get you into so
much trouble."

She knew that he was just playing
with her to frighten her into willingly
submitting to him, but she could feel the
hysteria mounting within her just the
same. She wanted to scream aloud when
he took the blade and repeated the
identical move on her opposite cheek.
"*Mon Dieu*! You have two such little
ears! One really has need for only one."

"I know what you are trying to do,
Captain, but it won't work. You aren't
frightening me. If you want to sell me,
you can't afford to mar my appearance."

"That is true, my pigeon, but
accidents can happen so unexpectedly."
She heaved a sigh of relief when he
leaned back and pulled the knife away
from her face, even though she knew it
was just a momentary reprieve.

Laurette lightly touched the tip of
the blade to one of his fingertips. A
widening circle of blood appeared at the
end of the finger. "*Mon Dieu*! I have

pricked my finger! Do you see how quickly an accident can happen?"

She could only sit helplessly as he reached out the finger and rubbed a bloody trail along the smooth line of her jaw. She bit down on her lip to keep from screaming aloud when he then leaned over and licked it off with his tongue.

The evil leer was only inches away, the black satanic eyes gleaming into hers. Laurette lowered his mouth to hers, forcing her head back against the chair. She clamped her lips tightly shut as she felt the abhorrent slide of his hand into her chemise. His fingers squeezed the nipple of a breast until she was forced to open her mouth and cry out with the pain. His tongue snaked into the chamber of her mouth and both of his hands were now squeezing and pinching her breasts as she whimpered under the ravishment. She wanted to gag with revulsion as his tongue stroked and curled around her own. When the opportunity presented itself, she bit down on his tongue in desperation.

His head shot up and his eyes were feral with anger. Laurette slashed out viciously with a backhand across her face. Her head slammed against the chair from the force of the blow.

"You little bitch. That was a mistake—one for which you will pay painfully!" he snarled.

She remained silent as she faced him with loathing and contempt in her eyes. She knew that the die had been cast.

Laurette grabbed a fistful of her hair, yanking her head to the side and exposing her slim neck. He picked up the knife and began to lower it. She closed her eyes and braced herself for the shock of pain from the slash of the knife. At the sound of his manical laughter, she opened her eyes. He was dangling a lock of her hair that he had hacked off with the knife in front of her face.

"So, my pet, you are not as brave you would like me to believe."

Laurette picked up the candlestick from the nearby table. Patricia watched, horrified, as he began to swing the lock back and forth above the candle until the flame grabbed it and raced up the silken strands. They coiled up into round curls as the fire consumed them.

The stench of burning hair filled the small cabin as Laurette watched, fascinated, until the last strand had been incinerated.

My God! The man is completely mad! He is going to kill me, she realized with horror, as Laurette stood above her with his appalling leer, still holding the candlestick.

"I think we should shorten some of that long hair of yours," he snickered. She was consumed with panic and could no longer contain her scream when he grabbed some more strands of her hair and pulled her head toward the candle. He was about to lower her hair to the flame when there was a loud rap at the door.

"Sails sighted off the port stern, Cap'n. Closing fast," a voice called out.

"Damn!" Laurette cursed, slamming down the candle.

Patricia closed her eyes in thanksgiving as tears began to trickle down her cheeks.

He grabbed her jaw and squeezed it in his grasp until she opened her eyes. "Well, *ma petite*, we will have to postpone our diversion. I imagine that fool Kirkland has followed."

Just the sound of Stephen's name gave her a measure of hope.

Laurette blew out the candle. "His ship is no match for my guns. I will blow him out of the water as easy as I extinguished this candle. What a shame you will not be able to see it."

"Two sails off the port stern," a voice called out.

This latest news caused Laurette to throw back his head with laughter. "*The China Lady* must be following." His eyes were lit with a manical joy. "That fool lover of yours has done it now! He's got himself trapped between us."

Laughing wildly, Laurette grabbed his cutlass and ran out the door.

When Stephen slowly opened his eyes, he found himself staring into a pair of dark hazel eyes. "What happened, Captain?"

Stephen sat up and discovered he was sitting on the wharf surrounded by the Scottish captain and several of his crew. He clutched the man's arm frantically. "Laurette. Laurette has Tory. I've got to get to my ship."

"Relax, Captain Kirkland. One of your crew was here when we found you. He has gone to round up the rest of your men. You can do nothing until they return, so tell me what has happened to you."

"*The Serpentine*! Has she sailed yet?" he asked desperately.

"Yes, Captain," one of the men replied. "I just caught sight of her sails in the moonlight. From the glimpse I got she looked to be under a full press of canvas."

"It is still not too late. My ship is much lighter. I can still catch her," Stephen said relieved.

"I am certain you can, Captain. If my memory serves me correctly, and it usually does in matters pertaining to the sea," the Scotsman replied confidently, "that ship was carrying twenty-four cannon, ten six-pounders on each side and two nine-pounders at her bow and stern. How many do you carry, Captain Kirkland?"

"Eight," Stephen said irritably. This was all wasting valuable time.

"I am aware of that," the Scotman said with a crooked grin. "I was hoping to remind you of that fact. I am curious to know what you intend to do when you do catch up with her." He shook his head hopelessly. "Because, Captain Kirkland, I am afraid she can blow you out of the water before you get your grappling hooks within fifty feet of her."

27

Stephen had no idea how he would accomplish his rescue of Patricia. He knew only that he had to get her away from Laurette as soon as possible. God knew what the scurvy bastard would subject her to before she would ultimately end up on an auction block on the Barbary Coast or some crib in China.

"Tell me, Captain Kirkland," the Scotsman asked, "can those gunners of yours hit anything with those eight six-pounders you have?"

"Enough to have gotten us out of some pretty tight scrapes," Stephen said defensively.

The young man reflected for a few minutes longer. Stephen thought he would burst from suspense. "Then I think I have thought of something that should work. We will form a line of battle with *The Betsy* making the first pass. They will undoubtedly unleash the full force of their cannon on my ship and I will return their fire. While they are reloading, you can come up and, naturally, they will expect you to make your pass. Rather than do it, I want you to swing to their stern for raking fire. Put the full firing power of your six-pounders loaded with grape-shot directly along the length of the ship and blow away her lower sails and anyone fool enough to be on deck."

He grinned broadly. "Without that mainsail and with most of their people on the main deck injured, they will be helpless. Then you swing to their starboard side and get your grappling hooks into them."

"What about your ship, Captain? If you take a full blast of their fire, your ship could be damaged."

"Don't worry, Captain Kirkland. I'm not foolhardy! I will make certain I keep a safe enough distance so that their shots can't do me much harm." He frowned intently. "You must understand that the whole success of the maneuver depends upon the fleetness and maneuverability of your ship—and on the accuracy of your gunners. If your men miss their marks and you give *Serpentine* time to recover, they will regroup and swing about. You'll be a sitting duck with your weak fire power."

A *sitting duck!* Stephen thought with a wry smile, remembering his chat with Tory. The words had come home to haunt him.

He eyed the intense young man with

a suspicious curiosity. "Why are you doing this, Captain? It is really not your quarrel."

"Let's say it is difficult for me to turn my back on a fellow Virginian in need of help." He grinned roguishly. "Another reason is that I just can't resist a fight."

The dark hazel eyes sobered grimly under the tricorn that shadowed them. "But my main purpose, Captain Kirkland, is to keep you alive. Very soon America is going to have need for a navy and for men like you. I do not want to see you scuttled before that time comes. I have plans for you."

Stephen was uncertain whether he should be flattered or insulted by the remark. The man's vanity was unbelievable! Stephen knew he was an older and possibly more experienced seaman than this brash young man. But the Scotsman's unfaltering faith in himself, coupled with what appeared to be an indomitable courage, immediately inspired Stephen's confidence in him, and, he recognized the man for what he was—a born naval officer.

Stephen nodded in acceptance. The plan was a sound one. His greatest concern was Patricia's safety. He was gambling that Laurette would have her imprisoned in his cabin under the quarterdeck. He would make certain that his guns would be aimed above the captain's cabin. *The Betsy*'s guns would be striking along the deck of *The Serpentine*.

"*The Betsy* is ready to sail. I suggest we leave at once."

Stephen nodded. "I have a small matter of some unfinished business before I leave port. Have no fear. *The Liberty* will be right behind you."

He returned to his ship and wasted no time in collecting some spikes and a mallet. Stephen quickly placed them in a pouch and tied it to his waist. He regretted Tom's absence, but after some quick instructions to the Second Mate, Stephen removed his boots and slipped into the water, as his crew began to prepare the ship to sail upon his return.

The *China Lady* bobbed lazily on the water, the undulating movement of the ocean causing her to drift and lightly tug at the heavy cable that held her anchored.

Stephen approached the black hull of the ship cautiously, slicing through the water with barely a ripple. He pulled a knife from his belt and clenched it between his teeth, then began to scale the anchor chain hand over hand, the powerful muscles of his arms and shoulders straining tautly under the effort. When he reached the top, he peered over the railing in search of the watch. Satisfied there was no sign of him, Stephen jumped to the deck on silent cat's paws.

He squatted in the shadows, his ears straining for the sound of a voice or tread of a foot. Then, in a low crouch, he stole across the deck and stopped by a dimly lit companionway leading to the crew's quarters. He closed the doors and slipped the bolt, locking them to prevent anyone's interrupting him.

A noise nearby attracted him and he stepped back into the shadows. He spied the man on watch just a few feet away. Obviously having over-imbibed, the man was slumped on the deck sleeping, a spilled bottle of whiskey lying beside him.

Stephen moved to him and gave him a tap on the head to make certain he would not be a threat to his scheme. He crossed swiftly to the foot of the quarter-deck steps and listened to the sounds emanating from the companionway leading to the captain's cabin. After distinguishing the giggles of two females, accompanied by ensuing groans, he knew Billy Wong was occupied with his favorite diversion, a *Menage a trois*. As much as he would have enjoyed spoiling the scoundrel's pleasure, Stephen knew he dared not take the time.

He left the quarterdeck ladder and hurried over to a cannon on the port side of the ship. He drove a spike into the touchhole, that vital opening through which the charge was lit. He repeated the process with the remaining five cannon, then did the same to the six cannon on the starboard side.

Stephen then returned and unlocked the doors leading to the crew's quarters. Within thirty minutes from the time he had set foot on the deck, Stephen was back in the water swimming toward *The Liberty*.

All twelve of the cannon on the *China Lady* had been rendered unusable and no one knew he had even been on board. It could be days, or even weeks, before anyone would be the wiser.

The sun had just begun to rise and the far horizon glowed with golden light. Helpful hands were waiting to pull him on board *The Liberty*.

They quickly weighed anchor and, under full sail, with studding sails unfurled, the ship began to glide across the water.

From the crow's nest above, the lookout bellowed that *The Betsy*'s sail was in sight about five miles away. He could also see *The Serpentine* a short distance beyond. *The Betsy* was under reduced sail, holding back just out of the range of the cannon of the larger ship.

Soon the tall white sail of *The Betsy* could be seen from the quarterdeck against the brightened sky and, an hour later, *The Liberty* had come within several cable lengths.

Stephen trained his telescope on *The Serpentine*. He could see Laurette directing the frantic activity that was underway. His eyes swept the deck, but could see no sign of Patricia. He directed his attention to *The Betsy*. Her captain was clearly readying his vessel for the coming fight. The crew had begun to haul out their guns and secure the sails on the ship, while other members of the crew were lining the bulwark with pails of water and spreading sand on the deck to prevent men from slipping in the gore that could soon be liberally spread across the deck.

Stephen had already taken such preparations. All available buckets and casks of water were on deck, in the event they were hit and had to squelch any fires. He needed to keep all of his sails flying to maintain the needed maneuverability that was so critical for the success of the action.

He brought *The Liberty* in line with *The Betsy* and they moved nearer to the pirate ship.

Laurette had run out all of his cannon on the port side of his ship in the hope of blasting *The Betsy* out of the water as she drew abreast. He had seen the damn-fool captain of *The Betsy* haul down most of her sails for fear they would be blown away during the battle. By the time they could be unfurled to come about for her second pass, he would be reloaded and ready for her. He was not worried about *The Liberty*. He knew that Kirkland's ship carried only eight light cannon. She was no threat to his more heavily armed vessel.

As soon as *The Betsy* began her pass, Laurette opened fire. Bright red flame and dense clouds of black smoke appeared as the other ship returned her fire.

The captain of *The Betsy* had wisely chosen the windward side to make his pass. That way he knew that the inevitable black smoke from the cannon would not blow back into the faces of his own gunners, which was exactly what was happening to the crew of *The Serpentine*. They could not see through the dense black bank that drifted into their faces that their shots were falling slightly short of their mark. The gunners on *The Serpentine*'s last two cannon were able to see enough to adjust for the change in the distance and managed to put a shot into the hull of *The Betsy*, causing very little damage other than splintering some of the timber on the forecastle.

Laurette's crew had begun to reload as *The Liberty* approached for a broadside run. When the lighter vessel suddenly swerved across their stern, the pirate crew scampered to try to run out their starboard side battery.

All of the guns of *The Liberty* were trained on the main deck of *The Serpentine*. At Stephen's command, the first two cannon erupted in a burst of grapeshot and fire. They missed their mark, dismantling the mizzenmast instead. The blast from the next two guns, loaded with solid shot, struck the thick mainmast about twenty feet above the deck, gouging a large section out of her diameter. The remaining four cannon unleashed their fire power with withering effect on the poor souls caught in its path. Some of the shot cut the mainmast's supporting stays, which was sufficient to bring the mast tumbling down, ripping and pulling the rigging down on the heads of the few remaining pirate crew still on their feet. They scrambled away from their guns to avoid the rain of cordage, sails and yards.

The Liberty swung to windward and drew up within a few feet of the now sluggish ship. A dozen grappling hooks flashed across the distance and found their marks in the rigging and bulwark of *The Serpentine*. The two ships were now locked together.

The two dozen men of *The Liberty*, led by their captain, clambered across to *The Serpentine*, leaping onto the deck wielding their cutlasses and swords, pikes and billy clubs, and whatever other weapons they could grab. Several carried pistols, which they fired into the cut-throats who attempted to repel them.

Stephen caught a glimpse of Laurette on the quarterdeck, and he began cutting a swath through the struggling men in an attempt to reach him. When he saw Laurette head for his cabin, Stephen knew the pirate leader was going for Patricia.

He lashed out ferociously at the pirate who was attempting to thwart his effort. The sailor was no match for Stephen and immediately fell under his sword, but not before Laurette had succeeded in slipping into the cabin and closing the door.

Stephen leaped to the quarterdeck and rushed to the door, but was halted when it would not budge. He drew his pistol and shot off the lock, then smashed open the door with his foot.

Laurette was about to cut the ropes binding Patricia. He whirled and fired a shot at Stephen.

Stephen ducked, avoiding the shot, and in frustration Laurette threw his useless pistol at him, striking Stephen in the head. He fell back under the force of the blow and struggled to shake off his dizziness.

Laurette saw his plight and Patricia screamed out a warning when the pirate leader lunged at Stephen with his cutlass, but Stephen was able to raise his sword and thwart the jab.

"So, Yankee, you are anxious to die!" Laurette sneered, his evil eyes gleaming with malevolence. Patricia's spine was wracked with a convulsive shudder at the sight of it.

"Has he hurt you, Tory?" Stephen asked. His eyes remained locked on the pirate.

"No, Stephen," she half-sobbed. Her heart was pounding so rapidly that it felt as if it would bludgeon through the wall of her chest.

"That was wise of you, Laurette, or your dying would have been prolonged," Stephen taunted.

Laurette spat in contempt. "Do you think you frighten me with your useless threats, Yankee? Save your breath—you will have need for it when I cut your throat."

My God! Patricia sobbed in anguish. *Why must they rattle their swords at one another. Can't this nightmare end?* She watched frantically, praying for Stephen's safety.

The two men began to circle each other warily, the small room restricting the movements. Laurette's mouth was curled into an evil sneer. Stephen's face remained inscrutable as he assessed his enemy.

Patricia cried out when Laurette
made a quick lunge with his cutlass.
Stephen stepped aside to avoid it and
swung up his sword, knocking the blade
aside. He picked up Laurette with his left
hand, as if he were a sack of clothing, and
slammed the pirate against the wall.
Laurette's cutlass fell through his fingers
and dropped to the floor.

With a feral snarl he pulled a large,
wicked-looking knife from his boot and
attempted to drive it into Stephen's
stomach. Stephen stepped aside, releasing his hold on Laurette, and the
pirate chief fell to the floor, where he
crouched like a cornered rat.

Stephen threw aside his sword, and as
he was drawing his own knife out of the
top of his boot, Laurette sprang at him.

Patricia screamed as the two men
fell against the table. It splintered under
their weight and they crashed to the floor
of the cabin. She watched helplessly as
they thrashed and rolled, their bodies
locked together in a death struggle.

A curdled cry escaped from Laurette
and he began to crawl across the floor
toward her, his knife glinting menacingly
in his hand. His villanious eyes gleamed
with an evil that was mesmerizing.

She screamed again when his hand
reached out to grasp the skirt of her
gown, but suddenly, his mouth gaped
open and the dark eyes seemed to roll

upward. He fell back, the front of his shirt saturated with blood from the wound in his chest. Patricia stared, transfixed, at his lifeless body. Stephen got to his feet, still holding the blood-stained knife, and cut her bonds.

She threw herself against him with a strangled sob and his arms enfolded her. For several moments she remained huddled within their protection, sobbing out of control. Stephen just held her, allowing her to spend her tears, savoring the feel of her in his arms again.

Finally, reluctantly, he whispered, "I have to get back to the fight, Tory." Patricia sighed deeply and stepped out of his arms. She smiled up at him through the tears that were still staining her cheeks. "Will you be all right until I get back?" he asked gently.

"I'm fine now, Stephen. Truly I am," she assured him with a brave smile she did not feel.

He picked up his sword and, with a final backward glance, stepped out on the quarterdeck.

The air was black with smoke because some of the spilled gunpowder had inadvertently been ignited when one of the cannons exploded. Tongues of flame had spread along the deck of the ship to the remnants of sails and riggings that were scattered about. The ship was burning out of control. The fight was over, and

Stephen's crew were transfering the wounded to *The Liberty*.

The Betsy had come about and now lay alongside to assist *The Liberty* in her endeavors. The young Scots captain and his crew were rounding up prisoners, retrieving the pirates who had jumped or been thrown overboard.

Once on board, several of them stepped forward, claiming to be English and American seamen whose ships had fallen victim to *The Serpentine*'s guns. They asked for passage to Virginia, and the captain agreed. The others were taken to the brig.

The Liberty released its grappling hooks from the burning ship and the crew of *The Betsy* returned to the safety of their own deck.

Patricia waited at Stephen's side as the last of the wounded were placed in the longboat.

Laurette's body had been pulled from the cabin and was lying on the deck. Mesmerized, Patricia stared down at him. The terror she had endured was still too vivid in her mind, and it was hard for her to accept that this villainous scoundrel was no longer a threat to her.

Laurette's face still wore its evil smirk, frozen now in death; his black eyes appeared as cold and merciless to her as they had been when he was alive. The sight of the gleaming blade still clenched in his hand caused her to shudder and draw the cloak that Stephen had thoughtfully placed on her shoulders more tightly around her.

Stephen saw the terror on her face as she looked down at the lifeless body.

"Well, Tory, I hope now you will finally recognize the difference and admit your mistake."

Her eyes swung to him questioningly. He pointed to Laurette's body. "*That* is a pirate."

The grin that followed was too irresistible for her to ignore. She was so totally in love witht this man. *Let him have the last word*, she thought lovingly as she laughed up into his handsome face. She could feel all the tension easing from her body as he took her arm and helped her into the longboat.

The two ships unfurled their sails; *The Betsy* was bound for a port in Virginia, *The Liberty* was to return to Jamaica.

"A safe voyage, Captain Kirkland," the captain of *The Betsy* called out as the gap between the two ships began to widen.

"And you, too, Captain . . ." Stephen shot forward in alarm and cupped his hands to his mouth. He called out in a loud voice, "Captain, I don't even know your name. To whom do I owe this debt of gratitude?"

The young captain of *The Betsy* flashed a disarming smile that changed the fierceness of his visage to a boyish charm.

"The name is Jones, Captain. John Paul Jones."

28

The first thing Patricia did when she arrived safely on board *The Liberty* was to hurry to her cabin and take a hot bath. She scrubbed her body and hair furiously in her attempt to wash away any lingering evidence of her experience. The mental image and its horror would linger, however, as a reminder to execute caution. There would be no more running off haphazardly on any of Barbara's impulsive forays, she vowed to herself. She now knew the danger and folly of those excursions.

She slipped on her nightgown and robe and leisurely dried and brushed out her hair. Just knowing Stephen was nearby gave her a feeling of security that was quickly eradicating the unpleasant memories of the past twenty-four hours.

She lowered the brush as she remembered a glaring fact that had slipped her attention at the time. Stephen had watched *The Betsy* sail away and had made no effort to put her on the ship. Did that mean he was taking her with him?

Well, after her experience he would have to bind and truss her to get her off *The Liberty!*

A light tap at the door snapped her out of her musing and she swung it open. The Second Mate, William Higgins, was standing there with a big grin holding a cup of hot tea.

"Feeling better now, Madam Fairchild?" he asked.

"Haven't I told you to call me Patricia?" she said with a feigned frown. He had been one of her patients during the measles epidemic.

He handed her the cup. "Thought you would like this."

"That was very thoughtful, Will," she said with a grateful smile. "It's the very thing I needed."

"It was a good fight, wasn't it, ma'am?" he said with a broad grin.

Patricia winced. "If there *is* such a thing as a good fight. I certainly am thankful for the outcome. Were any of our crew seriously injured?"

"Just some scratches, ma'am. Enough to give them something to brag about over an ale. It's not often you can send the likes of a scurvy bas—ah, scoundrel like Laurette to Davy Jones's locker."

"Well, I personally intend to thank every one of you. I love you all," she declared fervently.

"That reminds me, ma'am. Cap'n

wants to see you as soon as you finish your tea." He started to turn away and then turned back with a shy smile. "I'm glad you're safe now, ma'am."

"Thank you, Will," she said with a tender smile.

Patricia drank her tea and then, tucking her robe tightly around her, she went up on deck and crossed to Stephen's cabin. In response to her light rap he called out for her to enter.

When she stepped into the cabin Stephen was standing at the commode shaving, naked except for a towel wrapped around his waist. He obviously had just bathed because his hair was damp; she waited for him to turn around, fascinatedly watching the ripple of muscle across his shoulders as he dipped the razor in and out of the basin of water. *Lord, he has a magnificent body!* she thought appreciatively.

As if sensing her thoughts, he turned and walked to her, wiping away the few remaining traces of the shaving soap. Now the added scent of bay rum began to play a provocative tease with her senses. His eyes ravished her in a blistering appraisal and Patricia felt a hot flush creep up her entire body. He saw the blush and his brow quirked at an amused angle.

"Are you climbing into that bunk, or shall I put you there?"

Patricia knew she was aflame and felt completely intimidated by his hovering above her. She swallowed nervously.

"I think we have a great deal to discuss."

"There has already been too much talk, Tory."

Patricia's nervousness gave way to irritation when she saw the pleasure he was deriving from her predicament.

"Now don't feign maidenly modesty, Tory. I gave you every opportunity to leave. In Boston. In Virginia. When you stowed away on this ship, you knew there could only be one way it would end."

Stephen reached out and leisurely drew her into his arms. His mouth was warm and teasing at her ear as he slid her robe off her shoulders. "Besides, this is what we both have been waiting for."

It was the straw that broke the camel's back. His whole attitude was too smug—too arrogant! He was making her feel like a cheap whore under his confident guise of complacency. Disgusted, she brushed aside his hands.

"Take your hands off me." The look in her eyes matched the frigid tone of the command.

Stephen's control slipped slightly and he grabbed her. His strong fingers bit into the soft flesh of her shoulders and his eyes marbleized with a chilling glare.

"So! You are going to play this part to the bitter end," he taunted. "How much more of this do you expect me to bear?" His hands tightened and she felt as if they would crush her bones, but she refused to cringe. This moment of reckoning between them was long overdue, and she was not about to allow his obvious strength to determine the outcome.

"You're hurting me, Stephen," she declared with biting contempt. "I think I've suffered enough tonight at the hands of insensitive men!"

There was almost a brutality to his smile as he glowered above her, but he eased his grip. "I think you like it, Tory. I think this is what you want from me. That is why you keep prodding me—pushing me to the brink. You want me to hurt you, don't you, Tory? Is that what you've been waiting for?"

It wasn't true. She wanted to cry out how wrong he was. She didn't want his brutality; she wanted his love.

His head plummeted down like a bird of prey's and captured her mouth with a hard and punishing kiss that forced back her head until she thought her neck was going to snap off her shoulders. She wrenched her mouth from the plundering pressure. In the attempt, her head slammed against the cabin wall. She felt dizzy as her head began spinning from the jolt, and she fought to focus her vision on his taunting lips. There was no compassion in his face. There was only an unrelenting determination that twisted his handsome face into cruel and menacing lines. He was treating her in the same fashion Laurette had done. This knowledge frightened her more than any words.

She turned her head aside to avoid his descending mouth and his warm lips nuzzled into her neck. His teeth began to nibble at the slender column, each bite sending shocks of the most exquisite pain surging through her.

She would not allow him to do this to her. This time she would not permit herself to give in to the potency of his persuasive kiss. She twisted her head from side to side to avoid his marauding mouth and squirmed against him in an effort to free herself from the weight of his body pressing her back against an un-yielding wall. She could feel the heated hardness of him crushed against her, and her breath escaped in a sob of panic that caused her to struggle more fiercely against the fiery bulge.

"Damn you, Stephen, release me!" she hissed through gritted teeth. "If I wanted to be treated like this, I would have been satisfied with a Laurette or a Billy Wong."

"I'm not Laurette or Billy Wong and you know it, Tory. This has gone on too long between us."

Stephen pulled her tighter against him, one arm encircling her like a band of steel. The fingers of his other hand clamped on the nape of her neck like a vise and forced her head around to meet the descent of his mouth.

Her mind was reeling under the assault. Was this, finally, how it was going to happen? After all the prolonged waiting, was he going to take her like one of those same blackguards who had tried to misuse her?

His kiss was hot—so hot her lips felt blistered beneath it. She clenched her teeth to keep his tongue from invading the chamber of her mouth. Undaunted, he began to trace the circle of her lips with provocative sweeps that seemed to soothe as well as tantalize her inflamed mouth.

She couldn't seem to get her breath. The strength in the arms holding her, the masculine smell of him, the heat from his body pressing against her, and the demands of those unrelenting lips, all combined to weaken her resistance. Her lips parted, and her vanquished groan of surrender coupled in a husky duet with his guttural growl of victory as his tongue speared through her parted teeth and pierced the honeyed chamber of her mouth.

She ceased her struggle and slipped her arms around his neck. His mouth was on hers in a hot, assaulting kiss that left her mindless to everything except the throbbing ache at the junction of her legs, building with an increasing intensity that threatened to explode within her.

She drew a shuddering breath when his mouth released hers and she opened her eyes to meet his sapphire gaze. He stepped back and her arms felt like lead as they slipped off the muscular slope of his shoulders to drop uselessly to her sides. Her back was pressed against the cabin wall and she stood on trembling legs watching like a snared rabbit as his hands slowly and deliberately reached out and slipped the gown off her shoulders. She felt it slide to the floor where it lay in a crumpled heap around her ankles.

Now, naked, she stood trembling, the feel of the cold timber against her back. Her eyes were wide with fright and, yes, anticipation, as the sapphire gaze followed a long swanlike neck to the firm and thrusting globes of her breasts. She could feel them swelling under the smoldering intensity of his dark eyes. Then his eyes moved on to examine the dips and curves of the silken sheen of her stomach and hips. When they paused momentarily at the vee of her legs, the dark eyes seemed to pierce the throbbing nucleus. They continued to slide slowly down the long slim legs that were trembling so much she feared they would collapse.

In a sudden move, confusing to her, he stepped away momentarily. Her garter was in his hand when he returned. He kneeled and slid it up to her knee. Rising to his feet, he stepped back, his dark eyes aflame with desire.

"I knew you would look like this. You're so perfect, Tory. So perfect," he murmured in a husky whisper.

She felt like a naked harem girl on an auction block, and some inner strength within forced her to raise her chin in defiance. Stephen sensed this subtle change and his eyes swung back and met the mutinous look in her emerald eyes. His mouth curved with a slight, barely perceptible smile, and then, with damnable deliberation, he reached out to deliver the killing blow. His palm cupped her right breast and his thumb began to rub the hardened peak. Her stomach seemed to contract into a knot and she gasped with the ecstasy of it. She bit down on her lip to stifle a moan of pleasure. When his other hand closed around its twin, she could no longer contain her groans. For several mindless moments—or was it only seconds?—she stood trembling with exquisite rapture as his hands and abrasive fingertips created sensations in the sensitive tips that drove her to the brink of madness.

"Stephen." It came as a half-sobbing plea when his hands left her breasts. Her eyes, now hardened with passion, opened in protest, but closed immediately in ecstasy when the warm, moist chamber of his mouth enveloped a breast and his tongue began to toy with the turgid peak.

Her whole body began pulsating, throbbing. The ache at the junction of her legs became unbearable. She pleaded for him to stop—but prayed he wouldn't. She lost whatever feeble hold she had on her sanity when he slid to his knees and his hot, marauding mouth began to press moist kisses down the flat planes of her stomach, until it reached the pulsating heat of her passion.

Her groans became incessant when his mouth closed over it. She clutched his shoulders, her nails digging into the taut tendons, and slumped helplessly against him.

The invasion of his tongue shot a wave of liquid flame through her body. It incinerated her mind and consciousness and she tottered on the edge of blackness, spinning in a black void.

She cried out his name over and over until the sound was silenced by the return of his mouth. Now she clung to him, returning his kiss, devouring the taste of him in an explosive, uncontrollable response.

He began to cover her face and neck with quick, moist kisses. "Tory. My Tory. My beautiful, beautiful Tory," he whispered. Patricia returned his kisses, her hands clutching at the muscular chest and the corded brawn of his shoulders. She fought for the return of her sanity, but in vain. She wanted more of him. More of his hands, more of his mouth, and she wanted his hot, throbbing manhood inside her.

"Stephen, please." She was pleading mindlessly.

He swept her off her feet and carried her to the bunk. She lay shamelessly, watching him release the towel that was covering him. Her eyes glowed with added hunger and her heart began pounding wildly in her chest when he tossed it aside. She felt consumed by the smoldering embers of his dark eyes as he stared down at her, and she raised her arms to receive him. The long lashes of her eyelids swept her cheeks when he lowered himself to her. His head dipped and his mouth met hers.

"Stephen." His name was a sigh of love on her lips as their breaths mingled. His mouth devoured hers, seeming to consume the word from her mouth. She arched against him, her taut breasts pressing against the wall of his chest.

His mouth slid in a moist trail and closed around the bud of a breast. She could feel it swelling under his mouth as he suckled it like a feasting babe, before giving equal attention to the other. But rather than release their fullness, the action seemed to cause them to swell greater, until she was writhing senselessly beneath him.

The scent and feel of him was intoxicating and she soon was drugged by an indescribble sensation of pure pleasure. She could no longer deny him. but abandoned herself to him and the pleasure he was bringing to her. Her love and need for him exploded in uninhibited reciprocation. She stroked and explored the taut muscles of his shoulders and felt them jump beneath her fingertips. Her hands slid down the powerful sloping biceps to the steel might of his chest, and her fingers curled into its downy fur. Finally, when her roaming fingers sought the hot probing phallus, his moan of response was as satisfying to her ears as the sound of his name in her rapturous sigh was to him.

Unable to prolong his control for another second, he parted her thighs and drove into the tight moist chamber and the knot that had been stretched to tautness finally snapped with her cry.

She strained against him, clutching him to her and crying out his name at the moment of their shared rapture as they were transcended to a divine plane far beyond the earthly limitations of their bodies.

Patricia lay quietly for a long time, uncertain whether Stephen had fallen asleep. She could feel the sheen of perspiration that coated his body and knew her own was the same. She gloried in it! Just the thought of their two bodies cleaving together with the blending of the salty moisture thrilled her, excited her.

My God! Maybe I am a depraved whore! she thought with shock.

Stephen was still slumped on her, his head resting on her breast. She slid her arms around his waist. Even the heavy weight of him felt glorious. She never wanted to let him out of her arms. He stirred slightly and began to idly rub his leg along hers. Its hairy roughness was tantalizing. The nipples of her breasts hardened and her body shook with a quick tremor. The knot in her stomach had been retied.

His hand slid to her breast. His movements were slow and leisurely as he played with it. He seemed so unaffected by what he was doing, but her own body had burst again into flames.

Her hands swept lower and she lightly grazed his spine with her nails. It was as effective as an aphrodisiac. She could feel him swelling again within her, and a soft sigh slipped through her lips.

Stephen raised his head. "I was determined, no matter what you said, to get you into this bed. Someone could have blown the ship out from under me, and I wouldn't have been deterred."

"I'm glad you were, or we might be still discussing it." She dipped her head and her teeth began to nibble at his ear.

Stephen's mouth curved with a devilish grin as her lips began a moist trail across his chest and curled around a nipple. "But you know, Tory, I believe I might have just opened Pandora's box," he groaned hoarsely.

29

Sometime during the night they fell asleep.

Patricia awoke to the sight of sunlight streaming through the porthole. She stretched contentedly and lay back reflecting on the previous night.

It had been glorious!

They had loved intensely throughout most of the night, both of them trying to retrieve the time they had wasted. What had come before, and whatever was to follow, could never touch those shared moments of discovery.

Patricia shook aside the arousing memories and slipped into her gown, retrieving her robe with the intention of returning to her room. She reached for the handle of the door, then halted abruptly. To get from Stephen's cabin to her own, she would have cross the deck. The whole crew would see her and know she had spent the night in his cabin. What did she care? She loved him! What did it matter who knew it?

She drew back, deciding at least to

improve her appearance. A quick glance in the mirror above the commode confirmed the fact that her hair was a fright. Patricia poured some water from the pitcher into the basin and reached for a nearby cake of soap. She sniffed it appreciatively. It smelled like Stephen. *I mean, Stephen smells like it*, she thought with a wry smile.

She removed her robe and gown and completely sponged herself and washed and rinsed her mouth. Now clean and refreshed, she pulled on her robe and attacked her hair with Stephen's brush. A painful bout succeeded in returning it to its usual silky sheen. Laurette's brutality had done very little damage. The spot where he had hacked off some of her hair was easily concealed beneath some longer strands.

Satisfied with the results, Patricia cleaned her hair out of his brush; everything in the cabin was too meticulously clean to leave any part of it otherwise.

Patricia was about to remove the robe to replace her gown when the door swung open. Stephen entered, carrying a tray. Their eyes met and the memories of their lovemaking blazed in their locked gaze.

"Good morning," he said softly.

"Good morning, Stephen."

Patricia couldn't take her eyes off him. He looked incredibly handsome in the morning light, wearing a white shirt, with black breeches tucked into knee-high boots, his dark hair tied neatly in a queue.

"I thought you might enjoy a cup of tea." He put the tray down on the table.

"That is very thoughtful of you, Stephen." She wanted to run into his arms, but didn't have the courage. It would be too brazen, even after her un-inhibited response to his lovemaking the previous night.

"Can I get you anything else?" Stephen asked formally. He seemed as uncomfortable as she.

"I could use some clothes. I would be too embarrassed to return to my cabin in just my robe and nightgown."

Stephen tried to gauge her mood. He could sense she was uncomfortable. Was it regret? Or was it just that charming naivete that would often surface, that winsome child within her that had been deprived of an existence?

He sat down in the stuffed chair. "Why would you be embarrassed?" he asked.

He knows why I would be em-barrassed. Why is he making this so difficult for me? she wondered. "I would hate for your crew to see me dressed like this. They would all know that I spent last night here in your cabin." She blushed, unable to continue.

Howeever, it was the sign he was looking for. "Come here, Tory," Stephen said gently.

She moved across the cabin and stood in front of him looking like a disobedient child about to be reprimanded. Stephen's hand closed warmly around hers, and he pulled her down onto his lap. His hand cupped her back and he smiled tenderly into her eyes. "Do you really care whether or not my crew know you spent the night in my cabin?"

His nearness intensified her longing for him. They were sitting eye to eye and her gaze met his boldly. Satisfied with what she met in his probing gaze she nestled on her side against him, curled up her long legs, and rested them on the arm of the chair. "No, I really don't care what anyone thinks, Stephen. I've had to learn to live with that concept for a long time." She slid her hand up and began to run her fingers along the chiseled line of his jaw, her eyes and mouth returning the warmth of his smile. His head dipped and their lips met. She relaxed in his arms and surrendered to the excitement of the kiss.

His provocative mouth began to extract the response that lay dormant beneath the surface of her control, waiting for him to summon it. Her eyes were hazy pools of desire when they were forced to separate.

"Lord, Tory! I can't get enough of you!" he murmured softly. His lips slid to her ear and down the column of her neck.

She closed her eyes and lolled back, her body throbbing with blissful sensation. He parted her robe and his hand cupped her breast.

"What are you thinking about, Tory?" he whispered softly, his breath rippling the hair at her ear. "I can't read your mind when your eyes are closed."

Her emerald eyes were a sensuous invitation when she raised the lids. "It is just as well. They aren't proper thoughts for a lady. I was thinking of what a brazen hussy I am, because I am enjoying this so much."

He chuckled lightly and she basked in the warmth of his gaze. His hand continued its sweep down the curve of her spine and halted on her thigh. His gaze shifted down and he began to stroke her leg.

"Do you know you have the most beautiful legs I have ever seen on a woman, Tory?" he declared huskily. "I haven't been able to keep my mind off them ever since the first time I saw them."

Her breath began to quicken as he continued to stroke her leg slowly. He leaned down and pressed a light kiss on her thigh. "I have wanted to do this ever since the first night we met."

Patricia felt a sudden change come over him as his face sobered and his eyes hardened to blue marble. His voice deepened with the intensity of his thoughts. "God! What would I have done if that animal Laurette had succeeded with his plan?"

She raised a hand to his chin and forced his gaze to meet her own. "But he didn't, Stephen. That is all that matters now."

A knock at the door prevented him from replying. The voice of Will Higgins announced, "We're ready to shove off, Captain."

"Very well, Mr. Higgins. I will join you at the dock in one hour. We will begin loading cargo at that time."

"Aye, Captain," he replied.

Stephen got up and set her on her feet. "Well, Madam, are you going ashore in just that robe?"

Patricia's memories of her last experience ashore were still too vivid in her mind. She shook her head as she firmly belted her robe. "I think I will remain on the ship. I've seen enough of Kingston."

As if sensing her reason, Stephen put his hands on her shoulders and smiled down into the worried frown on her up-turned face. "Honey, the danger has passed. There is no one there who will hurt you."

Her eyes clouded with doubt. "What about Laurette's cohort, Billy Wong?"

"*The China Lady* sneaked out of port during the night, Tory. We are the only ship in the harbor. Come on and see for yourself." He grabbed her hand and pulled her out on the deck.

Just as Stephen had said, the harbor was empty except for *The Liberty*'s longboat headed for the wharf.

"Well, I suppose I could go back and retrieve my clothing," she relented.

"Well then, you brazen hussy, put on some clothes and let's get going," he declared, giving a solid swat to her derriere.

In her absence the room at the inn had been restored to its proper order. Stephen saw her safely settled there, then quickly departed with a promise to return as soon as he could get away. He had arranged to take on a cargo of sugar, rum, pineapple, cinnamon and several other spices, and he would have to spend his day supervising the loading of it.

Patricia put on the native sarong that Stephen had bought her earlier and busied herself laundering and pressing her clothing. There was barely a moment, though, that her thoughts did not stray to

Stephen.

She had a view of the harbor and wharf from the balcony of her room, and she caught an occasional glimpse of him as she strung out or removed a garment from the railing.

By sundown she had bathed and was completely dressed awaiting his return. When a light tap sounded on the door she sprang to it and swung it open with a wide smile. Her smile grew even wider at the sight of Thomas and Barbara Sutherland.

By the time the women had exchanged their hugs and kisses, Stephen had joined them and they moved downstairs to dine at the inn.

"You should have seen how beautiful it was in the mountains," Barbara said as they ate their meal. "Aren't you glad, Patricia, that I convinced you to come down here?" Her brown eyes narrowed in contrition. "I realize, of course, just sitting around in your room is probably not quite as exciting as a honeymoon."

"Well, it hasn't exactly been what you would call dull," Patricia responded.

Barbara turned to Stephen. "Stephen, I hope you have tried to keep Patricia from becoming too bored."

"I've been doing my best to keep her pleasantly occupied." Stephen and Patricia's gaze locked with secretive amusement.

"Well, you know, Stephen, sometimes you can be very stuffy," Barbara continued, sampling a concoction of lime and coconut, oblivious to the byplay between the two of them.

Patricia was beginning to derive a great deal of enjoyment out of the conversation. Her slender brow arched delicately in reflection. "Well, now that you mention it, I suppose it could have—"

"Don't you dare say it, lady, or I'm putting you over my knee," Stephen interrupted with a stern frown. However, the amusement in his eyes was evidence of how hard he was trying to restrain his laughter.

Her eyes, dancing with mischief, remained locked with his. "All I was going to say was that it did get a little dull after you rescued me from the pirates."

Stephen's expression did not alter. "That's funny. I thought that was about the time it really began getting interesting."

Barbara turned to her husband. "What are they talking about, Tom?" she asked confused. "What is all this talk about pirates?"

Stephen had already briefed Tom on the events that had occured in his absence. "There was a little trouble while we were gone," he said offhandedly.

Barbara leaned across the table, covering Patricia's hand with her own. "What happened, Patricia?" Her pert face was etched with a serious frown.

"Well, cousin dear," Stephen answered, before Patricia could respond, "while you were in the mountains blissfully enjoying your honeymoon, Tory was snatched by a pirate. You missed all the excitement."

"Well, I wouldn't say she missed *all* the excitement," Tom said defensively, getting into the spirit of the conversation.

At this point everyone at the table was playing this conversational game—everyone, that is, except Barbara Sutherland, whose eyes were wide with disbelief.

"Snatched by a pirate! You mean that repulsive Billy Wong?" Barbara exclaimed.

"No, not him. He was a tadpole compared to that snake, Francois Laurette," Patricia said with a shudder.

"Francois Laurette! You mean *he* is the one who kidnapped you?" she squealed, aghast. "Why, he's the worst blackguard in the world!"

"Not anymore. Thanks to Stephen. He rescued me," Patricia said with an emphatic nod of her head toward Stephen.

Barbara clasped her hands together

in delight. "Oh, how gloriously romantic!" Her young face was aglow with enthusiasm. "Just like a knight of the realm riding up on his white charger to rescue the fair damsel!"

"Well, that's very true, if you want to think of *The Liberty* as a white charger," Patricia agreed.

"*The Liberty*! Are you saying it all took place on the ocean? Oh, I can't believe it! It must have been so exciting."

"Not quite, Bab. It was very frightening. The sound of the cannon was deafening. I thought the ship was being blown apart. And then there was all the black smoke, and the clash of swords with the yelling and shouting as the men fought." Patricia shook her head. "No, it was very frightening at the time it was happening."

Barbara drew back abashed with a chagrined smile. "I understand. You all are joking, aren't you? You're making all this up to teach me a lesson because you think I'm too impetuous. I'm really going to change, I swear. I am going to start conducting myself with the proper decorum that is expected of a young married woman of my station."

Tom leaned over and clasped her hand. "Honey, I love you just the way you are. I just don't want your impetuosity to get you into a situation you can't get out of." His handsome face sobered. "I don't want you to come to any harm, sweetheart."

"And we have been telling you the truth, Bab. I *was* kidnapped by Laurette, and Stephen *did* come to my rescue. There was a battle at sea and Laurette's ship was sunk.

"But I'm grateful for your impetuosity, Bab," Patricia said kindly. "Because of it I have had the most exciting adventure I've ever known. I've done things I never dreamed of doing. I never had a normal childhood, I never had a close friend. I'm grateful to you, Bab, for giving me that." Tears were glistening in the eyes of both of the women as they smiled at each other.

"This dinner is turning too melancholy," Stephen chimed in. He winked at Tom. "I think these two ladies need a walk in the moonlight, don't you Tom? We sail tomorrow and there will be only a deck to walk for a long time."

He shoved back his chair and grasped Patricia's hand. "Come on, Tory. Let's leave these honeymooners to themselves. I'll give you another lesson in how to read the stars."

Later in her room, amid the splendor of a tropic night, with the soft breeze stirring the leaves of a towering palm, the sweet fragrance of jasmine floating on the air, and the distant sound of silver-capped waves breaking on the sands of the shore, Stephen took her in his arms and loved her.

30

The Liberty weighed anchor and glided out of Kingston with sails blossoming under a fair wind. By midday, Jamaica's tall peaks were just a shadowy hump on a distant horizon.

Ever since the battle with *The Serpentine*, the relationship between Stephen and Patricia was no secret to anyone, so she moved into his cabin. Tom Sutherland was then able to reclaim his cabin with his bride.

Stephen's cabin was roomier and more comfortable than she had been accustomed to, and Patricia enjoyed the added freedom of movement. She especially enjoyed curling up in Stephen's stuffed chair with a book, although, if he weren't occupied on deck, Stephen would often show her the pleasures of curling up with him in it instead.

The days passed idyllically, and *The Liberty* skimmed across the water under the guidance of a strong southwesterly wind. Islands with pale sandy beaches and lush green peaks beckoned invitingly against the blue shimmering water.

In the evening when Stephen was not at the helm, Patricia often sat on his lap while he worked at his desk. He would spend hours carefully scrutinizing the shoals and reefs on the many charts that lay in the rack that hung above his desk. Often he would map a course with his drawing compass and protractor, or patiently trace their route for her on a huge globe that stood in the corner.

Without his saying, Patricia could sense, just by the way Stephen touched or held them, how much he treasured these instruments.

Once, when she teased him about it, he shrugged and grinned, "These are the tools of my trade, Tory. I would be as lost without them as a carpenter without his hammer or a doctor without his scalpel."

Her favorite times, though, were those spent with him at the helm. All the crew would be asleep except for the man on watch in the crow's-nest. She would stand in the circle of his arms as he steered the ship, as if they were floating on a sea of shimmering stars. She would feel all the tension ease from his body and he would become a man totally at peace with himself and the elements.

If I were an artist, this is the way I would want to capture him on canvas, she thought to herself one night as he stood at the helm.

"Will you ever be able to love anything as much as you do the sea?" she asked wistfully.

"The sea is like a woman, Tory. She wears many faces, posses many moods. Her eyes can be blue with warmth, green with iciness or black with mystery. She can be generous one moment and treacherous the next; calm and serene, then stormy and wild. There are days when she can be incredibly dull and nights when she can be inconceivably exciting, beautiful and frightening.

"In moments like this, she will soothe you to slumber with her tranquil hands, then, without warning, lash out at you in all her fury."

His voice deepened with huskiness. "She will lure a man into believing he can control her, but she is always unpredictable, always challenging. He can weather her, but he will never conquer her."

"It sounds as if it were useless, then, for another woman to try to compete against her," she said softly.

His incredible blue eyes swung in her direction. "Some women can succeed in making a man give up everything he cherishes, Tory, even his honor."

Patricia tenderly cupped his cheeks in her hands and stared up into his wary gaze. "A woman who is truly in love will never demand that sacrifice from the man she loves. She will waive her own honor before she allows him to forfeit his. You have yet to learn that about a woman, Stephen Kirkland."

She rose on her toes and kissed him gently on his lips, then left him and returned to the cabin.

Several times during the voyage a Union Jack was sighted in the distance, and the nearer they drew to Boston, the more numerous these sightings became. Patricia could tell that Stephen's added tension stemmed from her and Barbara's presence on board. A shifting wind had slowed their progress, but it was anticipated that they would reach their destination the following day.

At sundown, an electrifying shout rang out from the crow's-nest. "Sail on the starboard! Another to port. A third dead ahead."

Stephen raced along the deck and was on the quarterdeck in seconds. Tom Sutherland, on duty, already had his telescope trained on three sails in the distance.

"They're flying Union Jacks," he said grimly, as he handed Stephen the glass.

The British ships were closing rapidly, with a favorable northeasterly breeze in their sails, from the direction in which *The Liberty* was headed. They were between them and the coves or reefs *The Liberty* could slide into to avoid detection. Stephen had no option but to swing his ship around and head back out on the course he had just sailed.

An hour later Stephen's worst fear was confirmed when they were able to identify the three vessels. England's 100-gun warship, *Royal George*, sat snugly in the center of the triangle with the frigates *Augusta* and *Liverpool* as a convoy.

There wasn't a man below deck. Patricia and Barbara had remained on deck watching as anxiously as the rest of the crew. Their cloaks had become wet from the fine mist that had begun to fall.

The crew's eyes were turned on their captain, who stood on the quarterdeck deep in thought. He knew it would be disastrous to meet the British head-on because of their superior fire power. Should he strike his colors before any one was hurt or killed?

He glanced heavenward, as if looking for guidance. The misty spray immediately coated his face and he brushed it aside in irritation.

It was a starless night. The moon was concealed behind black clouds, which threatened to burst open in a torrent at any moment. His mind was spinning as it grappled for some faint vestige of hope.

As if an ancient spectre whispered in his ear, the word *Dundee* played across his mind. He shrugged aside the thought. Why at a time like this, should he be losing his concentration? The Battle of Dundee hadn't even been a naval engagement! It had been a battle that his ancestor, Robert Kirkland, had fought in during the time of Cromwell's overthrow of the Crown. The battle was an oft-repeated story that had been passed down through generations of Kirklands, relating how the brilliant young Scottish general, James Graham, when surrounded and pursued by an overwhelming enemy force, had turned his beleaguered troops around at night and slipped past his pursuing enemy in the darkness.

A faint smile tugged at the corners of Stephen's mouth. "Take the women below, Mr. Sutherland. Douse all lights and secure everything on the ship. No one is to speak or make a sound." At the sight of the confused look on Tom's face, Stephen grinned. "The Battle of Dundee, Mr. Sutherland."

For a few seconds Tom Sutherland did not grasp his meaning. Suddenly the younger man's face broke into a broad smile in comprehension.

"We are going to turn this ship around and try to slip past them in the dark!" Stephen said.

In pitch blackness *The Liberty* hauled about, her experienced crew as familiar with the complicated riggings as they were with the lines on their own faces. Now in dead silence, she moved toward the enemy.

The crew stood motionless, each man unconsciously holding his breath, as one of the frigates passed by, unaware of *The Liberty* on its starboard side.

Now Stephen faced his next serious test. In the darkness, he could not identify which ship had passed them. The *Liverpool* had been to his port side and the *Augusta* his starboard. If it was the *Liverpool* and he tacked starboard, he would then be in the direct course of the *Royal George*. On the other hand, if the frigate had been the *Augusta* and he did a port tack, the same thing would occur. Even if the warship didn't ram them in the dark, *The Liberty* would be at the mercy of her broadside guns.

Stephen elected to remain on course. Close-hauled, he moved very slowly, with the men straining their ears for the slightest sound that would reveal the location of the huge warship.

The huge black hull of the *Royal George* loomed out of the darkness on their starboard and began gliding past them like an enormous sea behemoth. They watched anxiously as the long hull, spanning over two hundred feet in length, slide by.

Suddenly the moon peeked out from behind the drifting clouds and a beam of moonlight snaked across the water and caught the stern of *The Liberty* in its path. Stephen swung into immediate action, ordering a tack to port. The warship opened fire from her quarter-deck. A near-hit hurled a spray of water onto the deck, drenching some of the crew.

"Be glad it's only water, men, and not grapeshot," Stephen shouted.

The Liberty continued to tack, her crew pulling and hauling, slackening and tightening the many lines that were necessary to execute the complicated zig-zag movement required when trying to catch the wind while sailing against it.

The frigates, attracted by the sound of fire, began to tack about, but the warship, heavier and bigger, failed in her attempt to tack and drifted astern and now lay head to the wind. A blast from the light chase guns on her bow, however, hit its mark and some severed rigging dropped down like snakes onto the deck of *The Liberty*.

With the fickle hands of nature, the wind shifted to the southwest as Stephen steered for the Massachusetts coastline. The frigates had come up and passed the *Royal George*, but *The Liberty* was far out of the range of their guns. However, that same wind that had come to her rescue was also aiding the English ships.

Patricia and Barbara had sat silently during the whole incident, holding hands to bolster each other's courage. Patricia was reminded of the fright she had suffered when Laurette had had her head shrouded in a pillow case. She was sorry for Barbara, sensing the younger girl's torment.

"Don't worry, Bab. I know Stephen will get us through this," she whispered.

Barbara's eyes were as wide as saucers when she turned to her. "I'm not worried about myself, Patricia, but I couldn't bear losing Tom now. I love him so much," she said softly. The tears were streaking her cheeks.

Patricia put an arm around her shoulder. "Nothing is going to happen to him, honey. Stephen won't let anything happen to any of us," she said confidently.

The Liberty had lost her mizzen topsail and her spankers. Several of the crew had already scampered up the yardarms in an attempt to repair the damaged rigging and rehoist them. Without them, the ship could not maintain the necessary speed to stay out of cannon range.

The girls had come on deck once the immediate danger had passed. Stephen was at the helm, following the coastline. He rounded Point Allerton and ducked in close to Stoney Point. Soon the frigates, sailing in advance of the slower warship, passed the point and continued on toward Georges Island.

It was almost daylight, and Stephen wanted to reach his destination, a secluded cove near Quincy Bay. He steered *The Liberty* cautiously along the coast.

However, the captain of the *Royal George* had not been taken in by his ruse, and the huge warship rounded Point Allerton in pursuit.

The cry of "Two sails off the starboard!" sounded from above. The frigates had turned about and were coming back to rejoin the warship. They were about five or six miles away, so Stephen knew his only problem at the moment was the *Royal George*, which was gaining speed as it came downwind.

"What are you doing, Captain?" Tom Sutherland cried in alarm when Stephen swung the ship into a narrow straight between Windmill Point and Peddocks Island. "This water is too shallow; we can't possibly get through."

"Throw out a lead line, Mr. Sutherland. I've studied the charts of these waters. I can make it through with eight feet of water. The *Royal George* draws at least twenty. It will take her hours to get around the point." His eyes gleamed with fervor. "I'm going to lose them. They are not going to get their hands on *The Liberty*. I'll run her aground and burn her before I see that happen."

Will Higgins climbed down the rope ladder on the bow aft of the anchor and hung from it as he heaved out the leaded line that was used to measure the depth of the water.

"Mark twelve," he called out, as the ship moved into the passage.

"Mark ten," Higgins shouted. Tom threw a worried glance at Stephen. If the water got any shallower, they could easily run aground.

Patricia marveled at the impassive mask Stephen was able to maintain. She wondered what was going through his mind. She knew the depth of his feeling for this ship and her heart ached for him.

"Mark eight," Higgins cried out. The bottom of the ship was kissing the sand below it. Any change in wind direction, without water to draw on, would thrust the ship into the jagged reef.

"Mark nine," Higgins called out. Stephen's expression remained unchanged, but Tom broke into a wide grin.

"Mark ten," Higgins shouted, excitement ringing in his voice.

They were through it. They had reached deeper water.

"Return to the deck, Mr. Higgins," Stephen ordered, as they sailed into the bay.

They followed the bay and were anchored in a snug cove, hidden from any vessels approaching from the north, before the *Royal George* even rounded Peddocks Island.

31

Patricia marveled at how swiftly the cargo was unloaded. The smooth operation ran completely undisturbed while some of the crew worked on the repair of the rigging. Several carts toted the contraband away as quickly as it reached the shore.

Tom had taken Barbara back to Boston to be with her family until *The Liberty* was ready to return to Virginia. Stephen had asked Patricia to remain with him, so despite her eagerness to get back to Boston and settle her business affairs, she willingly stayed behind to be with him.

When Tom did return, he brought news that the situation in Boston was getting worse. Every day there was some incident between the citizenry and the soldiers. The whole city of Boston was a powder keg about to explode.

Stephen decided to get *The Liberty* out of there before serious trouble erupted. He told Patricia so one morning while she was brushing her hair after dressing.

"Well, I hope you are going to give me enough time to pack my clothes. I don't care about the club, but I would like to get my money out of the bank before we go to Virginia."

Stephen did not reply, and she swung around. He had a shocked look on his face. She walked toward him, laughing and shaking the hairbrush at him. "All right, we'll forget about the bank, but you will allow me to pack, won't you?"

"Whatever gave you the idea I would take you to Virginia with me?" he asked softly.

Her blood must have turned to ice because her body felt frozen, numb. In the span of a single breath, her world had come crashing down upon her head.

"I just assumed you would. . . ." She faltered, unable to continue. Unable to even look into his cold, unrelenting eyes, she turned away.

"I have no intention of marrying you, Tory, and I certainly would not take you there under any other arrangement."

Patricia walked to the armoire in a daze and began to remove her clothing. She folded it up in a neat pile on the bunk. Her mind felt disassociated from the actions of her body, as she meticulously folded each item.

"I thought you understood, Tory, that I would not marry with the country on the brink of war. And I am not going to ask you to wait for me. I might as well marry you, as do that. I could get killed, or worse, return a cripple. I would never ask my wife to be my nursemaid for the rest of my life."

"I understand," she said impassively.

"No, you don't! I can tell you don't understand at all. It has nothing to do with my feeling for you. It is because of it that I am taking this stand.

"Tory, when this war breaks out, America is going to need every ablebodied seaman she can muster. We have no trained navy and we will be facing the greatest naval force in the world! My chances of surviving are very slim. I won't leave you, and possibly a child, behind."

"Your nobility is an inspiration, Captain," she said caustically.

Stephen came over and grasped her shoulders to stare down at her. "There is a solution, Tory. You could go to France. I would buy you a house there. I could then visit you from time to time with no strings attached if you found someone else."

"You mean you want me to become your mistress," she said scornfully.

"Well, it would free you from making a commitment."

"No, Captain, it would free *you* of any commitment," she blazed out. "And tell me, what makes you think we wouldn't have a child from that arrangement? Is it different if your orphaned child is a bastard?" Her indignation had grown now to full fledged fury.

"Oh, come on, Tory. Women have ways of preventing children. They take some kind of potion. I am sure you will be able to find out how to keep us from having a child."

She brushed aside his hands and stormed to the cabin door. She turned back, her eyes blazing with contempt. "Oh, I know the perfect solution for preventing us from having a child, Captain Kirkland. It's called complete abstinence!"

She slammed out of the cabin and raced along the deck, blind with fury and heartache. How could he have hurt her like this? She was obsessed with one driving thought—her need to get away from him. She never wanted to see him again.

Her eyes swung around in panic at the sight of him storming across the deck after her. She had to get away from him. The coastline was just a short distance away. She ran to the rail, hesitating for an instant.

Stephen saw her intent and cried out too late to prevent her from jumping into the water.

Patricia thought she would never surface. Her shoes and sodden gown seemed to be dragging her down deeper and deeper. When her head finally broke the surface, her aching lungs gasped for air. A strong undertow kept tugging at her feet, trying to pull her beneath the water's surface. Stephen was already in the water, swimming toward her as she struck out and headed for the shore.

She was beginning to feel completely exhausted, yet she was certain she had not swum more than twenty strokes. Her head broke the surface again, and suddenly Stephen's arm closed around her waist, holding her head above the water as he towed her to shore.

They collapsed on the beach and for several seconds just fought to bear the searing pain in their lungs. Finally, when he was able to speak, he lashed out at her. "You crazy, insane, idiot! You might have been drowned!"

"I was never in danger at any time," she declared haughtily. "I happen to be an accomplished swimmer."

"Well, that makes swimming and horseback riding at which you excel! Tell me, madam, what other extraordinary talents do you possess, so I know what fool scheme you will next attempt in trying to kill yourself!"

His tirade was cut short at the sight of the approach of a distant sail bearing down on the cove. If *The Liberty* didn't get out now, she would end up being trapped.

Stephen ran to the shore, waving off the boat they were getting ready to lower into the water. There wouldn't even be time to weigh anchor if the ship were going to get out. He cupped is hands and shouted. "Get out of here, Tom. Cut the line and get out of here fast."

The ring of an axe carried across the water as they chopped the line and the heavy anchor dropped to the ocean floor. *The Liberty*'s sails billowed into flight and she moved off. She had reached open water when the rumble of cannon fire shook the air.

Stephen watched in frustration as his ship disappeared around the curve of the bay with the *Royal George* in pursuit.

"Oh, God, Stephen, will she make it?" Patricia asked in horror.

"She's lighter and faster, and she has an empty hold. I just wonder where those escort frigates are waiting," he said worriedly.

At the sight of Patricia's shivering in her wet clothes, he turned away. "I guess we had better get out of here. I know where we can go to get dry."

They walked about a mile through the woods until they came to a huge stone building surrounded on three sides by a crumbling wall.

"It looks like a castle!" Patricia exclaimed at the sight of its crenelated turrets.

"It once was," he said ruefully, pushing aside a rusty gate. "It's called Canaan."

"Canaan? You mean like the Biblical Canaan?" she asked, looking about in wonder.

There was no question that the edifice had once been a magnificent structure. Now, deserted except for an occasional rodent, it was gradually crumbling to rubble. Several of the rooms, though, were still liveable, even though they were stripped of furniture.

Stephen took her to an upstairs room containing several blankets and candles. He shook out one of the blankets and tossed it to her. "Take off those wet clothes and wrap this around you to keep warm. I will be going away for a short time." At her look of panic, he added, "I'll be back, Tory. I am just going to try to get us some horses."

"Why can't I come with you now?" she asked, looking around uneasily.

"Tory, you have nothing to worry about here. You will be safe." He disappeared without another word.

Patricia was at her wit's end. She felt too uncomfortable in the room, so she finally put on her damp clothing and wrapped a blanket around herself. She stepped outside, feeling more at ease outside of the house than inside it.

The gate was hanging by a single rusty hinge and it crashed to the ground when she pushed it aside. A cloud of gray dust rushed up to envelop her.

Patricia looked around with interest. The place was certainly intriguing. She wondered about the people who had lived in the mammoth structure. *Canaan? The Promised Land. Good Lord!* she thought sadly, looking around at the crumbling rubble, *Was this some man's dream of a promised land?* The sight of several crosses on a nearby rise attracted her attention and, out of curiosity, she strolled over to them.

Strangely enough, the cemetery was in a much better condition than the house. It was as if someone were actually tending the tiny plot. She read the name of Philip Elliott on the largest marker. *I think this must have been your Promised Land, Mr. Elliott.*

Her glance swung to another marker bearing the name of Elliott and she moved to the next one. She pulled up in surprise at a wooden cross, still standing. The name Kirkland was carved across it with the name of Andrew and Sarah below it.

Kirkland! It couldn't be a coincidence. That is why Stephen knew about this place.

She was back in the house nervously pacing the floor by the time Stephen returned.

"I can't stand this place, Stephen. There is something incredibly depressing about it. It has an aura of sadness. Why did you bring me here?"

He laughed wryly. "You have a convenient memory, Tory. If you hadn't jumped off the ship, we wouldn't be here now, and you know it."

"Well, I certainly didn't plan it this way. Who are Andrew and Sarah Kirkland?" At the look of surprise on his face, she added. "I walked down to the cemetery and saw their graves."

"They were my great-grandparents. I told you that my grandfather was a half-breed. Those are his parents. Andrew Kirkland was a Scottish doctor and Sarah was a full-blooded Wampanoag Indian. Their story is quite tragic, but unfortunately, I do not have the time to relate it to you."

He paused meaningfully. "It is time to leave now."

All the pain that had been shoved to the back of her mind pushed forward to encompass her.

Stephen's palms gently cupped her cheeks, forcing her wounded eyes to meet the anguish in his own. His rough thumbs traced the line of her jaw, before his hands slid up into the thick honey silk of her hair.

"I will never be able to forget you, Tory. I wish there could have been a time for us. A time that would have been only ours, free of all conflict and commitments except to each other."

His head lowered and his mouth claimed hers. The kiss was exquisitely gentle, and yet it transmitted more love than all the passionate sex they had shared together could ever have done. Her arms slid up and encircled his neck, her senses flooded with the reality of how much she loved him.

There were tears streaking her cheeks when he pulled away, because she knew from the kiss what he was about to say.

"There is a mount outside. Follow the road north and you will come to an inn in about two miles. Now get out of here, Tory."

She raised her hand and touched his cheek, knowing it would be for the final time. Her chest was throbbing with an ache too painful to bear. All the words of love she wanted to say to him were caught in a suffocating ball in her throat and the only sound she could release was a strangled sob as she turned and fled from the room.

Long after her departure, Stephen remained rooted to the spot. The thought of a future without Patricia filled him with overwhelming despair. Could any cause be worth the price of losing her?

Finally, unable to dwell on the thought another moment, he turned to depart. He stopped abruptly at the sight of the ring of muskets trained on him.

A British officer stepped forward with a crisp salute.

"Will you please identify yourself, sir?"

"My name is Kirkland," Stephen replied. He knew it was useless to pretend otherwise.

"Stephen Kirkland? Of *The Liberty*?" the officer asked.

Stephen nodded in admission.

"Captain Kirkland, you are under arrest for suspected acts of treason against the Crown. May I have your weapon, sir?"

Stephen grinned in concession and slowly pulled the pistol from his waist. With a curt bow he handed it to the officer.

32

Patricia was thankful for the privacy as she rode away, because it allowed her to openly shed her tears. As a matter of fact, she thought she would never stop crying. The tears continued to flow in a stream that left her eyes swollen and her nose red. Normally, she did not give way to self-pity, but she was incapable of checking the flow of tears.

Ironically, despite Stephen's earlier arguments, she was the one who now felt betrayed. How could he just let her walk away? His admission that he loved her was of very little comfort to her. Had their roles been reversed, could she have sent him away? Never! she told herself emphatically. *I could never do it to him, no matter what the cause!* The hopelessness of her love for Stephen overwhelmed her.

She was still crying when she reached the inn. Unmindful of the hour, or the fact that she had not eaten, she deliberately rode past it. In her present mood she did not have any desire to talk to anyone.

When the road reached a fork, a sign pointed out the direction to Boston and Patricia turned her mount on that road. She had no idea how far she was from the city, but in her state of malaise, she really didn't care.

The sun had long set and a steady drizzle snapped her out of her depression enough to force her to take shelter in a nearby farm. A rust-colored mongrel announced her approach by running alongside her horse, barking loudly. It looked more friendly than ferocious. When she climbed down the dog padded over to her. It eyed her warily and Patricia leaned over and patted its head.

"Hi there, fellow," she cooed. "What are you doing out here in the rain?"

The dog began to wag its long tail in response to her touch, following at her heels when she climbed onto the porch and knocked at the door.

All of the shutters were closed and her rapping produced no results. She finally tried the door, but it was locked.

"Well, fellow, they're either very sound sleepers, or nobody's home," she said aloud, with a desolate glance at the dog. "Don't tell me they went away and left you on your own!"

Patricia could see the outline of a nearby town, so she took the reins of the horse and crossed the yard. A heavy bar secured the barn doors, but she managed to unlatch it. She stepped gratefully into the shelter, and the horse and dog did not need any encouragement to follow.

The dripping dog immediately shook himself off and Patricia squealed in protest as water sprayed in all directions.

"Listen, you old mutt, I came in here to get out of the rain," she chastised him affectionately.

In a short time her eyes adjusted to the darkness and she soon was able to light a lantern and survey her surroundings. The barn appeared to be dry and secure. A cow occupying one of the stalls greeted them with a disinterested lowing. The dog went over to it, sniffed several times in recognition, and then curled up on a pile of hay and watched Patricia as she unsaddled the horse and rubbed it down with an empty sack that was hanging on the stall. In a short time the horse was chewing contentedly on some oats and hay.

Patricia investigated the barn but could not find anything she was willing to eat, no matter how severe her hunger. However, she did find a horse blanket. She shook it out thoroughly and wrapped herself in it after shedding her wet clothing.

Finally, exhausted, she sat down next

to the dog on the pile of hay. He crawled over to her and put his head on her lap. Patricia smiled and began to scratch the dog behind the ears. The dog obviously loved it, because everytime she attempted to stop, he slid his nose under her hand to encourage her to continue.

"Hey, you old mutt, do you think I'm going to sit up all night scratching your ears?" she scolded. She hugged the dog affectionately, and he began to lick her face.

"That does it!" she announced, pushing him aside. "You stay on your side of the bed, and I will stay on mine!"

She settled back into the hay, but within seconds the dog was snuggled up against her side and was soon sleeping contentedly. Patricia reached out and began to stroke it gently. "I guess you and I are in the same fix, fellow," she said softly. "We both are deserted by the people we love."

Her thoughts returned to Stephen Kirkland. There were no more tears left in her to cry over him. Besides, she told herself with a wave of resentment, she was not going to spend the rest of her days crying over a man who did not love her enough to want to marry her. Perhaps, all his noble talk was just an excuse he used to avoid a commitment to a woman. Well, he's the loser, not I, she told herself with a renewed spirit. I was willing to give him my love, so he has lost a great deal more than I. *You can't lose what you obviously never had to begin with!*

With a resigned sigh she relaxed, but sleep evaded her for a long time after she closed her eyes.

Patricia was awakened the following morning by the dog jumping up and barking at a figure standing in the doorway of the barn. Her initial alarm disappeared when it ran over and leaped up playfully into the arms of the young lad.

The boy was ten or eleven years old, with hair the color of straw. His face had a generous smattering of freckles. He laughed and tried to draw his head away from the dog, who was licking his face. The boy hadn't seen Patricia and dropped the dog in surprise at the sight of her when she sat up. Startled, he stared at her.

"Who are you?" the lad asked, drawing back in surprise. His blue eyes were round and wide.

"I'm sorry if I startled you," Patricia apologized. "I came in here last night to get out of the rain."

The boy relaxed with a wide grin. "Oh, I wondered why the barn door wasn't hitched. I was afraid I'd left it open."

"I knocked on the door, but I couldn't wake any of you. That's why I came in here," she explained.

"Nobody's home, ma'am," the lad replied. "The Parkers went to Marshfield cause Mr. Parker's brother is ailing. My name is Jeremy Sloan. I live on the neighborin' farm, and I've been coming over to milk the cow for the Parkers."

"Well, I'm glad to meet you, Jeremy. I don't suppose you have anything to eat with you?" she asked hopefully.

He reached into a pocket of his trousers. "I've got an apple here." Jeremy handed it to her and Patricia began to munch on it ravenously. "Be glad to give you a drink of milk soon as I empty old Queenie here."

"That sounds delicious, Jeremy. I would appreciate it if you would go outside so I can dress. It will only take me a few minutes."

"No bother, ma'am. There's an apple tree behind the barn. Yankee Doodle and I will just go and pick you a couple more apples," he said obligingly.

Patricia shook her head, chuckling delightfully. "Yankee Doodle? Isn't that an unusual name for a dog?"

The boy regarded her with a guarded curiosity. "You ain't no Tory, are you, ma'am?"

Just the mention of the name was enough to remind her of Stephen Kirkland. She frowned in disgust. "I am beginning to hate the sound of that word."

Apparently her answer satisfied the youngster, and he sped off with Yankee Doodle scampering at his heels.

Patricia dressed quickly and was washing her face in the rain barrel when they returned. Jeremy had filled his hat with apples. Patricia ate another one while she saddled the horse and led it outside.

Jeremy brought her a ladle of rich, creamy milk and she drank it thirstily. The apples and milk succeeded in abating her hunger and she thanked Jeremy for his kindness.

"How much further must I go to reach Boston, Jeremy?"

" 'Bout a six-hour ride, ma'am. But you'll need a pass to get by the guards. The city has been closed off since June."

Pondering this new difficulty, Patricia mounted the horse and rode off. She stopped at the end of the road for one final wave to the boy and dog, who were standing in front of the barn.

It was late afternoon by the time Patricia reached Boston. Luckily, one of the guards at the outskirts of the city had recognized her from the club and let her through without the required pass. She rode directly home.

Salir opened the door and grinned broadly at the sight of her. "We have missed you, Missy." The huge man's face glowed with undiguised pleasure.

She stepped into the familiar hall and realized that she had been away for two months. An unforgettable two months! Sixty days that would probably affect every succeeding day of her life.

The first thing she wanted was a hot bath and a hotter meal. After a few words with Salir, she headed straight for her chambers and Salir went to the kitchen to order her water and food.

Her eyes swept the comfort of the familiar room. She drew back in surprise at the sight of the empty wall, where her portrait had once hung. *What in the world have they done with it?* she wondered briefly.

Salir arrived with her bath water and as he was departing she posed the question to him.

"Salir, what happened to my portrait that used to hang on that wall?"

"I have not seen it, Missy, since the night you left Boston. I thought that you took it with you."

"That's ridiclous, Salir. You saw me leave. I didn't take any portrait. I didn't even take any clothes with me that night."

"That is true, Missy," he reflected.

"Perhaps Mr. Reardon has the answer."

"Well, I certainly hope somebody does," she said.

An hour later, clean and refreshed after soaking in a hot tub, she finished eating the first decent meal she had had in over a week. She dressed carefully, fortifying herself for the unpleasant task that lay ahead of her when she confronted Charles with Stephen's accusation.

The club was already open by the time she strolled down the stairway. Salir was busy at the doorway and she stopped for a quick question.

"Has Çharles arrived yet?" Salir nodded in reply. "Did you tell him I'm back?"

Salir shook his head. "I was about to, but Colonel Milton arrived. He seemed very excited and they disappeared into Mister Reardon's office."

Patricia frowned. What urgent business would bring one of General Gage's adjutants to the club? Damn Stephen Kirkland for instilling these suspicions about Charles into her head! "Are they still in his office?" she asked.

"I believe so, Missy. I have not seen them since."

Patricia hurried down the hallway. She had to talk to Charles before the evening got too busy. His office door was slightly ajar, and she was about to rap when she heard the mention of Stephen's name.

"Did Kirkland say what he has done with Patricia Fairchild?" Charles asked.

"We are still interrogating him," Colonel Milton replied. "He insists he does not know the whereabouts of your partner."

"I'll kill him myself, if he's harmed her," Charles declared.

"That won't be necessary, Reardon," the Colonel said smugly. "We're shipping him to England on the morning tide. We will try him and hang him there. It would be folly to try him here. These Colonials are openly rebelling now. Those accursed Sons of Liberty would probably storm the gaol to free him."

"What about his crew? Did you arrest all of them, too?" Charles asked.

"We will when we find them. His ship outran our vessels and disappeared. We suspect it is near Marshfield, because a patrol stumbled unexpectedly upon Kirkland while they were checking an abandoned house in that vicinity. He was alone when we captured him, and he will not tell us what he was doing there."

"Then perhaps Patricia is with his crew," Charles said hopefully.

"You deceive yourself, Reardon. If she has remained with them, then she has become one of them," the Colonel said with disdain.

Charles Reardon denied it immediately. "I think Kirkland kept her his prisoner. Patricia would have come back to Boston if she were able. She is a wealthy woman, Milton. She wouldn't throw it all away." He shook his head emphatically. "No, there's been no sign of her since *The Liberty* left Williamsburg. That bastard knows where she is. Where do you have Kirkland now? Take me to him at once. I'll find out what he has done with her."

"We have him at headquarters, but he will be transferred to *The William* at midnight. We are not taking any chances on moving him in the morning. I am certain the Sons of Liberty are not aware that we have even taken him prisoner. This will be a coup for the Crown."

Patricia had heard all she wanted to. She was about to turn away when the door swung open. Charles Reardon drew back in shock at the sight of her. He appeared as startled as she was.

"My God, Angel! Is it really you?" he exclaimed in surprise. He grabbed her and hugged her tightly before she could even utter a word. "When did you get back? I was just telling the Colonel that I suspected you had met with foul play."

'I've been back for about an hour," Patricia said breathlessly. "I took a bath and dressed. I was about to join you, but I didn't mean to shock you."

"Patricia, you've met Colonel

Milton," Charles said.

"Of course. It's a pleasure to see you again, Colonel," Patricia said gracefully, offering him her hand.

"Your obedient servant, my lady," Milton said as he kissed her hand. "You have been absent for a lengthy time, Madam Fairchild. I must ask you how you returned to Boston."

Patricia had to have time to think. She did not want to reveal too much of Stephen's activities, but she could not see what would be gained by lying at the moment.

"I was a prisoner on board the vessel *The Liberty*. Somewhere south of Boston I jumped off the ship. The Captain followed me and kept me in an abandoned house. I finally managed to escape and make my way here."

Charles patted her shoulder consolingly, but the English colonel regarded her suspiciously. "You say this Captain Kirkland left his ship to follow you." She nodded. "And you know nothing of his whereabouts at this time?" he asked skeptically.

"The last time I saw him, he was alone in that old abandoned house. It was a mammoth structure with crumbling walls. I've never seen anything like it before, here in the Colonies. It reminded me of a castle."

"And when did all this occur,

madam?" Colonel Milton inquired. He appeared to be openly skeptical of her story.

"I escaped from Captain Kirkland yesterday. I spent last night in a farmer's barn."

"Why didn't you stop and seek official aid, madam?"

"Are all these questions necessary, Milton?" Charles Reardon asked angrily.

"I am afraid so, Mister Reardon. Madam Fairchild spent a considerable amount of time in the company of a notorious rebel. It is necessary that she explain her actions."

"Colonel Milton, Madam Fairchild was with Kirkland because I asked her to go with him. That is the only reason." Charles was becoming angrier at the Colonel's officious attitude.

"Nevertheless, I prefer that Madam Fairchild accompany me to headquarters. It is important that we get her testimony and dispatch it on the ship sailing in the morning."

Patricia threw her hands up in resignation. "I can't believe that anything I have to say is important, Colonel. But, very well, if you insist."

"I will personally be responsible for Madam Fairchild, Milton. I will bring her to your headquarters myself. It will not be necessary that she be treated like one of these rebels. Besides, I have a great deal to discuss with her before I sail tomorrow." There was an authoritive command in his voice that even the Colonel could not ignore.

"Sail tomorrow? Where are you going, Charles?" Patricia managed to ask in a surprised voice.

"I am returning to England on some official business, Angel. I am glad you got back before I left."

"Well, Charles, I will expect you and Madam Fairchild at my headquarters within the next two hours."

"As you wish, Colonel Milton," Charles replied with cool graciousness.

They moved to the foyer and were saying good-bye to the Colonel when Salir opened the door to admit an arriving guest. Patricia almost gasped aloud at the sight of Thomas Sutherland dressed in formal dining clothes. Their glances locked for several seconds before she turned away hastily.

Charles had obviously missed the exchange between them. He took her arm to return to his office when several English officers rushed over at the sight of Patricia.

She was soon surrounded by red uniforms. She had no idea what she replied to their enthusiastic greetings, because her mind was spinning on how she could get Thomas Sutherland alone, to tell him about Stephen's capture.

Obviously, he wouldn't be there now if he knew of Stephen's whereabouts. He must have taken the chance of coming here in the hope of finding out something from her. At least someone believed in her!

She found herself being pulled into the main lounge. "Come on, Patricia, we haven't heard you sing in weeks," one of the men declared. The others echoed his demand, and Patricia found herself at the harpsichord.

Her glance swept the room and located Thomas Sutherland at the bar. To her distress, Charles Reardon was standing just a few feet away from him. After overhearing Charles's conversation with Colonel Milton, there was little doubt that Stephen had been right about him. Charles was obviously working for the Crown. He had deliberately used her in an attempt to have a man assassinated.

Patricia had no idea how she managed to get through the song. The men applauded and shouted for more. In an effort to stall for time, she honored their request and sang another song. When she finished, she walked boldy to the bar.

"All right, gentlemen. Inasmuch as I have been away for so long, I am going to pour each and every one of you your favorite drink. And I'll bet you all another free drink that I can remember what they all are."

The offer was met with a roar of approval, and the men crowded to the bar. Patricia stopped at the first young officer.

"Now, let me think. Captain Bridges, your favorite drink is Scotch whiskey. Am I right?" At his nod she quickly filled his glass.

She moved to the next man at the bar and eyed him shrewdly. "Lieutenant Carlson, you like a glass of port." She filled a wine glass full of the sweet red liquid and passed it to him with an enticing smile.

Charles Reardon was watching her intently, uncertain of her motive. It wasn't like Patricia to ignore his wishes. She knew how anxious he was to talk to her and could not understand why she was wasting all this time.

Patricia continued down the bar. The men were beginning to wager among themselves whether or not she would succeed in her attempt to match them all to their favorite drinks. When she reached Thomas Sutherland, she raised a delicate brow in concentration.

"Let me remember." A slim finger tapped her cheek as she studied him. "I seem to recall that you like a particular brandy." Her eyes suddenly opened in elation. "Oh, yes, of course. It's cognac. French cognac," she declared triumphantly.

Thomas Sutherland weighed her words. Patricia knew that he didn't like the taste of cognac; they had laughed about that fact. Cognac was Stephen's favorite drink. *My God! She's trying to tell me something about Stephen!*

"You have no idea how difficult it is to get cognac these days, *William*. The French aren't too willing to *ship* it to us."

Who the hell is William? Thomas asked himself. *What does he have to do with Stephen and a ship?* Was she trying to tell him something about *The Liberty?* he wondered. *Come on, Patricia, you've got to tell me more. Damn, if only Bab were here. Those two women always seem to be able to read each other's minds!*

Suddenly his young face broke into a wide grin. It was all beginning to make sense. Patricia was trying to warn him about *The William*. It was in port right now!

Thomas understood her message and he grinned in assurance. He sniffed the liquor appreciatively and raised his glass in a salute to her. "Then I will savor each drop, Patricia." He took a few sips of the costly brandy.

"I am afraid if you drink it that slowly, sir, we will all be here until *midnight*," she teased lightly, as she moved on.

It took her over thirty minutes before she finally finished pouring each man his drink. By that time Charles Reardon was clearly agitated, and he took her arm angrily as he led her into his office.

Thomas Sutherland watched them disappear, then quickly departed. Patricia's message had been cryptic, but some facts had been evident. They involved Stephen, a ship which was obviously *The William*, and the word midnight. He read his pocket watch beneath a lamplight and discovered it was already half-past the hour of ten. Whatever he had to do, he only had an hour and a half to do it in.

33

O nce in his office, Patricia jerked her arm free from Charles's grip, her own anger an easy match for his.

"What is your problem, Charles?" she fumed. "You know how much I hate to be manhandled, and I have just spent two months being just that!"

Charles was contrite, but impatient. "Patricia, it is late and I do have some important things to discuss with you."

"Well, I certainly have a few things to cover with you, too," she retorted bitterly. "However, I believe your Colonel friend has a prior demand on my company."

"Colonel Milton is no fool, Angel. Don't try to lie to him or you'll only get yourself deeper in trouble."

"Everything I told him was the truth, Charles. I have no idea where to find Stephen Kirkland or his damned ship! He's wasting his time if he thinks I do."

Charles regarded her with a closed look. "Did you ever give Emil Thackery the packet I sent with you?"

"Why do you ask? Was your brother hung after all?" she asked sarcastically. Her eyes flashed accusingly. "How could you do that to me, Charles? How could you use me like that?"

"It was a desperate measure and I regret it deeply. I had no right to involve you," Charles said honestly.

"That's right, Charles, you didn't," she lashed out. "I had no loyalty to one side or the other in this fight between the Crown and these American rebels. Your cavalier usage of me put me right in the middle of that issue!"

"That was unfortunate, Angel, and I will try to explain it to you when we return. However, I think we had better get down to headquarters now. Milton is not a patient man."

They made no attempt at conversation as they rode in a carriage to the British headquarters. Patricia was praying that Thomas Sutherland had understood her complete message to him. But even if he did, would there be enough time to do anything about it?

Colonel Milton greeted her with a reserved courtesy as he showed her to a seat. Charles declined the offer to sit and remained standing behind Patricia's chair. They both waited nervously for Milton to speak as he reseated himself behind his large desk.

"Now, Madam Fairchild, perhaps we

can go over some facts again relating to Captain Kirkland," the Colonel began patiently.

"Colonel Milton, I have told you everything I know regarding Stephen Kirkland," she said with exasperation.

"You were with him for two months, madam. In the course of that time you must have met some of his associates."

"Yes, I got to know several of the members of his crew quite well," she retorted.

Milton's eyes narrowed. "I am referring to his contacts off the ship, madam. Perhaps *you* could mention some dates and places?"

"Other than a brief stay at his family's home in Virginia, I spent most of my time confined to a cabin. I was his prisoner, Colonel."

The Colonel's attempt at a confidential smile resulted in his face curving into an unpleasant sneer. "Well, I am certain it wasn't a solitary confinement, madam. You are a very lovely woman and I cannot believe that Captain Kirkland would not be attracted to you."

"Whether or not the Captain was attracted to me is irrelevant, Colonel Milton. I certainly didn't encourage him to confide in me." His attitude was becoming insulting, and she was fighting to keep a rein on her temper.

"Perhaps not, madam, unless in the

course of that time, you had the opportunity to become intimate with him."

She glared defiantly, even a cursory attempt at drawing room civility forgotten. "I really fail to understand the line of your questioning, Colonel. Are you hoping that Captain Kirkland talked in his sleep?" She threw a mocking glance over her shoulder to Charles Reardon. "Really, Charles, you didn't tell me I was expected to take notes!"

The Colonel leaned across his desk in an effort to be discreet. "A man does have a tendency to speak more frankly to the woman with whom he is having an affair."

"Are you speaking from experience, Colonel?"

He drew back, his face inscrutable. "You are taking this matter surprisingly lightly, Madam Fairchild. Too lightly, I might add. Apparently, you fail to recognize that your own position is precarious."

Charles Reardon stepped forward and banged his fist heavily on the desk. "I will not stand for your threatening her, Milton."

"I realize your position with the government gives you authority, Mr. Reardon, but you must understand that I also have a duty to perform."

"Colonel Milton, I did not have any

control over the actions of Captain Kirkland," Patricia declared. "I repeat, I was his prisoner. When the opportunity presented itself, I attempted to escape. I fail to understand why that makes me an accomplice, or even a suspect. Your insinuations have been snide and degrading."

"And I am not allowing you to subject her to any more of them," Charles announced. He returned to Patricia's chair and put a supportive hand on her shoulder.

A firm rap at the door interrupted their conversation. "Come in," Milton called out irritably.

A young officer stepped into the room. "We have the prisoner ready for transfer, sir."

Patricia turned her head toward the door. Her face paled and her eyes widened in surprise to see Stephen Kirkland brought into the room flanked by two soldiers. His hands and ankles were fettered with iron shackles, and he looked rumpled and tired. She jumped to her feet instinctively as her eyes met his. She saw the initial shock in the sapphire eyes deepen to confusion, as he was struck with the incriminating implications of her presence in the Colonel's office. *Dear God! Does he think I have betrayed him?* she thought with horror.

After the initial shock of seeing her,

Stephen realized she was probably being questioned about their relationship. For her protection, he thought it would be best to maintain a hostile attitude.

She started to step to him, unable to contain the denial that leapt to her lips, but Charles Reardon put a hand on her arm to restrain her. "Stephen, it's not what you think. I didn't—"

"—Spare me any more of your duplicity, Madam Fairchild. We are both gamblers, and you hold the winning card." His dark head dipped in a mocking salute. "My compliments, madam. You've proven yourself to be the better player in the end."

Milton's mouth compressed into a ruthless grimace. "You have your orders, Lieutenant."

The sound of the closing door was as decisive and isolating as a clanging cell door sealing her heart inside. Patricia sank down in the chair and shut her eyes to try to erase the image of Stephen's final look of contempt. Her ears rang with the remembered echo of his scorn.

She could feel a wave of near-hysteria wash over her and wanted to scream in panic, a panic induced by despair.

Why? Why, if their love was doomed from the beginning, did they have to part like this? Why couldn't there have been, at least, a final moment of tenderness to treasure in the endless days to follow? Endless days, each more empty and bleak then the one before, because Stephen's laughter would not be there to lighten it. Endless days of frigid desolation looming before her, because his touch would not be there to warm her. Endless days void of passion, of desire, because his lips would not be there to inflame her.

Her pallor was enough to alarm Colonel Milton and he quickly poured a small amount of brandy into a glass. "I think you should drink this, Madam Fairchild."

Patricia's hands were trembling as she took the glass from him. She forced the scalding liquid down her throat.

"Damn it, Milton, I am taking her out of here," Charles declared. His face was florid with anger.

Colonel Milton was deliberating on the whole situation. It was evident to him that Patricia Fairchild was not feigning her anxiety. Apparently, she had been telling them the truth about not knowing Kirkland's whereabouts. He assumed that her distress was due to discovering that her lover was now their prisoner. It was also obvious to him that she had lied to them about her true feelings for the Yankee scoundrel. He nodded in concession to Charles's demands.

"Very well, my lady, you may leave for the time, but I must insist that you return in the morning for further questioning. There are quite a few questions that still remain unanswered.''

Charles took her arm and assisted Patricia to her feet. ''Thank you, Colonel Milton,'' she said with a weak smile.

He rose to his feet and bowed politely. ''My lady.''

His eyes followed their departure. In the morning Reardon would be gone, and he would no longer have to suffer his annoying interference in his investigation of this woman. He would just have to wait until morning.

Charles was assisting Patricia out of the carriage in front of the club when the stillness of the night was shattered by the sound of musket shots. Patricia's frayed nerves jumped in response to the sudden explosion as Charles swung around in alarm.

''Did those shots come from the harbor?''

''I think so,'' she said weakly. The faint color that had just begun to return to her cheeks drained rapidly, and her frightened eyes gleamed like two shiny green pools against the paleness of her face. Her instincts told her that Stephen was in the thick of the firing. *Dear Lord, please don't let anything happen to him*, she prayed silently.

''Let's get you inside, Patricia,''

Charles said brusquely. He saw her safely inside the door and then turned to depart. "I must investigate those shots. I will get back here before I sail."

"Let me go with you, Charles." Her face was wreathed in anxiety, and he guessed her reason.

"No, it might be too dangerous, Angel." His brow knit reflectively as he studied her. "Promise me you will remain here until I return."

"Where else would I go, Charles?" she asked confused.

He kissed her on the cheek and disappeared on foot in the direction of the waterfront.

Patricia paced the floor nervously, waiting for Charles to return. There had been no further sound from the direction of the harbor. What news would he bring? How would she bear it if Stephen had been killed?

Salir remained with her, and she brewed them each a cup of tea to help pass the time. If he were aware of the cause of anxiety, he gave no indication when she set a cup of the liquid before him.

"Why don't you go to your room and try to sleep, Missy. I will wake you when Mr. Reardon returns."

She shook her head and curled her hand around the hot cup. The warmth was comforting to her fingers and she realized that her hands were as cold as ice. "I am too nervous to sleep, Salir, but there is no sense in both of us missing our sleep. This isn't your problem. Why don't you go to your room and go to bed."

"Your problem is mine to carry, too, Missy. My people believe that if you share the burden of your problems with one who cares about you, the weight of it will be cut in half."

Patricia was shaken by his words. She was about to pour out her woes to him when there was a commotion outside.

A moment later Charles Reardon stormed through the door. Patricia bolted to her feet. At the sight of the frantic look on her face, he strode across the room and glared down at her.

"Your rebel lover has escaped."

She sank back down into the chair in relief. "Was anyone hurt?" she asked with dread.

"A few minor wounds on both sides," he snapped. "The rebels boarded the ship before the patrol even arrived. Most of the crew were ashore, so it was a simple feat. The patrol relaxed their guard when they got on board and that's when the rebels struck."

"Well, I am relieved to hear that no one was seriously hurt."

"How did you do it, Angel? How did you engineer it all? The moment we heard those shots, I knew, by the look on your face, that you knew what was happening."

"I don't know what you are talking about," she denied with a defiant thrust of her chin.

Charles was enraged. In his anger he grasped her arm and pulled her to her feet. Salir jumped up to come to her defense.

"Keep out of this, Salir. He won't hurt me."

"I must insist you release her, Mr. Reardon," Salir said ominously. His hands were balled at his sides.

The sign of returning sanity reappeared on Charles' eyes and he released her and turned away. "How did you accomplish it, Angel?" he said sadly.

He suddenly looked broken and old to her. She could not help but be reminded of the closeness they had once shared. Charles had always been there, supportive and understanding, whenever she needed him. Her compassion surfaced. Whatever his cause or loyalties, those memories would not change.

The man had been instrumental in almost destroying the life of the only man she would ever love. He had blatantly used her in a scheme to murder an innocent man. But now, she found herself actually feeling sympathy for him.

"I was outside your office door and heard you and Colonel Milton discussing Stephen's arrest. I passed that information to a friend tonight at the bar."

He turned back to her with a spark of respect gleaming in his eyes. "Of course, I should have guessed it the moment it happened." He shook his head. "You know, Angel, I never would have believed it! As a matter of fact, I even believed you when you said you weren't committed to their cause."

"And I believed you, when you told me your brother was going to be hanged!" she retorted.

Their gazes locked, both wincing from the smart of betrayal. Old friendships die painfully, and each of them was struggling with the awareness that there could be no other alternative for them.

"I suppose Stephen was right about Jeffrey Cunningham, too. Were you involved in his death?"

"No, Angel, believe me. We never heard of him until after he died. There was a rumor that he was an American spy, so we investigated his death. All we were able to find out is that the woman who loved him was so grief-stricken that she returned to England."

"At least I can be thankful for that," she said with relief. Patricia reached out and put a hand on Charles's arm. "I foolishly believed that I could remain neutral. As a result, Stephen accused me of being a Tory, and you think I have become an American rebel. Each of you put demands on a personal relationship that denied me the privilege of allegiance to either cause. How was it possible for me to be true to Stephen and to you? It was a perfect example of being damned if you do, and damned if you don't."

Her eyes pleaded for his understanding. "Can't you see that I'm not the transgressor? I have become the victim! I've lost the man I love and I have lost my best friend. I no longer even have a country that I can call my own."

"Since time immemorial, Angel, a man's duty to his country has had to take precedent over his love for a woman. I cannot believe your Yankee captain did not have to struggle with that duty, too. So try to understand that whatever I did, I did for the welfare of my country. I don't wholly approve of some of the demands the Crown puts on the Americans, but England is my motherland, and I feel compelled to stand by her, no matter what it costs me."

"You mean even at the price of your honor and integrity, Charles?"

"I guess that is all in the eyes of the beholder, Angel. You see these rebels as men of honor. To me, their actions are treasonable. But it is the motives behind a man's actions that determines his honor and integrity. I am sure this coming revolution will be fought on both sides by such men."

He put his hands on her shoulders and smiled down tenderly at her. "I never wanted to use you, Angel, but sometimes there are no other options. That, unfortunately, is the kind of business I'm in."

His glance swung to Salir. "Get her out of here, Salir, as quickly as possible. I don't think I can stall Milton for more than an hour."

Charles leaned down and kissed her on her cheek. "Take care, Angel."

She remained standing silently after he left. Stephen, and now Charles. *Is it all just a dream?* she asked in desperation. Salir's hand on her arm shocked her back to the reality that it wasn't. He recognized her grief, but he knew that there was no time to honor it.

"Mr. Reardon warned us to leave, Missy, as quickly as possible. I think it will be difficult to get past the British. You are well-known by some of their officers."

"If I had some men's clothing, I could disguise myself as a boy. I did that on the ship and it worked."

"Well, mine are obviously too large for you." He started to move to the door. "But I know where I can get some. I have a friend nearby who has a son close to your size."

Patricia's eyes opened wide in astonishment. "Why, Salir, you have been keeping secrets from me," she teased.

The big Moor grinned broadly. "Man does not live by bread alone, Missy. I will be back shortly. You gather what you want to take along, but do not take more than a small bundle."

Patricia sighed deeply. "Do you think it will work, Salir? It all seems so hopeless. There are English soldiers everywhere."

Salir grinned. "This is a big country, Missy."

She put a restraining hand on his arm. "Are you certain you wish to be involved in this affair? You can get out now, before it is too late."

He smiled down at her with a patient smile. "As long as I can be of help to you, I will stay by your side."

34

Patricia paced the floor, nervously waiting for Salir to return. She tried to formulate a definite plan in her mind. She was uncertain which direction to go, but felt her only hope was to try to head South. She would let Salir make that decision.

She jumped, startled, when Salir suddenly appeared at her chamber door. She had not heard his approach and was always amazed at how swiftly and quietly the huge man could move about.

"Quickly, Missy, we must hurry. Here are the clothes you asked for." He shoved a bundle of clothing at her. "I have a horse and cart waiting," he announced as he hurried away.

Patricia pulled off her gown and began to slip into the boy's garments. Everything she put on was slightly too large, but she blessed the loose-fitting shirt for concealing the swell of her breasts. She gathered her long strands of hair and tied them with a ribbon, then tucked them under the tricorn that Salir

had given her to wear. The shoes were so
large on her that they almost fell off her
feet, but the pair of woven hose she
pulled on helped to fill the gap.

Patricia grabbed the small parcel
containing her jewels and some money
and scurried down the stairway.

Salir was already sitting on the
wagon seat, the reins of the horse held in
his hand. He reached down a huge paw
and lifted her effortlessly up beside him.
With a quick flick of the reins, the wagon
moved forward, just as a patrol of
English soldiers appeared at the top of
the hill.

The wagon, being driven by a negro
with a young lad sitting next to him,
attracted little notice as it rolled past the
patrol.

Patricia sneaked a covert glance
behind her as they crested the hill and
saw the patrol halt at the front of the
house.

They followed the coastline the rest
of the day. When it became too dark to
travel, Salir pulled the wagon into a
copse of trees.

"We'd best rest the horse now,
Missy." He jumped down from the
wagon, then lifted her to the ground.
Within moments, he had retrieved a
parcel of food and some blankets, which
he had wisely procured while waiting for

her to dress, and spread them on the ground.

Patricia barely nibbled at the food. She had not eaten the entire day, but she had no appetite. She succeeded in forcing down a few bites of the bread and cheese as Salir consumed his meager portion.

"Thank you, Salir. It was delicious," Patricia said. The danger of her position was secondary to her heartache. Stephen was gone. Charles was gone. She could not turn to Barbara for help because Tom was probably at risk the same as Stephen. Salir was the only friend she had left, she thought sadly, as she watched him kneeling at the fire. Her conscience began to nag her for involving him in her troubles.

"Perhaps, now would be a wise time for you to go, Salir."

He raised his head in surprise, and she could see the intelligence and humor that rested in the depth of his dark eyes. "Go? Go where? My home is here, MIssy. With you. A man's home is where he has found contentment. He can not chart it with maps, or the sands of the deserts, or shores of the seas. Its boundaries lie within his heart."

"You are a remarkable man, Salir," she said humbly.

"You sleep now, Missy," he ordered.

"I will keep the watch."

"I can't sleep, Salir. Truly, I can't. I have too much on my mind. We have a long journey ahead of us. Why don't you sleep? I will sleep tomorrow, when we are farther from Boston," she argued.

He saw the determination on her face and knew there would be no sense in arguing with her. He nodded wisely and turned away to pour her a cup of tea.

Salir covertly pulled a tiny packet from his pocket and added it to the liquid. It was a potion to induce sleep that his Togolese woman in Boston had given him, in the event he was hurt or wounded. He smiled, recalling the many nights the wild and fiery woman had warmed his blood and bed.

He returned to Patricia and handed her the cup. "Drink this, Missy, it will do you good."

Patricia accepted the cup with a distracted smile. "Thank you, Salir." She began to sip from it, her thoughts wrestling with the emptiness of a life without Stephen. Should she try to find him in Virginia and accept his offer to go to France? At least that arrangement with him would be better than none at all.

Soon her eyes began to droop from the effects of the drug, and within minutes she was sound asleep.

An unusual noise in the stillness of the night attracted Salir's attention and he cautiously moved through the trees until he reached the source of the sound.

He parted the brush and peered through to discover a ship anchored in the nearby cove. It was apparent to him at the sight of the flurry of activity by the crew, that the ship was preparing to sail on the ebb tide.

Salir spied the captain standing on shore issuing orders and the Moor's broad face broke into a wide grin. He hurried back to where Patricia lay sleeping. Salir released the horse and swooped up the sleeping woman into his arms. Deep in a drugged slumber, Patricia barely stirred, but merely settled against the warmth of his chest.

The crew of *The Liberty* had never seen Salir before and several of them stopped their activity to stare in astonishment when the mammoth Moor came out of the woods carrying a lad in his arms.

Stephen Kirkland straightened up slowly at the sight of him and stood with his hands on his hips, watching Salir's approach with a suspicious eye.

"You're a bit far from Boston, aren't you, Salir?"

"We are fleeing Boston, Captain. It has become quite dangerous," Salir said.

"We would be most grateful if you would allow us refuge on your ship."

Stephen nodded toward the sleeping bundle in his arms. Patricia's face was concealed against the broad chest. "Who is the lad?"

The Moor thought he would remain cautious until he discussed everything with Patricia. "He is the son of one of the attendants who worked for my mistress. His father has been arrested as a suspected rebel and the boy has fled with me to avoid arrest." Whatever explanation would be necessary in the morning, he was certain the Missy could handle it.

"And just where is your mistress now?" Stephen asked, distressed.

"She has left Boston," he replied, in all good conscience. "If you have need for a crewman, I am strong, Captain, and familiar with the sea."

Stephen considered the wisdom of taking him along. "What is wrong with the lad? Is he ill?"

Salir grinned. His dark eyes dropped to the bundle in his arms. "Just exhausted, Captain. It has been a long and tiring day for the youngster."

"Very well," Stephen relented. "A few of my crew have been wounded and I could use another able-bodied hand. Perhaps I can even make use of the lad. We had to leave my cabin boy behind on this last voyage with a case of measles. Let the lad get a good night's sleep and send him to me in the morning."

Salir nodded with a grin. "We are most grateful, Captain."

The arrival of Tom and Barbara Sutherland interrupted their conversation and Stephen hurried over to them with a worried frown. "I see you didn't find her."

Tom shook his head. "I'm sorry, Stephen. There was an armed guard posted outside the club, so we just kept riding past it. The place looked deserted, though."

"Where in hell can she be?" Stephen pondered. He forced a smile. "How did your parents react to the news of your wedding?" he asked Barbara.

"They couldn't be happier, Stephen," Barbara replied. "They are making arrangements to visit Virginia."

"What is Salir doing here?" Tom asked surprised. "I thought for sure when I saw him with you that he had brought you word from Patricia."

"Who is Salir?" Barbara asked curiously. Her wide eyes swung to the Moor with interest.

"Salir is Tory's devoted servant," Stephen answered. "He said she has left Boston."

"Well, just how devoted is this Salir to her?" Barbara asked suspiciously.

"Tory claimed he would kill for her," Stephen said, his mind so preoccupied with his worries about Patricia that he was blinding himself to the obvious.

Barbara shook her head. "Then you are being very naive if you believe he doesn't know where she is." With a forceful stride she walked over to Salir, who was standing in the shadows. She glanced briefly at him, still holding the sleeping form in his arms. The big Moor winked meaningfully at her, and Barbara immediately grasped his meaning. Her brown eyes were dancing with mischief when she turned away.

"Well, I guess we better board or we'll miss the tide," Stephen relented, with a final backward glance. Salir climbed into the longboat with the remaining members of the crew, and in a short time *The Liberty*, her sails unfurled against a moonlit sky, sailed into the open sea.

It was over an hour before Stephen left the quarterdeck to go to his cabin. He was surprised to see Salir slumped on the floor in front of the door.

"What are you doing here, Salir? Surely there must have been an extra bunk for you below?"

"I like it out here, Captain," Salir replied with a grin.

"Did you find a bunk for the lad?" Stephen asked.

"Yes, Captain, I found the perfect bed," he said. His mouth widened into a broad smile of amusement at some secret thought.

A strange man, Stephen thought to himself as he entered his cabin.

A single candle glowing in a sconce on the wall revealed a sleeping form in his bunk. *So that's what Salir found so amusing*, he thought with irritation as he turned back to the door and pulled it open. His dark eyes were blazing with anger. "Damn it, Salir! Get that boy out of my bunk."

The Moor threw up his hands in a gesture of helplessness. "The lad is tired, Captain, and I wanted to make certain he was comfortable."

"Well, I'm tired too. I haven't slept in forty-eight hours. Either you get him below, or I am waking him and kicking his sleeping ass out of here!"

"I can't wake him," Salir protested feebly. "He is sound asleep."

"Well, we will soon see about that!" Stephen raged, storming over to the bunk. He threw aside the quilt and was about to yank the boy out of the bed when he froze at the sight of the sleeping figure.

"Tory?" he asked incredulously. He turned back to Salir in disbelief. "Is it really Tory?"

Patricia sighed deeply in her sleep

and a soft smile tugged at the corners of her mouth, as if responding to the sound of his voice.

Stephen shook her gently, but she remained undisturbed. His dark eyes swung worriedly to Salir. "What's wrong with her?"

"It's only a harmless drug."

"You drugged her!" Stephen sprang to his feet, his hands balled into fists.

"Just to make her sleep, Captain. She will wake soon, I can assure you. You will take care of my mistress?" he asked.

Stephen controlled his initial anger and turned back to Patricia. "Yes, Salir, I will take care of your mistress."

"Then the time has come for me to go to bed."

He started to close the door, but stopped when Stephen called out, "Thank you, Salir."

The big Moor's eyes met the grateful warmth in Stephen's, and he nodded as he closed the door.

For a long time, Stephen just sat on the edge of the bed staring at her, remembering his feeling of frustration when Thomas Sutherland had described to him Patricia's involvement in his escape from the British.

He had cursed himself for being ten times a fool. Hell, he loved the woman passionately! Why hadn't he convinced her of that when he had the opportunity to do so? He had vowed to get his wounded crew members back to Virginia and then return to Boston, because even if he had to fight the whole damned British army and navy, he had been determined to find her.

Stephen got to his feet and removed his clothing, then pulled back the quilt and climbed in beside Patricia. With a strangled sob he gathered her into his arms. Patricia snuggled against him with a contented sigh.

She was gradually drawn back to wakefulness by the pleasant sensation of warm lips sliding down her neck. She moved her head to allow the moist mouth a freer access. Her long lashes fluttered as her mind told her that, regretfully, the dream would soon end. Her emerald eyes slowly opened to find a pair of sapphire eyes gazing down at her adoringly. For a few seconds she savored the sight of them, enthralled to know the dream had not ended.

The lips on hers were bruising; they seemed to devour her. The pressure of them increased as Stephen's passion grew. She could feel a warmth spreading through her and a nervous fluttering began in her stomach.

"Oh God, Tory, how I've missed you," he whispered aas his mouth lowered to cover hers.

Patricia opened her eyes to discover

that, somehow, miraculously, the dream was a reality.

"Stephen," she moaned with passion as his hand began to rip away her shirt as if it were paper. She was powerless to move, held immobile by his arms. "I don't understand. How did I get here? What happened?"

"Hush, darling, you're safe on *The Liberty*," he whispered. "I will explain it all later."

Stephen's head dipped to claim a breast and his mouth closed around it. The sensation that had begun in her stomach now raged out of control when his tongue began tantalizing the sensitive peak.

A groan was forced between her quivering lips and his mouth returned to claim hers. She parted her lips to accept his probing tongue. The pressure of his mouth increased as he felt the rising response in her.

"Oh, Tory, Tory, how I love you," his husky voice moaned in a new assault at her ear. His hand slid down to release the trousers and he slipped them off her hips. She trembled under a shudder of ecstasy when his firm hand closed around behind her hips and drew her tighter between his thighs. She knew she was beyond control. Her need was as great as his and she parted her thighs to accommodate him as she slipped her arms around his neck and clung to him.

Her eyes opened and she glowed under the blazing passion she read in his dark eyes. For a few seconds their gazes locked, her emerald eyes glittering with a sensuous invitation.

Stephen did not ignore it. He lowered his head to hers and once again his mouth covered hers. Her passion matched the power of his and their tongues coupled in a heated duel. Her urgency intensified as his mouth returned to her breasts.

He stopped to play with each quivering mound before moving down the satin sheen of her stomach. She began trembling and writhing under the agonizing ecstasy of his mouth. By the time he reached the junction of her thighs she was moaning helplessly. Her thighs opened to the dark head, as his mouth closed over the core of her need, his tongue a fiery poker that threatened to incincerate her.

Her nails raked the sinew of his shoulders and he rose and sheathed himself in the moist velvet softness of her. Their bodies melded together, the perfect rhythm building to its culmination.

It was many moments before he raised his head and gazed down at her. He dipped his head and pressed a light kiss on the end of her nose, before brushing back the strands of hair that clung to her cheeks.

Her emerald eyes met his loving glance with open frankness, and a sensitive smile tugged at the corners of his mouth.

Stephen raised his head and grinned down at her with an endearing boyish grin, entirely alien to his usual sophisticated guise. "I should have suspected it was you last night. Salir would never have deserted you if you were in trouble."

His expression softened, and he raised a hand to tenderly caress her cheek. "Thank you for saving my life, Tory."

A gentle smile captured her face and her finger returned to play with the corners of his mouth. "I was left with no other choice. I'm in love with you, Stephen."

He couldn't conceal his quick smile of pleasure, before adding, "I thought we might have succeeded in making a rebel of you after all."

"I'm still uncertain what I am, Stephen, but I agree with Salir that the problem is everyone's, and doesn't just concern a chosen few. Do you understand?" He groaned when her teeth lightly nipped his shoulder.

Stephen captured her hands and pulled them above her head. "I understand, but I should remind you that you're on the high seas now, and it's considered mutiny to mistreat or disobey the Captain."

"And suppose I do?" she challenged, a dangerous gleam dancing in her eyes. "Just what will the Captain do to me?"

Stephen's mouth slid to a breast and curled around it. Her body responded instinctively with a quivering shudder. "He could have you stretched on the yardarm," he murmured. His mouth began to pay homage to the other twin peak, his tongue toying with the tautened bud until his moist mouth closed around it. Patricia gasped at the exquisite sensation sweeping through her.

"What . . . what else might the Captain do, if provoked?" she asked throatily.

"He could have you flogged."

Stephen's head lowered to her stomach and his tongue began to caress it; each stroke felt like a hot, moist lash to her flinching nerve ends. She began to squirm helplessly beneath him, her hands still pinned to the floor above her head. When his hand slid between her thighs and began to caress her, she begged him to release her. Her body began to convulse under wave after wave of ecstasy.

Stephen watched the changing expressions on her face and in the incredible green eyes as she was gripped by passion. He marveled at the exquisite loveliness of her and his own passion leaped hungrily at her response.

He released her hands and his body trembled as her arms entwined him. She molded her soft curves against him and her hand reached down to his manhood, fondling it gently as she directed it to the opening that waited for its invasion.

Once again the dancing rhythm began between them. The tempo of their movements increased as his thrusts built in intensity. His mouth closed over hers, smothering her cry of fulfillment when the hot evidence of his love flowed into her.

They remained entwined for a long time until Patricia broke the silence. "Stephen, I have thought about France. I have decided I would rather have you in a small part of my life than no part at all."

He rose to his feet. "We'll talk about it when I get back. As much as I hate to leave you, it is time for me to take the helm."

Patricia rolled over to gaze admiringly at the magnificence of Stephen's nude body as he retrieved his clothing. She watched him with unabashed admiration as he dressed. When he was finished, he turned back to her with a crooked grin.

He sat down on the side of the bunk and reached out and stroked her cheek.

Patricia smiled up at him, her eyes glowing with her love for him. "Go back to sleep, Tory. I will be back in a few hours."

She sighed with happiness as he disappeared through the door, then rolled over and within minutes, was sound asleep.

35

Patricia felt as secure as in the warmth of a cradle. She opened her eyes to the gentle rocking beneath her. It certainly did not feel like the hard earth or the creaking bounce of the rolling wagon. She raised her head and gazed around to discover that she was lying in a bunk.

Her eyes swept the empty cabin in astonishment and recognized the room immediately. It had not been a dream! She was on *The Liberty* and Stephen had made love to her. The confusion of how she got there no longer mattered. What mattered was that she was here in Stephen's cabin. In his bunk! The thought of it sent electrifying shivers up her spine.

The huge room was as neat and tidy as ever. The small wooden table and two chairs were still standing in the corner, and the commode with its basin and pitcher rested against a wall. Her gaze swung warmly to the large upholstered chair that he loved so much beckoning to her to come and sit. She slipped out of the bunk and padded barefoot to it, sat down and tucked her knees under her chin in contentment.

The sight of his huge sea chest at the foot of the bunk was a reminder of her own nudity. She glanced hopefully at the nearby armoire. Was it still filled with her clothing, or had he destroyed it in his anger with her?

Her eyes continued their probe and swung to the tools of his trade, those untouchable items he cherished more than gold. Nothing had been moved, from the round globe of the world still resting on its stand in the corner, to the large compass encased in its brass pedestal. The barometer still hung on the wall above the rack of neatly rolled maps.

She smiled tenderly at the sight of his drawing compass and protractor lying in their familiar places on his desk. He was such a creature of habit!

When her glance idly swung to a portrait hanging above his wide desk, her mouth gaped open in astonishment. Her eyes were wide with shock and she was thankful she was sitting down, because she could only stare with her mouth agape at her purloined portrait hanging above his desk.

She sat motionless for a long time, with her arms wrapped around her legs and her head resting on her knees, just staring at the portrait.

Finally, she got to her feet and quickly found some of her clothing in the armoire. The tempo of her movements increased with eagerness as she finished brushing her long hair before scurrying out the cabin door.

A last thought caught her fancy, and she hurried back in and quickly rifled through a drawer in the armoire until she found what she was seeking. She slipped the red and black garter up a slim leg.

Patricia stepped on the quarterdeck and paused to watch Stephen at the helm. He was absorbed in studying the stars, unaware of her presence. The moon cast a glistening swath across the deck and Patricia stood in its glow, the tips of her long tawny hair silvered with moonlight.

She walked to him and slipped her arms around his waist, nuzzling her cheek against his back. She could feel the power of all that contained strength through the fabric of his shirt.

"You're late, Mr. Sutherland. You were supposed to relieve me a half hour ago."

"You're such a fraud, Stephen Kirkland," she scolded, stepping around into the circle of his arms. She turned to face him as he steered the ship, her back pressed against the big wheel.

Stephen leaned down and placed a light kiss on the tip of her nose. "You are right, moonbeam. I knew it wasn't Tom."

"That is not what I mean, and you know it," she chided lightly.

"All right, madam, explain it to me while you can, because in a few minutes I expect to be relieved and it appears you are going to need another lesson in the proper respect due the captain." He dipped his head and began to nibble at the slim column of her neck.

"I really believed all that noble talk of yours about shipping me off to France and visiting me once or twice a year. I actually was prepared to go along with it!" He raised his head and eyed her dubiously, as if to ask what had changed her mind.

"My picture!" she responded to his silent inquiry. She shook her head in disbelief. "I am amazed that a man who professes to be such a cardshark can still believe he is holding the winning hand after such a misplay." Her eyes flashed impudently. "Not this time. Captain Stephen Kirkland! This time I'm holding the winning card. I've won the hand, after all."

His dark eyes danced with amusement. "I haven't the faintest idea what you mean, Tory."

Her slim finger beat out each word against his chest. "My picture, you fraud! My picture that you stole from me to hang over your desk because you are so mad about me."

He threw back his head with laughter and slipped an arm around her waist, pulling her against the length of him. "Mad! Insane! Crazy! Bewitched! Demented!"

"You can make all the jokes you wish, Stephen, but you are never going to deceive me again. I know now you can't bear to be away from me for any length of time. You wouldn't last a week before you turned into a quivering, worthless hulk."

He groaned at her smugness. "Just because I hung your picture over my desk?"

A complacent smile caught the corners of her mouth and her finger began to trace the outline of his lips. "The picture you went to a great deal of trouble to steal from my bedroom in Boston." She stopped, and her smile turned into an adorable pout. "By the way, just how *did* you get my portrait on this ship?"

He chuckled warmly, "I had two of my crew get it the night you and I left for Virginia. I was going to steal it before I even knew you would be sailing with me."

"I should be furious with you, but I love you too much—even though I am now convinced you are a thief and a pirate."

"I am *NOT* a pirate. I am a priva—"

Her lips covered his before he could finish the word.

The sound of Thomas Sutherland clearing his throat finally forced them to break the kiss and pull apart.

Stephen nodded to his second mate. "Take the wheel, Mr. Sutherland." He swooped her up into his arms and carried her to his cabin.

They got no farther than the red rug in the center of his cabin floor. They rapidly undressed one another, amid kisses and oaths of love.

Stephen pressed a kiss to the knee above the familiar black and red garter. His scorching glance devoured the sight of her stretched out, tawny and golden against the bright red rug, the honeyed perfection broken only by that provocative garter hugging her leg.

"I love you, Tory," he whispered huskily, then lowered himself into her outstretched arms.

Sometime during the morning Stephen carried her to his bunk. They both fell asleep in each other's arms and the sun was high in the sky when they finally awoke.

Dressing quickly amidst their laughing and kissing, they finally opened the door to go on deck. Salir was standing there, waiting patiently. He eyed Stephen with a stern frown.

"You have not harmed my

mistress?" he questioned threateningly.

Stephen shook his head. "She has come to no harm, Salir. I can assure you, I have emerged the weaker."

Salir looked to Patricia for confirmation. "Are we home now, Missy?"

Patricia understood his meaning and nodded, her happiness in glowing evidence. The big Moor grinned, revealing white teeth in a broad smile. He had long been certain of the outcome between his mistress and this rebel Captain. Tory or Whig, he knew the passion between them could not be denied. Remembering their earlier struggles together, the tall Moor suddenly exploded with loud laughter.

The wind had blossomed the sails into billowy white clouds that floated against the splendor of an azure sky. Stephen's arms encircled Patricia's waist and drew her back against his chest. The two stood on deck with the feel of the wind on their faces as it whipped the golden strands of her hair.

There was still so much to be said between them, but for now there was only the indisputable reality of their love for each other.

Thomas and Barbara Kirkland leaned over the bridge and smiled at the sight of the couple at the rail. "I guess you're right, Bab," he conceded with a crooked grin. "Looks to me like there will soon be another wedding in the clan."

Two dimples danced in her cheeks as she slipped her hand into his. "Well, *I* never doubted it for a moment."

"Captain, what course shall I steer?" Tom called out.

Stephen hugged the woman in his arms in a tighter grasp. Patricia twisted her head and smiled up into the dark sapphire of his gaze. His head dipped to place a light kiss on the lips of the woman he loved before his voice rang out jubilantly.

"Full sail, Mr. Sutherland. We're going home. Home to Virginia!"

EPILOGUE

St. John's Church
Richmond, Virginia
March 23, 1775

A hushed expectancy quieted the crowd as the unobtrusive man rose to his feet. For a moment Patrick Henry's glance shifted to his devoted disciple, Thomas Jefferson, who was seated in the room. Jefferson's steady gaze returned his stare. Beside Jefferson sat his close associate, Richard Henry Lee, who was waiting just as patiently for Henry to begin. George Whythe, also in attendance, settled back as comfortably as possible on the hard bench, his scholarly mind deep in thought. Next to him, Benjamin Harrison shifted in his seat, nervously waiting to hear what the country's most eloquent orator would speak of today.

Massachusetts was preparing to take up arms against the British. All day the Burgesses had been arguing the pros and cons of such open rebellion. It was no secret to anyone in the room that Patrick Henry advocated that Virginia follow her sister colony's example. Whether one agreed or disagreed with the philosophy, no man present doubted that whatever Patrick Henry had to say to them this day would be a masterful declaration.

"*Mr. President,*" Patrick Henry began, addressing the Virginian Burgesses, "*No man thinks more highly than I do of the patriotism, as well as the abilities, of the very worthy gentlemen who have just addressed the House. . . .*"

The rich timbre of Henry's voice carried through an open window to the street, where Patricia Kirkland was seated in a carriage next to her husband. Stephen held her hand as he waited with the same anticipation as those assembled inside.

Thomas and Barbara Sutherland were sitting opposite them. The steadfast dedication on their earnest faces expressed the sentiments of all the nation's young patriots.

The flame of freedom had been kindled across the nation. Soon it would blaze into a fire that would pit neighbor against neighbor, son against father.

And, as in the past, the Kirklands' commitment to freedom would make their choice a simple one.

This was evident to Patricia as she studied the determination on the faces of her three companions in the carriage. Her lovely brow creased with a troubled frown and her hand slid down protectively across the slight swell of her stomach. She was carrying Stephen's child within her, a child soon to be born into the midst of this conflict.

Her worried glance swung to the strong profile of her husband seated beside her. He turned his head and saw the disturbed look in her eyes, and his chiseled face softened with love. His hand reached down and closed over the hand that was lying on her stomach.

"Aren't you feeling well, honey? Is that son of ours giving you a problem?"

Patricia's face relaxed into a smile. It was a radiant smile, reflecting the intuition and wisdom of a woman in love. Whatever turmoil lay ahead, Stephen would always be there when she needed him.

The emerald warmth of her eyes glowed with love as she slipped her fingers through the comforting strength of his.

"I'm just fine, Stephen, and so is your son. I think the little rebel is worried that this war will start before he can get out to join it."

Stephen chuckled warmly and slipped his arm around her shoulders. "I think, between the two of us, we're going to make a real patriot of you yet, Tory."

Patricia leaned back in contentment against the strength of him as he turned back to listen as the voice of Patrick Henry rose in fervent declamation:

> "Gentlemen may cry peace, peace, but there is no peace. The war has actually begun! The next gale that sweeps from the north will bring to our ears the clash of resounding arms! Our brethren are aleady in the field! Why stand we here idle? What is it that the gentlemen wish? What would they have? Is life so dear or peace so sweet as to be purchased at the price of chains and slavery? Forbid it, Almighty God!
>
> I know not what course others may take, but as for me, give me liberty or give me death!"